THE
PATRIOS
NETWORK

THE PATRIOS NETWORK

CLASSIFIED DOCUMENTS

O.I.T. ONLY

ANTONY JOHNSTON

Lightning Books

Published by
Lightning Books
Imprint of Eye Books Ltd
29A Barrow Street
Much Wenlock
Shropshire
TF13 6EN

www.lightning-books.com

First edition 2022
Copyright © Antony Johnston 2022
Cover design by Ifan Bates

Typeset in Minion Pro and Knockout HTF28

British Library Cataloguing in Publication Data
A catalogue record for this book is available from the British Library

ISBN 9781785633034

Humbly dedicated to the memory
of John Le Carré

The shipping container's door inched open with a grinding lament. It stopped just wide enough to reveal a face Yuri had never seen before, framed by elasticated white plastic.

'*Red admiral*,' Yuri said, quiet but firm.

The man inside the container nodded, satisfied, and opened the door wider to allow Yuri through. He slipped inside, making a mental note to consider making future protocol more secure. Then again, it seemed unlikely he was accidentally walking into a *different* shipping container whose occupants expected someone to knock on the door, say a code word, then come inside to discuss the results of their torture methods on the pathetic, bleeding prisoner strapped to a chair and whimpering in the centre of the floor.

Still. *Moscow rules*, as the old guard used to say. Assume nothing, trust nobody.

A second interrogator wore an identical thin plastic full-body coverall. Two to ply their trade on a third, and from what Yuri saw they enjoyed their work. He wondered if red coveralls would make more sense; they were already halfway there. But seeing the pristine white slowly turn crimson, coupled with the awful knowledge of precisely why and how that was happening, probably formed an effective part of their method.

He marvelled at the ingenuity of the set-up. A location as anonymous and temporary as could be imagined, large enough for its intended use but no larger, inside which you could do almost anything. The walls were covered with silver heat-reflective material, and while Yuri wasn't about to break out his swimsuit, it had kept the temperature above freezing – presumably helped by one of the occupants sweating and screaming in pain for hours at a time. Soundproofing material behind the insulation was supposed to take care of that, though he wondered how successfully it masked the noise. People could be surprisingly loud over nothing more than a peeled fingernail.

The chair looked as if it had been lifted from a dentist. Perhaps it had. Modified for purpose, though. Not many dentists strapped their patients down with leather cuffs over the wrists and feet. Speaking of cuffs, Yuri almost banged his head on two metal restraints chained to the ceiling. He looked down and saw two more chained to the floor.

The first torturer turned from closing the door, saw his expression, and shrugged. 'Sometimes we make them stand up.' No further explanation was forthcoming, or necessary.

At the back of the container – behind the chair, so its occupant couldn't see what was being prepared, because sometimes the anticipation was worse than the final pain – was a portable table with folding legs, the kind one might take camping in the Urals, and upon it a canvas holdall, zip open to afford access to its contents. Most of which were very sharp, though some were deliberately very blunt.

A separate bag, a small backpack, leaned against the back wall. The second man bent down now and from this bag snatched a water bottle, next to which was what looked like a plastic box for sandwiches. The man drank from the water bottle and winked at Yuri. *Thirsty work.*

There was nothing else in the container, so he turned to the prisoner. A young man, north-east Asian of appearance, perhaps

Mongolian or even Yakut. Hard to tell after the beating that had been delivered. He reached out with a gloved hand and tilted the man's semi-conscious head this way and that. Doing so dislodged blood from the prisoner's gums as he whimpered in pain, fresh flow escaping the slack corner of his mouth. His eyes swivelled; not the animal, instinctive panic that had probably consumed him earlier that evening, but now the tired delirium of a man who knew pain was merely a state of existence. One with which he had become intimately familiar over the course of the day, and if he had any fear that he might come to know it even more closely in the hours ahead, it was buried so deep within him it wouldn't surface in time to show.

Still peering at the torturers' handiwork, as if preparing to grade it, Yuri said, 'Did he talk?'

'Eventually,' said the first. The second hadn't spoken yet, and showed no intention of doing so. Perhaps this was their thing, or perhaps the mute one was a moron who transformed into a multilingual prodigy when speaking via handheld implements.

The first torturer retrieved a piece of paper from the folding table and handed it to Yuri. A name, and an address. One he expected, the other he did not, but his expression betrayed nothing. He pocketed the note and looked at the prisoner.

'How reliable is he? I mean...' Yuri gestured at the blood, the tools, the bodily wreckage. 'Some people will say anything.'

The torturer shrugged again. 'That's why we prefer young targets. You take an old man, someone who's seen life, and they know this is the end. They tell you nothing, or nonsense, and wait to die. But a young man who thinks his whole life is still ahead of him will play the game. Defy you, then lie to you, then tell the truth because he always thinks there's a chance he can make it out to fight another day. Maybe even take revenge.'

'Ah,' Yuri nodded, 'naïveté.' He turned the prisoner's face

towards him, though the man's eyes still couldn't focus. 'He's right, you know. If you were older, maybe you'd have seen a few of these from the other side. Enough to teach you that escape is for the movies…and revenge is for people who don't get lifted in the first place.' He retrieved a folded cloth from inside a coat pocket, shook it out, and clamped it over the prisoner's mouth and nose.

Now came the final struggle, the absolute fear, the instinct that overrode all pain and suffering and exhaustion. Every last ounce of energy expended to fight for life, desperate for existence to continue, no matter how painful. At last the prisoner's eyes found focus, his throat found voice, his muscles found strength; reserves previously unknown, depths previously undiscovered, willpower previously untapped, no matter how shallow or weak. Circles of blood stained the cloth, expelled with force from mouth and nose but trapped in its weave. Yuri still wore his gloves, but the cloth wasn't to remove evidence, it was to prevent spatter and blemish. He needed to be able to walk out of here unmarked and return to polite society as if he'd never left. Blood stains on his shirt cuffs would rather spoil the illusion.

Nevertheless, of course he wanted to do it himself. He was old-school enough for that. It had been a long time since the last time, but the memory came easily, skill and movement that were his to summon. The sensation and experience of killing another human with one's own hands could never truly be forgotten. Not that it kept him awake at night. He wasn't a person much afflicted by remorse or regret.

Consumed by revenge, though. The type not found in movies, but in a lifetime of righteousness and anger; that was his strength and his weakness. One day, he assumed, it would kill him. But today it would kill this young man, whose only mistake was being one of a handful of people with the information he needed to enact that revenge.

Light fled the prisoner's eyes a moment before the fight fled his body. Yuri waited for the final exhalation, and suddenly remembered the pretty young doctor, many years ago in Zurich, who had named it for him: *postmortem agonal respiration*. A muscular contraction that occurred following cessation of the heartbeat. The shock of his dead father suddenly appearing to breathe had distracted him from the details, to be honest. And later, in Yuri's hotel room, hadn't been an appropriate time to ask her to repeat the explanation.

The prisoner relaxed, in the way only a truly dead body could. Yuri removed his hand, leaving the cloth. Instead he took another one, gaily patterned, and mopped his face. That insulation was better than he'd guessed.

The other men were already gathering their tools into the holdall, while removing other items; a metal tube, and a small plastic bottle filled with grey liquid. Yuri asked, 'How long before somebody finds this container?'

'Months, maybe years. By then he'll be long gone.' The speaking man held up the tube and bottle. 'Caustic agent. The gas will corrode anything traceable, and dissipate as it escapes the vents.'

Yuri nodded. 'Fire would attract too much attention.'

'Exactly. Tomorrow this box begins a long transshipment journey around the world. It will spend months at sea, then a few days at a port somewhere, before transferring to a new ship, where it will do the same again. Two years, if security doesn't force it open before then. There's no reason they should.'

'Good.' With one last look at the body, Yuri left them to clean down and decontaminate the container with the practised ease of experienced operatives.

He returned to the gate and exited the port. The guards ignored him, as they'd been paid to, and he continued into the night. His hire car was parked a kilometre away, a precautionary habit ingrained over many years. In the distant sky over Hamburg, bright, silent fireworks exploded to celebrate New Year. Yuri allowed himself an internal celebration too, letting fantasies of where tonight would lead, and what would follow, warm him during the cold walk back to his car.

Some people needed to be taught a lesson. He would relish playing the role of teacher.

2

@ToTheFathers
7:00 AM January 1

LAND OF HOPE AND GLORY
NEVER TO BE SLAVES
66408726102204878
16611636666158410
81760216047699996
98452426655275963
31678602813496935
24266552759633167
86028134969356107
29596332133951796
56964998345629311
30163096284016047

Posted via Twitter on the web

Six weeks later

3

It made a nice change to travel on her real passport. No cover ID, no disguise, no fake contact lenses or wigs, just the real Brigitte Sharp. The wrong side of thirty to pass for a student; the wrong side of five-ten to easily blend into a crowd; the wrong shade of complexion to pass for anything other than English, despite the French passport tucked in the inside pocket of her trusty black leather jacket. Twenty years in London would do that to you.

OpPrep had offered to give her a cover identity, a *legend* as they called it, but it was a half-hearted gesture and there was little point for such a brief trip. Eurostar was running more services now, and she didn't need to pretend to be someone else today. She was on her way to confront a traitor, hopefully catch him red-handed with an enemy of the state, and take them both back to London by the same route.

Besides, like everyone else on board, she wore a mask. Even if Simon Kennedy had stood up from his seat at the other end of the carriage, turned around, and looked her straight in the eye, he wouldn't have recognised her. They worked in different departments and, despite Bridge's limited fame within SIS, there remained thousands of officers and staff who not only didn't know her but who, upon seeing her pale skin, black hair, black clothes, black boots, and generally surly demeanour, would place her in many other categories before thinking to file her under 'intelligence officer'.

She'd never heard of Kennedy either, before Giles Finlay summoned her to a meeting in Broom Eight two days ago. Giles was head of the CTA, MI6's *Cyber Threat Analytics* unit; at least she assumed he still was, despite several promotions in the years since he'd created it. Bridge wasn't sure of his official title these days, but he remained her boss – despite her own promotion to lead SCAR, the inter-agency board she'd helped bring into being. *Shared Cyber Anti-terror Response* was created to pool developments across SIS, MI5, GCHQ, and the Ministry of Defence, to stay one step ahead of attacks and espionage. Bridge hadn't wanted to lead it, but then she had, but then it had been taken away from her, but then that had turned out to be a sort of cruel test on Giles' part. She still hadn't fully forgiven him. But much of her time since had been spent either working at home or fucking her new CIA boyfriend at *his* home, both activities enjoying increased frequency thanks to the pandemic, and they'd brought with them new problems. First among them was the lack of sleep she endured these days, and not only for the most obvious reason. It was a rare night that Bridge didn't wake up several times from violent, frightening nightmares. Karl was sympathetic, but nobody's patience was endless.

Nevertheless, Giles remained her immediate boss, and when he summoned she attended – in this case to one of the smaller secure briefing rooms at SIS headquarters in Vauxhall, with a small conference table and space for half a dozen people. Like all Brooms it was soundproofed, windowless, and hardened against wireless signals. A screen and keyboard at one end of the table were connected by physical wire to their computer, which lived in a secure SIS server facility in the building's basement. When not in use, every Broom's screen looped through the same screensaver, a slow, gentle pan over deep green fields that Bridge had come to loathe within months of joining the Service. Years later, and despite several generations of computer upgrade, it hadn't changed. She often wondered if someone in the IT department was playing a joke.

Bridge and Giles entered to find Emily Dunston already waiting. Dunston was Head of Paris Station, controlling the Service's activities in France from her London desk. She drummed her fingers on the table impatiently and glanced subtly at the computer screen – which to Bridge's surprise showed not the screensaver but a man's face, white-haired with reading glasses perched at the end of his nose, looming over his laptop camera. Devon Chisholme, Senior Executive Officer at the MoD.

'Is that secure?' asked Bridge as she sat down.

Giles shrugged. 'If it isn't, heads will roll downstairs. Similar to our phone apps, so they tell me.'

'Feels like half a SCAR meeting. What's going on?'

On the screen, Chisholme shook his head. 'Not so much inter-agency intelligence, I'm afraid, as rooting out a bad apple.' Dunston snorted quietly, but if Chisholme heard it he didn't react. 'Put simply, we suspect one of yours is about to sell military secrets to the enemy.'

'What you neglect to mention,' said Dunston with an arched eyebrow, 'is how those secrets came to be in the hands of an SIS officer in the first place.'

'Yes, yes, we have our own bad apple to deal with as well,' said Chisholme. 'But we can handle that internally. What we can't do is follow your man to Paris and arrest him. Unless you'd prefer we trample all over Emily's turf and ruin her cosy relationship with the *gendarmes*?'

Bridge cleared her throat and turned to Giles. 'Perhaps you'd better start at the beginning.'

'I should coco,' Giles muttered, taking the mouse and keyboard. On the screen, Chisholme's face was replaced with a slide showing the career profile of a nondescript forty-something man, an SIS officer called Simon Kennedy.

Bridge scanned his history. Former signals officer in the British Army, good analyst track record, five months in Ljubljana several years ago before returning to London. 'Short assignment in Slovenia. What brought him home?'

'Family,' Giles replied. 'His wife became pregnant shortly after arrival, and didn't want to raise the child there. We had additional concerns, so brought them home and all was well.'

'Additional concerns?'

'All in good time. Devon, we can't see you, but would you care to enlighten Bridge?'

The civil servant sighed. 'Ms Sharp, do you know what an EMP is?'

'*Electromagnetic pulse*,' she replied, and reeled off what she knew. 'It knocks out all electronics; networks and computers, obviously, but also alarm clocks, cars, microwaves – anything with a circuit board. Can even wipe hard drives if it's powerful enough. Two ways to get one: either set off a nuke, or if you're less keen on mass destruction, rig up a huge generator on wires. But they're cumbersome and imprecise.'

'Quite so. Except now, or I should say in the very near future, we will have a third option that fits inside a briefcase, with an area effect of three hundred metres.'

Bridge whistled. 'That's a real breakthrough.'

'Yes it is,' Chisholme said, 'so you can understand our dismay when we discovered an MoD researcher appears to have passed the designs to your officer, with intent to sell them to the highest bidder.'

She looked back at Simon Kennedy's nondescript photo. 'Old army connection, I assume?'

'So it seems. And now Kennedy is preparing to make use of

another connection.'

On cue, Giles displayed several surveillance photos on the room's screen. In them Kennedy stood on the banks of a river – the Ljubljanica, Bridge guessed – with another man, making apparently casual conversation that was surely anything but. 'Boštjan Majer,' said Giles, expertly pronouncing it *bosht-yan my-uh*. 'Information broker and auctioneer of international secrets. He was our additional concern about Kennedy.'

'The name rings a bell,' said Bridge. 'But if you knew Kennedy was friendly with this guy, why did you let him come home?'

'We only had evidence of this single encounter. Obviously a red flag, but nothing came of it that we could tell, and with Kennedy re-stationed here in London we were able to keep an eye on him. Majer himself has been on UK Borders' watchlist for years, so we'd know if he tried to enter the country. But he hasn't, and Kennedy's been clean as a whistle ever since.' Before Bridge could say it, he continued, 'Until now, obviously. The impetus appears to be his impending divorce. Kennedy's wife is leaving him, taking their child with her and taking him to the cleaners.'

In her mind, Bridge assembled the disparate pieces into a whole. 'He needs money his wife won't know about. He remembers a man who'll pay for secrets, and an old friend who might be able to supply them.' She turned to Dunston. 'And now he's on his way to a rendezvous in Paris. I assume you'll have Henri Mourad watching?'

Dunston shook her head. 'Afraid not. Before he came to Paris station, Mourad spent a year working alongside Kennedy on the Balkan desk here in London. He'll be standing by as backup, but he can't be the primary shadow, and nobody else I have in the city is up to the job.'

'Meaning you think I am?' said Bridge, with half a smile. She and Dunston had crossed swords several times in the past, but the

Paris head let this one go with a silent frown.

Bridge matched it. Mourad was the Anglo-Algerian Paris station chief, and a colleague in whom she had complete trust. Not so long ago SIS had maintained officers embedded in cities all over France, any of whom they could have called on. But ever-tightening budgets had cut and cut until those regional officers dwindled to zero.

Being half-French herself, though, this wasn't the first time Bridge had helped out across the Channel. She contemplated another life in which she'd diverted to Paris, working for Dunston instead of Giles, and suppressed a grimace.

'What do we know about this upcoming meet?' she asked as Giles closed the photos and returned Chisholme's face to the screen.

'Very little. Majer is on Interpol's PTS list, and was seen arriving in Paris yesterday.' *Personnes Toujours Surveillées*, or People Always Monitored, was a list of individuals in whom Interpol had a perpetual interest, supplied to bureaus and local police around the world. Any reported sighting of someone on PTS was added to their file. 'Meanwhile we flagged Kennedy buying a Eurostar ticket for Saturday.'

'In his own name? How did this guy pass training?'

'No rule against officers travelling to Paris for the weekend. Remember, he doesn't know we're watching.'

Bridge turned to Dunston. 'What's your instinct? Brush pass along the Seine, or back table at a café?'

'The possibilities are endless,' Dunston admitted. 'That's why we need an officer on the ground, someone who knows Paris but won't be recognised, to follow, intervene, and apprehend. I have a friend – in the *Police nationale*, Devon, not the *gendarmerie* – ready to assist once you call it in.'

'But not before you grab them all red-handed,' emphasised

Giles. 'Obviously we want Kennedy, but we've also been trying to bag Majer for years. Two birds with one stone will do very nicely.'

'I'll need a firearm,' said Bridge. 'Otherwise I won't be apprehending anyone, let alone keeping them there while *les poulets* catch up.'

'Already authorised. You're booked in with OpPrep tomorrow morning.'

She turned to the screen. 'Devon, what sort of buyers will Majer approach to sell the designs? Are we talking nation-state resources only, or could you build one of your new EMPs in a shed?'

'Somewhere in between, I gather. The materials are very expensive, especially the battery formulation, and assembly is tricky. You'd require both funding and specialists.'

'The sort a terror group might have access to?'

Chisholme didn't move for five seconds. Bridge couldn't tell if he was thinking or his screen had frozen. Eventually he said, 'Let's try to ensure it doesn't come to that. Giles knows my feelings on this matter.'

'Devon wants to arrest Kennedy before he even gets on the train,' Giles explained. 'But this is the best chance we've ever had to bag Majer, and we'll still get him before he can sell to Beijing or whomever.'

'Surely Moscow's a more likely buyer for this sort of kit?'

Giles looked at Bridge as if she'd suggested he fly a rocket ship to Mars. 'Ordinarily, yes. But unlikely in this case, given Majer is widely suspected of handling Sasha Petrov's escape from Russia.'

'Oh, that's why his name rang a bell,' said Bridge, kicking herself for not making the connection. 'I haven't thought about Petrov since before Covid.' Sasha Petrov was Moscow's very own whistleblower, a Snowden-like infosec staffer who released a trove of classified Kremlin documents into the wild. He'd been headline news for a short time, hunted by Moscow. But Bridge had spent that same time mourning her mother's sudden death, drinking enough to cope with the loss, and energetically screwing Karl at every opportunity. Current affairs were the last thing on her mind. Then the pandemic had begun, worldwide lockdown followed, and everyone forgot about the embarrassing leak. 'Wasn't the Home Office considering his sanctuary claim? He'd be a catch.'

'Officially they're still considering it, but that bird has flown,' said Giles. 'Too much Russian influence in London these days to rubber-stamp it, and Moscow doesn't forget. So assume Boštjan Majer remains persona non grata, and he's more likely to sell to the Chinese.'

Bridge sighed. 'I'm definitely going to need that gun.'

An officer on the ground, Dunston had said. Bridge's OIT status – *Officer in Theatre*, the licence to operate as an SIS field officer – had been a rollercoaster ride. She worked hard to finally obtain it; immediately lost it when her first-ever op went south; spent years trying to get it back; decided she didn't want it after all; was forced back into it; feared it would be taken away again when she was demoted; and finally received a promotion, instead. It wasn't so long ago she'd tell anyone who'd listen she was happiest when sat in front of a keyboard, but lockdowns and quarantines had made her restless, even despite her early decision to 'bubble' with Karl. They hadn't been together long, and neither of them was ready to start living together. But the only other option had been to simply stop seeing each other, potentially for a year or more. So they'd alternated between their two flats, mostly using Karl's because Bridge's had an uncanny ability to remain messy no matter how many times she tidied it. It had worked out, mostly. They hadn't tried to stab each other yet, which she considered a success. But the stir-craziness was a constant looming presence, especially for

Bridge. Being unable to travel made her understand how much she'd come to expect it as part of being OIT, even if technically it was work.

'Mesdames et messieurs, bienvenue à Paris Gare du Nord.'

The Eurostar announcement interrupted Bridge's reverie and returned her to the present. Pretending to focus on her iPhone, she stole a glance at Simon Kennedy. He had no luggage, not even a briefcase. She assumed the stolen plans were on a USB thumb drive, tucked safely in a pocket.

She stayed a good distance behind him as they exited and made their way downstairs to the local trains. Kennedy took a Parisian Navigo card from his pocket and breezed through the turnstile, suggesting he'd been here recently. Perhaps to scout the meeting location? Bridge followed, grateful she wasn't the only passenger keeping her mask on. Kennedy still wore his, too.

Then they were on a platform, southbound into the heart of the city, where Bridge positioned herself twenty metres from Kennedy outside his peripheral vision. A train arrived, and Kennedy stepped on board. From here it would cross under the Seine to the left bank, past the Sorbonne and south to Saint-Rémy-lès-Chevreuse. Bridge entered the next carriage along and stood by the adjoining window, watching him through the glass.

She checked the map and saw this line connected with the *Orlyval*, a shuttle to the airport. Bridge wondered if Kennedy had arranged to meet Majer there. Few places were as anonymous as an airport, especially with passenger numbers rising again. If so, Henri would have one hell of a drive on his hands. The Paris chief was waiting in a car above ground, ready to track Bridge's location when she re-emerged on the street, but that plan assumed the street in question would be within the city. She was glad she'd chosen comfortable boots over fashionable ones, because she might be here for a while.

Loud music suddenly blared from further down the carriage. Bridge turned, expecting to see a busker, but instead she and the other passengers watched a trio of young black men begin to dance as their boom box played an upbeat polka. '*Mesdames et messieurs, bienvenue à Paris! C'est une belle journée aujourd'hui, nous sommes là pour vous faire sourire!*' they shouted in unison.

It was smooth, co-ordinated, and practised; the lead dancer filmed it all on his phone for TikTok, the second carried the boom box, the third brandished a cup for coins, and none of these duties hindered them as they expertly danced along the carriage and around passengers, perfectly in time to the music. Bridge smiled, preparing to fish out a euro when they drew near, but suddenly they stopped. Another group of young men, four white guys with cropped hair and beards, moved to block their way. One of them shoved the lead dancer back into the others. Another yelled at them to shut the fuck up and get off the train; in fact why not get out of France and go back home? Voices rose across the carriage, some in defence of the dancers and some agreeing with their harrassers. Racist insults followed, and one of the bearded men even shouted '*Heil Hitler!*' in their faces.

Bridge's height gave her a stride advantage. She took two quick steps, reached for the *sieg-heiling* man's arm and twisted it back behind him, forcing his elbow the wrong way. With her other arm she circled the neck of another beard, pressing hard on his windpipe...

No. She shook her head to clear the image from her imagination and turned away, keeping Kennedy in sight through the window to the next carriage. She couldn't afford to draw attention to herself or get sidetracked. That her first instinct had been to start breaking bones unsettled her, but regardless, she was working. Much as she didn't like it, Bridge had to play the part of an ignorant bystander who didn't want to get involved. She was hardly the only one.

The dancers and racists tumbled out together at Châtelet–Les Halles, still shouting at each other and the surrounding public, while Kennedy remained seated in the other carriage. Bridge wondered again if they were destined for the airport.

But to her surprise Kennedy disembarked soon after, at Port-Royal. She followed him out, maintaining distance as he climbed to street level and turned west along the Boulevard de Montparnasse. Too wide and open for her liking, so she crossed the road and pretended to check her phone before continuing to follow. She didn't have far to go. After a brief walk, Kennedy buzzed an apartment building door between two small shops. Bridge hung back behind a restaurant truck unloading on her side of the street and watched as he spoke into the grille. The door opened, Kennedy entered, and the door closed again.

Shit. They hadn't anticipated a private apartment. According to local informants, Boštjan Majer was staying at a hotel off the Champs-Élysées. If he had a bolt hole here on the Boulevard, SIS didn't know about it.

Or did they? She pulled down her mask, took out her phone, and called Giles. He answered on the second ring. 'Line?'

'Secure. Kennedy's entered an apartment. I can't tell which one, but can you run the building for me?' She relayed the address and waited, leaning against a lamppost outside the restaurant and adopting the look of a bored local. She heard the tell-tale *click* of a third line connecting.

'Bridge, this is Emily Dunston. That building is home to a safe harbour, but it hasn't been used for months.'

She swore. *Safe harbour* was the code name for a network of apartments in major cities, owned by SIS – or rather by anonymous shell companies in the Caymans financed by SIS' shadow fund – and available for any officer in need. Worried about being lifted by the enemy? Head for the local safe harbour. Passing through, but overnighting at a hotel isn't safe? Stay at a safe harbour. Need to arrange a clandestine meeting somewhere you can guarantee isn't bugged? Use a safe harbour.

The apartments were managed by local caretakers, normally senior officers approaching retirement. It was a quiet appointment, no footwork required, no diplomatic declaration necessary. While the caretakers were employed by SIS, they weren't conducting operations or following mission orders. All they had to do was clean the apartments, regularly sweep them for surveillance devices, and be on call 24/7 at an emergency number.

'Can't be a coincidence that this is one of ours, can it?' Bridge said. 'Where's Henri?'

At the mention of his name, the Paris chief cut in to the conversation. 'On my way; fifteen minutes max.'

'That apartment isn't booked today or any time in the future,' said Dunston. 'And Farrow, the caretaker, is a Cold War relic. Stickler for procedure.'

Giles mused, 'Which means either Kennedy is breaking into the apartment...'

'Or Farrow is compromised,' said Bridge, completing the thought. 'Maybe he was offered a cut. Give his pension a boost.'

'The apartment number is 4C,' said Dunston. 'How do you want to play this?' One thing Bridge liked about the Paris head – perhaps the only thing, if she was honest – was Dunston's willingness to trust the judgement of whoever was on the ground, rather than micro-managing from behind a desk. Bridge ran through the potential scenarios in her head, and they were all bad. The street was growing busy as lunchtime approached, and in the few minutes she'd been on the phone several people had already left or entered the apartment building.

'Can you send me a file pic of Farrow?'

'Of course. Give me a moment.'

'In the meantime, I'd say don't contact him or local police yet. If the caretaker's in on it and sees you call out of the blue, or if one of them is scanning police radio and hears the call, they'll abort. I can't cover front and back door by myself, but the one thing we have on our side is the element of surprise. Blow that, and Kennedy and Majer will evacuate – assuming Majer's even here, yet – while Farrow will say he's just cleaning the place, and we'll have nothing.'

Her phone vibrated as Farrow's file photo landed in her inbox. He looked like a hundred other senior SIS officers; slim, around sixty, thinning white hair. She didn't *think* she'd seen him exit the building while she was watching, but given his everyman look and the prevalence of masks, she couldn't be sure.

'Photo received. Henri?'

'Still ten minutes out,' he said.

Bridge weighed her options. If Majer wasn't already in the apartment, she could secure Kennedy and Farrow in the meantime and wait for him. But if he was there, how long before he left again? 'Every minute I wait increases the risk we lose them altogether. I'm going to blag my way into the building.'

'No blag necessary,' said Dunston. 'That building has keypad entry, I can give you the code. You're on your own getting into the apartment, though.'

Bridge was already crossing the road, pressing a single AirPod into her ear and pulling her mask back up. When the earpiece beeped to confirm its connection she said, 'I'll rely on my winning personality. And I'll leave this line open, so I won't have to reconnect to call you for that police backup. I don't fancy fiddling about with my phone while trying to watch three targets.'

'Understood,' said Giles. 'We'll mute until you give the word.'

'Meanwhile I'll call my police contact and tell him to stand by, but no movement or radio for now,' said Dunston. 'Ready for that code?'

Bridge was. She tapped it into the building's keypad, pulled open the buzzing door, and slipped inside. OpPrep had issued her with a subcompact Glock 26, small enough to be unobtrusive in a shoulder holster under her jacket. She'd had to wait for thirty minutes in a private room at St Pancras while security checked her special dispensation to carry a firearm on Eurostar, but she was glad of it now as she climbed the stairs. There was a good chance nobody else would be armed; information brokers worked on trust, and an experienced operator like Majer might not even need backup muscle. Belatedly, she wondered how Kennedy was planning to receive the money. Could he have opened a Swiss account? Surely he wouldn't ask Majer to transfer a few hundred grand to his local branch of Barclays.

The building was more spacious than it looked from outside, with half a dozen apartments on each floor. She passed several people on the stairs; they were all masked, but none resembled Kennedy or Majer and the building had no elevator. Finally she reached the fourth floor, quiet except for the tinny din of daytime television coming from 4A to her left. She turned, following the doors round to the unremarkable and unobtrusive 4C. That being rather the point.

Now she was faced with getting into the apartment, and even as she stood there figuring out her next move, Bridge heard someone in the stairwell pass this floor on the way to the fifth. The door lock was a regular Yale, which she could pick inside ninety seconds, but that was more than enough time for someone to pass on the stairs and raise the alarm. She also couldn't hear any noises from inside the apartment, and while lock-picking was quiet, it wasn't silent. Anyone inside might hear it.

On the other hand, if she knocked and someone called out from behind the closed door, what could she say? '*Livraison spéciale*' wouldn't cut it; nobody using a safe harbour apartment would order any kind of delivery, special or otherwise. They'd immediately be suspicious.

Then again, she did have a gun.

Bridge drew the pistol, held it inside her jacket pocket, then bent her knees to make herself look shorter through the peephole. None of the men inside that apartment would recognise her, face mask or not. She knocked on the door with her free hand and waited, deciding to pose as the daughter of a concerned neighbour. Farrow wouldn't have needed to visit much during the pandemic, so the neighbours might not have seen him for months. Long enough to grow worried about an older man who seemingly lived alone.

But nobody called out from inside the apartment, or came to the door. Even over the other flat's television monotone Bridge expected to hear voices, footsteps, scraped chair legs, something from inside 4C to indicate movement. Had Dunston given her the wrong apartment number? Impossible. The Paris head didn't make that kind of mistake. But Bridge had now been standing here, a highly visible stranger in the building, for too long. Only one option remained.

Like all SIS officers, Bridge had trained for field work at The Loch: an MoD facility in the Scottish highlands where Sgt Major Instructor 'Hard Man' Hardiman and other specialist tutors trained everyone from civil servants to security staff in dangerous work. It was where she'd learned to pick locks, fight in close quarters, and fire the gun she now gripped in her pocket, loose but ready as she'd been taught. She'd also been taught that firing a handgun at a lock was more likely to ricochet and kill the shooter than open the door, as even a basic lock was built from hardened solid metal.

The wooden frame *around* the lock, though, was a different

matter.

'No answer, no indication of movement,' she whispered into her earpiece. 'Prepare for breach.'

Bridge stood back from the door, sighted the jamb above the lock, and slowed her breathing. She fired one shot – immediately re-sighted, now aiming directly below the lock – second shot, and now she was moving, twisting into a side kick that forced the lock bolt through the now-splintered wood and onward, slamming the door against the apartment's side wall as she reset into a ready crouch. She raised the Glock from her low position, covering anyone who stood in the hallway.

But nobody did. Bridge waited three seconds, still hearing no sound or movement. Were they waiting for her, hoping she'd walk into a crossfire? Possible, and now unavoidable. The door was breached; there was no going back.

She stood up and inched forward into the hallway, pushing the door closed behind her. Even the television-watcher in 4A must have heard the shots. They might be calling the police right now, but Bridge couldn't let the thought distract her. Her more immediate concern was not getting shot in the next five seconds.

Still no sound as she reached the sitting room door and stopped, her back against the wall. She crouched again, hoping anyone shooting was inexperienced enough to instinctively aim high. Most people did. Something solid pressed into her back, and she turned to find a scented air freshener plugged into an outlet. She pulled it out and flung it ahead of her into the room, to draw their fire.

As it hit the back wall and clattered to the floor Bridge swung around the door frame, position low and pistol up, seeking targets.

There were none. At least, none standing upright.

Three men lay on the floor, silent and bloody. Two held guns. None moved, not even the rise and fall of shallow breath. Bridge swept the rest of the apartment, confirming it was empty. She holstered the Glock and returned to the sitting room. Then she pulled down her mask, and regretted it when stale iron and body odour washed over her, clinging to the back of her throat.

'Bridge, abort!' Giles suddenly shouted in her ear. 'Get out, now.'

Caught by surprise, she reeled in confusion. 'Nearly gave me a bloody cardiac. You were supposed to be on mute. What's going on?'

'Word from my police contact,' said Dunston. 'Someone heard shots, and an armed response unit is en route.'

'Fuck.' The neighbour must have called them. 'Tell Henri to stay back. How long have I got?'

'Police ETA unknown, but imminent. Mourad is holding his position, five minutes away on Rue Guynemer. What's the situation?'

'Total clusterfuck. Three dead.' Bridge stepped around the bodies, careful not to touch anything or step in blood. Kennedy was nearest the door, face down with a small Browning pistol in one hand, his shirt soaked in blood from a chest wound. Majer sat across the room, slumped on the floor with his back against an easy chair, wielding a Heckler & Koch pistol. His chin rested on his chest as if asleep, but the wreckage of his own chest said otherwise. The final body was an older man, hair as grey and thin as his clothes, matching the photo of Farrow. He lay on his bloody front, face turned to the side, hands empty of weapons but reaching out for rescue and salvation. 'Kennedy, Majer, and Farrow are all off the board. Looks like a double-cross of some kind...'

'Move now, think later,' Giles urged her.

'Hang on, hang on,' said Bridge, looking around the room. Bloody smears and handprints stained the furniture and walls, suggesting some or all of these men had been given time to take final breaths, heavy gasps of desperation and regret. Who shot first? Who wouldn't back down? Who attempted the double-cross in the first place? Those questions might never be answered, but she could still salvage something from this carnage. 'If they all shot one another, then the plans are still here.'

'To hell with the plans, just get out,' said Dunston, but Bridge was already crouching by Kennedy, turning his body over.

She pulled his jacket open, ignoring the blood-soaked cloth slipping between her fingers. His inside left pocket contained his passport and a Samsung phone. She pocketed the latter, hoping her CTA colleagues back in London could crack it open, then turned to the other side. It held a thin credit card wallet and Navigo card. She was about to look in the outside pockets when she noticed a narrow opening halfway down his inside left pocket lining. A spectacles pouch, complete with thin zip enclosure. Bridge gripped the bloody material and pulled at the zip.

'Et voilà,' she murmured as a USB thumb drive slid out onto Kennedy's chest. Hearing distant shouts from the apartment stairwell, she pocketed it and turned to leave. There would be one hell of a mess to clean up – not just the physical scene, but the political ramifications and explanations the Service would have to provide, both private and public. But SIS was well-practised at concocting vaguely reassuring official explanations to spare families, and the public, from the sordid truth. No doubt Giles was already working that angle back in London.

All she had to do was go up a floor and wait out the cops. There might even be a fire escape down from the rooftop.

She made it to the hallway before three *Police nationale* officers stormed in, guns raised, screaming at her to drop to her knees with her bloody hands in the air.

4

'Holy shit. Casey, you seen this?'

Casey Lachlan didn't hear. He was wearing earmuffs, focused down range, the stock of his Colt MT6601 nestled into his shoulder, and head cocked to sight along the barrel. No mount or scope, no bench support to steady the rifle. 'Shooting clean,' his father had called it, ever since he first took young Casey to a range. Of course, that was with the old man's hunting rifle, an M1, which was never designed to take scopes unless you were a sniper anyway. Over the years 'shooting clean' had come to be a sort of family catchphrase for doing a job right, without fuss.

Casey wished he was here now. Maybe he was watching somehow. Casey eased out the tension in his shoulders to focus on the target. He inhaled deep, exhaled steady, squeezed the trigger. The crack of a single shot, still loud through the earmuffs, and a split-second muzzle flash. Letting his shoulder move with the stock as it bucked in recoil. He remembered the first shot he ever made, how stiff he'd been, trying to prove the recoil was nothing. All it bought him was a shake of his father's head and three days of aching shoulder.

Today, by the time his shoulder even moved, the bullet was a hundred yards down range and buried in the target. At least, he hoped that's where it landed. He placed the rifle safely on the bench in front of him, slipped off the earmuffs, and picked up his binoculars to check.

'How's it?' asked Mike, now standing next to him.

Casey passed him the binoculars. 'Inch left of centre. Not bad for first shot of the day.' He said that last part a little louder, so anyone nearby would hear. But when he glanced around to see who that might be, nobody was close enough. Freedom Hills Range was a no-frills kind of place, nestled in a shallow valley. The owner supplied the space, the targets, a bathroom, and refreshments. You wanted anything else, you brought your own – including beer and chairs, which was why the other early risers were still tailgating at their trucks instead of over here shooting.

'Get a bench support and you'd have been dead on,' said Mike. Before Casey could reply he handed back the binoculars and said, 'I know, I know. Shooting clean, all that bullshit. Me, I prefer being accurate.'

Casey smiled. 'I like both,' he said, putting the earmuffs back on to signal the conversation was over. Mike Alessi was a year older than Casey, a nerd who'd forgotten more about computers than Casey would ever know. But, useful though he sometimes was, the Flag Born wasn't about computers. It was about defending America, and that took marksmanship. Casey had him licked but good in that area. As he reached for the rifle again, though, Mike held out his iPhone to show Casey something.

'Wait, you gotta see this,' he said. Then, realising the screen was blank: 'Shit, hold on. Trust me, it's worth it. You need to listen, too.' Casey removed his earmuffs again while Mike unlocked the phone. The screen lit up on a page at Frank, the patriotic version of YouTube, ready to play a video. The preview image showed the former president, looking serious and committed as always, facing the camera in a darkened room. Old Glory hung behind him, its stars and stripes artfully draped. Mike tapped the screen, and the video played.

'My fellow patriots. You true and loyal Americans. Everybody knows this is a dark time, a terrible time. It's a crisis, what the liberals are doing to our country. Right now, in cesspools like San Francisco and Los Angeles, they're paying black women to have babies. Can you believe it? Those of us who understand, we can see this for what it is – white genocide in action, right? The great replacement. And it's not only happening here in our great country. This is all over the world, our beautiful heritage, being destroyed and wiped out by people who want the white race to disappear. One day we'll all be gone if they have their way, believe me.' His voice rose. *'But true patriots will not stand for it. And now we have a chance, a perfect chance, to show the world that we will not lie down and let our culture be destroyed. We will not abandon our people to the liberal nightmare!'*

Casey glanced at Mike. 'Is this a campaign?' Mike waved *shush* and pointed at the video.

'You know I can't go on TV and tell you this. They don't want you to hear the truth, not even our so-called allies. This country is so bad, I have to deny my own words if they call me out. And if you try to do anything about it, the fake news media will call you traitors and other bad things, instead of the heroes you are. But like I said, this is happening all around the world.' He smiled sadly. *'And some places, well, the liberals aren't so much in control. I hear from leaders in Europe every day, they call me and say, "Mr President," because they respect me, "Mr President, we need your help. The EU, full of terrible people, they won't do anything. We've got immigrants flooding our borders every day, thousands of them, they walk in and take over. We can't build a wall, the*

EU won't let us, and our own people aren't trained for this. We need strong, loyal American patriots to come and help us deal with this invasion. Please send your best men." They're crying, these big, strong men, leaders who never cry, but they're so grateful for everything we've done, and everything we can still do. The media is watching, so I can't say any more, but I want all of you, loyal warriors, to think about how you can help our brothers in the old fatherlands. The time for Operation Patrios is coming soon. Watch for the signal. God bless me, and God bless us all.'

The video ended. Realising he'd been holding his breath, Casey covered it up by spitting on the ground. 'Fucking EU. Dumb liberal motherfuckers are helping the enemy wipe them out, and they don't even know it.'

Mike smiled. 'So you think it's real?'

'Was there a word of a lie in what he said?'

'I guess not, but they can do a lot with computers these days.'

Casey shook his head. 'They can't fake that, Mike. I didn't see any cuts, did you? Besides, why would the president post fake news of himself?'

'He didn't post it. It was, hold on...' he tapped on his phone screen. 'Patriotic And True Rebels In Our Service. It's the first video they've ever posted.' He showed the screen to Casey, who read the user name, then laughed.

'P-A-T-R-I-O-S,' he said, pointing at the user name's initials. 'That's what he called the operation, right?'

Mike's eyes widened like Casey had shown him the hidden arrow in the FedEx logo. 'That's right! Holy shit, you got marksman's eyes all right.'

The range was quiet, as it often was early on a Saturday. Only a dozen other people hanging out, and none of them close enough to have heard what they were talking about. Casey said, 'Who else has seen this?'

'Everyone,' Mike laughed. 'It's viral, man. A guy linked to it on the Eagles & Aviators board last night, but it was already spreading. By now the whole world's seen it.'

Casey grunted and prepared to resume shooting. 'Then I guess those guys in Europe are gonna have plenty of help coming their way.'

'But not everyone got sent a bunch of money.'

That got his attention, as Mike must have known it would. Casey paused mid-grab for his rifle. 'What money?'

'It was wired to the Flag Born account this morning, from the same people. Look.' Mike launched his bank's app and showed him a transfer to their militia's fund that morning: thirty thousand dollars, from an account labelled simply PATRIOS.

Casey whistled. 'Who are these guys?'

'I don't know, but not everyone got money like this. One board went to hell this morning when a couple groups who'd been paid asked about it, 'cos they assumed everyone else did too. But most guys didn't get anything, and they're pissed. There's like a thousand replies already.'

'Did you tell them we got paid?'

'Hell, no. Not when I realised they were picking and choosing.' Mike looked offended. 'I'm not stupid.'

'You tell any of our guys about it yet?'

'About what?' A voice spoke behind Casey, startling him. He turned to see Brian, the Flag Born leader, walking up.

'Oh, hey, Brian,' said Mike. 'We were just talking—'

'About the president's video,' Casey interrupted quickly, before Mike could open his big mouth. 'You seen it?'

Brian nodded. 'Damn straight. That man's got a way with words, ain't he? Can't say I agree with him this time, though.'

'Don't agree? Every word he said was true.'

'Damn straight, but it ain't our fight. Not our business to get involved in other countries' business, right? They got a problem with towelheads, it's up to them to figure out the answer. Hell, it don't take a genius.' He pointed a finger down range and mimed firing a pistol.

'That's exactly why we should go over there and help them,' said Casey. His opinion of Brian's 'leadership' was no secret. If he could be bothered he'd have staged some kind of coup by now to take over – he was sure the others would support him, if he did – but it seemed like a lot of work, and he did what he wanted anyway.

Brian shook his head. 'Uh-uh. Don't you think we've got enough problems of our own right here in America? Sun Tzu said, "*Only an idiot fights a war on two fronts.*" Let's fix our own problems before we start helping others. America first.' He turned and left.

Mike looked like he was trying not to laugh. 'What's funny?' asked Casey.

'That quote wasn't... never mind.' Mike shook his head. He watched Brian walk back to the tailgate gathering. 'No European vacation for us, I guess.'

'Bullshit. None of those guys know about the money, right?'

'No, but Brian said—'

Casey almost vibrated with anger. 'Screw what Brian said. What else is the Flag Born for, if not to preserve the white man's heritage and integrity? We're a global brotherhood, and I got plenty of vacation due. How about you?'

'How long for? There's no instructions or nothing.'

'Not yet, but I bet you can figure out how to contact someone with that internet brain of yours. Must be somebody's job to tell us where to assemble once we get there, right?'

Mike looked at his phone, as if the answers might flash up on-screen. 'Thirty grand... I mean, that's enough to fly a dozen of us there and back, easy.'

Casey followed Mike's gaze to the other members, but shook his head. 'Sure,' he said slowly, 'if all we need to do is fly there and back. But think about it. We'll have to rent a car. Sleep somewhere. Eat, drink. Europe ain't cheap, Mike.' Casey had been to Dublin five years ago, on vacation, making him the voice of authority on all things European. 'Besides, be honest. How many of those guys do you think got the balls?'

Truth was, Casey wasn't a hundred per, cent sure he had the balls himself, but he was damned if he'd let Mike see that. And what he'd said was true; the Flag Born had been formed for exactly this purpose, waiting for a call like this. He'd spent months telling anyone who'd listen that the way to solve Europe's problems was to go in there, Iraq-style, and lead their brothers into battle against the encroaching immigrants. Casey had passed up protesting at the Capitol because he wanted to take action, not freeze his ass off carrying a home-made sign. By the time he saw shit was going down there for real, it was too late. But now their American president – the *real* president – had given them a mission, and Europe was finally ready for them. Patriots didn't shirk from their duty.

Especially if it meant reminding the lower races who was in charge.

'You and me, man,' he said. 'We can be goddamn heroes. Get online and ask for details. Tell whoever's co-ordinating from Europe that we're standing by and ready to fly.'

Casey put on his earmuffs, picked up his Colt, and fired three quick shots without resetting. Checking through the binoculars, he could almost feel the old man's hand on his shoulder, nodding in approval at the tight triangle of holes.

5

Bridge was used to being arrested.

The first time had been when she was fifteen, after she hacked the local council's website and defaced it with vegetarian animal rights propaganda. Her mother was mortified at the scandal of a police car outside their house, while Bridge was merely angry at whichever of her so-called friends ratted her out. There had been a couple more times as a teenager, and the University hack at Cambridge that led to her being recruited for SIS. Since taking on field work, though, she'd come to know the inside of cells and interrogation rooms in a surprising variety of countries, and the most fascinating thing about them was how stubbornly un-fascinating they all were.

Paris was no exception. They'd taken everything from her pockets, including the USB drive, then thrown her in a cell three metres square with a poured concrete floor, old plaster walls, a moulded concrete bench, and a small high window covered by steel mesh. They left her to stew there before dragging her to the interrogation room which, like the cell, could have been anywhere in the world. Another concrete floor, plain walls, table bolted to the floor with fixing points for shackles, uncomfortable wooden chairs, and the ubiquitous recording devices; cameras high in every corner with red activation lights blinking passively, and a regulation audio recorder on a wall-mounted shelf.

'At least the cell had a window,' she said to the officer as he gently but firmly pressed her into one of the chairs. He rolled his eyes and moved back to the door, watching her.

If the wall clock wasn't a lie, Bridge had been in the cell for two hours without water or a toilet break. She was pretty sure that violated her human rights, but good luck getting any sympathy from a Paris cop, or even a judge, after being apprehended trying to leave a scene with three dead bodies. A cursory exam would prove her own gun hadn't been fired, but she didn't blame them for assuming the worst.

More worrying was how quickly the police had arrived at the apartment. They weren't Emily Dunston's friendlies, which meant someone else had heard shots, dialled 17 for emergency, and called them to the address. At the time Bridge had assumed the TV-watcher in apartment 4A did it when she broke down the door. But given time to think in the cell, she remembered she'd barely been in the apartment for two minutes when armed police charged in. Even an emergency response unit wasn't that fast. Instead, the caller must have heard the crossfire between Kennedy, Majer, and Farrow. Bridge kicked herself for not following Kennedy inside immediately, but could she have stopped the massacre if she had? Or would the police have arrived to find her body alongside the others?

Most of all, though, she was concerned that nobody had come to collect her. Surely Henri had a line to the local cops? What about someone from the British embassy? Giles and Dunston had heard the commotion, but one of the cops ripped out her AirPod before Bridge knew where she was being taken. Did the police know who she was? If they'd allowed her a phone call she'd have dialled Giles already, but like toilet breaks, such niceties weren't afforded those suspected of multiple murder.

A senior officer, plain-clothes type, entered and sat opposite her. He had a pen and notepad, a thin moustache, and a bored demeanour. Only the last surprised Bridge; again, three dead bodies, armed woman without a scratch on her. Perhaps it was because he'd already guessed her only response to every question would be *aucun commentaire*, the French equivalent of *no comment*. Someone from London would be here soon enough. All she had to do was wait this out.

The officer began recording and questioned her in French. 'You're a dual national. Says here you were born in Lyon.'

'No comment.'

'What were you doing in that apartment?'

'No comment.'

'You work for the British Department of Trade and Industry. Does your Government know you're here?'

'No comment.'

'Why did you kill those men?'

'No comment.'

'What's your relationship with the apartment's owner?'

'No comment.'

A knock at the door brought relief from the monotony, and some hope of escape. Even Giles couldn't have got here this fast, but perhaps someone from the embassy had finally come to save her from this pointlessness. Or Henri had persuaded the cops to put her on the first Eurostar back to London.

The officer gathered his pen and notepad, paused the recording, and left the room. Bridge heard muttered voices on the other side, and wondered what deal was being worked out. If she was stuck here then the *Police nationale* would demand jurisdiction, but perhaps someone from London would be allowed to shadow them to satisfy the bureaucrats. She just hoped they'd let her have that USB drive back.

The door opened and a large, wide-shouldered man entered. A man she recognised, but hadn't thought she'd ever see again.

He cocked his head at the police officer standing guard inside the room, who got the message and left, closing the door behind him.

To her dismay, the newcomer carried an Asus laptop and the USB drive she'd taken from Kennedy. He placed both on the table between them, sat in the chair opposite, and glowered at her. He didn't restart the tape recorder, and the CCTV cameras' red lights were now dark. The man took a pack of cigarettes from inside his jacket, removed and lit one, then dropped the pack on the table. He gestured at it, while blowing a cloud of smoke.

'Brigitte Joséphine Sharp,' he said. 'Care to join me?'

Bridge scowled. 'Thank you, Monsieur Voclaine, but I quit.'

'Serge Tolbert, if you please.'

'So that *is* your real name. I thought it might be another alias.'

'No more than yours.' He glanced down at the USB stick. 'Before we get to this, perhaps you'd like to save us all a lot of time and effort and tell me why you killed three men this morning?'

Bridge leaned back and folded her arms. 'I'm innocent.'

'I doubt that very much,' said Tolbert. He was DGSI – *Direction Générale de la Sécurité Intérieure*, France's equivalent of MI5 – but Bridge hadn't known that when she first met him. Then he'd been François Voclaine, world-weary programmer, wife-beating misogynist, and second-in-command at a secret military drone project called Exphoria where she'd been tasked to find a mole. At one point she'd thought he was the leak, before discovering Tolbert's identity was fake; he was in fact hunting the same mole. They were on the same side, and ultimately helped one another with mutual off-the-books favours. Perhaps he thought that would be enough for her to confess to murder.

Tolbert shrugged and plugged the drive into the laptop. Its icon appeared on the desktop, and to open it the system demanded a password. Tolbert looked up from the keyboard at Bridge, as if waiting for her to tell him. She returned his shrug, secure in the knowledge that she really didn't know the password.

But he did, apparently. Tolbert smiled as he typed, and the drive opened. Inside were hundreds, maybe thousands of documents, all with inscrutable alphanumeric file names.

Bridge leaned forward, unable to hide her curiosity. 'All right, I'm impressed. How did you know the password?'

'You're not the only one who can use a computer, *mademoiselle*. My men have been on this for the past hour until we cracked it.'

'So that first cop knew he was only marking time? No wonder he looked bored.'

'As I'm sure you can imagine, your name set off all sorts of alarms when it was entered in the system, including at the DGSI. I came down here and saw the drive in your possessions bag. So now that we're talking, tell me this: why are you so interested in nuclear power stations?'

Bridge opened her mouth to respond, then belatedly realised that wasn't at all what she'd expected him to say. She pointed at the laptop and tried again. 'I don't know what that is.'

Tolbert snorted. 'You expect me to believe you killed three men for this drive without even knowing its contents?'

It was plain that *aucun commentaire* wouldn't cut it here, so she decided to pass the buck instead. 'I didn't kill anyone. Just call Giles and get this over with, will you?'

'Who?'

'Giles. My boss, in London.'

Tolbert was confused. 'I thought you worked for Emily Dunston.'

'Which shows you don't know everything. I promise you, François – sorry, I mean Serge – I swear to you those men were dead when I arrived. Do you really think I'd have hung around long enough to be caught?' Now it was Bridge's turn to hope their past encounter might persuade Tolbert to extend her the benefit of the doubt.

He thought about it for a moment, then opened several documents on the laptop. Blueprints, accompanied by scientific formulae and data spreadsheets several grades above Bridge's know-how. Tolbert gestured at the files. 'Nuclear reactors, control rooms, specifications. But here's the strange thing: as far as we can tell, these aren't secrets.'

'What do you mean?'

'What I say. These are the plans for Belleville-sur-Loire, a plant that was opened before you were even born. It's hardly information worth killing for.'

'I. Didn't. Kill. Them.' Bridge took a deep breath. She didn't want to trust Tolbert blindly, but was it really blind? He'd trusted her during Exphoria, even when she unwittingly blew his cover, and there seemed to be more going on here than either of them understood. She made the decision and spoke carefully. 'Two of those bodies are ours; Farrow and Kennedy. Our intel said Kennedy was here to sell plans for…well, not an old nuclear plant, that's for sure. Something new and secret.'

'Selling to Boštjan Majer, presumably? He is known to us. But he wouldn't even take a meeting for this garbage.' Tolbert gestured at the screen. 'You can download these plans off the internet for free.'

Bridge frowned. 'It doesn't make any sense. Kennedy wouldn't have tried to sell Majer rubbish. You can tell from the scene that one side tried to rip the other off, and everything went *bang-bang*. But I'd have thought Majer double-crossed Kennedy, not the other way around.'

'How would Majer know he was being double-crossed? We found no computer in the apartment.'

'Of course not. Those apartments are –' She stopped herself, realising she'd almost given away that it was a safe harbour. Then again, after today SIS would remove it from their books anyway. 'That apartment is clean. No surveillance installed, including a ban on computers.'

'Ah, one of your little dens,' Tolbert smiled. 'We know about those. A good place to conduct some clandestine business, eh?'

Bridge pictured the apartment in her mind. Tolbert was right, there was no computer present, and she hadn't seen a laptop bag or briefcase. Kennedy hadn't carried one, but was it possible Majer had brought a laptop, demanded Kennedy unlock the USB stick, and pulled his gun when he realised he was being sold a lemon? But if so, why was the stick still in Kennedy's pocket? He was nowhere near Majer when he'd been shot or returned fire –

'Wait a minute.' She straightened, running through the scene again. Tolbert said nothing, giving her time to think. Bridge quickly replayed events in her mind, over and over, looking for the anomaly. When she found it she said, 'Why did he have a gun?'

'A man like Majer is always armed.'

Bridge shook her head. 'Not him. Kennedy. I shadowed him from London, and he wasn't carrying. Even I had to jump through hoops to get a firearm on the Eurostar, and I'm a field officer. Kennedy was a pen-pusher.'

'Then there was a gun in the apartment. I expect all your little "safe havens" have them, yes?'

'For Farrow, sure. But he wouldn't hand it to Kennedy, leaving himself unarmed. Unless...' Bridge leapt to her feet. 'Fucking hell; unless he didn't. We need to take another look at that apartment.'

Tolbert remained seated, looking bemused. 'Mademoiselle Sharp, may I remind you that you're under arrest.'

'Oh, for God's sake.' She rolled her eyes. 'Don't you get it? The whole thing is a stage, a set-up. Someone else was there.'

'A fourth man?'

'Or woman, thank you. But whoever it was, they took the real thumb drive and planted that one to throw us off the scent.'

Tolbert swore, closed the laptop, and walked with her to the door.

6

Sasha Petrov didn't believe what he was seeing.

No, that wasn't true. He could believe entirely what was being broadcast on the screen. He even knew how it was done, and he should. But that was how he knew the news anchors were mistaken.

Outrageously racist, they called it. An antagonistic slap in the face, from a man they had once trusted, but now showed his true colours. And while the action he called for was in Europe, how long before this infantile, offensive man turned his attention to the rest of the world?

They were wrong. Not about the former president's character, or that his words were an outrage. Of course they were; someone wrote that speech with its precise effect in mind. The person who wrote it could even be someone known to Sasha, if his assumptions were correct.

But they'd all been fooled. The former president didn't actually say those things. The video was so successful because everyone knew he *might* say them, if he thought he could get away with it. It wasn't hard to imagine that his own staff were persuading him, right now, not to publicly disavow the video. It was after all merely saying what his supporters wanted to hear. The question those staff would ask was, of course, why? Who benefited from this video being seen around the world?

Sasha knew. He was probably – no, certainly – the only person in this building who did. He might be the only person in this city, this region, even this entire country who knew the answer to that question.

And this TV, this ridiculous propaganda machine, was his only source of information about it. They wouldn't let him leave; the suite was guarded night and day. But this was too much. He had to get out somehow, even if only virtually.

He muted the TV and turned to the door, hearing its magnetic lock *chunk* open. A short official entered, accompanied by a burly guard he hadn't seen before. The official carried a case, which he opened on the coffee table to reveal a medical kit and syringe.

Sasha snorted. 'At last, you're giving me a vaccine?'

The official offered a quizzical look. 'It is required,' he said, missing the sarcasm. 'Your arm, please.'

Sasha rolled up his sleeve and offered his shoulder. He didn't like needles much – who did? – but he liked dying even less. It was in and out in a moment, replaced by a cotton swab which the official pressed against his skin.

'Hold this firm for one minute.' The official returned everything to the case and closed it up. 'The dose takes time to be fully effective. Then you will be transported.' He and the burly guard left without another word. Sasha remained on the couch, wondering how his life had come to this. Not so long ago, it had all been so clear and simple.

But this was no time for self-pity. He'd wasted enough energy on that, before realising that even screwing the junior girl who brought him food and drink didn't help. He'd laughed at the thought that the suite was probably wired for vision, and some security guard had to sit through video of it. Maybe even the same guard who now made deliveries instead of the girl. He wondered if she even still worked here any more.

The assumption of cameras also made his life difficult, limiting what he dared to do. One more way of cutting off his access to the outside world. But there was an old saying that limitations force creativity, and Sasha Petrov was very creative indeed when he put his mind to things. It was time to consider his options.

7

'*Bonjour, monsieur Tolbert,*' said Giles, his voice tinny through Bridge's phone. 'Sorry, that's about the extent of my French. *Mein deutsch ist besser, ist das nützlich?*'

Tolbert dismissed his concerns. 'I speak English well, Mr Finlay. It's good to meet you at last.'

They were in the back of a speeding car, unmarked but with grille lights flashing and siren blaring to cut through Parisian traffic. Bridge and Tolbert gently rocked from side to side in the back seat while she tried to hold her phone steady. She'd called Giles as soon as they climbed into the car, to arrange a video conference with him and Emily Dunston.

'Why don't you fill us in, Bridge?' said Dunston.

'Not much to tell. Two hours in a cell, then finally my name caught DGSI's attention.'

'If you'd told us you were coming, we could have helped,' said Tolbert. 'You've made quite a mess, and I still don't even know why.'

Giles was silent for a moment, then said, 'Classified documents, is all I can tell you. Kennedy was trying to sell them to Majer.'

Bridge turned to Tolbert. 'What was the response time, from the first emergency call to the police reaching the apartment?'

'First? There was only one. Response time was six minutes and thirty seconds.'

Bridge ran the timeline back in her mind and shook her head.

'Six and a half minutes before the cops arrived, I was still standing in the street. Is there a recording of the call?'

'Naturally. A man reports hearing shots from the apartment, then cuts off before giving any other information. We traced the number, but it was a pre-paid mobile. We located the signal, though, and confirmed it came via a cell tower that serves the apartment building.'

Giles stroked his beard in thought. Even hundreds of miles away Bridge felt a sense memory, imagining the familiar waft of his hazelnut grooming oil. 'So someone heard the shots, called the police, and instead of the killer they got you, Bridge. Rather bad timing.'

Bridge shook her head. 'Or very good timing if that call was made by whoever killed Kennedy, Farrow, and Majer. A fourth man.' She could almost see cogs whirring in Giles' mind, no doubt asking himself the same questions Bridge had pondered in the police interview room. She wondered what would happen to her arrest report, and the recording of her being questioned by the bored detective before Tolbert arrived. DGSI would probably either seal them *Top Secret* or simply destroy them. It's what MI5 would have done.

Giles spoke at last. 'Bridge, you watched Kennedy enter, so the shooting must have happened while you were outside. If you're right about a fourth man, there's a good chance you saw him leave the building.'

'I might even have seen them enter,' she agreed. 'But I was only really watching for Kennedy or Majer, and nobody else stood out as obviously suspicious.' She turned to Tolbert. 'Is there CCTV on the Boulevard? Maybe outside Port-Royal?'

'I'll get someone on it.' He took out a Pixel phone and began dialling.

'Don't assume it was a man. Have them look for women, too.'

Tolbert rolled his eyes. 'With you sitting here, how could I not?'

'But we've lost too much time,' said Dunston, annoyed. 'Whoever did this could be anywhere in France by now, or even out of the country. Belgium, the Netherlands, and Germany are all less than two hours by train. By the time we know who we're looking for, they could be anywhere in Europe.'

'Including the UK, with the right documents,' said Giles.

Tolbert was enquiring after the CCTV on his phone, so Bridge answered. 'All true, but we have to assume this was a pro. If DGSI focuses facial recognition on their database of known operators, we might get a lucky hit.'

The car turned into Boulevard de Montparnasse, but soon jerked to a halt. The road was closed, a phalanx of emergency vehicles filling the street outside the apartment building. 'We're here. I'll let you know,' said Bridge, ending the call. Tolbert swore under his breath as he ended his own call. 'Problem?' she asked.

He made an all-encompassing gesture at the scene around them and climbed out of the car, pulling on a disposable mask. Bridge exited her side and took out her own mask, grateful the police had returned her possessions. To her surprise, though, as she walked towards the apartment building Tolbert crossed the street in the other direction. She caught up with him, careful to stay outside of the police cordon. 'What's up?'

'Cameras at Port-Royal aren't operational,' he said, walking quickly towards the Italian restaurant outside which Bridge had lingered. A security camera was mounted over its entrance.

'There's a *tabac* on the other side of the road, too. They might have something.' She was about to offer to go and check, then remembered she had no jurisdiction.

'They let you go, then?' called a familiar voice.

Startled, Bridge turned to see Henri Mourad approaching. 'You should probably stay away,' she said. 'This will be a shitshow for your station.'

Henri laughed. 'Technically I outrank you, so let me worry about the politics. I assume that's Tolbert?' He nodded at the big Frenchman, looming over the restaurant owner to demand their CCTV recordings in the name of national security.

'Have you been inside?' asked Bridge, looking up at the apartment building. Giles was right; she'd probably seen the killer with her own eyes as they exited onto the street. She cursed herself for not having noticed anything amiss, for being so focused on the people entering she'd paid no attention to those leaving. The killer might even have passed her on the stairs. If Bridge had been a few minutes faster, she would have caught them red-handed. Instead she'd found herself in the frame, and now she wondered: why call the police so soon? Why not wait an hour, or even call at all? Why not let the bodies rot until someone noticed the smell and broke down the door?

But it made sense if the killer had seen Bridge shadowing Kennedy. The apartment's living room window looked down onto the boulevard. She imagined the killer lying in wait, perhaps on the fifth floor stairwell, for Kennedy – the last arrival. When Farrow opened the door to admit Kennedy, the killer emerged and shot both men, then went inside to finish Majer. He looked out of the window, saw Bridge, made her for a tail, and called the police.

No, wait. Stop. That didn't make sense.

If the killer had shot Kennedy and Farrow when he opened the door, she would have seen blood outside. So the killer must have somehow entered the apartment without bloodshed. Were they known to one of the men inside, and invited in? Bridge imagined someone entering, being introduced as a friend...then shooting everyone, staging the scene, and leaving. Had whoever let them in expected to be spared? Was this a *triple* cross?

'Earth to Bridge. You still with us?' Henri waved a hand in front of her face.

'Sorry, I was miles away.' She shook her head. 'Something's not right about this, but I'm going round in circles trying to figure it out. I need to get inside, possibly talk to forensics.'

Henri puffed his cheeks. 'As I said when you weren't listening, the cops are keeping this one to themselves. Even threatening diplomatic blowback didn't get me anywhere, despite two bodies being British.'

'They can't keep me out,' said Tolbert, returning from the restaurant. 'The DGSI needs to know what happened in that apartment, and no jumped-up *poulet* will stop me.'

Bridge introduced Tolbert to Henri, then said, 'How did they know?'

Tolbert looked sideways at her. 'Come again?'

'The killer. How did they know about the deal?'

'Are we sure he did?'

'They took the thumb drive.'

'Thieves steal things.'

Bridge rolled her eyes. 'And replace them with a lookalike they just happen to be carrying?'

'OK,' Tolbert conceded. 'So one of them leaked. London knew about your officer coming here to sell, so maybe someone else did too.'

Henri considered that. 'Or Majer had already set up a buyer, but they decided to cut out the middle man and just take the goods.'

Tolbert nodded, agreeing that was possible. 'You stay here,' he said to Henri. 'We're going in.'

Henri was taken aback. 'I'm station chief, so technically Farrow worked under me. I should be in there.'

'I don't know you,' said Tolbert, as if that justified everything. 'I'm sure Ms Sharp will make a full report.'

Bridge shrugged at Henri in apology and followed Tolbert. He flipped open his DGSI wallet and brandished it at a police officer manning the cordon, demanding to be let through. The officer stepped aside. Bridge entered the building while Tolbert ordered the officer to get on with requisitioning recordings from the *tabac* and any other shops and businesses with cameras looking this way.

Something continued to nag at her. She'd almost had it a moment ago, but now it drifted out of reach again. She climbed the stairs, trusting it would return when she saw the apartment. Police officers, crime scene investigators, and paramedics came and went as building residents watched from their doorways, hollering unanswered questions at the uniforms. To avoid scrutiny Bridge tried to look like a bad-tempered officer who didn't want to be here but had a job to do. Close enough to the truth to be convincing.

Tolbert caught up on the third floor, and they mounted the final stairs together. The fourth floor was now filled with officers and examiners. If 4A was still watching TV, they'd struggle to hear it above the din of people issuing orders and reporting in. Tolbert's ID got them inside 4C, though not before pulling on plastic hooded coveralls and booties.

The scene was untouched, if rather more crowded than before. But the three dead men still lay on the floor, blood pooled around them. Tolbert turned to the lead investigator, a middle-aged man, and asked, 'What's your thinking?'

'It'll be in the report.'

Tolbert glowered at him. 'I'm not asking for your verdict, I'm asking for your thoughts. And, to be blunt, I'm not asking.'

The forensic investigator sighed. Bridge figured he was used to detectives pulling rank on him at crime scenes. Nevertheless, he complied.

'They died in order of age,' he said, gesturing at Farrow. 'Oldest man first. The state of his body and blood suggests he was killed long before the others, maybe early this morning. Next was this one.' He pointed at Majer, nearest to them. 'Later in the day, but rigor condition indicates some time before the third.' Finally he nodded across the room at Kennedy. 'He was recent, presumably not long before your colleagues broke in and arrested the bitch who did it.'

Tolbert half-smiled at Bridge, but she let it go and said, 'You're implying they weren't all shot at the same time? How can that be?'

The investigator looked at her sceptically. 'None of these men were shot, *mademoiselle*. The guns are for show. They were all stabbed, at different times.'

Bridge groaned as the pieces clicked together in her mind. She'd missed it because she'd been rushing, and her timeline was all wrong. She walked out of the apartment, disposing of her plastic cocoon in the bin as she exited, and descended to the street. Stepping outside, she wasn't entirely surprised to see that Henri had left, presumably to vent at Dunston about Tolbert's attitude. She leaned against the building wall, taking deep breaths. Tolbert emerged from the building a moment later, took out two cigarettes, and offered her one. This time she accepted it.

'What's on your mind?' he asked, lighting hers, then his own.

'Noise and surprise,' she said after a long first drag. 'I've been wondering why there was only one call to the police. You know how loud guns are, even with a silencer, and this isn't the sort of area where people ignore gunshots. But because the pistols were in their hands, I didn't consider other possibilities. If I'd looked closer I'd have seen they were stabbed.'

'You didn't have time.'

Bridge took another long drag and blew out a cloud of smoke in frustration. 'Because I thought they'd been shot, I assumed it must have all happened at once. They couldn't have been shot earlier, or the cops would have been called long before Kennedy and I got here, right? But a professional can stab someone without making a sound, in complete silence. Then they position the body just so, and patiently wait for the next victim.'

Tolbert whistled. 'You really think the killer stabbed the old man first, then sat with the body for hours until the others turned up one by one? That's cold.'

'Not only that, they staged each body in turn without haste or mess. Then for a last poke in the eye they called the cops on me, slowing us down while they escaped.' She half-smiled. 'We're definitely dealing with a pro, but on the bright side that means they'll be on a watchlist somewhere. Your boys are going to have a long night with those CCTV recordings.'

8

Andrea Thomson was walking with her son Alex when the lights went out.

They were visiting her in-laws, and Alex suffered the perpetual boredom typical of all young boys forced to endure their family, despite the menagerie of games and puzzles they'd brought to keep him entertained. So, both to occupy him and to escape the equally perpetual disapproving gaze of her mother-in-law, she took him for a walk through the Fens, on the pretext of looking for local birds. He was still just young enough to enjoy that.

Her partner Joan stayed behind to help prepare tea. She'd said a walk would 'help Alex build an appetite', which sounded absurd to Andrea, considering their son's ability to eat half the refrigerator between meals. But Andrea didn't mind. She jealously tried to guard her private hours, and ensure she was home from work in good time most days, but being a senior MI5 officer was no more a nine-to-five than her Army days. She and Joan had met in Afghanistan, when the latter was an embedded journalist shadowing the battalion, and sometimes it felt like they'd seen more of each other while they were in a war zone than after they returned home.

Dusk was long out here, the sun's afterglow stretching to the horizon, and the imminent onset of full darkness had taken Andrea by surprise. She circled them around, emerging from the fields into a local village, its sole shop closed and visible only by the dim glow of a security light. Alex sighed melodramatically, appalled that this backwater couldn't supply him with an ice cream past six o'clock in the evening. Andrea tried not to laugh, and reassured him that his grandparents definitely had ice cream, and pudding, and a hundred other grandson-spoiling foodstuffs ready and waiting for his voracious appetite.

'Now,' she said, 'do you have your torch? There's no streetlights between us and home.'

She might as well have asked him if he was carrying an egg whisk. 'You didn't tell me to bring it.'

'I didn't think I'd have to,' said Andrea. 'Well, my phone's got plenty of battery. Should be enough to get us back to the cottage.' At least they didn't need it quite yet, thanks to the light from houses and the single streetlamp standing guard over the village green.

Until they all suddenly went dark.

It took her a moment to understand, because there was no sound, no *pop* of a failed bulb or short-circuited wire. One moment they were navigating the narrow roadside kerb by the curtain-diffused light from a house; the next Andrea couldn't see the garden wall, let alone the road. Her first instinct was to stop walking and reach out for Alex, clutching at his shoulder. That was when the cry went up, every house on the main street shouting in frustration as they peered out and realised the whole village's power was gone. TV viewings interrupted, half-cooked meals ready for wasting, electric heaters cooling.

'What happened?' Alex gasped. 'Shit, is it an attack?'

She squeezed his shoulder. 'Mind your language. It's only a power cut; nothing to worry about.' It occurred to her that he'd probably never experienced this before, living his whole young life so far in London. She couldn't blame him for getting a little over-excited, but made a mental note to keep an eye on what kind of video games he was playing. To be fair, it was the first cut they'd experienced while visiting Joan's parents as far as she could recall. But they were relatively common in places this rural. Her own grandparents' place in Kinnesswood used to black out regularly; she remembered them grumbling that 'this place seems to run off a car battery and piano wire'.

Her eyes adjusted at last, and she was glad of the long dusk. Just enough light remained to make out silhouettes of the road, houses, and streetlights once she got her night eye in. She took out her phone and activated the flashlight.

'Don't worry. When we get home it'll all be back on.' She pulled Alex in for a reassuring hug. 'And if not, we brought some jigsaws.'

Andrea didn't need to see in the dark to know his eyes were rolling all over again.

* * *

In fact the power didn't return for two hours, during which the cottage settled into a candlelit silence with Joan doing her Sudoku puzzles, Alex playing cards with Granddad, and Grandma reading a magazine. Meanwhile, Andrea sat on the landline phone – thank goodness they still had one, so she could make calls even in a power cut – trying to get an answer out of someone, anyone, about what had happened. It was fruitless; even when she eventually pulled security rank it only earned a vague explanation that 'a relay had tripped' and power would be restored 'soon'.

When the lights finally came back on, Joan and Alex cheered. Joan's mother said it was about time, as if it had somehow all been Andrea's fault, then marched into the kitchen on a mission to rescue tea even though they'd all been scoffing bags of crisps in the dark.

All was back to normal. Nothing to worry about.

9

The Eurostar took two hours and twenty minutes from Gare du Nord to St Pancras, and Bridge spent two hours and eighteen minutes of it fast asleep. She jerked awake as they pulled in at London, disorientated and flailing, with the sparse and mournful cries of *The Writing on My Father's Hand* playing in her AirPods. She apologised for startling the couple sitting opposite, first in French, then in English when she realised they were local, and hurried off the train ahead of them before she embarrassed herself any further. Thank goodness there'd been nobody sitting next to her, or she might have accidentally whacked them.

Adrenaline had kept her going throughout Paris, even when banged up in a cell or being questioned by Tolbert, but as soon as she took her seat on the last train home, Bridge felt it drain away. She remembered putting on her mask, inserting her earbuds and starting a Dead Can Dance playlist, declining a drink from the attendant, nodding at the couple (who now probably thought she was a psycho)...then nothing until she woke at St Pancras. She hadn't dreamed at all, or if she did she had no memory of it. As far as she was concerned, that could only be a good thing.

It was late, she was still tired, and the cold London air was damp enough to warn of incoming rain. Nevertheless she decided to walk to Euston rather than take the short Tube connection, to clear her head. She didn't want to dwell on the apparent conclusion that maybe what she needed to ensure a night of dreamless sleep was to spend the day stumbling over dead bodies and being interrogated by the police.

She turned onto the Euston Road and removed her mask and earbuds, wanting to hear, smell, and taste the city. It was a dirty old town, as they said, but it was home, and life had almost fully returned to the old girl.

She wondered what lockdown had been like in Lyon. She hadn't been back to visit since her mother's funeral, and while her sister Izzy kept in touch with some of the old family over there, Bridge had hardly spoken to her lately either. That wasn't in itself surprising; Bridge had been away on a mission while Izzy sat at their mother's side in hospital, then arranged the funeral as well. Bridge had made it to the service, but even on her most defiant days couldn't deny she'd acted poorly and left her big sister to pick up the pieces.

Their conversations since had been strictly business concerning the will, the house, Maman's savings and pensions. Bridge didn't care about any of it. Izzy was the one with a family; she could have the lot. But of course it wasn't that simple. There were forms to sign, receipts to acknowledge, and frustrating conversations with French bureaucrats to navigate, so the sisters were required to stay in touch. Izzy had wavered over selling off the house in Lyon, then couldn't due to the pandemic anyway. It remained unsold, its future uncertain. The money they'd both received was simpler; the first Bridge had known about it was when a payment arrived in her bank account. She promptly transferred half back to her sister as a nest-egg for Izzy's children, Stéphanie and Hugo, and intended to spend the rest travelling. Covid had other ideas, so instead Bridge distributed chunks of it around local animal charities before shoving the rest into a savings account and trying not to think about it. Karl had banged on about investments and funds for a while, but eventually stopped after she threatened to burn it all in a Scottish boathouse if he didn't shut up.

He didn't get the reference, but that was OK. It was part of his charm; he could name every bloody elf, dwarf, and goblin in *Lord of the Rings*, but he knew nothing about British pop culture before he'd come to work here. She'd once spent an evening telling him about an old TV game show from the 2000s, every round growing increasingly outrageous and improbable, until she had to admit it didn't exist and she was winding him up. He hadn't seen the funny side, but she'd laughed all night. Perhaps she was going a little stir-crazy after all.

It made the unfairness even more acute. The suddenness of her mother's death had been what drove her to Karl in the first place – that desire to live, *sans attendre*, to not be timid or put things off until tomorrow – but then the whole world was forced to do just that. The cruel irony of being denied the chance to live at the moment she'd decided to do so wasn't lost on her. Thank goodness a lifetime of gothdom had prepared her to laugh at such tragedies.

Maybe that was why she and Karl hadn't yet tried to throttle each other. They were peas in a pod when it came to technology – Giles had once called him an American version of Bridge – but their outlook on life couldn't have been more different. His Stateside brand of relentless positivity grated at times, but she couldn't deny it was an effective counterbalance to her own inherent fatalism – and vice versa. The old *uk.london.gothic-netizens* newsgroup she'd relied on as an anchor to the real world had finally died, a victim of lockdown apathy, now just another ghost town of spam and porn binaries. Without Karl to keep her spirits up, she didn't want to think about where her mind might have gone during isolation.

She wondered if she'd make it through tonight without nightmares. Or maybe her two hours on the train would be all the peace she got.

There wouldn't be much peace tomorrow; Giles had allowed her to return home and sleep, given the circumstances, but ordered her in for a debrief at ten the next morning. She'd half-heartedly pointed out tomorrow was Sunday, but Giles didn't even acknowledge the objection. Early in Bridge's career he once said that for Service officers weekends were a privilege, not a right. At the time her French side had bristled at this outrageous encroachment on her free time, and wondered if he'd been joking. It didn't take long to realise Giles' sense of humour didn't run in that direction.

She made up her mind and took out her iPhone to text Karl.

Back in London. Going to my place. Work in the morning.

He replied immediately:

Too bad, but understood. How was it?

He didn't expect details over text, of course. But when they first decided to bubble together they'd tried to keep their respective jobs private and secret, and it had proven impossible. Unable to be in the same room in case of accidental screen glances, and not being able to discuss anything they'd spent whole days working on, was absurd within the cramped confines of a London flat. They might as well have not bubbled in the first place.

Besides, they were already bound to one another by a shared secret, one that would likely get them both fired and perhaps even prosecuted if revealed. In Estonia they'd escaped the clutches of the Russian agent Maxim, and prevented the Tempus computer system's attempt to release data stolen from politicians and civil servants all over the world; emails, spreadsheets, classified documents, the works. Both SIS and the CIA had wanted that data for themselves instead, but Bridge and Karl mutually agreed that was a terrible idea. They'd deliberately corrupted the data and told their bosses it was an accident. After that, deciding on a 'no more secrets' policy between them had been easy.

Chatting at home was very different to using electronic communications, though, so they remained circumspect over calls and text. Bridge could at least let him know she hadn't been injured, tortured, or traumatised, the occupational hazards of her job. She found the 'thumbs down' emoji, followed it with:

Not great! But

A horn blast almost made her drop the phone. She recoiled from the noise, and an angrily gesturing taxi driver, as his cab narrowly missed her on the crossing into Euston Square. Bridge retreated to the pavement, took a deep breath, and resumed.

Not great! But I'm OK. See you soon.

She'd have liked nothing more than to spend the night in a warm bed with Karl, but it wouldn't be fair on him if she spent the whole time fretting about the debrief and, inevitably, failing to sleep.

A drop of rain landed on the screen, then another, and another. Bridge put her phone away and turned up the collar of her leather jacket. Ignoring the still-red crossing light she hurried across the road, through the square, and into the station.

10

'Well, this is a grand old fuck-up, isn't it?'

Giles tutted. 'Careful, Devon. The statues might take offence.'

These being their only confidants on a brisk Sunday morning in Whitehall Gardens, which Giles instinctively disliked. He preferred his clandestine meetings in well-trafficked places, to hide in plain sight amongst crowds and commuters. Two men in greatcoats, ponderously walking together in front of the Ministry of Defence building, were an open invitation for someone to strap on a pair of headphones, hoist a parabola, and point a shotgun mic their way.

Devon Chisholme shook his head in disbelief. 'How am I supposed to explain that your officer let classified plans for a breakthrough weapon fall into hostile hands?'

Giles bristled. 'Some of us have actual dead bodies to explain away, if we're comparing lengths. Nobody expected a third party to burst in and slaughter all concerned. According to the pathologist, Farrow and Majer were dead long before Bridge arrived in Paris anyway.'

'Where is Sharp now?'

Giles checked his watch. 'On her way into the office, I should think. We're debriefing in a little over an hour. Why do you care?'

Chisholme stopped and spoke quietly. 'We must keep a lid on this, Giles. We can't let it be known the plans are out there on the market. You have to get that drive back.'

'And we will, but you and your office in turn have to understand that anything digital can be copied, perfectly and without limit. For all we know Kennedy has already uploaded those plans to the internet, from where they might by now have been *down*loaded to a hundred different enemy databases.' Chisholme paled with horror, so Giles hurried to reassure him. 'But I don't believe that's the case, or that we'll see them online. Whoever did this went to a lot of trouble; it wasn't young boys having a lark. They'll want to make good their investment. We're assuming details of the meeting leaked, and what we saw was premeditated enemy action.'

'But who would have leaked it?'

'Take your pick,' Giles shrugged. 'Kennedy may have been too loose-lipped in his efforts to sell. Majer may have spread the word among his own buyers, one of whom perhaps decided to go direct to the source.'

'You really don't think they'll have made copies?'

Giles resumed walking. 'Not what I said. I doubt they've *distributed* copies, because the plans are clearly of high value to them. All I'm telling you is that getting the USB drive itself back is no guarantee of solving your problem.'

Chisholme's tone turned icy. 'I think you'll find this is *your* problem, Giles. Your officer was on the scene, and need I remind you that I advocated arresting Kennedy before he even left the country. It was you who wanted to scalp this Majer chap into the bargain.'

Giles didn't rise to the bait. Instead he asked, 'Tell me, how *is* the Ministry staffer who happily gave Kennedy access to classified development plans?'

Chisholme grimaced. 'Neither you or I will be hearing from him for a while. Wonderful thing, the Terrorism Act. Which I'm sure a man like you knows all about.'

Giles did, and also knew better than to enquire further. The unlucky staffer was probably warming a cold isolation cell inside an offshore MoD black site, being interrogated as to how many other classified secrets he'd stolen and sold to associates. There was a first time for everything, but rarely a last. He said, 'SIS, SCAR, and our officers acted according to protocol and mission regs at all times, acting on information you brought to us after your department was compromised. If anyone's going to fall on their sword, Devon...well.'

'I don't think you'd enjoy testing that theory, Giles. Demotions in the Ministry are almost unheard of. Within the security services, however...well.'

Giles regarded Chisholme in something of a new light. Nobody rose to Senior Executive Officer at the MoD without a certain ability to negotiate the corridors of power, but this 'if I go down I'm taking you with me' threat was a level of raw politics he'd not previously encountered in the civil servant. 'All right. Keeping secrets is in our job description, so we can keep this internal while we try to fix it. But what about your side?' Giles nodded back at the edifice behind them. 'When reports of bodies cross certain desks, questions will be asked.'

Chisholme shrugged. 'I fail to see why such reports should concern us. None of the bodies are MoD, and neither was anything found in their possession.'

Despite himself, Giles was impressed at the man's moxie. 'You can't pretend Paris had nothing to do with the MoD. We have mission briefs.'

'None of which need see the light of day until long after this mess has been resolved, don't you think? As you said, you're rather good at keeping secrets across the river. How many Cold War dossiers have you still got squirrelled away?'

Giles ignored the question and thought about what Chisholme

was proposing. Finally he said, 'A lie is always more effective when couched in reality.'

'Meaning?'

'Meaning when we do let this particular cat out of its bag in Whitehall, we put your staffer firmly in the frame, assuming he can still stand upright, and tell the truth...except for the part where we don't yet know the killer's identity, and aren't currently tracking him across Europe.'

'You mean let people think we did? But then why wouldn't we have arrested him the moment he stepped onto the street in Paris?'

Giles smiled. 'Because we wanted to see where he was going, of course. Following people without apprehending them – indeed, without them even knowing it – is something else we're rather good at. So long as we collar him before any real damage is done, the timeline can be...retrospectively corrected.'

'You say that with the air of a man who's done it before,' said Chisholme. Giles said nothing. 'What if real damage *is* done? What if this mystery killer makes a hundred copies, as you suggested, before we catch him? What if he builds the bloody thing and uses it?'

Giles' smile faded. 'Then, my partner-in-cover-up, you will see how a true blame game plays out.'

11

'Come in, Brigitte. I believe this is the first time you've requested a session with me. Should I pop some champagne?'

'I could turn right around and leave, you know.'

Dr Nayar smiled. 'Please, sit down. You know I'm here to listen, and to help.'

Bridge had spent years in sessions with SIS' resident psychiatric therapist, reluctantly trudging in to this warm, soft, gentle, pastel room. All officers underwent routine psych assessments twice a year, but after Bridge's first field mission in Syria went badly wrong she'd been ordered to visit weekly. Over time she and the calm, understanding, frustratingly insightful Dr Nayar had come to a sort of mutual arrangement. She would turn up and do her duty, the doc would probe at the parts of herself Bridge thought were much better left alone, thank you, and occasionally she'd storm out rather than talk about them.

But during the pandemic everything changed. For one thing, sessions were held by video call rather than in person, and it was difficult to storm out of your own lounge. But the bigger change came when Dr Nayar said Bridge no longer needed weekly sessions. Their calls were reduced to one per month, and soon even those had dropped off.

Bridge barely knew what to do with herself. Dragging herself to therapy had become such a part of her identity, she felt lost without it. But the doc pointed out that lockdown kind of suited

Bridge – travel frustrations notwithstanding, staying indoors and staring at a computer screen was hardly a radical change of pace. More importantly, Bridge's life had stabilised to a degree neither of them could have foreseen. She knew her own mind better than ever; she had a boyfriend who accepted her, warts and all; and while she still had family problems, even Bridge had mentally downgraded those from 'existential' to merely 'annoying'.

She hadn't visited Dr Nayar since they'd returned to work at Vauxhall. The doc hadn't summoned her, and Bridge hadn't been about to make an appointment.

Until now.

She sank into the familiar soft armchair and gathered her thoughts. She'd been trying to gather them the entire way here, but they'd slipped through her mind's fingers like so much water.

'How was your post-mission briefing?' asked Dr Nayar after a minute of silence.

'That's not what I came here to talk about.'

'No, but it'll get your mouth and brain in sync. Give it a try.'

Bridge took a breath. 'It was fine. I mean, the mission was a shitshow. But it wasn't my fault, and now dealing with the fallout is in someone else's hands. Mostly the MoD's, I expect, but we're hardly blameless.'

'Sometimes missions go bad, no matter how carefully you prepare. And, "shitshow"? Really?'

'Yeah, just a spectacular failure. Everything that could have gone wrong did, and – oh.' She stopped, realising what the doctor meant. 'Yes, it's an American idiom. If it's any consolation, Karl says *oh, bugger* now as well.'

Dr Nayar smiled. 'Is that what you wanted to talk about? Or your family, perhaps?'

'Izzy's the same as ever,' said Bridge. 'I suppose I'm the roadblock there. She needs me to sign forms for the lawyers – something to do with our mother's house – and I haven't got around to it.'

The doctor was silent for a moment, then asked, 'How have you been sleeping?'

'Um, not great,' said Bridge, caught off guard by the question. 'But, you know, state of the world and all that. Nothing to do with Izzy.'

'I was thinking about the house, not your sister.'

Bridge frowned. 'That's not what I wanted to talk about, either.' Dr Nayar raised a silent eyebrow in reply. 'Look, Izzy's never going to sell it. Every time she makes plans to sell a house, something conveniently happens and she winds up keeping it. It's like she's collecting a set.'

'What's wrong with that?'

'Because all she's going to do is keep moving around them, spending a few months here and a few months there, and convince herself it's a lifestyle!' Bridge took a breath to calm herself, and the doctor gave her the space to do so. Of course she did. 'Izzy's turning into our mother, giving up her life for her husband and kids. I know it's none of my business, but...'

'You've always told me you and Izzy are nothing like each other.'

There it was, the heart of the matter. How did she do that?

'We're not. When Izzy met Fred they were both working for the same mission in Africa, but when they got married it was never in doubt that he'd keep his job and she'd give hers up.'

'Are you planning to have children?'

'No! God, no. Well, I don't know.' Bridge gestured around them. 'Hardly a good time to bring a kid into the world, is it?'

Dr Nayar smiled. 'I've never met a woman who felt ready and prepared to raise a child. It's not like karate, where you can practise for years and then take an exam.'

'Trust me, even when you do it all flies out the window as soon as someone kicks you in the face,' Bridge snorted. 'But look, this isn't – it's not about kids. It's about…' She trailed off.

'Has Karl asked you to give up work?'

'He knows I'd knock his block off if he even suggested it.' Bridge took a deep breath. 'But *I've* been thinking about it.'

Dr Nayar looked surprised. 'Does Giles know?'

'I don't mean like that.' Bridge paused. 'You're right, I haven't been sleeping well. Hardly sleeping at all, to be honest. I have nightmares. I know they're the usual anxiety points; the extra work responsibility I have now with SCAR, fear of letting people down, all that.' She smiled. 'I've been coming here long enough to finally recognise what's on my mind, I guess. But now I'm worried it's going to drive Karl away.'

'Have you talked to him about it?'

She might as well have suggested Bridge ask Karl's feelings on genocide. 'I'm not going to plant the idea in his head.'

Dr Nayar paused for a moment, then said, 'Do you know what the number one cause of relationship breakdowns is among Service personnel? Not just here. It's the same at MI5, Defence Intelligence, GHCQ, even Special Branch. Probably the CIA, too, but they're not inclined to discuss it. Which is ironic.'

'I don't understand. Why is burnout ironic?'

'It's not. But the main cause is *trust*.'

Bridge shook her head. 'I trust Karl completely. Even I know this is about me, not him.'

'One affects the other. Your lack of self-confidence makes you worry he'll break up with you over work, but you don't trust him enough to talk to him about it.' Before Bridge could reply, she continued, 'What do you think he'd say if you did?'

Bridge hesitated. 'I…suppose I don't know, not for sure. It's not really something you ask people, is it?'

'Why not?'

'Well, because you shouldn't need to.' A second thought struck her: 'Besides, nobody would admit they're thinking of leaving, would they? Even if they were. They'd tell you what you want to hear.'

'Do you think Karl would lie to you?'

'I don't know.'

'Would you lie to him, if the roles were reversed?'

Bridge slumped in the chair. She wanted to say no, of course she wouldn't. But there had been that guy at university, hadn't there? The one who'd seemed really nice, but then nice had quickly turned into boring, and instead of being an adult about it she'd deliberately behaved like a shit to try and drive him away, all so she wouldn't have to be the one breaking up with him. It hadn't even worked, because he'd believed every excuse she served up, until Bridge finally came clean and ended it. What a disaster.

'You can't have a relationship built on lies.'

'We all have secrets, Brigitte. Many people believe a lie that harms nobody and serves the greater good is perfectly acceptable.'

Bridge scowled. 'Well, those people aren't me.'

'I think the problem here might be one of obsession,' said Dr Nayar. 'You're analysing the minutiae of your relationship instead of just enjoying it. Perhaps you need a distraction.'

'...Are you seriously telling me to get a hobby?'

12

Fréderic Baudin stared at his phone screen, trying to figure out what he was looking at. A white man, holding the hand of another, who was the first in a chain of brown people, with… 'Is that a boat?'

'*Oui, papa,*' said his daughter Stéphanie, lowering her drawing and beaming at the camera. 'It's you, and the people you're helping. Maman says we must be very proud of you.'

Fred smiled back. 'It's beautiful, Stéphanie, well done. How is school?'

Stéphanie's smile faded. 'Cold. I don't like it here in England, papa. I want to come to France with you.'

Isabelle appeared on the screen and put a comforting arm around their daughter. 'We would only be in Papa's way, Steph,' she said. 'Besides, Marseille is a long way away from the farm. So it wouldn't make any difference.'

'How long?' Stéphanie demanded.

Fred briefly considered exaggerating just to end the line of conversation, but he knew the girl would look it up online anyway, so the truth would have to suffice. 'Five *hundred* kilometres!' He stretched his arms wide for emphasis. 'Almost half of France. Imagine how long that would take to drive every day.'

At one point Fred had considered selling the old family farm in Côte-d'Or. It held a lot of memories within its walls, and not all of them were good, thanks to Isabelle's younger sister Brigitte.

But after everything that had happened in the world, and between Britain and Europe, he was glad he hadn't gone through with it. When Médecins Sans Frontières no longer needed him here at the camp, he intended to take his family there for a long vacation.

Stéphanie's expression turned glum. 'OK...I *suppose* you're right.' Behind her, Isabelle stifled a laugh at the girl's audacity, and Fred had to do the same. While their daughter was growing to be the spitting image of her mother, Isabelle insisted she was more like Fred in character. He wasn't always sure she meant it as a compliment.

'Besides,' he said, 'it won't be long before I'm home for a break. Only a couple of weeks.' Stéphanie rolled her eyes at this eternal span of time, and now he really did laugh. 'It will pass before you know it. Now, go do homework or whatever you have to do, and let me talk to your mother.'

Stéphanie slid out of the kitchen chair and made way for Isabelle to take her place. Fred couldn't help noticing how tired his wife looked, but knew better than to mention it. Instead he simply asked, 'How are you coping?'

Isabelle shrugged. 'I *am*, which is more than can be said for some of our neighbours. At least the schools are open again, so I only have to deal with Hugo during the day. I'm meeting with the kindergarten place next week.'

'I still have a hard time believing he's almost ready for school.'

Isabelle smiled. 'It's happening right in front of my eyes and I can't believe it. But listen...' she hesitated, and Fred knew from her expression she had something more serious to talk about. He leaned forward and waited for her to continue. 'This video of the president... People are saying it's going to cause trouble for places like Camp Sud. Is that true?'

'Where did you see that video?'

'Fred, I'm not blind. Just because I'm chasing after children, it doesn't mean I'm oblivious to the world. Are you OK over there? You look—'

'What? I'm fine,' he said, perhaps too quickly. 'Nobody is coming around here waving the stars and stripes.'

Isabelle gave him that look, the one that said *I don't believe you*, but didn't say it. Instead she said, 'You know what I mean. They might be wrapped in the *tricolore*, but they still want to see everyone at your camp thrown back in the sea.'

'Relax, will you? And don't worry about that farting fool. He's a moron, all wind and noise, and his acolytes are no different—'

'Fréderic!' The shout came from Louis, one of his staff, who threw open the trailer door and hurried inside. 'We, um, could use your help at the south gate. Urgently.'

'I'm on break,' said Fred, indicating his phone. 'Talking to my wife.' But Louis' expression was truly worried. The man shook his head and thumbed back over his shoulder, saying nothing more. Fred realised he didn't want to explain further while Isabelle could overhear. He turned to the screen and apologised. 'This looks important. I'm sorry.'

She shook her head and waved him away. 'Go, work. Call me again tomorrow. *Bisous.*' She blew him a kiss, which he hastily returned before ending the call and turning to Louis.

'What the hell is so urgent?'

Louis held the trailer door open. 'What else? Protestors.'

Fred followed Louis out and through the camp, hurrying towards the south gate. Anticipating trouble.

Médecins Sans Frontières had called Fred to Marseille several months ago. The organisation had begun to work with the government and UNICEF when it became clear Marseille was now a favourite landing spot for refugees fleeing Syria, Libya, the Congo, Sudan... Even Fred had trouble keeping track of the sheer number of countries represented here at so-called Camp Sud, despite that being part of his job. As an MSF logistics manager he'd been around the world, working in the bleakest and most deprived areas of humanity. It should have been different in one of the largest cities in twenty-first century France, yet the camp's chainlink fence felt like a national border. Cross through the gates and you entered a place little different to camps in Algeria, Egypt, or Turkey that housed the people fleeing horror in neighbouring countries. Every day Fred was amazed that Camp Sud was within city limits; ironically it had been easier, and faced less local objection, to set up camp here than in the original proposed location to the south, on the rocky coast. That area was more sparsely populated...but the sparse population was wealthy, and included many people who either ran Marseille or dined with those who did. The UN would have had an easier time if it had walked in carrying a blow torch and proposed burning the marina's million-euro yachts.

Camp Sud started as a small camp for a single boat of refugees who'd been refused sanctuary in other cities, even other countries. That was when Fred had still been in London, crossing his fingers for an escape from lockdown like everyone else. But some people were escaping more immediate problems. By the time MSF called him here, word had spread among those shipping refugees across the Mediterranean. Now the camp held several thousand, periodically arriving by boat and landing on the rocky coast, or sometimes even bussed in from Italy when they deemed their own camps too full.

Fred's job was to oversee vaccinations in the camp. Isolating new arrivals in bubbles, enforcing social distancing, and ensuring everyone was vaccinated before mixing with the rest of the camp. Some insisted they'd already been jabbed before fleeing their homes. Given where they were coming from, Fred and his team estimated nine out of ten such claims were nonsense, made for the same reason they hadn't been vaccinated in the first place; anti-vax propaganda that had spread like wildfire though poor and oppressed communities, sometimes initiated by governments with an agenda, sometimes the result of superstition and rumour that got out of hand. Regardless, Fred's team took nobody's word for it, and the lack of outbreak in the camp reassured him they were doing the right thing.

If that had been Fred's only responsibility, it was already a full-time job. But he also found himself keeping track of camp numbers, co-ordinating with the city to arrange and distribute food and water, securing other medical aid... He'd even been put in charge of the language tutors – volunteers with the impossible task of teaching a basic level of French in a few short lessons to people whose only second language was broken English.

All of this was made more difficult by the periodic influx of new arrivals and the occasional disappearance of some already here. But that was the job. Some of Fred's small team were men and women he'd worked with before in Africa or Asia; some were relatively new but committed to MSF's ideals, even as they began to understand the challenges they faced and the reality of helping refugees. All year round the heat and stink from cramped bodies and neglected effluence threatened to become unbearable; and if those didn't get you, the heartbreak and tragedy of any given refugee's family story would. But that was true everywhere Fred had been. Someone had to take a stand, to prove humanity was not entirely lost.

This empathy, however, proved hard to come by. Fred couldn't tell Isabelle because she would worry, but for the past week he and his team, as well as other camp organisers, had been sleeping in their trailers rather than trying to return to their hotels each night. The camp had slowly been surrounded by a growing protest group, idiots and xenophobes who wanted to see it shut down and asylum seekers 'sent home'. As if any of these people had a home to return to. The protest started out small; annoying, but not a real problem. Then more and more people joined, and a semi-permanent 'base' had been set up. They had tents, refreshments, even places to sleep – an irony that Fred assumed escaped the protestors themselves – and soon they turned their frustration and outrage on the camp organisers, harassing Fred and others as they began and ended their shifts.

Things had come to a head when two protestors assaulted Louis, pelting him with seashells. When he naturally reacted angrily, they shoved him to the ground and claimed self-defence. It had been a tense moment, with Fred and other camp staff facing down a mob and calling on the police, even though half the force in Marseille was sympathetic to the protests. The mob eventually backed off when Fred pulled out his phone and began recording. Calling for foreigners to be left to drown was one thing, but attacking a Frenchman apparently wasn't something they wanted broadcast to the world.

Perhaps that would change today. The five young punks pushing their way in through the south gate certainly didn't seem concerned by appearances. Fred had often thought to himself that at least here in Marseille he wasn't ducking bullets and mortars every other day, but he wondered what it might take for that to change.

Other aid workers, and some of the burlier refugees, were arguing with the young men and trying to prevent their advance. Flaps and entrance coverings on nearby tents were held firmly closed from inside. Fred noticed two of the young men carried clubs; a baseball bat and, bizarrely, a hockey stick. The others weren't armed, but that hadn't stopped them pushing their way past the gate staff. The city had posted a small police presence, but insisted it would 'send the wrong message' for their officers to guard the gates, so it was left to staff. Most of the time it wasn't a problem, because the protestors weren't trying to get inside. They simply wanted to harass anyone going in or out. Meanwhile, the refugees knew there was nothing waiting for them outside anyway until aid workers helped them negotiate France's labyrinthine bureaucracy. But sometimes...well, sometimes it was a problem.

'Has anyone called the *nationales*?' Fred asked loudly, holding up his phone as if to do so.

'Not yet,' said a UNICEF worker, blocking the hockey-stick wielder from entering the camp.

Fred turned to the young man who looked most likely to be the leader. Second tallest, second widest, but he didn't look to the others for reassurance every five seconds. 'Do you want me to? Protest or not, they take a dim view of anyone carrying a weapon besides themselves.' It was half a bluff, and everyone knew it. On any given day it was a coin toss whether the cops would arrest these kids or join them.

'Well, we take a fucking dim view of these filthy cockroaches filling up our country,' said the young man. 'We don't have room for them here! France is full!'

The others heard and began chanting, 'France is full! France is full!' and trying to get round the aid workers' loose human chain. The one with a baseball bat swung it at an African man who stood defiant; the refugee caught it with surprising reflexes, and with a twisting motion took possession of the bat. The punk who'd swung it blanched in surprise and took a step back, but Fred quickly ran over to place himself between them.

'Half these people will go on to England anyway, because they already speak English. And Marseille has always been a city of immigrants and refugees. Learn some damn history. Your own ancestors probably came here on a boat.'

'That's right,' said the leader, getting up in Fred's face, 'And it wasn't a problem, because back then there were jobs for everyone. Now there's nothing! How much does the government spend on these fucking vermin? But when it comes to helping out Frenchmen like us, who were born here, suddenly there's no money in the pot!'

'You still have a roof over your head, don't you?' Fred threw up his hands in despair. 'These people have lost everything. It sounds to me like you should be protesting to the government about your own situation, not here shouting about someone else's.'

'They didn't *lose* anything, they left it behind. Nobody forced them to leave!'

That was too much for Louis, who shouted, 'Are you so fucking stupid? How about the militias with machine guns threatening to kill their families? "Nobody forced them"? Now I've heard it all!' Fred wished his colleague might have been a little more diplomatic with his words, but they were all true.

He was losing patience himself; Fred expected France's young to be intelligent enough to see through the transparent lies and propaganda they were force-fed every day online, in newspapers, and these days even on TV news. He was glad Isabelle and the children were still in London. The English media was no better, but at least there his children couldn't see that France was turning as ugly as its neighbour across the Channel.

The leader of the young punks turned on Louis. 'All they've done is walk from one war into another.' He turned to his fellows, rousing them. 'Because we fight for the fathers, you see? To honour our own countrymen, who fought to preserve *our* way of life!' He lashed out and punched Louis. Caught by surprise, the aid worker collapsed to the ground.

A lot of things happened at once.

The African refugee who'd commandeered the baseball bat swung it at the nearest of the young men, who threw up an arm in defence and got what sounded like a broken bone for his trouble. The punk with the hockey stick aimed not for a person but for the nearest tent, pulling on the hooked canvas to bring it crashing down to the ground, collapsing around the frightened people huddled inside. One young man kicked at Louis, now prone on the ground. The last charged at another refugee, Syrian by the look of him, colliding headfirst. The Syrian staggered back and fell on another tent, tearing through the thin fabric. A twinge in Fred's gut made him hesitate – even though it was several years since he'd been shot in Côte-d'Or, the phantom sensation had never fully disappeared – but he tried to put it out of mind and ran at the leader, ready to fight.

Then a gunshot rang out, and everyone instinctively ducked. Many refugees, their reactions born of traumatic experience, threw themselves flat on the floor and played dead. Fred looked up to see the dark blue uniforms of police officers rushing in through the gates. The African dropped the baseball bat and followed it to the ground, automatically locking his own hands behind his head. That didn't stop a female police officer firing a Taser at him for good measure. A second officer Tasered the young man with the hockey stick. Both convulsed on the ground, and the remaining punks raised their hands in surrender.

'You shouldn't be firing at us,' shouted their leader angrily. 'We're on your side! We fight for the fathers!'

Unimpressed, the lead police officer kicked the young man's legs out and trained his pistol on him. Then he turned to the aid workers. 'Who's in charge here?'

Fred shrugged. 'That's something of an existential question. But you can talk to me.'

13

@ToTheFathers
3:00 PM February 14

ALLONS ENFANTS DE LA PATRIE
LE JOUR DE GLOIRE EST ARRIVÉ
37594226173811069
88272469120419708
64872063588894173
72369499337460894
17439461152613227
33957150378390021
16166704488465578
64830778201210431
57498024619572413
41725652417623058

Posted via Twitter on the web

14

'We've got him,' said Tolbert.

Bridge sat bolt upright at her desk. 'Does he have the thumb drive?'

'No, no, sorry. I don't mean we've got him in custody. But we know who he is.'

She slumped back down in her chair, deflated and disappointed. 'You really know how to let a girl down.' She and Tolbert had parted ways after they examined the safe harbour apartment, and she'd messaged him upon returning to London to make sure the CCTV examination was underway. Now she was prepping for a SCAR meeting when her phone rang and switchboard asked if she'd take a call from the French officer. Naturally Bridge had hoped for good news, but it seemed she'd set her hopes too high.

'So my wife tells me,' he laughed. 'Anyway, you and I were both right. The restaurant footage includes the building entrance across the boulevard, and we're pretty sure our man is on it. It took time to identify him, but he is a man, and he's definitely a professional.'

'You're *pretty* sure he's on it? You're not certain?'

She shared the cramped Cyber Threat Analytics room with her colleagues Ciaran Tigh and Monica Lee. They'd been listening from the moment she picked up the phone, but now caught her disappointment and returned to their screens. Ciaran had spent the morning cracking open Kennedy's phone, but so far it had revealed nothing of interest. His preliminary conclusion was that the wannabe seller of secrets had used a burner phone to communicate, as any sensible officer would. A black-bag team had searched his home, but found nothing.

Meanwhile, Bridge could almost hear Tolbert shrug at the other end of the line. 'We checked the recordings from one hour before Kennedy arrived, to thirty minutes after you entered the building. For safety, in case we have the timings wrong, you understand?' Bridge murmured assent, and he continued. 'Well, that's a busy building. Fifty-four people entered and exited during that time, and as I say, it took a while to identify each of them. First we had to go door-to-door and get everyone's *carte d'identité*, to identify legitimate residents. Then we had to investigate those residents, in case one of them was involved. Then we had to identify the visitors, delivery drivers, and postmen, and eliminate them as well…'

'My heart bleeds for you, Serge. Now please, put us both out of our misery and give me a name.'

He tutted loudly. 'Young women today are so impatient. Luckily for you, a man left not long before you were apprehended who doesn't fit any legitimate criteria. His name is Ilya Kazhdan, and he is a known SVR officer.'

Bridge groaned. She'd tussled with the SVR, Moscow's foreign intelligence service, several times before. 'So much for not needing to worry about the Russians.'

'What do you mean?' Tolbert asked.

'Nothing. Let's see what he's about.' She found Kazhdan in the SIS database and looked at his profile on her screen. Heavy-featured and clean-shaven, Kazhdan looked every bit the stereotypical Russian thug. She didn't remember seeing him exit the Paris building, but he might have worn a hat or wig, grown a beard or moustache, lost or gained weight… There were a hundred ways to change one's appearance, and Russian field officers knew them all. She skimmed his bio. 'Five years in Poland post-Iron Curtain, three in Romania, three in Italy… He's been around, hasn't he?'

'More pertinent to our concerns, he hasn't occupied an official position for the past decade. In fact he's had no public profile at all. It's like he disappeared.'

'He might have quit. Lots of former SVR wind up as private security for oligarchs.'

'Those positions are publicly visible. The officers who take them have jobs and houses, and we see them with their clients. But this is the first confirmed sighting of Kazhdan in several years. French analysts have long suspected he was promoted to black ops, working undeclared.'

'An off-the-books assassin? Bloody hell. That would explain a cold-hearted killer who's prepared to knife someone, stage the body, then sit with it for hours waiting for the next target.'

'Exactly so. On reflection, it is probably better that you didn't confront him. I fear I would be talking to your replacement.'

Even though Tolbert had never seen Bridge fight, she felt slighted by the remark. 'Let's hope we can find him and bring him in without too much damage. You have people looking?'

'All of France is on alert, but his profile suggests he's not that stupid. I've given everything we have to foreign intelligence, and they're informing our colleagues in other countries as well. We'll get him.'

She breathed a sigh of relief. In theory there was nothing to stop Kazhdan from uploading the EMP device plans somewhere, or even dropping the thumb drive in an envelope and posting it to Moscow. But those were amateur moves, too obviously intercepted. After the trouble he'd taken to obtain it she expected the drive, and its contents, would remain on his person until the moment he placed it in his superiors' hands.

Of course, catching him before that happened was easier said than done. But it was something tangible Bridge could hold on to – a solution to the problem. Kennedy's death wasn't her fault. Kazhdan escaping wasn't her fault. The loss of the EMP designs wasn't her fault. She knew all of this, but until now the combined errors had still eaten away at her. Ultimately, she was the one on the ground, in Paris, when it happened. She was the one who had apparently been only metres away from Kazhdan without even realising it. And SIS did love a fall guy – or gal – if one was available. Bridge already had several black marks on her record, for going AWOL or failing to protect assets, and while she'd always managed to climb back out, at least they were holes she'd dug herself. To suffer here, when her only mistake was stopping to consult her superiors before acting, would have been ironic and unfair.

But now they had a name, a photo, and every agency in Europe watching out for Kazhdan. She thanked Tolbert, made her excuses, and gathered her notes for the SCAR meeting. Some good news, at last.

15

'It's nothing but bad news, I'm afraid,' said Andrea Thomson.

Bridge had asked her for MI5's update of matters relevant to SCAR: terrorism both domestic and foreign, unusual online activity, and any form of espionage. The broad remit underlined the point of the cross-agency group, to co-ordinate information and pool resources from different departments rather than working in isolation.

'Far right chatter online continues to increase exponentially,' Andrea continued, nodding at the main screen where Steve Wicker from GCHQ occupied one half of a video call. 'There have also been attacks traced back to such conversations, many of which include foreign participants. Whether those people are agitators or ordinary joes, though, we can't know for sure.'

Steve picked up the baton. 'Perhaps not, but we're reasonably confident. Most people taking part in such discussions, either on message boards they think are private, or WhatsApp chat groups and similar, either don't hide their identity or are only capable of rudimentary obfuscation.'

'They think they're being clever, but you can see who they are,' Giles clarified.

'Precisely. But every so often we come across someone, often a vocal rabble-rouser, who knows how to conceal their identity properly. Quite often their posts and timing suggest they're based in eastern Europe. We think those are the experienced actors, egging the others on.'

Giles shrugged. 'Belarus, Hungary, even Poland is starting to lean that way, sadly. Can we shut these message boards down?'

'They'll only pop up again on another server,' said Bridge. 'We've noticed the up-tick in activity too. I set up a fake online account months ago to monitor boards like these, and if they get shut down for terms-of-service violations they just move somewhere else and carry on like nothing happened. It's better to leave them be, so we can keep an eye on them.'

Andrea nodded. 'That's Five's position, particularly as intel from those boards has led to some arrests for arms smuggling. There are a lot of guns floating around Europe, and a worrying amount are landing here. Mostly small arms, which I suppose is better than the alternative.'

'Is it co-ordinated?' asked Devon Chisholme, from the other half of the video call. 'Do the police have a handle on where they're going?'

'Not that we can tell, which is worrying. We've worked with customs and the police to intercept and remove a number of weapons caches, but we haven't been able to determine who's buying them. Yet.'

'Read me in on that when you have time, would you?' asked Giles. 'If we can use our sources to work backwards, it might solve the problem in both directions.'

Bridge nodded, pleased to see the cross-departmental group working as intended. She was less pleased about the next item on the agenda. She took a breath, tapped a key, and moved on.

'Next up; this horrible video. I assume you've all seen it.' She doubted there was a person on the planet who hadn't seen the former president's rallying cry for race war in Europe by now. It had been released while she was cooling in a police cell in Paris, but days later was still being discussed online. She turned to the final member of the group, here in the Broom with them: Karl Dominic, representing the CIA. It was no secret he and Bridge were a couple – keeping it hidden would have been impossible – but they tried to maintain a purely professional air when at work. She asked him, 'What's the Agency's assessment? Should we be worried?'

Karl shook his head. 'No. It's obviously fake.'

'Yes, but recent events have shown that whether or not something is true doesn't really matter to a lot of people,' said Bridge, turning to Giles. 'These are the same wackos who believe the moon landings were faked, or the government killed Obama and replaced him with a lookalike. You can't even beat them with facts. They dismiss anything that runs counter to their bias as part of the same cover-up. It's impossible to disprove a conspiracy.'

'We do live in rather strange times,' said Giles.

'Hang on, though,' said Andrea. 'Why are we so sure it *is* fake?'

Karl shrugged. 'He's sitting behind the presidential seal, for God's sake. Former presidents can't use that.'

'I think *can't* is doing a lot of heavy lifting in that statement,' said Bridge, reaching for the room keyboard. 'Shall I look up how quickly I could knock up a seal with a 3D printer and some modelling paint?'

Karl relented. 'No, point taken. But dammit, it's not allowed.'

'What about his voice?' said Steve. 'Surely that's harder to fake.'

'Perhaps an impersonator,' suggested Andrea.

'They might have a hard time finding a good enough impersonator who's willing to say all this horrible stuff.' Bridge turned to Karl. 'Presumably those who know him can tell. Has Edison Hill given an opinion?'

Hill was Karl's CIA boss here in London. He nodded. 'Yeah, everyone who met the real guy says the voice is off. But not by much.'

'Perhaps they hired an actor and told him it was a joke,' said Giles. 'Like those "celebrity voicemail" recordings you can buy for someone's birthday, where a bad Al Pacino impersonator shouts "*hoo-ah*" down the phone at you for fifty quid.' Bridge and Andrea both turned to look at him. 'Not the wisest gift choice I've ever made. You take my point, though. You can't fake someone's voice with a computer.' He raised an uncertain eyebrow at Bridge. 'Can you?'

She shrugged. 'There are AI machine learning projects working hard on voice imitation. Some TV shows and films have already used it to recreate a line or two for dead actors, so it won't be long before it works for entire speeches. It's a question of firepower, not concept.' Met with several blank looks, she explained. 'Think about computer games. When *Pac-Man* was released, something like *Grand Theft Auto* was impossible, almost inconceivable. The state of the art was pushing a yellow circle around at ninety-degree angles; the idea of taking part in a fully-animated interactive movie was literally science fiction. But it happened, and it happened fast, because it didn't require a conceptual leap like *Pong* and *Space Invaders* had in the first place. All it took was for the same technology to become vastly more powerful.'

'You're saying the same applies to these deepfakes, voice and all.'

Bridge nodded. 'Remember that early demonstration, where someone took a video of George W Bush and replaced his facial expressions with their own?' This time, most people nodded in agreement. 'It was really primitive. No speech, no lip sync, just a fake Dubya silently gurning at the camera. That demo may feel like a long time ago, but it was only 2016. Now people are making Tom Cruise deepfakes on their phones. It's moving faster than anyone imagined.'

'Forget the technology for a moment,' said Andrea. 'Yes, I

know, that's why we're all here. But whether or not it's real is a question for the FBI, not us. We should be more concerned about the content, because you're absolutely right that there are plenty of people out there who'll believe it regardless.' She turned to Karl. 'If I was in Quantico right now, I'd be very worried about so-called patriotic militias taking this as a call to arms.'

Karl nodded. 'We stay out of the FBI's business, but I know they're monitoring it, and they've informed us several individuals on their watchlist have flown to Europe. Naturally we assume they're following the directions in the deepfake video, and we've begun alerting local law enforcement.'

'All the video says is to come to Europe and be prepared, though,' said Bridge. 'Hardly comprehensive instructions.'

'Apparently some domestic militias have received travel payments and detailed directions. If the Bureau knows what those directions are, though, they're not telling us.'

'How helpful,' snorted Andrea.

Bridge shot her a look. 'The whole reason this committee exists is because we're not much better about that ourselves, remember.' She turned to Steve Wicker on the video screen. 'Can you get GCHQ watching online chatter for these subjects? Militias in Europe, Americans arriving to join in, that sort of thing.'

'We've already seen and flagged discussion of the video, and the usual related racism.' Steve hesitated, then typed a note on his laptop. 'We'll take an active look at the militia question specifically.'

Bridge sensed he had more to say. 'Is there anything else new from GCHQ?' she asked, hoping to coax him out.

'Nothing specific,' he said. 'It's like Andrea said before, there are a *lot* of new young fascists crawling out of the woodwork. The past few years have empowered them, and now with crap like this urging them on… It's a lot, you know?' He smiled sadly. 'The stuff we pass on to you is the tip of the iceberg. You wouldn't believe how much shit we wade through, trying to separate the keyboard warriors from the ones who might actually pick up a Molotov and do some damage.'

'Hopefully a lot more of the former than the latter?'

Steve raised an eyebrow. 'More of both these days, unfortunately.'

Giles had been lost in thought, but now leaned forward and peered at Karl. 'If the FBI is monitoring militia groups in the US, presumably they have people embedded?'

'I'd expect so,' said Karl. 'Like I said, we stay out of their business. There are legal issues, you know?'

'Oh, I'm very aware of the legal quagmire in which US security embroils itself. Which is why I'm wondering if any of those embedded agents have, as part of their cover, flown to Europe with their comrades.'

Karl began to speak, then stopped and thought for a moment, his eyes unfocused. Bridge knew this look well; he was following through the implications of what Giles had said in his mind, figuring out the best response. She did it sometimes too, only she hoped it wasn't quite so obvious.

Karl said slowly, 'Federal agents aren't authorised to operate on foreign soil.' It wasn't lost on the others that he'd stated a rule, rather than offer an opinion on whether it had been broken. Bridge could practically see gears turning behind his eyes as he spoke.

'Indeed,' was all Giles said in response, though his look spoke a thousand words.

Karl avoided his gaze and typed furiously on his laptop. 'I'll... push that up the chain,' he said. What he really meant was, 'I'll corner Edison Hill in his office and yell *why the hell didn't the Feds inform us about this bullshit*?' Bridge wished him luck trying to get a straight answer.

'Next up,' she said, 'This EMP business.' She related the good news that Tolbert and the DGSI had identified Ilya Kazhdan, which was met with a murmur of hope. Andrea looked like she had something to say, so Bridge gave her an opening.

'Andrea, I meant to ask: your lot normally takes point on interrogating any of ours who go bad, right? So were you already looking into Kennedy? Any insights to share?'

Andrea shook her head absent-mindedly. 'No, he wasn't on our radar yet. But I was wondering...we visited my in-laws this weekend, and the power suddenly went out for a few hours across the Fens. All I could get from the energy company was guff about a tripped switch, but could it have been this missing device?'

'Sorry, I completely missed this story. Was the blackout localised?'

Andrea nodded. 'Hardly a national event. It's a pretty unlikely place for an attack, as there's nothing there, but I couldn't help wondering.'

'They'd have had to build it in record time,' said Bridge. She made a note to follow up anyway, but doubted it would come to anything. 'Devon, didn't you say this device is short-range?'

Chisholme nodded. 'Approximately three hundred metres. But also remember its capabilities. Andrea, did your phone continue to work? Your laptop, perhaps?'

'Well, I couldn't charge anything, obviously, and the TV was out. But yes, our devices worked until the batteries ran down.'

'Then it wasn't an EMP,' Bridge reassured her. 'They fry circuit boards too, and let's face it, everything's electronic these days. So your phone and laptop would have stopped working, and even your oven and toaster would have been kaput when the power came back on.' Bridge couldn't quite tell if Andrea was relieved or disappointed, and smiled in sympathy. 'No drama, sorry. Just crappy infrastructure.'

Karl spoke up from the end of the table. 'We're assuming the Russians will try to build that device, right? That's why they stole the plans?'

'Undoubtedly,' said Giles. 'The real question is whether they'll succeed. MoD device tests had around a seventy-five per cent success rate, and that's both with their enormous resources and the scientists who designed it on hand. Nevertheless, if Kazhdan truly is working for Moscow, no doubt they'll attempt to build the device.'

'Or sell the plans on to China, or North Korea?' said Karl. 'All three could have it in their arsenal before we know it. Back in the US they're asking if the device could bring down a plane.'

Bridge nodded. 'If you set one off during a flight, absolutely. But getting it on board would be almost impossible. You couldn't disguise it as a laptop, right, Devon?'

'That's correct,' said Chisholme. 'The new design is a miracle of miniaturisation, but it's still the size of a briefcase and would set off every alarm conceivable on an airport scanner. You'd have an easier time smuggling C4 explosive on board.'

'What about a train?' Andrea suggested. 'Or a motorway full of cars. Like Bridge says, everything's electronic these days. So even on the ground it could lead to a potential disaster.'

Bridge had a horrible vision of a motorway pile-up as dozens of cars all shut down at the same moment. Or trains colliding because their systems were blown out and signals couldn't be changed.

'I'm not convinced they'd sell to the Chinese,' said Chisholme. 'The Moscow-Beijing relationship has cooled recently.' He turned to Giles. 'At least, that's what it says in the reports I get from your lot.'

Giles nodded. 'Mostly due to corona virus, but we don't believe a sale is likely, regardless. If the motive was money they could have simply outbid whatever Majer was offering for the plans. No matter the amount, they'd have made a profit when selling on. Instead Kazhdan took a huge risk, drawing attention to the event.'

'I've looked into Majer since I got back,' said Bridge. 'He was no fan of Russia, and even had a history of agitating against the USSR when Slovenia was still part of Yugoslavia. That might also explain why he offered to handle Sasha Petrov, the whistleblower. Perhaps a loyal comrade like Kazhdan just couldn't resist killing Majer – as a bonus, or to send a message.'

'How could it send a message if we never knew Kazhdan was there? They even planted that fake USB drive to make us think it was a mutual killing.'

Bridge nodded. 'But the smoke screen only had to last while he escaped. They must have expected we'd figure it out eventually.'

'You did figure it out pretty fast, though,' said Karl, and Bridge tried not to smile at the compliment. 'Do we know where Kazhdan is?'

'Not right now, but our allies across Europe are looking for him, and I assume Paris station is fully briefed?' Bridge looked to Giles, who nodded in confirmation. 'Good. One way or another, we'll get him.'

She hoped she sounded as convinced of that as Tolbert had.

16

Yuri stood on the bridge and chuckled. A pile of rags in the shadow of the railing stirred at the sound, revealing a pale and emaciated face from within its folds. Seeing an old man standing alone and laughing to himself, the face concluded he was no threat and retreated into the pile, becoming still again. Vagrant or junkie? In this city, they were often one and the same.

Yuri had laughed because being here in Zurich reminded him of the pretty young doctor again, and for a moment he'd entertained the fantasy that he might research her online, see what she was doing now. It was an absurd thought, of course. He couldn't even remember her name. It would be in his father's medical records, but he had no desire or intention to check those. Besides, how old would she be now? She was young then, but now she'd be...

About the same age as me. He thought of her as pretty and young because that was the only time he'd known her, all those years ago. Now they were both older, wiser, and uglier. Such was life.

He looked out across the river, to the streets and quays lining its banks. One o'clock in the afternoon, with many people shopping and eating lunch. Even in the cold, some ate on benches by the water. Most still wore masks. A cautious people, the Swiss. Except for the occasional idiot junkie, of course.

Yuri hadn't expected to be here at all. He'd been in Warsaw, preparing for a stint in Minsk, when the pandemic hit. Without diplomatic cover to allow him ease of travel he'd been forced to remain in Poland while Moscow focused on using existing assets at home rather than building new ones. There were worse places than Warsaw to sit out most of a year, but it didn't come naturally to him, so he continued to work his network of online contacts, spotty-faced hackers, and young believers. It was one of these who turned up the promising lead that had saved him from the drudgery. Yuri had fed the lead to Moscow, who had fed it out to the community, who had relished the chance to vigorously question their various informants...one of whom supplied information which led to Yuri visiting a shipping container at midnight on New Year's Eve.

It was inspired, really. When the idea came to him, and the plan unfolded in his mind like the petals of a beautiful flower, he appreciated its cruel irony. He'd given it the code name *Red Admiral*, a reference to the theory that a butterfly flapping its wings in Brazil could ultimately cause a tornado in Texas. Yuri's target would never even know until it was too late. 'An audacious plan,' his superiors had called it then and many times since, along with regular reminders that it was strictly speaking outside his remit. One old Kremlin crank had even suggested it would be simpler to use Sarin gas. But Yuri stuck to his guns, because part of Red Admiral's purpose was to make a *statement* and warn the world not to fuck with Moscow. Besides, it was foolproof by design. It would cause so much trouble, in so many different ways, that it would take the enemy years to untangle – long after the main objective had been quietly achieved, lost amid enough sound and fury to distract a naive world.

It might even increase demand for Russian energy exports. Never a bad thing.

A man came to stand by Yuri on the bridge, leaning on the rail and looking across the water. He was masked, and wore a fleece-lined cap and sunglasses to boot. Even people who knew this man well might struggle to recognise him.

But not everyone.

'Have you seen the forecast?' Yuri asked.

'They say the eastern bear doesn't feel the cold,' came the reply. Anything else would have been a warning sign, a signal that something had gone wrong and the meeting should be aborted. But Red Admiral continued to go according to plan.

Yuri smiled and said, 'It's good to see you.' Underneath his mask, the assassin Ilya Kazhdan replied with a non-committal noise. Yuri continued, 'I must congratulate you on staging it well. The official story is that they killed each other, like a bad movie. Everyone is speculating, of course, but nobody will admit why those men were at the apartment in the first place. Soon it will be forgotten.'

'Someone followed Kennedy to the meeting,' said Kazhdan, 'and it happened on Paris soil. They won't forget.'

Yuri peered at him. 'Who followed? Did they see you?'

'A woman, but she wasn't looking for me. I could have asked her the time and she wouldn't have known. It all went to plan, and I switched the drives as instructed. They may never realise it wasn't a mutual killing.'

'*Maybe* is not a word I rely on,' said Yuri. 'It won't take them long to discover the drive is fake anyway, and if Kennedy was followed they'll now also have an approximate time for his death. That means they'll check cameras, and *that* means you, my friend, should return home for a while.'

Kazhdan shrugged again, this time combining the gesture with the retrieval of a small USB drive from his pocket. 'I'd rather go somewhere warm for a change.'

Yuri took the proffered thumb drive and slipped it into his own pocket. The movement was so deft and well-practised that not even the nearby vagrant could have seen it. 'Wouldn't we all? But we go where we're told. So I'm telling you to return to Moscow and accept the commendations I'll make sure you receive. Spend a year working on your beard.'

'And you?'

'My beard is doing just fine, thank you.' He stroked it absent-mindedly, remembering how much it had itched when he first started to grow it out during quarantine.

'I meant *that*,' said Kazhdan, nodding at Yuri's newly-filled pocket. 'What's it all for?'

Yuri smiled and patted him on the shoulder. 'When the tornado makes landfall, my friend, you'll know about it. You and the whole world.'

That was almost certainly true, but it wasn't the whole truth. It had always been the case for men in his position that the more successfully they carried out their task, the fewer people would know they'd done anything at all. But this time it was imperative. There was an art to obfuscation and distraction – as the staging of the Paris apartment had proven – and this would be Yuri's biggest canvas yet.

He left Kazhdan standing on the bridge and walked to the Hauptbahnhof, to catch an afternoon train to Prague. As he waited on the platform Yuri turned the thumb drive over and over inside his pocket. Audacious, indeed.

17

So far, Europe was working out a hell of a lot cheaper than Casey had predicted.

Mike had made arrangements and bought their plane tickets from the US – two-way, with a return flight in twenty days, like the guys he talked to on the internet said. It was only when they were in the air, already flying, that Casey started to worry about language. That trip to Ireland had been easy because they spoke English. This could be a whole different ball game. But it turned out everyone here did too, at least enough to get by. Mike had written down the address he'd been given and showed it to a cabbie, who looked at them as if to check they were sure. But Mike nodded, so the driver shrugged and pulled away. Fifteen minutes later, after a much lower fare than Casey had expected, they were sitting at a bus stop in front of a church on some back street as night fell. For the first time he wondered if maybe this had been a mistake. Christ, they came here on the word of strangers on the internet, and neither he nor Mike had told anyone where they were or what they were doing – although he reckoned some of the other Flag Born might guess. Now they were freezing their asses off at a goddamn bus stop, in a foreign country neither of them knew anything about, waiting for a stranger to come pick them up.

It was simultaneously the dumbest and most exciting thing he'd ever done.

And the money was real. Mike said a dozen groups had been

funded, all from the same mysterious PATRIOS account. Thirty grand each. Nobody would spend half a million dollars on a prank, would they?

'You hear from any of those other guys on your internet, yet?'

Mike shook his head and shivered against the cold. 'Haven't tried. Radio silence, they said, remember? No exceptions.'

Casey grunted and stood up to pace, swinging his arms to put some warmth back in them. 'Then this had better be the right damn bus stop, because if we're still here when night falls, I'm calling that cabbie back to find us a hotel. Damned if I'm gonna freeze my ass off 'cos somebody gave us bad intel.'

'They'll be here. We did everything they said.'

And right at that moment, as Casey's doubts reached their apex, halogen headlamps pierced the dusk and swept around the corner. Their source was an old European jeep, military style, stripped down and ready to roll. It came to a stop in front of them, and the passenger window rolled down. Casey saw two men inside, both wearing wool hats. The passenger didn't even look at them, but the driver leaned across and called out.

'Gentlemen,' he said in thickly accented English, 'There is no bus tonight. Can we offer you a ride?'

Mike called back, 'We're, uh, we're waiting for the Admiral.'

The man grinned – calling it a smile would be too kind – and hopped out of the jeep. He was tall and rangy, wearing plain fatigues and combat boots, and the cold didn't seem to bother him. He offered Mike his hand, but Casey stepped in front and shook it. 'Welcome to *Patrios*,' said the man. 'I am Captain Popescu, but everyone calls me Eagle.'

'Works for me,' said Casey. 'I'm Sergeant Lachlan, and you can call me Casey. This here's Sergeant Alessi. We call him Mike.'

Mike hesitated, then shook Eagle's hand too. 'Are you the guy I spoke to online?'

Eagle laughed and pulled open the jeep's rear doors. 'That is not my area. Our co-ordinators handle this side of things, and we simply follow orders.' He took their heavy suitcases, one in each hand, and tossed them in the back like they were tissue boxes. 'That is what soldiers do, yes? Where did you serve?'

Casey had been expecting that, and had an answer ready. 'You know we can't tell you. Ask us no questions, we'll tell you no lies.'

Eagle laughed again and held out his hand. 'Your phones.'

Casey handed his over without a thought, but Mike hesitated. 'We maintained the blackout,' he said. 'What do you need them for?'

Eagle took a half-step closer. Mike actually had maybe thirty pounds on him, but Casey knew who he'd put his money on. 'They can be traced, even when they are not used. For success, we must ensure that does not happen.'

Mike still hesitated, and Eagle shrugged. 'If you have changed your minds, it is unfortunate. I was told Americans are reliable, willing to fight for victory. If that is wrong, you can call a taxi and go home.' He turned his gaze to Casey. 'Or you can stay and fight.'

Casey hissed at Mike. 'Come on, man. Don't pussy out 'cos you can't check Facebook or whatever. This is the job, right?'

Mike's shoulders slumped as he handed his phone to Eagle, who turned to the jeep window. The passenger held out a silvery-looking bag, and Eagle dropped the phones inside it. The passenger took the bag inside and Casey heard a zipper being closed.

Eagle was all smiles again. 'It is, as you say, the job.' He walked back round to the driver's door, so Casey and Mike climbed into the back. Inside, Eagle thumbed over his shoulder at them and said, 'You see, Dmitri? True American patriots. They are exactly the men we need.'

Dmitri, the passenger, grunted in reply as Eagle put the jeep in gear and drove into the night.

* * *

Eagle drove for almost an hour, deep into the country and through a forest, finally arriving at a camp amongst the trees. It had a sign, but Casey couldn't read it, and didn't care anyway. The ride here had been dark, uninteresting, and bumpy as all hell. The only time anyone spoke was shortly before they arrived, when Eagle had a quick radio conversation with someone in a foreign language. All Casey wanted was to lie down somewhere, but they hadn't passed any hotels on the road. When Eagle pulled their cases from the jeep to carry them into a low building on the edge of the camp, Casey finally understood. Oh, well. Money they didn't have to spend on hotel rooms meant more left over for him and Mike after they were done here. Hell, for all he knew those Patrios weirdos might pay them a bonus for taking part, too. They were obviously loaded.

The low building was a long dorm of cheap beds and zero privacy. Free or not, Casey didn't relish that and was relieved when Eagle showed them to a separate room with two bunks, a desk, a clothes rail, and a small bathroom. Fatigues lay folded on each bunk. The concrete floor, breeze block walls, and single light bulb hanging from the ceiling finished off the prison-cell vibe. But the door had a lock, and it beat the hell out of sleeping in rows of two by ten.

It made sense for the camp to be out here in the middle of nowhere. Combat training was noisy; if they were close to a town or city people would be calling the cops every day. At least, that's what Casey assumed, because this was Europe, where they hated guns. Making everyone live and sleep in the same location would build camaraderie, and allow them to train for longer. He wondered how much training a guy like Eagle really needed, though.

As they unpacked, Mike hissed, 'Why the hell did you tell them we had ranks?'

'He started it,' said Casey with a shrug. 'That guy's obviously a veteran. You want him to respect us, don't you?'

Mike hung his last polo shirt on the clothes rail and kicked his suitcase under his bunk. 'And what happens when he finds out it's bullshit?'

'How's that gonna happen?' Casey didn't bother hanging anything. He stacked his t-shirts and pants on the shelf above the rail. 'I'm not gonna tell him.'

Mike groaned and lay back on his bunk. 'Hello...the internet? It's not hard to look people up.'

'Relax. *That is not my area*, remember?' Casey did a bad impression of Eagle, making Mike laugh. 'Look, why do these guys want us here? What are they funding us for? They don't need warm bodies to shoot straight. You saw that dorm, there's ten, fifteen guys already here. And this ain't the only location, right? Manpower, they got.'

Mike yawned. 'Then why?'

'One word, man. Leadership.'

'Seriously?'

Casey placed his combat boots next to his bunk, hung his toiletry kit from a nail by the sink that anticipated the need, then closed his case and shoved it under the bed. 'A hundred per cent. Who led all these countries into Afghanistan? America. Who led them all into Iraq? America. We lead, they follow. It's the natural order of things.'

'I guess you're right.' Mike took a deep breath, exhaled. 'Tomorrow we should ask them the mission details.'

'Uh-uh,' said Casey. 'Don't ask. *Order* them to tell us.'

He hit the room light and climbed into the top bunk. Despite his excitement, sleep came easy.

18

Karl's hand gripped Bridge's elbow. 'Hey, isn't that the guy from – damn, what was the movie…?'

Her fork paused halfway to her mouth as she followed Karl's gaze. She saw who he meant and nodded. 'Stop staring; this isn't LA.' Bridge had never been to Los Angeles, but assumed their attitude towards celebrity sightings was less circumspect than the accepted London practice of completely ignoring them.

'Surely you must meet actors and celebs at work,' said Julia, holding her wine glass while her husband Douglas refilled it. 'Don't they come to you lot for visas, or visit you at the embassy when they're over here?'

Bridge tensed. Julia was an old friend, but neither she nor Douglas knew what Bridge and Karl really did for a living. Like intelligence officers everywhere, they had long-standing cover stories designed to sound as boring as possible to deflect questions and suspicion: Bridge was a civil servant at the Department of Trade and Industry, while Karl was an IT geek with the US State Department.

It worked, too. If anyone asked Bridge about her day at work, or to tell a funny office story, she had a dozen ready-made anecdotes that would make the questioner regret their curiosity, and possibly consider their life choices. So did Karl, and they'd once spent an evening comparing their stories to see whose was dullest. Karl won handily, because he was allowed to get nerdy about computers. Bridge said that was unfair because, much as she was interested in that stuff, most people would rather lick sandpaper. By contrast she could reel off stories about trade mishaps and net import quotas, which used to be greeted with similar yawns, but in a post-Brexit world everyone and their aunt now fancied themselves an economics professor, and to Bridge's horror people occasionally wanted to discuss the topic. The increased research she'd had to undertake to maintain her cover was mind-numbing.

Karl deflected Julia's question with a self-deprecating smile. 'Some of the big guns have handshake photos taken with the ambassador, but they don't invite the guy running ethernet cable through the floor to photo-bomb them.'

Julia had first invited them to her Soho club for a double-date dinner more than a year earlier, and after being forced to postpone multiple times they'd agreed to wait until everyone had been vaccinated and venues re-opened properly. Bridge had expected such places to struggle to stay open, but she'd been there before with Julia and recognised some members who could probably keep the place afloat with their pocket change.

Julia wasn't one of them – she'd been a TV producer since leaving uni, where she'd read English in the same year as Izzy, but insisted she remained firmly mid-level. Bridge suspected their definitions of 'mid-level' differed, considering how often Julia ordered from the bottom half of the wine menu, but that was par for the course with her sister's friends. Douglas was literally a model, for heaven's sake.

Izzy herself had declined repeated invitations to join them, which didn't surprise Bridge for a moment. So had Karen, the fourth of what had previously been their regular dinner group, and Bridge wasn't honestly surprised by that either. Karen had been Izzy's closest friend at uni, so it was inevitable she'd take Izzy's side if choosing between the sisters. But it still saddened

Bridge. Karen had been something of a role model for her; a single woman, ambitious and successful, who lived life to its fullest – and, despite bemoaning a tumultuous love life, was under no illusions that she needed a partner to be complete. Karen put her work before everything else.

'Ground control to Bridge...can you hear me, Major Sharp?' Julia waved a hand in front of Bridge's face to catch her attention. 'Are you still with us?'

Bridge smiled, embarrassed. 'Sorry, yeah. Just, um...' She cast about for a mundane explanation. 'Hoping I get to see my niece and nephew again before they have kids of their own, that's all.'

Julia reached across the table and squeezed Bridge's hand. 'She'll come around. When was the last time you called her?'

'I can't even remember,' said Bridge automatically, then realised it was true. Had she called Izzy when Maman died, or the other way around? It had been such a whirlwind. Thinking she was going to visit her mother in hospital, then hearing she was too late; the funeral where Bridge had felt like a pariah; a drunken graveyard visit before returning home to throw herself at Karl; the clipped phone conversations with Izzy about the house, the will, the money. 'It can't have been long ago. Probably something about the house documents.'

From the corner of her eye she saw Karl give a tiny shake of his head. He called his mother in Puerto Rico every night when he wasn't working in the field; every single night, just a two-minute call to tell her he was doing OK and he loved her. He sometimes argued with his siblings, but within hours they were talking again like nothing had happened. Bridge's up-and-down relationship with Izzy, not to mention the almost non-existent relationship she'd had with her mother, bewildered him. But he knew enough by now not to call her on it. 'It is what it is,' she'd once said to him, hating herself even as the words slipped from her mouth.

Now Julia was hoeing that same row. 'Try actually calling,' she said. 'You're all vaccinated, right? The little communists, too? So you could suggest getting together. Has she even met Karl?'

Karl laughed. 'I don't think she even knows my name.'

'It's not like I ever regularly took boyfriends round to Izzy's place,' Bridge protested.

'Not like you had one that lasted this long before,' said Julia with a knowing smile. 'Just call her, Bridge. She's on her own with the kids right now, so Stéphanie's probably driving her up the wall.'

'Why's she on her own?' asked Douglas, between mouthfuls.

'Fred's working in France. Médecins Sans Frontières is helping out with refugee arrivals somewhere on the south coast. Marseille, I think?' Julia looked for acknowledgement to Bridge, who shrugged to indicate she was no better informed. 'You know how badly the pandemic fucked up Africa.'

Douglas, whose family had immigrated from Ethiopia in the eighties, grunted agreement, and Julia continued, 'Vaccinations have been a nightmare, so Izzy said they're trying to jab everyone who comes in as a precaution.'

'How are they taking that?' asked Douglas.

'I have no idea.' Julia turned back to Bridge. 'But Izzy would, and that's one more reason you should reach out to her. Make an effort, you know?'

Bridge pushed her food around her plate, feeling like a berated teenager. Perhaps finally deciding to back off, Julia turned to Karl. 'Bridge mentioned you play *Dungeons & Dragons*. Is that right?'

'Uh, sure,' said Karl, thrown by the sudden change of subject. 'Every few weeks I stay up late and play online with friends back home. It's social time as much as anything.'

Douglas smiled. 'She's brought it up because I got into it during lockdown. Started watching some YouTube sessions, then tried playing with some friends, and now I'm addicted.'

Karl leaned into the conversation, finding someone new to geek out with. Julia smiled at Bridge, who tried to relax as Dr Nayar's suggestion to find a distraction rang in her ears.

19

First exercise: firing range.

Not *everyone's* first exercise, of course. Turned out many of Casey and Mike's fellow recruits had been here already, some for a couple of days, some for a week. And more were coming; as they filed through the cold, hard-packed yard to breakfast, Eagle's jeep rolled up with another young man in the back, a pack slung over his shoulder.

The fatigues were more like thick canvas jumpsuits. Uncomfortable, but at least they were the right size. Mike said that was probably what Eagle had been doing over the radio on the drive here.

Only a handful of the other recruits spoke English well enough to hold a conversation, but Casey and Mike were the oldest people there outside of Eagle and his pals, giving them a natural seniority. None of the other recruits looked older than twenty-five, tops. They wanted to know about America, expressing their disgust at what the country had become under liberal elites. Casey gladly held court, telling them about the Flag Born and other militias, how they were taking their country back and returning to traditional values. A couple asked if they'd been at the Capitol protests, and were disappointed they hadn't until Casey told them the whole thing was a bullshit gesture, and they were here because they wanted to take *action*, not shout and wave banners. That got a round of shouts and smiles. Many of the young men were local, and had been recruited online like them; some had even been members of the same secret message boards as Mike, and like typical nerds they complained together about having their phones taken on arrival. Casey rolled his eyes and finished his breakfast.

When they were done, Eagle introduced the new kid – Casey forgot his name, something Russian-sounding – and said they were going to start the day at the firing range. Casey looked around at the recruits, wondering if any of them could outmatch him. He doubted it.

At that moment, through the window, he saw Dmitri lead a group of older men from the camp into the surrounding woods, all of them carrying rifles and packs with a practised air. 'We joining them?' Casey asked.

'No,' Eagle replied, 'That is a different exercise. Come.' He turned on his heel and led them through the camp, past a street of fake buildings, to an open area with targets propped about thirty yards down range.

They stopped at two tables of weaponry, watched over by another older man in fatigues who nodded at Eagle. Casey wondered who these older guys were. Last night he'd been sure he and Mike were brought here to lead the young recruits, but the older men gave off the same vibe as Eagle himself; experienced veterans. Were they the leaders? If so, why had a half dozen of them left camp to take an armed hike through the forest?

'Holy shit, look at this stuff,' said Mike, breaking Casey's train of thought. 'It's fucking ancient. Like out of the Cold War.'

Casey looked over Mike's shoulder. He was right; the armoury table was all AK-47s and pistols he didn't recognise. The recruits picked them up, feeling the weight under the older veteran's watchful eye. Casey did likewise, taking a rifle and shouldering it, aiming downrange.

'Suits me, man. Iron sights'll never run out of battery.'

'Yeah, yeah, *shooting clean*. But seriously, what gives?' Mike called out to Eagle. 'What's with the old-school equipment? Did we travel back to the nineteen-eighties or what?'

Eagle took the AK-47 from Casey in his gloved hands, racked the charging handle, and sighted down the length. 'Do you know how many people have been killed by Kalashnikovs like this?'

Casey nodded. 'Been around since the forties, right? So, a shitload.'

'A shitload,' Eagle repeated, smiling. 'Mikhail Kalashnikov was a genius. A soldier may drag this rifle through the darkest jungle, bury it in the thickest mud, carry it across the deepest river, and still it performs. I have seen AKs set on fire, yet continue to operate. But most importantly, my friends...' He held up the gun and laughed, 'They are dirt cheap! Our benevolent financiers are paying not only for us, but for all of Patrios, remember. We take what we can get, and we fight with what we have. That is the warrior's way, eh?'

Casey turned a pistol over in his hand, noting the Russian star moulded into its grip. 'All this Commie weaponry is fucking with my patriotism. You don't got any Colts or Brownings? Russians ain't the only ones with cheap guns, you know.'

Eagle ignored the question. He reached into a box on the table, pulled out a magazine with blue tape wrapped around its width, then handed it and the AK-47 to Casey. 'We are all patriots to the white race. That is what matters.' He pointed downrange at the targets. 'Let us see you shoot, Sergeant Lachlan.'

Casey smiled and walked to the firing point. He dropped to one knee and held up the magazine to check the ammo. 'What are we firing?' he asked.

The veteran watching the armoury table answered as if reading from a manual. 'Plastic practice ammunition. Shorter range due to reduced weight, but flight profile is consistent with standard seven-six-two.' He didn't need to add *so don't fuck around*.

Casey grinned at the other recruits. 'Watch and learn, boys.' He'd never fired an AK-47 before, but a gun was a gun. He loaded the magazine, shouldered the rifle, flicked the safety and selected single shot.

Brace, sight, squeeze.

His first shot was low and to the right; he heard some snorts of disappointment from the other recruits, but put them out of his mind and focused on correcting his aim. Brace, sight, squeeze. The second shot was two inches to the left, over compensated. He breathed, refocused, fired again and hit bullseye. Then, to prove it wasn't a fluke, he did it twice more.

20

Bridge delivered three kicks, followed them up with three punches, and barely noticed. The gym was still operating on pre-booked hourly slots to keep attendance numbers manageable, given nobody wanted to wear a mask while working out, and her regular time was early enough that she often had this end of the room to herself. Not that she'd ever been one for socialising at the gym, but the unusual lack of hubbub let her mind wander as she moved through her usual workout on the weights and heavy bag.

She'd almost called Izzy after getting back from dinner. Sat on Karl's couch, phone in hand, ready to tap the number. He'd persuaded her it maybe wasn't such a good idea with most of a bottle of red inside her, and she didn't know if she could go through with it anyway.

'You probably should,' he'd said, circling an arm around her shoulders and gently but firmly pulling her towards him. Bridge gladly relaxed against his chest, phone still gripped in her hand. 'Not tonight. But this way you get to be the adult in the room. On the call. Whatever.'

She rolled her eyes. 'You sound like Julia.'

'Because I agree with her. That's not news; you know how I feel.'

When they'd first met – which had been a week to remember, with flirting, interrogations, car chases, and hacking to boot – Bridge had the distinct and infuriating impression that Karl saw her as a broken doll he could put back together, a project on which he could apply his American can-do attitude. Since then, and after what now seemed like half a lifetime of living together, they'd both backed off. He was less insistent that she work on fixing everything wrong with her life through the power of positive thinking, and in return she controlled her angry knee-jerk reactions when he couldn't help himself. She'd also largely given up pointing out how he was just as messed up but in different ways; how he got majorly stressed out if he didn't talk to his siblings for a week, or how all his D&D characters were grunts with daddy issues.

'I'll call her tomorrow.'

'Will you, though?'

'I'll think about it.'

Bridge had switched to her music app, set an old Black Tape for a Blue Girl album playing quietly through the lounge's bluetooth speaker, and curled up against Karl's chest. He was more of a heavy metal guy, so it had taken a long time to find albums they could agree on, but at least they shared common ground in their families' endless prodding questions about when they would grow out of it. With Bridge's family it had always been rooted in a strange fear that no man would want to marry a black-clad goth; the idea she might not want to get married in the first place never entered their minds. Karl's family were more concerned that it wasn't proper for a government employee to go headbanging at the weekend, but there was also an undertone of how his lifestyle made it difficult to find a 'nice girl'. Bridge had yet to meet his parents in the flesh, but they'd had regular video calls. She didn't know if they considered her a *nice girl*, but they were pleasant enough and seemed relatively normal. They even took an interest in his life and work – which was actually an interest in his cover story of working for the State Department, but it was a step up from the indifference Bridge's mother had always shown. Or not shown, she supposed.

She kicked the gym bag again, a full-body strike whose momentum travelled up her root leg, through the hip rotation, and down her forward leg, driving into the canvas with a satisfying thud. Not that she'd ever imagine her mother or sister superimposed on the bag. Perish the thought.

Not even Karl knew why she'd been avoiding talking to Izzy: because Bridge still hadn't signed the papers to authorise an auction of their mother's house. Well, that and all the other usual reasons. That didn't make him or Julia wrong, though, and Bridge couldn't avoid it forever. She'd finish this session, have a shower, and call Izzy on the way to the Tube—

Her phone buzzed, its bright screen glowing from atop her holdall. She might not have noticed if the gym wasn't so quiet, but she did, and sighed when she saw who was calling. Of course.

'Izzy.'

'Bridge. How are you?'

'In the middle of a workout, as it happens. What's up?'

'I thought I'd call, as it's been a while. Julia said you're still with Karl.'

She should have known. Why pressure one sister into making up when you can pressure both? Bridge wanted to be angry at Julia, but really she was angry at herself for dithering. Now Izzy could say she was the one who acted like an adult and made the effort to call.

Bridge put those thoughts to the back of her mind and offered an olive branch. 'Yes, we alternate between his place and mine. Is Fred still at the camp? How are Stéphanie and Hugo finding that?'

'Oh, you know. Steph was getting used to him being away, and then the lockdowns happened and she got used to having him around all day instead. Poor Hugo never knew any better, so he's not taking it well. *C'est la vie.*'

'And I bet he's grown loads since I last saw him,' said Bridge, refusing to slip into French on principle.

'They both have,' Izzy said. For a moment Bridge wondered if her sister might extend some kind of invitation, but instead she changed tack. 'I suppose you've been busy with work too. Back to travelling?'

'Here and there, yes. Nothing exciting,' she lied.

'But you're home now.'

'For the moment.' Where was this going?

The answer came quickly enough. 'Then you've got time to sign those papers for Maman's house. The auction house has re-opened, and I want to get on with sorting it out.'

'I assumed you were keeping it. Yet another house for you to move between.'

Bridge regretted that as soon as she'd said it out loud, but if Izzy picked up on it she didn't rise to the bait. 'We're not made of money, Bridge. I finished the clear-out last time I was over there, and now it's time to sell the place. I've got some old stuff of yours waiting to send, actually. I'll courier it over.'

So much for not being made of money. 'What stuff?'

'From when we were kids. Maman kept boxes in the attic. There are things in here I'd forgotten all about.'

'I'm not sure I want to be reminded. You can chuck anything of mine. I don't want to live in the past like her.'

'Maman wasn't living in the past. She just didn't forget about her own family.'

Bridge rolled her eyes. 'Look, you were the golden girl who produced grandchildren. She didn't care what I did, and once we were old enough she buggered off and left us both here.'

'Can you blame her? We were a handful, and you know it. I was practically an adult, you were in trouble with the police, and suddenly she had to work out how to raise us by herself. It's hard enough when there's two of you, believe me. Sometimes I think about what I'd have done if I'd lost Fred, and I don't know. I just don't know.'

Bridge felt the weight of the implication behind Izzy's words, but she didn't want to get into that. She'd apologised for putting Fréderic in danger a hundred times over, for all the good it did.

'No matter how much you might feel yourself turning into Maman, I can't imagine you ever being disappointed in Steph and Hugo.'

'I'm not "turning into" Maman, what's that supposed to mean?'

'Izzy, you have a grumpy foreign husband and two bilingual kids, you spend your entire life being a wife-slash-mother, and you're happy as a pig in shit because it's all you've ever wanted. You couldn't be more like Maman if you moved to Lyon and sold your car.'

'Last I looked, Bridge, you and I were both still French. You're the one sleeping with a foreigner.'

'That's hardly—' Bridge stopped herself, not wanting to argue about Karl, and regrouped. 'I've never wanted that, and you know it. It's not my life.'

'No, your life is nothing but work and no time to spend with family, even when they're in hospital.'

Bridge had been cooling down from the workout, but now her face flushed again. 'That's not fair. I told you, I didn't know.'

'You didn't care to know. The same as you didn't care to help me sort out the will, or the house.'

'You made it quite clear you didn't want my help.'

'Can you blame me?' Izzy shouted. 'You talk about your life, but what's the point of all this work if it doesn't buy you the time to live? Who's going to remember all those hours at work, Bridge? Who's going to mourn you when you drop dead at your desk one day?'

From the corner of her eye, Bridge saw a couple of gym regulars doing their best to ignore her. She lowered her voice. 'That's a bit rich, Izzy, considering your husband isn't even there right now *because he's working*. Putting in every hour he has to help complete strangers, people you don't even know and never will.' Bridge felt bad for using Fred's work to argue her point, but those were the lengths Izzy drove her to.

'The key word there is *helping*. Even if people don't know his name, Fréderic is leaving his mark and making the world a better place. I will never stop being proud of him for it.'

'I do that too!' Bridge hissed. 'But you never even started being proud of me for it.'

She ended the call, threw her phone back on her holdall, and slammed a fist into the punch bag.

21

Second exercise: combat sparring.

Shooting had put a big smile on Casey's face. One or two of the other recruits came close, but in the end he was by far the best shot. Eagle looked impressed, even surprised, which Casey was only too happy to see. Mike had been average, as he always was on the range. It wasn't his speciality.

They'd returned to the dining hall for lunch. Even though they hadn't done anything physically strenuous, and the food was little more than bread and cold meats, everyone was buzzing so much after the shooting practice that they practically inhaled everything put in front of them. He couldn't follow the non-English conversation, but Casey saw enough gestures and heard enough slang to know they were imagining shooting up towelheads like the morning's paper targets.

Five minutes after eating they were back outside, forming a circle on the yard's semi-frozen ground under Eagle's direction. He'd retrieved an armful of headguards from the main building and handed them out. Eagle and Dmitri didn't sleep in the dorm, and Casey knew the only separate sleeping quarters in the block was the room he and Mike occupied, so he presumed the other men had bunks in that main building.

Two locals were eager to get scrapping. Eagle stated the minimal, simple rules in English: 'No biting, no gouging, you lose when anything except a foot or hand touches the ground,' then stood back and let them at it. The fighters circled one another inside the improvised human ring to cheers of encouragement, taunting each other in their own language. Once again Casey didn't understand the words, but he understood trash-talking just fine.

It was over in seconds. While one recruit was still busy jeering, his opponent punched him in the side of the face, grabbed his reeling body, and pulled it over an outstretched leg. The first guy didn't know what hit him and went down like a sack of potatoes. Casey winced as the loser's head hit the ground. The headguard saved him, both from the fall and the punch to his jaw, but he'd be nursing some nasty bruises.

The victor raised his arms in celebration and shouted at the others, challenging them. Another recruit wearing a headguard immediately stepped up and they squared off. This fight lasted a little longer, with some feints and near-misses, but the first solid blow to land was a boot from the challenger driving into the other man's stomach, and that signalled the end. The first guy doubled over, gasping for breath, and his opponent didn't have to do more than push him sideways. Casey laughed involuntarily at the absurdity of it.

Then felt Eagle push a headguard into his hands and say, 'Show them how it's done, Sergeant.'

Casey shrugged and strapped on the guard. He was no boxer, but he'd been in some scuffles, and the first two fights – if you could call them that – had made the winning tactic obvious. Get in fast, don't pull your punches, and follow up any contact with an immediate second blow. Like double-tapping a target, one strike wasn't enough to be sure. He stepped into the ring, faced his opponent, and said, 'You ready?'

It was a distraction. Before the other guy had even finished answering, Casey swung a fist at his head.

But all he connected with was air. His opponent ducked back out of reach, like he'd been expecting the blow, and Casey barely made contact with his headguard. Not enough to do any damage, and when he moved closer to attempt a follow-up he walked straight into the other guy's elbow, ramming into the side of Casey's head. He stumbled, off-balance, felt someone grab his shoulder to steady him, then tried to pull away when he saw it was his opponent. Too late. He turned Casey around and headbutted him. Padded headguard or not, Casey's vision exploded with points of light and he reeled back into the surrounding crowd. He was barely aware of the other guy moving, approaching, and then a familiar voice shouting.

'That's enough,' said Mike, stepping between them. 'You win, now stand back.'

'He is not fallen. It's the rules,' the opponent growled, advancing on Casey.

Mike shoved him back and stood his ground. 'What about fucking headbutts, are those in the rules?'

The other shrugged. 'Eagle did not say it was illegal.'

Casey focused on catching his breath and trying not to fall over, not in front of everyone here. If they were going to lead this group, he couldn't show weakness. Lose a fight, sure, whatever, but he had to show he could take it. Mike turned to Casey and removed his headguard, ready to don it himself. 'Shit, Mike, no,' Casey said between breaths. Mike wasn't cut out for this.

But his friend smiled, and was about to reply, when the guy in the ring kicked him in the back. Mike fell into Casey and the crowd, stumbling but managing to stay upright. Some of the crowd booed, but most of them laughed. Eagle said, 'At least wait until he has his guard on,' but made no move to stop anything.

Mike still had the headguard in his hand. He spun around and threw it at the other fighter, who instinctively raised his hands to stop it hitting him in the face. Mike took a short step forward and swung his leg, like a punter on fourth and long, into his opponent's balls.

A loud and simultaneous '*Ohhhhhh!*' rang out from the crowd as every man winced in sympathy. Mike turned to Eagle and shrugged. 'You didn't say it was illegal.'

Eagle burst out laughing, and after a moment the crowd joined in. Mike took Casey by the shoulder, turned him around, and walked him through the crowd to a nearby table and bench. 'C'mon, partner, let's get a look at you,' he said.

Casey was still seeing stars, and resented having to rely on someone else to stay upright. But Mike had surprised him. Maybe getting out of his usual routine was bringing the nerd out of his shell. For once, Casey thought better of saying that out loud.

The sparring resumed in the yard as Mike sat Casey on the bench to run through 'how many fingers'-style concussion checks. The truth was, Casey's pride had taken a bigger blow than his body, and after another minute his vision cleared.

Dmitri emerged from the trees, leading the same men who'd followed him that morning. There was no question they looked like veterans, and were older than the other recruits. They ignored Eagle and the younger men, talking quietly amongst themselves as they filed into the main building.

'Hold on,' said Mike, and got up to follow the men. He was stopped at the doorway, with one veteran blocking the entrance and Dmitri backing him up. Casey couldn't hear them talking, but the message was clear; *no unauthorised personnel*. Mike raised his hands and backed away. Dmitri pulled the door closed.

Before Mike could return to the bench, though, the recruit he'd kicked in the balls walked over to him. The guy was obviously still sore from the way he moved, but he was bigger than Mike, and Casey worried he'd bear a grudge. The two men faced off, and exchanged some words. Mike held out his hand in peace, and to Casey's relief, the other guy finally accepted. They shook, nodded in mutual understanding, and Mike walked back to the bench.

'No hard feelings,' he said with a shrug as he sat down. He thumbed over his shoulder at the main building. 'Command quarters is off-limits to recruits. I told them I wanted some aspirin, but no dice.'

'*Command quarters*,' echoed Casey. 'Shit, I guess that means we're not here to lead. So who the fuck are those guys?'

Mike grinned. 'I don't know, but look on the bright side. If they're in charge, they'll take the blame if anything goes wrong.'

22

It wasn't the first time Fréderic had been called to Marseille's new port for a shipping container.

The old port, not far away, was now a tourist attraction and yacht marina. Cargo ships came to the new port instead, laden with supplies and merchandise ready for distribution around France and Europe. Hundreds of containers were offloaded every day. Most of them spent less than twenty-four hours on the docks before they were collected by hauliers and transported away.

Most of them.

Sometime a container stayed longer. It might be part of a batch not yet scheduled to leave; it might be 'rolled' due to overbooking on its intended ship; it might even be the subject of a transportation dispute, or held by port authorities for investigation.

Or it might contain something other than goods.

Fred and Louis climbed out of their MSF car to be greeted by several port security officers, brandishing flashlights and lamps. Their grim expressions told Fred all he needed to know. He and Louis were led through the container storage area, an incomprehensible grid of ever-changing steel towers piled on unyielding concrete. In the dark of the evening, the only way Fred could orientate himself was by the floodlights and diesel noise coming from their destination.

'How long has the container been here?' he asked.

The senior security officer, a burly middle-aged woman, shrugged. 'That's the problem; we don't know. Somehow it slipped through manifest and was given an empty storage slot without us being notified. We have no record of it leaving a ship, and nobody will admit to placing it here.'

'Meaning money changed hands,' said Louis.

The woman shrugged again. 'It happens. Inspectors mentioned a bad smell in the area, but that's not so unusual. Then the shouting and banging started, and – well, here we are.'

The container in question was one of dozens in this area, and stacked high up, which made everything more difficult; for him and Louis, for the port workers and medics in attendance, and for the poor souls trapped inside trying to get out. The floodlights illuminated two ambulances and a cherry-picker, with which port workers slowly brought down the container's inhabitants two at a time.

'How many?' asked Fred.

'Nineteen,' said the security officer with her customary shrug. It accompanied every answer she gave. 'Twenty, if you count the dead one.'

'Languages?'

'They all speak African, and some of them sounded like English.' Before Fred could point out there was no such language as *African*, she shrugged again. 'I don't speak either of those, so don't look at me. I don't care who takes them, whether it's you, the police, or the gravedigger. But they don't belong here, and nobody's paying for container demurrage, so I want them gone.'

Fred gave up trying to find a shred of concern in the woman and instead turned his attention to the people already on the ground, surrounded by police and medics. The assumption that they were refugees bound for Camp Sud was fairly solid. They looked malnourished, exhausted, and ragged. No matter where they came from, or what they were fleeing, that look was universal.

'English?' he said hopefully to the healthiest-looking man in the group. The man pointed at a woman, presumably his wife, who was wiping tears from her eyes.

'Yes,' she said, sniffling. 'I speak English. We are four families from Darfur. They would kill us, you see? So we came through Libya, and there are…are…' she began to cry again, and her gaze flicked upward to the container. 'My father…'

Fred nodded, understanding. *Twenty, if you count the dead one.* People traffickers took money from these desperate families and promised them passage to the safe haven of Europe. What they actually got was stuffed in a cramped shipping container with insufficient food and water, and an undersized bucket. Sometimes the ones who looked young and healthy enough were trafficked to a country where they didn't speak the language, imprisoned by crime gangs, and made to pick fruit or clean toilets until they dropped. Sometimes the young women were forced into sex work. And sometimes the traffickers took the families' money then left them to starve in places like this, not caring whether anyone rescued them. Fred was mildly surprised only one, presumably elderly, passenger had died during the journey. He'd seen reports of containers where the entire contingent had succumbed, found too late after being abandoned.

Someone in this port had unloaded the container from a ship and placed it here off the books. It would require at least two compliant workers, both of whom had to be bribed. He wondered how well those workers would sleep at night, knowing what they'd done for a few extra euros. But judging from the senior woman's attitude, the answer was probably *fine, thanks*.

Fred sighed and took out his phone. The container's inhabitants were indeed bound for Camp Sud, but only if he could persuade the police they were victims rather than criminals. It was going to be a long night.

23

Third exercise: sweep and advance.

Seeing the sun go down after they ate dinner, Casey had expected lights out and sleep. But Eagle had other plans. He led the recruits by flashlight to a part of the camp they'd walked through but not talked about; a fake street with sketchy-looking wooden buildings on either side. Just as Casey wondered if they would have to learn the layouts he turned at a noise and saw the older guys, the ones Dmitri had led into the forest, approaching with lockboxes hoisted on their shoulders or carried between them. They dropped the boxes by Eagle, and he opened them to reveal weapons and equipment.

First he gave each recruit a full-face gas mask. 'Wear this, or you will immediately be disqualified. We have no medical facility here, and if I have to drive any of you to hospital I will blindfold you and leave you there.' Everyone, including Casey, did as they were told.

Next Eagle handed out AK-47s, and two magazines for each recruit. Once again the mags had tape wrapped around them, but this time it was orange. 'What's the difference?' asked Casey.

'Paint rounds,' said Eagle. He gestured at the veterans, who were taking masks and guns but also pulling on gloves and padded vests. 'This is a sweep-and-advance exercise. These men will be the hostiles. You see one, you shoot.'

'How come they get armour?'

'Because after you shoot them, they will move on to the next house and do it all over again. Your objective is to start at the top and clear one side of the street with minimum casualties. If you are shot, come outside, remove your mask, and wait.' He handed each recruit a Maglite. 'Sergeants Lachlan and Alessi, you are the squad leaders.'

The recruits grumbled, but nobody dared outright complain in front of Eagle. Casey was grateful for the mask; they couldn't see him grinning underneath it.

Mike tested the flashlight, shining the beam on the ground. 'One question. Why are we doing this in the dark?'

Eagle gestured to the sky. 'It is winter. When Patrios commences, it will also be dark. Now, get ready.'

Casey felt a moment of panic as he and Mike led the recruits to the top of the 'street', while Eagle's men distributed themselves throughout the houses. Eagle probably thought Casey had done this before, maybe even for real. But by the time they stood outside the first house he knew what to say.

'Listen up,' he said, dividing them into two groups with hand signals. 'Group one: on my count of six, we take the first house and split into three units, one per floor. Never go alone, understand? Always at least two, wherever you go. Group two: with Sergeant Alessi, while we're inside you cover outside. Next house, we switch: group two goes in while group one covers. Then we switch again, each house. Everyone understand?'

The recruits who spoke English murmured in agreement and translated for the others. As they were about to head out, Mike leaned in and whispered. 'Where the hell did that come from?'

Casey shrugged. 'Clearance mission in a *Rainbow Six* game. I forget which one.'

* * *

Five minutes later, sweating and gasping for breath under the claustrophobic mask, Casey reflected on the old saying that 'no plan survives contact with the enemy.' They were only halfway and he'd barely scraped through, getting lucky when he rushed into a room without checking properly but the waiting veteran shot wide; almost falling down a flight of stairs in the dark; losing half his group to hostile fire, orange paint splattered over their fatigues to display their failure for all to see. He had no idea if Mike was even still leading the other group, or had been eliminated.

It was mad, noisy chaos. He loved every minute of it.

24

Bridge wrapped her arm around the train agitator's neck, ignoring the bristles of his beard through her thin sleeve, and squeezed tight – he spluttered, choking, grew quiet as his breath turned ragged – she smiled, grim satisfaction, knowing he'd never do it again, never again, even as the other passengers ignored her – train lights flickered, turned red – Adrian, she had him by the shoulders, her hands slick with his blood but she wouldn't let go, couldn't let go – they were in the server room, cold below Syrian desert, gunfire and sparks strobing scattered light – through blue lips he grinned, blackened teeth crumbling with every word, whispering so quiet she had to lean in close, beg him to speak—

'*You love it.*'

* * *

Thirty minutes later her tea was growing cold. She'd mainly made it to warm up her hands as she sat in a bathrobe by the lounge window. East Finchley by night hardly belonged in a gallery, but she'd lived here long enough that the view was a comfort, a familiar sight to calm her heart rate and clear her mind.

She checked the clock. Two-forty am. She heard bedsprings creak as Karl turned over, then creak again as he swung his feet to the floor. Footsteps as he entered the lounge and approached behind her, the weight of his hands on her shoulders gently comforting. She leaned back into him, resting her head against his body. He didn't need to ask, and she didn't need to tell him.

The evening had started with a quiet night in at her flat. She was still angry about Izzy's phone call, but while she tried not to let it show, Karl knew her well enough to recognise something was up. He'd cooked mushroom bourguignon, a slow dish that gave him enough time to wheedle the details of the phone call out of her. He understood, of course. Sometimes he was so bloody understanding it made her want to scream. But talking about it lowered her blood pressure, and later she'd played through *Star Wars Squadrons* for the third time while Karl read the new NK Jemisin, before all that pastry got the better of them and they retired to bed.

She'd managed just under three hours' sleep. Not bad for her, these days.

Karl leaned over and took the cooling mug from her hands, retreating to the kitchen to make a fresh cup. His tea had been terrible at first, but she'd diligently taught him the proper method, and in return she'd bought a countertop coffee pod contraption – the infant relation of the same brand in Giles' office – for him to use when staying with her. She couldn't tell the difference between those pods and the fair trade instant coffee she bought in jars, but then Karl couldn't tell the difference between a decent cup of tea and some lukewarm water that had once had a bag waved in its general vicinity. *All relationships are a compromise*, she'd once read.

'So, ah, maybe this isn't the best time to ask. Or…maybe it is.' He returned to the lounge, a mug in each hand, and gave one to Bridge.

She drew her knees up and said, 'Bribing me with tea, are you?'

'Is it working?' Karl grinned.

She took a sip of the steaming drink and nodded her approval.

'Maybe. Pray continue.'

'It's a work favour. Kind of. But, you know…'

'But not one you want to go through Giles. Is this purely you, or for the company?'

'I'm offended you even have to ask.'

She didn't have to, not really. Karl was a 'company man' through and through, even more dedicated to the CIA than Bridge was to SIS. She simply wanted to stop bad people getting away with bad shit, but Karl was a true believer. Whenever he stayed up late to watch live American football games she half-expected him to stand up and sing along with 'The Star-Spangled Banner.'

'So here's the thing,' he continued. 'I know Giles didn't seem to care much about it at the SCAR meeting, but we're pretty concerned about Operation Patrios. There's a lot of potential for embarrassment.'

'You mean from those embedded FBI agents operating illegally.'

'No – well, OK, I suppose that too. But I'm talking about the ordinary citizens caught up in it. Like I said, we have verified intel of funding sent to American militia groups. Payments covering travel to Europe, offers of command positions at training camps for whatever the hell they're planning.'

Bridge took another sip and raised an eyebrow. 'Verified by whom?'

'The usual. NSA, Prism, some informants.'

'All right.' She wasn't sure where this was going, but he evidently wanted to talk it out, so she adopted the role of questioner. 'How many groups have been funded?'

'We don't know for sure. We do know some turned down the money, and that's good news for us because it suggests those militias are all talk and no gun. But others accepted. Payment was made and rendezvous dates were set. Now there are American citizens on European soil ready to take point in a race war because they watched a video of our former president telling them it's their God-given duty.'

'You've traced the payments?'

'Yeah, but it's the same old runaround. They all lead back to the Caribbean, fake companies and laundering operations, clandestine and anonymised. Same with the emails. All burner accounts from places like *emailxero*, relayed around the world to be untraceable. A lot of it smells like operations we've seen before from Russia, but naturally we can't prove anything.'

Bridge smiled. 'Naturally. So why are you reading me in, here? What's the unofficial favour?' She had to admit, she was on the hook. She should have shot him down immediately and insisted he go through Giles, but this was intriguing.

Sensing that, Karl became animated. 'Like I said, we know there are US citizens who've taken them up on it. What we don't know is whether this is all some weird propaganda fakery to embarrass the United States, or if it's real.'

'You say that like having Americans pretend to play at *Racist Rambo* in France and Germany wouldn't be embarrassing enough.'

'No, of course it would. But if we know the operation isn't a fake, we can make sure none of it happens. We can find it, and stop it.'

Bridge doubted it would be that easy, but again: company man. Karl firmly believed there was nothing the CIA couldn't do, and she wasn't about to argue the point. 'You want me to find out if Operation Patrios is real. If they really are training Americans and whoever else to go out and kill immigrants. How, exactly? What can I do that the CIA or FBI can't?'

Karl smiled, that bright American grin that melted Bridge a little inside. 'Be a convincing fake European.'

25

The jab knocked Sasha out for three days. He barely noticed time passing, existing in a liminal fever on the boundary between sleeping and waking. He was glad he'd been given a single-dose vaccine, because he really didn't want to go through that again. But in a way, it was a blessing in disguise. He left the TV on throughout the ordeal, state news with the volume muted and English subtitles. They touched on the video of the former president once or twice more, and their credulity amused him. They truly believed it was real.

Or did they? They could be playing propaganda mindgames. Perhaps it served their purposes to pretend they believed it was real, giving them reason to be outraged at the president's words. If they dismissed it as fake, they couldn't also condemn him. But showing the face everyone expected to see allowed them to hide their true face, and advance their true agenda, in plain sight. It was a good disguise, one that would enable them to reach the world while hiding the truth.

Somewhere in his fevered mind a connection formed, and he realised the answer had been staring him in the face all this time. The next time a guard came in with food – food Sasha could barely look at, let alone contemplate eating in his state – he had a special request, to make the side-effects more bearable. The guard ignored him, but he persisted every time someone brought him food, and through a combination of diplomacy and whining they eventually relented. Sasha wasn't even truly sure who *they* were; no doubt there were senior people here to whom he had never been introduced, or who might not even know he was here.

Nevertheless, someone finally granted him his wish: access to the decadent imperialist Netflix, and a bluetooth keyboard to more easily use it.

Predictably, they were delivered only as he was starting to recover. It didn't matter. He didn't give a shit about Netflix. That was a convenient cover story to make the scheme sound more plausible and distract them from his real goal: the keyboard. It was his passage out of here, in a virtual sense.

Most people had no idea that modern TVs were fundamentally computers with a big screen. The model in his suite was one such device; an LG, running Linux at its core. A stripped-down and optimised version for watching TV, true, but nevertheless a working computer system.

Even people who kind-of grokked that concept wouldn't necessarily make the next leap of understanding. Everyone knew the TV was connected to the local network in order to receive streaming and catch-up services. But that was all it was programmed to do, wasn't it?

For the average person, the answer was yes. But a hacker knew it was possible to bypass those restrictions and get to the root of the machine. In order to let a viewer sign in to streaming services, the TV contained code that could read web pages, like a browser with no interface. On this model he couldn't just 'open' a browser window. They'd made sure of that before giving him the TV. But merely signing in to a service like Netflix sent the TV whizzing off across the internet, visiting a hidden web page to authorise the service and ask for his password. It knew which page to visit in the same way any computer knew how to find a website; by using a domain name server, or DNS, to translate an address like *www.*

twitter.com into its 'real' numerical address of *104.244.42.129.* DNS services all over the world kept a directory of which address pointed at which number, and all the directories were the same.

Except for the ones run by hackers.

Sasha altered the TV's settings so that, the next time it went looking for an authorised web page, it wouldn't get the numerical address from a legitimate DNS service. Instead it would go to an altered lookup catalogue, clandestine but well-known in the hacker community, that sent all requests to a single website. A site made by those same hackers.

He launched Netflix. Sure enough, it asked if he wanted to log on. He clicked *OK* and watched as the app tried to visit the company's own authorisation servers. Instead it was redirected to a website that detected the TV model and automatically responded by forcibly injecting a batch of javascript code. The screen flashed three times, then rebooted itself. Hey presto, his $200 TV was now an internet-connected computer that greeted him with the beautiful sight of a command line awaiting input, all while Sasha's captors thought he was watching movies.

(He could still do that too; these being hackers, the flashed system update came with a free pirated login to every streaming service catalogue he'd heard of, and many he hadn't.)

But Sasha wasn't here to watch movies. He was here to edit them. His first task was to spoof the security cameras so they couldn't see what he was doing. They were on the internal network, passive cameras installed in every room with a central server recording on a seventy-two-hour loop-and-wipe. What more would a building like this need? It was hardly an epicentre of activity and forensic analysis. He was amused to find that not only was there a camera in his suite as he'd suspected, but its angle would have given the security guard watching him with the junior girl a real eyeful. *Lights, camera, action.*

This time, though, he didn't want them to see any kind of action. The TV screen wasn't in shot, which was a relief, but he still couldn't risk them seeing him work. So he waited twenty-four hours, spending the rest of the day doing as many normal things as possible. Then he made a copy of that day's recording on the server.

Sasha worked fast, cutting out some of the extended time he'd spent with the keyboard so it wasn't quite so obvious he was using it to code. Those cuts left him with only a twenty-hour recording, so he took the section from the previous night while he slept and time-stretched the six hours to ten. Then he did his best to match the remaining cuts during the day to moments where he picked up or put down the keyboard, and trusted that nobody watching the security monitor would pay close attention. The edits were jumpy, and the clock on the wall was now sometimes out by as much as ninety minutes. But to a layman's eyes it was twenty-four hours of Sasha sitting on the couch, eating, sleeping, and occasionally using the keyboard to control the TV. A completely ordinary day like any other, with nothing to merit close attention.

He set the recording on a loop, repeating every twenty-four hours to the monitor output, and disabled the camera. The loop would suffice until he finally left this place. In the meantime he needed to investigate. Sasha knew why that deepfake video had been released, and he wanted to see how far they would take it.

26

From: Prosper

Those of us with eyes to see the truth know we are being overrun and taken for fools. I have served in the countries of these people, and I have great respect for their land and culture. If only they showed it the same respect, but no! Instead they shit on it, then invade our homes and ask us for pity. We will not let the barbarians replace us!

Bridge stretched in her chair, then stood and stretched again. Posting this stuff made her want to throw up. But she'd had a lot of practice at compartmentalising her emotions and locking them away somewhere while she got on with her job. Pretending to be someone else and saying things she didn't believe was pretty fundamental to the spy business. Even if it meant pretending to be a middle-aged French racist.

That in itself wasn't difficult. The fake online persona she'd created months ago to monitor right-wing message boards was named for Prosper de Chasseloup-Labat, the notorious colonialist from the time of Napoleon III. Chasseloup-Labat had been glossed over in Bridge's history classes at school in France, airbrushed out by modern revisionism. When she'd come to England, her new school didn't even need the airbrush; the

Second Empire might as well not have existed for all she'd learnt about it here. But the historical Prosper had stuck in her mind since childhood as an example of the kind of person she hoped she would never become, and now the memory proved useful. Over time she'd established a fiction that the online Prosper was a blowhard, a stereotypical Marine Le Pen supporter who resented the 'brown invasion'.

Following Karl's request she'd stepped things up a notch; filling in fictional details about Prosper and his life, making him former military to give an air of authority when discussing Operation Patrios. In Bridge's mind he was a man who'd come to believe, after serving in so-called developing countries, that white Europe truly was superior. The kind of man who would insist he wasn't a *racist*, heavens no, he was merely a *realist*.

She fleshed him out further by drawing on Serge Tolbert's mannerisms for verisimilitude. Bridge knew the DGSI officer's voice and speaking manner well enough to imitate it, rather than writing posts in her own voice. She didn't know if Tolbert really was racist, of course. But he was twenty years older than her, so maybe his school had extolled the glories of expansionist colonialism and positioned Chasseloup-Labat as a hero. Tolbert's attitude towards Henri, whose roots were Algerian, suggested it was possible and that was enough for Bridge to work with. It enabled her to think and post things she never would have otherwise, speaking in vague, knowing terms about things Prosper had seen and done while a soldier – though never with the kind of detail that could be verified or investigated. That was partly to hide his fictional status, of course, but it also suited the style of the message boards, where people were told not to give away potentially identifying details in case 'the man' was watching.

Many of the boards Bridge had found and joined made similar claims to be completely secure, safe from internet snooping. Some were only accessible by invitation, with no public link; part of an ad hoc 'dark web' that had grown up around the online far-right movement to evade scrutiny and infiltration. Others claimed they vetted everyone who registered an account with them, to the same end.

But some of them didn't give a flying fuck, and were open to every racist and neo-Nazi who fancied spewing a bit of the old hate and bigotry around the internet. Even on these open boards, most users were savvy enough not to use their real names or post personal photos, mistakenly thinking it made them untraceable. Bridge was prepared to give the Operation Patrios organisers a little more credit, though. If they were indeed part of this online community – monitoring it, recruiting from it, perhaps even co-ordinating through it – they'd surely use the private, more secure boards.

Nevertheless the open boards she'd already joined, easily found through links in the comment sections of alt-right platforms like Frank, were her way in. Soon after stepping up Prosper's activity Bridge had received four separate invitations to private boards, and accepted them all. It didn't take long to trace a few IP addresses and link traffic from those boards to find the others.

Technically speaking, Karl could have done this just as easily. But having a pre-existing account – one that had been around for some time, and especially predated the wave of incomers thanks to interest in Patrios – gave the Prosper persona credibility. Credibility that equalled trust.

From: DieWahreGerechtigkeit
Our socalled-Leaders are LIARS and should all be executed!! They betray their own People and open our Borders to PARASITES but think we dont can't see!! But we have Eyes and Ears and we see the Truth for our selves ,thanks to the hard work of REAL Journalists who dare to speak out and REAL Leaders like Queen Didulo Of Canada who is EXECUTING all Traitors!! You won't hear the REAL News on the MSM not even here in Germany because our socalled-Leaders to busy kissing the Feet (dirty shit covered LOL) of the ISIS Leaders sending TERRORISTS to replace us instead of holding TRTIALS for their Crimes by Firing Squads!! THEY WILL NOT REPLACE US!! !!

Bridge should have been offended at Karl's implication that she could 'impersonate' a real European, as if she wasn't one already. But if these disturbed people were the ones claiming to be real Europeans she wanted nothing to do with them, and it galvanised her. They truly believed a war was coming. If she could help prevent that spilling over into the real world, she was only too happy to do so. Besides, none of this was illegal or classified. She was simply trolling a bunch of right-wing message boards with a fake persona, and telling her boyfriend about the horrible shit she found there. What he did with that information was, officially, none of her concern and nothing to do with SIS.

Giles would still be pissed off if he found out, though.

27

Andrea Thomson would have missed it if not for her morning routine.

Every day, after wrangling Alex to get ready for school and prepping Joan's breakfast, she was picked up by an MI5 driver. The driver, the car, and the route taken varied daily as a security precaution, but Andrea rarely saw the scenery anyway. She spent that time reviewing her calendar and agenda, scanning morning headlines, and thinking about the day that lay ahead of her. Occasionally she would have to put out a few fires or prepare a response to a morning emergency, but most days it was one of the few moments she had to herself. The drivers knew better than to strike up conversation, operating firmly on the basis of speaking only when they were spoken to. So when the car pulled into the secure garage underneath Thames House she was normally forewarned, forearmed, and ready to read the morning briefing.

But today as she sat behind her desk, neatly arranging its contents and sipping coffee, she had a hunch that briefing was incomplete.

She buzzed her assistant and asked, 'Is Paul Granger still in the building?'

'I believe so, ma'am. I saw him down the corridor five minutes ago. Shall I try his desk?'

'Please.' Andrea turned in her chair to watch the river, lost in thought. She was going out on a limb. But her instincts had served her well, both in the forces and later in MI5.

'Come in,' she responded to a knock at the door.

Paul Granger, MI5's lead analyst, entered and closed the door behind him. When they'd first met, Andrea was surprised that this broad-shouldered ape with a buzzcut was possibly the smartest man in the building. But Andrea herself was often underestimated, for standing a head shorter than most, and over the years they'd become friends as well as colleagues. She trusted him completely; but nobody was immune to error.

The daily briefing lay open on her desk. Next to it was today's *Financial Times*, open at a minor story Andrea had noted while reading in the car.

'Sorry to call you in before you head home,' she said. Granger's day started at two a.m., working with the analysis team to compile that morning's dossier; everything the security service needed to know about the previous twenty-four hours, ready and waiting on every senior officer's desk at eight o' clock. 'This didn't make the brief,' she said, holding up the *FT* so he could see the story. An energy provider's shares were expected to take a knock following a three-hour blackout last night in East Kilbride.

Granger peered at it and nodded in recognition. 'I read that. Power company said it was a regular malfunction, and it didn't cross the threshold of interest for inclusion. I assume you disagree?' He rarely prevaricated or beat around the bush, and Andrea liked that.

'I think it's worth taking a second look. I was in a blackout myself recently, in Norfolk. They said that one was normal too.'

Granger nodded, understanding where this conversation was going. 'Wasn't it?'

'No idea, but the explanation I got was a "tripped relay", and according to this story that's also the official line here. Personally, I had the distinct impression I was being fobbed off.'

'By a power company? Perish the thought.'

'Exactly. Once is happenstance, twice is coincidence, and so on. We have infrastructure experts in-house, don't we? Someone who could get a real answer out of them, and understand what it meant.'

Granger nodded. 'We do, but the retailers will refer us to National Grid. They do the actual hard work of running the lines, so it's probably quicker to go straight to them. Although...' He raised a finger in the air, and Andrea waited for him to complete the thought. 'Come to think of it, Scotland's grid is under a different operator. So if this is hostile action, they're spreading wide.'

'I'd imagine they use basically the same equipment, though? In order to be compatible?'

'Sorry, ma'am. We've reached the limit of my knowledge in this area.'

Andrea was out of her depth, too. She wished she could tell him about the missing EMP blueprints, but that was an SIS matter. If it became necessary, she'd call Giles across the river and get the nod from him first. For now, she had to trust someone at Five could look into this with a degree of knowledge, not to mention discretion.

'I want to know if this was an attack. Keep an eye out for similar incidents, would you? And find me whoever has oversight around here on national infrastructure security. I'm either going to brighten their day or ruin it, depending on their point of view.'

28

From: WHITECHAOS

You are wrong. The posts are written in the style of Gematria, an ancient form of numberology. It's principals have been taught by Jews for millennia. The February 14 tweet is significant, first because it is on the 14 which has special meanings to Gematria scholars. Then the numbers tell a story. The number 7 appears 20 times, exactly twice per row. In Kabbalah 7 is the number of Netzach, which means Victory, and 20 = 2+0 = 2 which is the number of Chokmah, which means Wisdom...

This went on for many (many!) more paragraphs, but Bridge's eyes had already glazed over. She'd been through the standard teenage fascination with hidden meanings and codes, and being a goth, that had inevitably led her to the Biblical Apocrypha, *Liber Null & Psychonaut*, reading up on Kabbalah and chaos magic – the usual. She still had a few Phil Hine books on her shelf, in fact. But Bridge had also been through the standard teenage disillusionment with it all, and come out the other side deciding to focus her energies on tangible social good, for real results in the real world. At the time that had meant things like hacking the local council's website and plastering the front page with pro-animal rights propaganda. Now it meant trawling through message boards like this one to try and understand fascists, and finding that some had never emerged from that same phase.

Or perhaps 'Whitechaos' was still a thirteen-year-old kid.

Regardless, this was a theme she'd found across several boards; discussion and dissection of a Twitter account called *@ToTheFathers* that was created on January 1 and since then regularly posted things like:

```
ALLONS ENFANTS DE LA PATRIE
LE JOUR DE GLOIRE EST ARRIVÉ
37594226173811069
88272469120419708
64872063588894173
72369499337460894
17439461152613227
33957150378390021
16166704488465578
64830778201210431
57498024619572413
41725652417623058
```

Which was either an elaborate code, or an online troll having some fun. It could even be someone like 'Whitechaos' themselves, posting nonsense in order to come on boards like this and 'decode' it for other people and look clever – although in their case it wasn't decoding so much as projecting.

Whatever the reason, the amount of conversation focused on the Twitter account showed it was working. She hadn't seen people so desperate to understand nonsense tweets since QAnon had gone the way of the dodo. And like Q, whoever ran this account wasn't hiding their allegiance. 'The Fathers' were commonly referenced on these boards as a tribute to white ancestors, or a general call to arms.

From: Starsnstripes
    You all want red blooded patriots to come help you out? Then help us help you. Talk is cheap, my friends, and we've got enough problems of our own right here in America. Fucking perasites everywhere and the pedofile baby-eaters in DC are laughing at it us all. Put down real money and I'll get on a plane tomorrow, teach you pussys how to fight back against tHe Great Replacement. To The Fathers!!!!

Posters like 'Starsnstripes' were, as they themselves might say, a dime a dozen. Americans who posted many times every day, on recurring themes – the white world was being invaded by foreigners, Europe was overrun, America would be next, Congress was a satanic ring intent on destroying the country, and so on. Exactly the kind of people the Patrios organisers had apparently paid to fly over. But how were they recruited? Were they already known to one another? How extreme did they want their recruits to be, anyway?

From: Feuerkrieg
    Kill all fucking politicians, now
    Did you know ever since the America civil war it is no longer a country
    It is a corporation owned by the Jew Pope because they were bankrupt
    Now they dance them to paymasters fucking tune and rig every elections

```
Hang all traitors kill all zion filth
YOUR HATE MEANS NOTHING WITHOUT ACTION
```

Feuerkrieg was one of the more extreme, plastering boards with Nazi images and memes filled with swastikas, death's heads, and nooses. Now he was taking credit for an attack the night before on a Syrian refugee camp outside Munich:

```
This is not instagram this is the real action
in our Fatherland
Marched to that camp and mowed down some fucking
muslims yeah
They cannot say they not warned
One day you put me on the Saints leaderboard
```

The 'Saints' were terrorists the board users saw as martyrs; Anders Breivik, Omar Mateen, Jake Davison, even the Zodiac killer, because the 'absolute legend got away with it'. Had Feuerkrieg really been involved? Was he even German? Bridge has seen a report of the Munich attack which confirmed injuries only; no fatalities. But on boards like this, people were only too ready to believe authorities would cover up the extent of such attacks.

Bridge's phone buzzed. Grateful for a distraction, she checked it – and was immediately less grateful when she saw it was Izzy calling. What the hell could she want to talk about, after their last conversation? Bridge's thumb hovered over the accept call button. It must be something important; it wasn't like Izzy would ever apologise.

She swiped her thumb. 'Izzy. What's up?'

'I want to apologise.' Bridge's world lurched sideways. 'I'm sorry for...what I said before. I mean, we both said some horrible things. But I should have known better.'

The patronising implication that Bridge herself couldn't possibly have known better wasn't lost on her, but hearing her sister issue a genuine, unprompted apology threw her too off-balance to be offended. Bridge almost responded by asking if Izzy was feeling well, but that would only lead to a renewal of hostilities.

Instead she cleared her throat, then said, 'All right, thank you. I'm sorry too. Now what about Fred and Stéphanie?'

'What do you mean?'

'I mean the last time I saw either of them was in Lyon, and Steph looked like she wanted to cut me.'

Izzy hesitated. 'Well...she'd probably overheard Fred and me talking. While we were with Maman.' Again, the unspoken implication: *and you weren't*. Bridge had a very good idea of the sort of thing her niece had 'overheard', but let that one slide too. She was trying to work on calming her reactions, not immediately assuming the worst and going on the offensive. Izzy continued, 'Actually, I wanted to talk to you about Fred. All this talk of fighting in Europe has got me worried. He's working at a refugee camp, and last night a gang of neo-Nazis apparently attacked a camp in Germany. What if Camp Sud is a...a target, as well?'

'I'm not sure these people even *have* a target beyond "anyone who isn't white", said Bridge. That wasn't entirely true. According to the Munich report, witnesses had heard people chanting '*For the fathers*' during the attack on the Syrian camp. Only a hair away from '*To the fathers*'. But whether the attack had been part of co-ordinated Patrios action, or spontaneous, wasn't clear. Besides: 'Izzy, you know I can't talk about things like this, especially not over the phone.'

'But does that mean I should be worried? There are hundreds of people in Camp Sud, all from Africa and the Middle East. Can't you...no, I suppose not. Never mind.'

Bridge rolled her eyes. 'Don't pull that one. Just out with it.'

'Well, don't you have people in France? Is there someone who could sort of check in on the camp, make sure it has good security, that sort of thing?'

'Izzy, we all see the same reports. Sadly, white fascists attacking refugees isn't anything new. I'm sure the camp organisers, and the Marseille authorities, are all aware and keeping an eye out. I don't really see what good asking one of ours...' She hesitated, stopping herself from saying anything too explicit on an open phone line. But in that moment of hesitation came a thought, and a realisation, and a swell of anger. 'I don't believe this. You're unbelievable.'

'What?'

Bridge laughed bitterly. 'Did you seriously only apologise because you *want* something from me? I knew it was too good to be true. Asking me to pull strings, call in favours...but you thought I wouldn't do it unless you apologised first.'

For a moment Bridge thought she'd deny it, and not so long ago she was certain Izzy would have, but not now. 'Well, would you have?'

'Now we'll never bloody know, will we?'

'This isn't fair. I never ask you for anything, you know that.'

'No, because normally you get everything presented on a silver platter. That's why I'm kicking myself for not realising as soon as you said "sorry" there had to be something behind it. Christ, it's so transparent.'

'I'm looking out for my family. You know that's the most important thing to me.'

'How could I forget, when you never stop reminding me? For God's sake, Izzy. Do you have any idea how much I wish I could turn back the clock? Rewind to the days when you had no idea what I did, when Fred thought I was a bad influence but didn't actively despise me for getting him shot…' She'd said too much already, almost trembling with nerves. 'I can't do that, Izzy. None of us can. All we can do is take responsibility and act like adults.'

After a moment's silence Izzy said, 'That's exactly what I'm asking you to do.'

'By trying to manipulate me, instead of simply asking? Great fucking job, sis.'

Bridge ended the call and stared at her phone, still trembling, willing herself to calm down. She took a deep breath, then flinched, startled, at a hand on her shoulder. Karl stood behind her, and she put her own hand over his.

'I'm sorry,' she said. 'I didn't mean to lose it. She just…'

Karl bent down to kiss the top of her head. 'Drives you crazy, I know. You don't have to apologise.'

'To you, or to her?'

'Either. Both.'

He was right. But the more Bridge thought about it, the more she knew that Izzy had been right, too. Not in her clumsy attempts at manipulation, but in her concern about Fred in Marseille. Even in the short time she'd been investigating Patrios online, Bridge had seen the excitement and anticipation among its supporters and advocates. These people were looking forward to a race war, egging on attacks wherever they happened, and the incident in Germany suggested it wasn't merely online chatter. Perhaps there was more fire behind all this smoke than any of them realised.

29

The former president adopted the same position as in the first video, with the seal prominently displayed and patriotic flags draped behind him. He fixed the camera with a steely glare, his body barely moving as he spoke.

'My fellow patriots everywhere…yes, not only in America, but all over the world, and especially in Europe. You know this is so big, bigger than anything we've ever seen before, it's everywhere. Because it's happening everywhere. But let's talk about Europe, and the horrible, terrible invasion they're facing, it really is the worst thing. I want to speak to those people, the people of Europe, and say look at what happened in Munich yesterday. That was so beautiful, wasn't it? To see patriots like that, real warriors, fighting for their heritage against a wave of enemy genocide, I mean, you can't even call them enemies, they're more like cockroaches, but enemies is what they are, sucking the life out of Europe. America stands ready to help, of course it does, but what happened last night showed that Europe can stand up to this menace just fine. Afterwards people called me up, leaders from every country in Europe, saying "Mr President, thank you for speaking up, thank you for inspiring our people," and I said of course, because I take this duty very seriously. You know, people tell me

I shouldn't speak out, that I'm putting myself in danger. But if I don't, who will? Who will? Someone has to stand up for what's right. Someone has to fight for what's right. Don't you think? Don't you want to fight for what's right? Well, you know what to do. Don't believe the fake news media, don't believe the communist left. They lie, and lie, and lie. Believe your heart, and what you know is true. God bless me, and God bless us all.'

30

It was his idea. He couldn't believe it.

Sasha had spent months working on the plan for Operation Patrios. Yes, others had been involved, but the spark was his. He created it. Then the Kremlin said it was unworkable, impossible, expensive. 'An unrealistic and childish notion.' He told them they were idiots who wouldn't know genius if it slapped them in the face.

Actually, he didn't say that. He'd wanted to, very much. Instead he said nothing, sulked, and planned his next course of action.

(Look where that had got him.)

But now they were proving him right. All at once he was filled with a strange, uncomfortable mixture of pride, vindication, jealousy, and fear. His stomach felt like he'd swallowed a sack full of wildcats. They were using his idea after all. Patrios was happening, it was working, and soon they would know they shouldn't have doubted him. But Sasha wouldn't be there to see it. Oh, how things could have been so different!

(Would they, though? Or would he have quit anyway?)

It was all happening without him, and he would never receive the credit he should have for such a brilliant plan. Who would take that credit instead? He had a suspicion, and they would bask in glory that should have been his. It reminded Sasha why he was here in the first place, of how that life was now lost to him forever. Oh, he'd made money from it, with some still stashed away in Swiss accounts or invested in Bitcoin. But lately, trapped in here like a prisoner, he'd started to wonder if it had been worth it. Through the TV he'd gained access to the external cameras and spent hours watching people and traffic pass by outside, sometimes feeling an overwhelming surge of envy.

These people, these sheep, knew nothing. They had no idea how the world truly operated, yet they were content. They walked without fear, without constantly looking back over their shoulders. They didn't worry that every stranger might be trying to kill them; every umbrella tipped with venom, every drink laced with poison.

Sasha could never return to such ignorance, but he would have liked to return to a life without fear. That would be nice.

Noise outside the door startled him. The on-screen clock indicated it was time for his evening meal delivery. He frantically tabbed over to Netflix, hiding the computer interface, hit play on whatever was selected and skipped forward fifteen minutes. He tossed the keyboard to the other end of the couch and flopped down, one foot up on the cushions, head resting on his elbow as the door locks buzzed and the door opened. His heart hammered in his chest, so loud that surely the guard bringing his food could hear it? Apparently not. Dull-eyed and bored as always, the guard placed the tray of food on the low table and turned to go without a word.

Then stopped when he saw what was on TV, and laughed with contempt. 'You are like a woman,' he said in accented English.

Sasha's face flushed. On the screen a young couple in old-fashioned clothes walked through a garden, making doe eyes at each other. He hadn't looked at what he'd selected to play; he just needed to make the guard think he'd been sitting watching TV, not reading internet boards and hacking their security cameras.

'I like this actor,' he said with a shrug, hoping that would be enough for the guard, because Sasha couldn't have named the actor in question with a hot poker held to his feet.

The guard shook his head and rolled his eyes, said something in his own language that was definitely not a compliment, and turned to leave. Sasha had a sudden wild fantasy of escape – leaping from the couch, smashing the keyboard into the guard's head to knock him out, taking the man hostage to gain passage out of the building, and demanding a car to take him…where? Where could he go? What could he do?

Nobody knew he was here. And as much as he hated it, the anonymity and isolation of being trapped in this suite was keeping him safe and alive. The fantasy faded and vanished, dissipating like unreal mist.

The guard closed the door behind him. The magnetic lock buzzed closed, and Sasha's heart slowed at last.

31

Sundar 'Sunny' Patel looked up from the Toshiba laptop with a worried expression. '*Patrios* is what he said in the deepfake, isn't it?'

Steve Wicker nodded and retrieved his computer. 'Deepfakes, plural, now. There's a new one doing the rounds and dominating the conversation. Same format, which is more evidence that we're right to call them fake. Honestly, it looks like exactly the same video source, they just have him saying different shit.' He corrected himself. 'Well, using different words. He's spouting the same shit as before, but it's even more inflammatory. Hold on, I'll show you.'

Patel's GCHQ office was small but neat. Fully internal and windowless, it was filled with daylight-simulating LEDs to compensate for the lack of natural light. He could have claimed an office on the external side of the 'Doughnut', a nickname for both the data-gathering agency's circular headquarters outside Cheltenham and its occupants, if he'd wanted it. But Patel dealt with enough of that same data, often confidential and always sensitive, that the risk of long-range surveillance was too high. Steve knew his boss didn't mind; like most Doughnuts, all Patel needed to feel outside was a computer with an internet connection.

Steve located the second video. He'd saved the file to disk in case it disappeared from the internet, even though that was pretty low-risk. A hundred different far-right websites now hosted their own copies, all paranoid that everyone else's would be taken down. They'd love that, or more specifically they'd love to complain about it. But Steve didn't want to give them any more traffic, and therefore advertising income, than he had to for research purposes. He pressed play on the video.

After it finished, Patel exhaled in resignation. 'You weren't kidding. Same old shite but times ten. Cockroaches? Really?'

'See what I mean about it being obviously the same source? But Bridge said at the last SCAR meeting that a lot of people don't care if it's real or not, and everything I've read suggests she's right.'

'The voice, though. It's a bloody good impression.'

'We reckon that might be faked with AI, too. Scary stuff.'

'So's this *Patrios* chatter you found,' said Patel. 'How widespread is it?'

'Very, and it's growing,' Steve replied. 'Enough that I think Vauxhall and Five should both be made aware, if they haven't seen it already.'

'MI5? Is there a domestic element to this?'

Steve shrugged. 'Unknown if anything is operational, but there are definitely Brits involved in the conversation.' He'd been watching the online chatter since returning from that SCAR meeting, and sure enough he'd found far-right message boards and chat groups across Europe discussing the deepfake videos with excitement. Many of the same people believed Operation Patrios was a real mission, and rivers of blood would soon flow across the continent. Conversations about weapons and tactics, some of them worryingly knowledgeable, rubbed shoulders with lurid fantasies of genocide and slaughter against refugees, immigrant populations, foreign students, anything deemed 'Non-European'.

It was ridiculous; Europeans had mixed and mated with people from all over the world for hundreds of years – thousands in the case of Africa. But, as with the deepfakes, too many people believed in a history that never was because it fitted their worldview. Probably the same people who insisted Jesus was white because classical artists had painted him that way, and now believed he was on their side because they saw *Thou shalt not kill* as more of a guideline than a literal divine edict.

And this was just the stuff in the public conversations, or on private forums hosted on what their owners thought were secure websites. Steve shuddered to think what was being said in private chats on services like WhatsApp and Telegram, most of which even he and his GCHQ colleagues couldn't see. Not all, though; he'd joined a few under false pretences, faking his identity with pilfered photos and details, and pinging his phone identifier around the world a few times in case anyone tried to trace it. The people in those groups thought Steve was a white, middle-aged American army veteran from Kentucky who shared their ideology. If they ever found out he was a black guy from Dalston...well, he was glad he was over here, and they were over there. Unlike Brigitte Sharp, Steve had no taste for field work.

On his own computer, Patel re-read the chatter analysis. 'Surely we're not the only people seeing this? At the very least, France and Germany must be monitoring activity as well. What about the Americans?'

'The CIA played it down at the last SCAR meeting. Said it was all talk. But I cross-referenced a random selection of these accounts, and more than a few are known actors. People with a history of real-world agitation, and the arrest records to prove it.'

'Not just keyboard warriors.'

'No, but that's good for us. If they were, they'd take more precautions online and probably know these message boards aren't as private as they think. Instead, most of them either don't know or don't care.'

Patel leaned back in his chair. 'All the more reason to kick it over to Vauxhall. Prep a briefing packet for SIS; they can reach out to the continental agencies. I'll call Giles Finlay.'

32

Andrea wasn't sure how she felt about being unable to shout at the power company who'd fobbed her off in Norfolk. On the one hand, an occasional reminder to treat their customers as something other than morons never hurt. On the other, it now seemed they'd been fobbed off themselves. Few things were worse than being unable to answer a question fully, even if you wanted to, because you were operating on low-quality information.

The staff in MI5's department for national infrastructure security had relished the task Andrea set them. They thought of themselves as firefighters – working days that mostly consisted of calm, regular check-ups, with a lot of sitting around waiting for something to happen. But when something did happen, klaxons sounded and suddenly it was all hands on deck.

The blackouts in Norfolk and East Kilbride had not sounded any klaxons, because National Grid considered them mere equipment failures. Unexpected, but within regular parameters. So when Andrea had asked the infrastructure group to look into it they were grateful both for something to do, and for the opportunity to grill the grid operators about a potential oversight.

The equipment failure at both blackouts had been the same, and really was a tripped relay. But nobody could give a rational explanation for why either of them tripped in the first place beyond, 'Sometimes they do; that's the point of fail-safes.' The operators had assured MI5 they were performing observance checks on all previously installed relays of the same type and manufacturer, but it would take months to cover them all, and besides, there was no history of widespread malfunction. Sometimes a coincidence was merely a coincidence.

Andrea didn't accept that. Something Brigitte Sharp had said came to mind: *everything's electronic these days.* So, not wanting to put the wind up the grid operator without due cause, she called Sunny Patel at GCHQ.

'We can't be sure without rooting through the grid's own service logs,' said Patel now, videoconferencing in via the flatscreen in Andrea's office. 'So this is all speculation. But it's certainly possible both incidents were attacks, and conducted by the same hostile party. Come to think of it, conducting one would make the next easier because those substations use the same software.'

'Is that normal?' she asked, surprised. 'Surely the grid isn't buying something off the shelf.'

Patel shook his head. 'Yes and no. Nationwide, the overall system is bespoke and closely maintained. But substation management is almost entirely remote. There are different software packages used according to a station's location, size, primary use, and so on.'

'And these "tripped relays" were at substations managed by the same package?'

'Precisely. It's quite widespread; in fairly common use here and in Europe. Originally developed in the Netherlands. Now, as I said, this is speculative—'

Andrea interrupted him. 'Hold on, Sunny. Go back. This software isn't only used in the UK?'

'No, not at all,' he replied. 'France, Germany, Spain, and more. As I said, it's fairly common.'

'Russia?'

Patel shrugged. 'I don't have that data, but it's possible. Plenty of Russian-language systems operate using the Western alphabet rather than Cyrillic, for compatibility reasons. What are you thinking?'

Andrea took a moment to consider. What *was* she thinking? That the Russians might have practised hacking their own power stations, to create an attack on European stations running the same software? That this might, somehow, be linked to the Russian theft of EMP device plans? But why would they need both, if they essentially did the same thing?

'You said this is all speculation, Sunny. What would you need to be sure it was an attack?'

'Access to National Grid's service logs, but we won't get that without high-level authorisation.'

'Leave that to me,' Andrea said. 'I have a horrible notion this might be linked to an ongoing operation. If I'm right, getting access will be the least of our problems.'

33

While Sunny Patel held a video call with Andrea, across the river at Vauxhall Giles took a call from Steve Wicker to talk about the report package he'd prepared and sent over.

'This *Patrios* stuff,' said Giles. 'How can we use it?'

Steve looked confused. 'That's your area. It was Bridge who asked us to follow up on the far-right chatter, remember. I assumed you had a plan.'

It was entirely possible Bridge had a plan she'd neglected to share with Giles, a state of affairs he wasn't entirely unused to. There had been times he'd gambled on her instincts and been wrong, but many more when he'd been right to do so. He wasn't quite an old-school boss like Emily Dunston, who gave her officers free rein and would forever trust their judgement over a hundred analysts. He'd created the Cyber Threat Analytics unit precisely so that modern technical analysis could be brought to bear on SIS' work. But Giles also knew the value of letting an experienced officer follow their gut. There were some things a computer simply couldn't calculate, and human behaviour was top of that list.

'I'll follow up with Bridge after we've spoken,' he said. 'But you're the one who's been sifting through the data. What does it tell you? What are your thoughts? There are no wrong answers, so speak freely.'

Steve took a moment to consider. 'I think we're looking at a small group of experienced and co-ordinated agitators recruiting a larger pool of keen young men to cause mayhem across Europe in a simultaneous event. I also think those experienced actors are working on behalf of a hostile party, either state or high-value individual, who's financing this whole shebang.'

'That's quite a theory,' said Giles, thumbing through the report. 'You're not that explicit in here.'

'I was advised not to be,' Steve said cautiously. 'The evidence is there, but not strong enough for GCHQ to officially stand behind it. All we can say for sure is those deepfake videos have energised the European right – who insist they're not fake at all – and they're being egged on by core actors, both European and American, encouraging fellow travellers to take up arms and fight back against the Great Replacement in the name of Operation Patrios.'

Giles picked up on his metaphorical capital letters. 'The "Great Replacement"? Explain.'

Steve shrugged. 'It's a long-standing white supremacist theory that gets rediscovered every few decades. Supposedly the ultra-far left is deliberately breeding non-white and mixed-race children in sufficient numbers that they'll outnumber white people and thus take control. It only takes one person of colour to make a mixed-race baby, you know? White man, black woman; black baby. Black man, white woman; black baby.' He laughed at Giles' confused expression. 'Don't you know your Public Enemy? *Fear of a Black Planet*?'

Giles didn't dignify that with an answer. 'It never ceases to amaze me how the right convinces itself the left can co-ordinate a global conspiracy, when in my experience they can barely agree which way is up. What makes you think this Patrios movement has a state backer? Another hunch?'

Steve smiled in apology. 'Like I said, I was advised to leave it out of the report. But some of the leaders we've identified are known agitators, operating in different countries and historically in very different groups. Now all of a sudden they're singing from the same hymn sheet, or at least attending the same church, while someone is throwing around a decent amount of money to fly Americans over *and* train the young white wannabes. But whenever anyone asks about funding, the question is either ignored, shouted down, or deleted.'

'So much for their vaunted freedom of speech. But isn't that just wise discretion, to avoid a paper trail?'

Steve shook his head. 'Remember, a lot of this chatter is taking place on private boards where they think they can't be seen. Besides, these aren't exactly wise and discreet people. Half the time they won't shut up about the latest immigrant they kicked half to death, or the sympathetic politician they persuaded to support white pride, or their grass roots fundraising targets.'

'But not where Patrios money's concerned.'

'Absolutely not. Sealed lips all round.'

Giles sat back in his chair. 'So I'll return to the start. How can we use this?'

'Andrea Thomson has a copy of the same package, because some of the actors concerned are domestic. We figured you'd want to handle getting the word out to foreign agencies so they can put their own monitoring into operation. But even here, we know online chatter isn't the complete picture. If it's true that they're training these kids at camps all over Europe…' He left the thought unfinished, because his point was obvious but well outside his remit.

'Understood, thank you.' Giles nodded. 'I appreciate your candour, and for what it's worth I think you're probably right about the backed funding. The question, as always, is who.'

'Like I said, it could be a state, or just a sympathetic billionaire.

Plenty of those around, these days.'

'Sometimes filling both roles, unfortunately.' The rise of anti-immigrant nationalism had been so widespread in recent years that Giles couldn't restrict even the possible nation-state suspects to the usual places like Russia, China, and North Korea. It was equally likely somewhere like Poland, Slovakia, or Belarus might fund a programme like Patrios.

'There's, um, one other thing,' said Steve reluctantly. 'Off the record, like.'

Giles nodded. 'Go on.'

Steve hesitated, then said, 'Tolbert, the French officer. I only know him second-hand, but I think you might want to have a word.'

'Concerning the EMP plans, you mean?'

'No, no. He's…well, I think he's on several of these far-right boards, supporting Operation Patrios. Not with his real name, of course, but there's a user called *Prosper* who fits the bill. He's said some things that made me wonder, so I've pieced his posts together, and it sure sounds like the same guy. Is it possible?'

Giles steepled his fingers in thought. 'I don't know him well enough to answer, but we both know a woman who does. Thank you, Steve.' He ended the video call, picked up his phone, and rang downstairs.

'CTA, Bridge speaking.'

'How likely is it that your man Tolbert is a fascist sympathiser posting support for Patrios under the name *Prosper*?'

A full five seconds of silence followed; a state of affairs Giles *was* entirely unused to. Finally she said, 'You'd better arrange a call with the CIA.'

34

Edison Hill and Karl Dominic sat uncomfortably at the small table in Broom Six. They'd been told only that the meeting concerned Patrios, and neither wanted to break the silence with speculation. Sitting next to Bridge, Giles patiently worked on that morning's *Times* crossword. She stole a glance at Karl, who winced when she gave the smallest of nods in response to his silent question. Finally Ciaran and Monica, the remaining members of the CTA unit, joined them. Giles put down his pen and folded the newspaper.

'Thank you for coming, gentlemen, though I suspect this meeting may not be a happy one.' He turned to Bridge with a stern expression. 'Bridge, why don't you explain why we're all here?'

She cleared her throat, swallowed, cleared her throat again, then thought *fuck it* and began. 'I've been using that online alias I mentioned, named *Prosper*, to post on far-right online discussion boards in order to research Operation Patrios and determine if it's something we should be concerned about.'

'We asked her to do it,' said Karl immediately. 'We, ah, we didn't want you guys to freak out.'

'Your concern for our mental well-being is duly noted,' Giles replied, though he was looking directly at Edison Hill instead of Karl. 'Naturally, it couldn't have anything to do with you not wanting to officially admit there are embedded FBI agents taking part in exercises that could potentially lead to violent hate crimes on foreign soil.'

'Bureau men are not going to start shooting up goddamn Paris,' said Hill. 'But someone might. I know you didn't think Patrios was worth much concern at the last SCAR meeting, but the company disagrees. Someone with deep pockets is funding this operation. They're using shell companies to pay for Americans to fly to Europe for three weeks. That's not the kind of thing you do without a reason. Whatever the hell they're planning, they're serious. This is unprecedented territory, Agent Finlay, and it's our job to keep our countrymen safe.'

'Indeed. Your job, not ours.' He raised an eyebrow at Bridge. 'I knew you two shacking up would cause trouble some day. Is this a good time to remind everyone present that the point of SCAR is to *share* information and activity? Or does the CIA not regard its commitment to the response unit with sufficient consideration?'

In Bridge's experience, when Giles slipped into political-speak it meant either he was secretly furious, or he was working out how to use the situation as leverage and get what he wanted. Sometimes it was both.

'In the same spirit, can I point out that I wasn't doing anything classified or illegal? All I did was post on message boards.'

Giles shot her a look and turned back to the CIA men. 'If there are embedded agents over here, surely you're in touch with them. What are they telling you?'

'That's kind of the problem,' Hill replied. 'You're right, the FBI has informed us there are a small number of agents who had no alternative but to go along in order to maintain cover. But they were told to maintain comms silence before arrival, and there's been no contact since.'

'That's not surprising,' said Ciaran. 'Cell signals leak like a sieve, and tracking a phone is child's play. If you're trying to stay hidden, you ban phone usage.'

'Which brings us to what I've found on these boards,' said

Bridge. 'Unless everyone wants to keep playing at finger-pointing for another five minutes?' Giles' expression implied she was skating on wafer-thin ice, but she pressed ahead. 'Because it was worth it. I've learned a lot about Patrios already, and if I keep digging I'll find more.'

Giles exhaled noisily. 'Tell me about this persona, first. Why did GCHQ flag it as Serge Tolbert? Surely you didn't use his name?'

'Of course not. But the most convincing legends are based in reality, and online is no different. Building the Prosper persona on someone I know allows me to consistently imitate speech patterns and behaviour. It's not like I claimed to be DGSI.'

'So who do they think you are?'

'Former French military, a racist old dinosaur who now does unspecified security work. It's uncouth on those boards to probe too deeply into people's identity, and so far it's working. I've got into a few arguments – deliberately, to provoke reactions – and I've read a lot of stuff I'd rather not have, to be perfectly honest. But it's giving me an insight into the mindset of these nutters.'

'One man's nutter is another man's martyr,' said Giles. Bridge remembered that he'd created the CTA in response to the London 7/7 bombings, which had killed an old friend of his.

'There's also a Twitter account,' said Karl.

That didn't get the reaction Bridge suspected he was hoping for, so she followed up for him. 'We can't dismiss the impact of social media, not after QAnon. Q has vanished into the digital ether, but they laid the groundwork for similar conspiracy thinking. A lot of the people talking about Patrios are excited about this new Twitter account, @ToTheFathers.' She navigated to the account's profile on the room computer, scrolling down the page to show its strange, nonsensical tweets.

'Presumably a code,' said Giles. 'Do the words indicate the cipher?'

'It's possible. Every tweet starts with two lines of verse, often lyrics from a national anthem or patriotic song. But I haven't had any luck decoding them with known substitution ciphers, or using the words to decode the numbers. Remember, though, Q didn't need to issue explicit instructions. People pored over everything like he was Nostradamus and interpreted his posts as they saw fit.'

'Interpretations which coincidentally suited their own agenda.'

Bridge nodded. 'This could just be an agitator – someone stirring things up, deliberately posting to prompt similar interpretations. If so they're doing a cracking job, because people on the boards are going crazy over this stuff.'

'But what if it's not?' said Monica. 'We can't dismiss the idea that these might actually be coded instructions.'

'Agreed,' said Giles. 'I'm rather surprised your former colleagues at GCHQ didn't mention this.' Nobody seemed to know what he meant, so he filled them in on Steve Wicker's briefing. 'It was Steve who noticed this Prosper character and suspected it was Tolbert,' he finished, nodding at Bridge.

'I'll look deeper into the Twitter account,' said Karl. 'If we can find out who's operating it, it could give us a big insight into how this is being co-ordinated.'

'Not likely, though, is it?' said Ciaran. 'You lot never found out who Q was.'

Hill's mouth twitched in what may have been a smile, but it was gone in an instant.

'It's worth a shot anyhow,' said Karl. 'Who knows, there might be a link to the deepfakes too.'

'Surely we're not still talking about those.' said Monica. 'They were debunked.'

'Try telling that to the people on those boards,' said Bridge. 'Until the president comes out and says "That's not me," they'll go on believing it.'

Ciaran nodded. 'Even if he did, there are people who'd insist he was only saying that because he couldn't admit it in public. To stop the "deep state" getting to him – that sort of thing.'

Monica was already searching the BBC News website for a story. 'No, I mean they were literally debunked. Look.' She clicked on a piece headlined *Researchers Prove 'Racist' Video is Fake*. As if the scare quotes weren't depressing enough, Bridge noticed the story was buried deep in the Technology section, rather than on the front page.

But the subject was encouraging. Researchers at the Massachusetts Institute of Technology had analysed the videos and released a statement, concluding they were definitely deepfakes. The researchers used a tool sensitive enough to detect minute changes in a person's skin colour brought about by blood flow around the body; infinitesimal variations that were completely invisible to the human eye, but could be detected in a video recording with sufficiently powerful technology. The latest deepfake algorithms were smart enough to simulate breathing, blinking, and all the tiny shifts of posture that people made without thinking. But they couldn't replicate the almost-invisible subdermal reddening caused by blood flowing under the skin – and the videos in question didn't have it.

'That's good enough for me,' said Bridge, 'but something tells me the Patrios supporters will simply claim MIT is part of the conspiracy.' She was relieved to find out the videos were definitely fake. Maybe even the former president had limits.

'Then let's figure out next steps,' said Giles. 'We have an unknown party funding and organising what appears to be a co-ordinated effort to cause racial unrest in Europe. They may or may not be using a Twitter account, of all things, to issue instructions. They're flying Americans over to help, for unknown reasons, which has led to FBI agents getting caught up in this mess. Meanwhile, neo-Nazis across the continent are cheering it all on. Edison, you said something about three weeks?'

The CIA man nodded. 'That's what the US militias who got flown over were told. Take twenty days' vacation.'

'So whatever they're planning will probably happen inside that time,' said Bridge, checking a calendar. 'We've lost one week, but that still leaves us some breathing room. Plenty of time for local security agencies and police to get their act together.'

'Let's hope so,' Giles harrumphed. 'Leave that side of things with me. In the meantime, Bridge, continue taking part in those online boards and gaining their trust. Perhaps the best way to find out where these camps are located is to get yourself recruited to one.'

'Whoa, now, hold on. Nobody said anything about going undercover.' She looked to Karl for some help. To her horror, he shrugged.

'Kind of too good to pass up, isn't it?'

She glared at Giles. 'Did you fucking plan this? Was this the game all along?'

'Absolutely not,' he said, offended. 'But you've made inroads with Patrios supporters, so this could be our best chance to get some solid intel. Especially as our incognito Federal agents appear to also be incommunicado.'

Bridge turned to Hill. 'Surely the CIA has people stationed in Europe.'

Hill shrugged. 'We do, and I assure you they're working hard on the same problems we are. Some of them are even trying to infiltrate, yes. But many hands make light work, Agent Sharp, and a genuine European-born mole will be a real asset to everyone involved.'

For flattery is the bellows blows up sin, thought Bridge, and suspected her fate was sealed the moment this meeting started. She and Karl were going to have words later.

35

Three times a day, and more than half of those were a waste of time. If anyone had asked former Sergeant Colin Sanders for his opinion, he'd have said it was a bloody stupid way to run an operation.

But nobody did ask, and he wasn't about to say so out loud. That would endanger his fee, and if there was one thing besides his own skin Sanders never knowingly jeopardised, it was his bank balance.

So three times a day, every day, he closed and locked his office door, sat at his desk, took a pad from his top drawer, and readied a pencil. He then opened his laptop, loaded a web page, and compared what he saw to the pad. Most of the time it meant nothing, so he closed the laptop, replaced the pad in the drawer, unlocked his door, and thought nothing more of it.

But on some days it did mean something, and those were worse. Encryption, ciphers, and other code bollocks was always his least favourite subject. He'd had to learn it anyway, of course; the Paras were a cut above your average squaddie, expected to have brains as well as biceps.

Still, he'd rather be outside training the lads. He hadn't yet been briefed on the big plan, but that didn't bother him. Like any soldier he was used to knowing only what was necessary. Besides, his employers paid well and gave him a lot of leeway to run the camp as he saw fit. A position that filled his coffers *and* taught a few young kids to fight back against the third-world Islamists invading Britain? Worth putting up with a bit of silly cloak-and-dagger.

So on the days Sanders had a message to receive – like today, it turned out – he dutifully spent ten minutes carefully decoding it, then read and digested the directive. More often than not, even the real messages were simple propaganda reminding them to be prepared and on the lookout for infiltrators. As if he needed reminding.

Today's had that. But it also had something else.

```
PATER  ENGAGE  ONLINE  AND  ENCOURAGE  CIVILIAN
ATTACKS  AS  PROTOCOL  MEANWHILE  PREPARATIONS  AND
TESTS CONTINUE T-13 DAYS
```

Thirteen days. Finally, an event date to work towards. Not that the kids outside could be made battle-ready in such a short span of time. He'd always known that, but when he raised the point his employer said enthusiasm and dedication were more important. That was true to an extent, but to a professional like Sanders it seemed wrong not to send your best men into combat no matter how imbalanced the odds might be. He could have called up fifty freelancers like himself, all ready and willing to action whatever was required for the right fee. For some reason the organisers didn't want that. Veterans were for tuition and leadership only. 'Training the next generation of patriots,' they'd said, or some such bollocks.

Sanders tore off the pad's top sheet, scrunched it up, and threw it in the wastepaper basket.

36

'Was this the plan all along? Get me active on the boards, then persuade Giles to send me undercover instead of one of your own? You've got some nerve.'

Bridge leaned in the kitchen doorway while Karl prepared dinner. She'd waited until he began cooking to bring up the subject so he couldn't escape. Not that his Highbury flat afforded the space to do so, but it was the principle of the thing. Much like the question of whether he and the CIA had intended this outcome from the start.

'OK, look,' he said, slowly stirring a pot. 'Was it a possibility we considered? Of course. That's our job. But I swear we didn't work something out with Giles beforehand. You saw he was hearing that stuff for the first time. Hill and I just happen to think it's our best option.'

'"Our"? I didn't know I'd transferred to the CIA.'

Karl let the spatula rest and turned to face her. 'I meant for SCAR. But you know what? I think it's our best option, too. And yours.' He approached Bridge and took her hands in his. 'You're going stir-crazy cooped up. You can't sleep, you can't relax, you sit and stare out the apartment window. When they sent you to Paris, it was a blessing. You haven't been that animated since Tallinn. I've seen this sometimes in our own guys, Bridge. You've got the bug.'

'I am not a bloody danger junkie.'

He smiled. 'You don't have to be addicted to enjoy getting high.' He brought her hands to his lips, kissed them, then returned to the stove.

Bridge said nothing, annoyed at his presumption, but also at herself because some of what he said was true. She really had been excited to shadow Kennedy to Paris, and speeding through the streets in Tolbert's car to investigate the safe harbour apartment killings had been a real buzz.

Karl ground pepper into the borlotti bean sauce, then stirred again. It hadn't taken long for Bridge to find out he couldn't cook anything more complicated than coffee, relying instead on a steady diet of takeout, fast food, and restaurants. If they were going to live in each other's pockets, she'd insisted he at least learn to make a decent Italian.

Perhaps inevitably, he'd overcompensated. Karl's YouTube history was now a litany of TV and amateur chefs, while his online shopping history quickly filled up with utensils, pots, and cookbooks. Within a month he'd been able to make a pretty good pasta – this same one he was making tonight – but he hadn't stopped there. Now his repertoire of veggie food was five times as wide as Bridge's own, and considering he was normally a meat eater she couldn't complain. He wasn't hard to watch, either, with a towel slung over his shoulder and sleeves rolled up to his elbows as he ground, chopped, and stirred.

'I've been thinking about these tweets,' he said. Bridge wanted to protest at the sudden change of subject, but what more was there to say? Giles had told her to find a way in, and even if that order was influenced by the CIA, so what? All of his decisions were influenced by politicians, other agencies, or external forces in some way. Getting inside Patrios was the best option to find out what was going on and shut it down. Maybe she simply recoiled at the thought of having to go even deeper into this horrible cover persona she'd created. She'd need to come up with a new one to infiltrate in person, anyway. Even a brain-dead neo-Nazi wouldn't mistake her for a middle-aged Frenchman.

She realised Karl was waiting for her to pay attention. From the look in his eyes she braced herself for An Explanation.

'Sorry, go on. You've been thinking about the tweets.'

He tasted the sauce with a teaspoon, then wielded it like a baton as he spoke. 'It occurred to me, what if it's like a modern version of a numbers station? You've heard of those, right?'

Of course she had. But she didn't want to spoil his moment, so she said, 'I think so. What about them?'

'Numbers stations are radio broadcasts on shortwave frequencies, so you can hear them almost anywhere in the world. They transmit sequences of numbers at particular times of day, and if you're a spy in the field you tune in using an ordinary radio, take down the numbers, and decode what they mean. Hey presto, you've got orders.'

'A very old spy in the field,' said Bridge. 'Surely nobody uses them any more.'

Karl shrugged. 'You'd be surprised. Sure they're old tech, mostly used during the Cold War. But there are some still in operation.'

Sensing they were finally approaching the point, Bridge said, 'You think the *ToTheFathers* Twitter account is operating like a numbers station, sending out instructions?'

'Think about it. A big advantage of shortwave radio was how basic the equipment was. All you needed to hear the numbers was a receiver, because agents weren't transmitting anything back. They just had to listen and take down the numbers. Even the Stasi couldn't arrest someone for owning a radio, or a pencil.'

'I wouldn't be too sure about that,' said Bridge. 'They were vindictive fuckers by all accounts. But regardless, they *could* arrest you for tuning in to a numbers station when it was broadcasting.'

Karl dropped pasta into a pot of boiling water. 'Absolutely. And you had to tune in at the right time, because obviously, it was live.'

Bridge followed the logic and saw where he was going. It made a weird kind of sense. 'With a Twitter post, timing is irrelevant. You can look at it whenever you like, from anywhere in the world, after it's posted.'

'All it takes is one of these.' He held up his phone, currently doubling as a kitchen timer. 'You don't have to tune in at a precise time. You don't have to know a frequency. Hell, the account isn't locked, so you don't even have to follow it to read the posts. You just visit Twitter-dot-com on any web browser. Even if someone sees your browsing history...'

'...Then so what?' said Bridge, finishing the thought. 'Looking at Twitter these days is no more incriminating than owning a radio was back then. Less so, because millions of people do it every day. If you start thinking everyone who opens Twitter on their phone is a spy, you're into lunatic territory.'

Karl nodded, pleased with himself. 'But those *ToTheFathers* posts sure look like a code, don't they?'

Bridge fetched her HP laptop from the lounge and opened it on the kitchen counter. She browsed to the Twitter account's web page – exactly as she'd described, an activity so innocuous nobody could think it suspicious – then scrolled down the timeline of mysterious tweets. 'They post three times a day, once every four hours on the hour. Hang on, though...'

'What have you seen?' Karl stood beside her and placed his arm over her shoulders to look at the screen. The weight of it, the solidity of him, felt good. She should still be mad at him, but knew she couldn't keep it up. All this and he could (now) cook, too. In a way, she supposed Maman would have been pleased. Or at least less disappointed.

'Every post is different,' Bridge said. 'I guess there's no point in repeating themselves, when tweets remain online for people to see at any time.' She swiped her fingers on the trackpad, scrolling back in time through previous posts. 'The three-times-per-day schedule is constant, ever since the account was created on New Year's Day.' She pointed at the timestamps on a selection of tweets. 'See? One post per day at each of seven a.m., eleven a.m., and three p.m.'

'Weird times. Why not centre them around noon?'

Bridge stared at the screen, then groaned in realisation. 'We're an hour behind. If these tweets really are aimed at Patrios camps all over the continent, they'll run on Central European Time.'

'So: eight in the morning, noon, and four in the afternoon. That's more like it. Still, that's three sets of orders per day. Seems a lot.'

'They might not all be instructions. Some could be status updates, maybe.'

Karl returned to the stove and stirred the pot. 'Or they're filler. That's standard practice for a numbers station, to counter traffic analysis. The operators don't want anyone listening to know how many instructions they're sending, or when action might be imminent, right? So they *always* send a message, even when they have nothing to say. Filler broadcasts are nothing but random numbers, but they use the same format as real messages. The only way to know real from fake is by the schedule.'

Bridge snorted in amusement. 'Imagine you're a codebreaker and your reward for nights of sweating blood over enemy messages is *Mary had a little lamb...*'

'How many people reply to these tweets? Could be worth checking those people out.'

She shook her head, already knowing the answer. 'It was one of the first things I checked. Nobody *can* reply to them. They probably have the account permanently set that way, so only people they mention can reply.'

'But they're not mentioning anyone, just throwing shit out there for people to read. Which means they're not expecting a reply...like a numbers station.'

Bridge tapped her fingers on the keyboard, not typing but thinking. 'But who's reading them, and how are they decoding the messages? There must be a system. A matrix, an algorithm, a decoder wheel from a box of cornflakes, whatever. If these tweets mean something, it must be possible to extract the meaning. If we can solve that, maybe we can find out who's behind it.'

'Or we could go to the source. Subpoena Twitter.'

Bridge shook her head. 'You know what they're like. They'd take weeks to cough up user details, and anyway, our tweeter's probably using a burner email account and a VPN to post.'

'Still worth a try. Leave that to our side, we have a relationship with the Twitter guys. The Feds once kicked around the idea of having a permanent agency presence in their office.'

Bridge looked sideways at him. 'What, undercover? Sending someone like you in to spy on them?'

'Hell, no,' Karl laughed. 'Everyone knows we work with them anyway. They proposed a crisis operator, so when something bad happened our guy could get directly into the database and extract whatever information the agencies needed.'

'You said they kicked the idea around. But they didn't go through with it?'

'No. Turns out there really are some things even the agencies won't do.'

Bridge nudged him. 'Or maybe they don't tell underlings like us. It's a conspiracy!'

Karl looked to the sky in mock anguish. 'Oh, no, I've lost her to the lizard-believers! *Madre de dios*, what did I do to deserve this?'

She laughed. 'Seriously, how do we crack it? The tweets

obviously have a format, but that's in plain sight. There must be something more to the pattern.'

They were both silent as Karl drained the pasta. Then he said, 'What if we looked for the opposite of a pattern?'

Bridge looked at him askance. 'The opposite of a pattern is random chaos. Impossible to crack.'

'All right, maybe that's not what I meant. More like the negative space around a pattern, rather than the pattern itself.' He slid the pasta into the sauce and gently stirred. 'You remember in the late 2000s, the FBI cracked a Russian sleeper ring and deported them back to Moscow?'

'Didn't they make a TV series out of that?'

'Yeah, I think so. But you have to attend counter-intelligence class at Langley to learn what really happened. See, the NSA monitors every numbers station it can find, including this big one in Cuba that's been transmitting for decades. A couple years before those arrests, they noticed something weird about that station; most of its messages didn't contain the number nine.'

Bridge shook her head. 'That's impossible. If you're assigning decimal integer blocks to alphanumeric characters there should be an even distribution from zero to nine. It would be like writing a book without using the letter t. You could force it, but it wouldn't happen naturally.'

'Therefore those messages weren't natural,' said Karl, waving his spatula. 'NSA theorised the station's random number generator had a bug. It simply didn't produce nines, but because the filler is automated and by definition unimportant, nobody at the station paid close enough attention. So now the FBI could watch the suspects and see if they were always at home to receive messages on nights when the broadcast was real – when it contained nines – but when it was filler they went out for dinner or whatever. Boom, sleeper ring exposed.'

'You're thinking there's something here we can use in the same way? Some way to spot which messages are real, and which are filler?'

'Maybe,' Karl shrugged. 'There's always new mistakes to be made in this field. It's like anti-terror, right? For us to win, we have to be right every single time. For them to win, they only have to get it right once. But here the roles are reversed.'

Bridge opened a blank spreadsheet and began copying and pasting the @ToTheFathers tweets into it. 'There are more than three hundred tweets already,' she groaned. 'This will take a while.'

'You can't write a script to scrape them all off the web?'

She mentally kicked herself. 'Of course. See, this is what happens to my brain when my stomach is grumbling.'

Right on cue, his iPhone sounded its timer alarm. '*Valkyrie needs food*, right?' He silenced the timer and shooed Bridge out of the kitchen. 'Then let's get you fuelled up before you start coding. Go on and sit down. We've got all night.'

Bridge closed her laptop, returned to the lounge, and poured wine for them both. As predicted, she couldn't stay mad at him for long. Besides, working through a problem like this with Karl was exciting. That was the real buzz, for her. She was a problem solver, not a doorkicker. It just so happened that sometimes, one led to the other. She watched him serve up, his long fingers gripping the pepper mill, and nodded to herself. They had all night.

37

'Why the hell am I only finding out about this now?' Giles shouted into his phone. It was late, he still had another meeting before his day was done, and his patience wore thin. Especially for a call like this, delivering a unique combination of good and bad news. The good news was that Ilya Kazhdan had been spotted in Zurich. The bad news was that it had happened two days ago, and since then the Russian had vanished again.

'We were only told ourselves an hour ago, sir, and your assistant said you were in a do-not-disturb meeting.' Giles had never even met this young man, a junior officer under diplomatic cover in Zurich, who had evidently drawn the short straw to call him. 'Local security identified Kazhdan and passed it to the Federal Intelligence Service. But instead of informing us right away, they requested local watch continuance. Said it was in order to give us more useful intel.'

'It would have been rather more useful when it was fresh,' Giles grumbled. 'Where was he last seen before they lost him?'

'Heading for the Hauptbahnhof. But they didn't have eyes on him inside the station, and from there he could have gone anywhere in Europe.'

'Did anyone see him actually enter the station?'

'That wasn't clear in their statement to me, sorry.'

Giles sighed. 'So in fact he might have hopped on a bus, or hired a car. Do we have anything solid at all?'

'The original spotter did get a picture of him conducting a meet. I don't know how useful it is, but maybe the techies can pull something out of it.'

'Send it over immediately, then give the FIS a kick up the arse from me. Continue active alert status, in case he pops up again. We have to get lucky some bloody day.'

No sooner had Giles replaced the receiver than his phone rang again. Andrea Thomson was waiting outside. He'd almost forgotten he asked her to join him. He said to send her in, then opened his laptop and checked the secure network for this picture of Kazhdan. Without looking up he waved as Andrea entered. 'Make yourself a coffee. With you in a moment.' He heard her using the fancy pod contraption at his office kitchenette.

'Meeting's in ten,' Andrea reminded him, perching on the edge of the leather couch so it didn't creak. 'Our DG's being escorted to the Broom, so I figured I'd come and see if there's anything I need to know before we get in there.'

'Indeed,' he said, turning his laptop to face her. 'Good luck getting anything out of that, though.'

Andrea peered at the screen. 'What am I looking at?'

'Ilya Kazhdan with an unidentified contact in Zurich. One of their watchers spotted him and snapped a long-range photo.'

'I don't think anyone says *snapped* any more, Giles. Not with phones.' Sure enough, it had been taken with a modern phone, but even with the attendant high resolution and detail it was so distant that little could be discerned. 'I wouldn't have even recognised Kazhdan if you hadn't told me.' He stood in darkness under a covered bridge, features hidden behind a mask, sunglasses, and cap. Beside him stood another man in a long coat, scarf, and woollen hat. He had a large, grey beard, and appeared to be about the same height as Kazhdan – though it was difficult to be sure, as both men leaned on the railing and shadows obscured too much detail. Andrea reached out and zoomed in on the picture, but that only pixellated it.

'Absolute bloody waste of time,' said Giles.

'Not entirely. That certainly looks like a contact meet, and if Kazhdan handed over the plans then finding this other person is now more important. Better to be two steps behind than lose sight completely.'

Giles closed the laptop and stood. 'You know your problem, Andrea? You're too optimistic.'

She laughed and followed him out of the room. 'Somehow I doubt our counterparts will agree with you.'

* * *

'Our analysts are concerned about this also,' said Maria Schmidt, from the German BfV. 'An attack took place recently against a Syrian refugee community near Munich, and we have seen reports of increased violent rhetoric since these videos.'

'But they are obviously fake,' said Serge Tolbert, speaking from Paris. Behind him two more DGSI people nodded. 'Why do people not see that?'

'Because it tells them what they want to hear,' said Giles, finally getting a word in edgeways. Whether in person or a video call, it remained a trial to find daylight between France and Germany's constant sniping. 'The true believers simply don't care. It justifies their existing prejudices, and that's all the excuse they need.'

'We have requested the identity of the Twitter user,' said Schmidt, 'but the company has been reluctant to supply that information in the past, and slow even when they have.'

Andrea Thomson sat next to Giles in Broom Three. Secretaries and researchers from SIS and MI5 sat nearby, but the room remained comically oversized for their needs. The reason could be found at the head of the table, where sat C and MI5's Director-General, or DG. Neither spoke, remaining silent and watchful, but their presence underlined the gravity of the situation.

'Time is one thing we don't have,' said Andrea. 'Based on information from sources, we believe whatever they're planning will take place at the end of next week.' Andrea didn't offer the sources' identity. Bringing the CIA into this would be like throwing a cat into the middle of a dog fight; they'd stop attacking each other, but only because they hated the cat even more.

'You talk like this is co-ordinated action,' said Rossi, from Italy's AISI. 'We haven't seen anything to suggest that. What is your evidence?'

'The Twitter account—' began Schmidt, but Giles interrupted.

'There are a number of factors of which you may not be fully aware. That's why we called this meeting.' He waited until all eighteen of his counterparts at the European agencies were listening, then explained the payments to American militia members, the official and unofficial reports from GCHQ, and what they'd found on the Patrios-supporting message boards.

Kovács, from Hungary's TEK, spoke up. 'We are chasing our tails on this hoax. There is no army training to shoot black men in the street. We do not even have any black men living here.'

Giles tried to hide his frustration. 'I really don't think we can afford to be so blasé. Every indication we have is that the threat is real, and serious.'

'Why is SIS involved?' asked Dabrowski, from ABW in Poland. 'What is your interest in this situation?'

'One of ours has infiltrated the online Patrios-supporting community,' said Giles. He wasn't about to name Bridge, but Tolbert's facial expression suggested that in DGSI's case he didn't need to. 'Contrary to what some of our ministers might tell you, we still consider events on the continent within our interests.

Our stationed officers are staying abreast of developments, and keeping their ears to the ground. A simultaneous event like this is bad news for all of Europe.'

'*If* it's real,' said García, representing Spain's CNI. It was the first time he'd spoken. 'We still don't know for sure.'

Andrea replied, 'Yes, it's possible this is an online fantasy. But they said that about the attack on the US capitol, remember? Following the attack in Munich, our own anti-immigrant rabble-rousers are causing even more noise than usual. And wasn't there some trouble in Calabria last week?'

Rossi shrugged. 'There's always trouble in Calabria.'

'That's as may be,' said Andrea, frustrated. 'Who knows what other incidents might have already taken place, but were overlooked because they didn't merit national attention? We should take the situation seriously until we know otherwise. Better to be over-prepared than caught napping.'

'I agree,' said Schmidt. 'Do you have an information packet?'

'I thought you'd never ask,' said Giles, having expected the question to come from the Germans. Andrea quickly passed him a manila folder stuffed with printouts. He took the cue and held it up for all the attendees to see. 'We'll send you this dossier by the usual channels. It summarises what we know, and what we suspect. The main takeaways are to look for camps of young men playing at soldiers; advise local police to increase watchfulness over refugee camps and immigrant populations; and trace any Americans who flew to your countries in the past eight days.'

Tolbert's eyebrows shot up. 'That's a lot of tourists. Perhaps the UK is not doing so good, but I assure you, the world is returning to France for their vacations.'

'*Touché*,' said Giles, earning a wry smile from several other countries. 'Then focus on males arriving without families, either solo or in small groups.'

'Presumably those with a military background, in particular?' asked García.

'Actually, no,' said Andrea. 'In our experience, the typical militia member of this kind is a civilian, not a former soldier. Most of the veterans I know have more sense.' Some of the other agency representatives were ex-forces like her, and they nodded in agreement.

'Thank you all,' said Giles, his tone making it clear the meeting was over. 'Let's consider the matter ongoing, and keep communications open. Hopefully we can nip this thing in the bud.'

One by one, the conference windows blacked out. Giles opened the manila folder Andrea had passed him, and smiled when he recognised Steve Wicker's GCHQ report. 'Excellent stagecraft,' he said, passing it back to her. 'Thank you.'

'Hopefully they won't notice the actual PDF is only half the size.'

Giles shrugged. 'The Germans are probably the only ones who'll bother to read it anyway.' One window remained open on the screen; the connection to DGSI. Tolbert was now alone in Paris, and his posture suggested he was waiting until everyone had filed out of the room at Vauxhall. Giles raised an eyebrow at him; Tolbert nodded in response.

Most of the secretaries and assistants had already left, while those remaining gathered notes and files. MI5's DG hovered by the door, waiting for C, who looked expectantly at Giles. He approached.

'Any update on the MoD business?' C asked.

'I rather think that's what France is waiting to enquire after.'

'Should I stay for this conversation, then?'

Giles shook his head. 'There's been one development, but it only came in an hour ago and is already cold. I'll report later today, but don't hold your breath.'

C nodded, understanding, and ushered the DG outside. Andrea followed behind, leaving Giles suddenly alone in the cavernous Broom. He closed the door, ensured the *In Use* light was still activated, and turned to Tolbert.

'It's Sharp on the boards, yes?' said the Frenchman. Giles simply nodded in answer. 'Is she still over here?'

'No, she returned immediately after you released her and has been in London ever since. Why do you ask?'

'Her sister's husband works at a refugee camp in Marseille. I saw reports of trouble down there recently.'

Giles hadn't known that, but then Bridge rarely talked about her relatives. 'May I ask why you're keeping tabs on Bridge's family?'

Tolbert laughed. 'Every time she comes to France there's trouble of some kind with them. Do you blame us?'

'I suppose not.' Giles mentally ran through SIS' own file. 'This is the MSF chap, yes? Baudin, I think?'

'Exactly. Is Sharp over-emphasising the Patrios threat because she thinks he is in danger?'

Giles shrugged. 'She barely speaks to her sister, so I rather doubt it. Besides, while Bridge is an important part of our efforts to get to the bottom of Patrios, she didn't initiate them. We're not chasing shadows, *monsieur* Tolbert. This is a credible threat, and we are simply not prepared for a well-organised, co-ordinated attack.'

'Why do you think they are well organised?'

'Like Andrea said, it's better to be over-prepared than caught wanting. *Au revoir.*'

In truth, Giles wasn't entirely sure how organised Patrios was. It certainly appeared to be, and this business with Twitter made him suspect there was a bigger picture that remained to be uncovered. If only one of those bloody FBI agents could get a message out somehow, it might crack this whole thing wide open.

38

Casey woke suddenly in the dark, somehow aware he was alone. Still half-asleep, he figured Mike must be taking a shower. But the bathroom was silent, and then Casey remembered it didn't have a shower anyway. He checked the time; not long past four o'clock. Nobody got up that early in the camp, least of all a nerd like Mike. What was going on?

Casey climbed down from the top bunk, slipped on his boots and jacket, then quietly left the room. He snuck a peek into the main dorm and found everyone asleep, as far as he could see in the dark. Not even pre-dawn light yet.

As he exited the dorm block and peered round the corner, that same darkness made it difficult to identify the almost-black shape sneaking out of the command quarters and moving across the almost-black courtyard. But Casey had known Mike for almost three years now, and recognised the way he moved. (If pressed, he might have admitted that the moon breaking from behind clouds and briefly illuminating the scene helped.) Luckily for Casey, Mike didn't stop to look around in the flare of moonlight himself, or he might have seen his friend standing there like a chump in sockless boots, pyjama pants and a jacket.

Something stopped Casey from calling out. Perhaps it was the feeling of true excitement. Everything they'd done up until now had been fun, new, and exciting in its own way but it was still practice, like range shooting with the Flag Born back home. You might miss, you might not, but you knew what the deal was.

Or maybe it was what Mike carried in his hand, that had reflected the moonlight and almost made Casey gasp.

Where the *hell* had that sneaky bastard hidden a second phone?

An answer offered itself in Casey's mind, and he wished it hadn't. Sure, Mike was an internet addict, and Casey had figured he'd start hankering for it before long, but surely even he wouldn't go to such an extreme. No, he must have borrowed someone else's phone. But wait – everyone's phones had been taken and put in those silver bags that blocked your signal. Casey understood the sense in that. Everyone knew the government was always tracking your phone's location, and the camp was somewhere any government would want to find. Eagle had said that if the cops ever came around, everyone should say loud and clear that everything they did here was legal. Even if that was true (and it probably wasn't) it didn't mean you put up a sign and invite them over.

That only left one option. Mike had gone into the command quarters and stolen his phone back.

Casey followed him into the trees, treading quietly. The cold, brittle branches of the undergrowth tugged at his pants and entangled his boots, but he kept his cool and didn't utter a sound. Mike, on the other hand, wasn't making much effort to stay quiet. Like he was confident nobody would follow him. And why shouldn't he be? If Casey hadn't woken suddenly he wouldn't be out here to see his friend suddenly stop, pull out a phone – a phone he absolutely, positively, should not be using – and crouch down by a tree to type something on it. Mike huddled to shelter the screen, but it still shone like a beacon. Three inches of daylight in forty acres of dark forest. No wonder Mike had walked well away from the camp before turning it on.

Casey circled around the tree, hoping to get a look at the screen before announcing his presence. In his mind's eye he imagined Mike flinching, startled, impressed at Casey's stealthy moves. He'd admit he was texting his girlfriend, or reading message boards, or even watching porn. They'd laugh about it, and Mike would ask him to keep his secret, and Casey would agree. What else were buddies for? Then they'd walk back together, and Casey would keep lookout while Mike returned the phone to its silver bag, before they snuck back into their room with nobody any the wiser and laughed themselves back to sleep.

Didn't quite work out that way.

Casey tiptoed up behind the tree. The screen glow was visible over Mike's shoulder, but he still wasn't close enough to read it. One more step—

Suddenly his world turned upside down and he couldn't breathe. He was staring up at the sky through the trees, two different shades of black. But then the moon slid out from behind a cloud again, and the pain in his stomach finally registered simultaneously with the surprise that Mike was leaning over him, his fist pulled back and ready to strike. Then Mike recognised him, relaxed, and looked confused. Not half as confused as Casey, though.

'What the fuck are you doing?' Mike whispered.

Casey's body chose that moment to restart functioning. He gasped in a lungful of air, his head spinning as he tried to sit upright. Mike kept a hand on his chest, pushing him back down. Casey nonchalantly replied, 'I could ask you the same question.' Or he tried to, anyway. It came out as a sort of pained wince of '*I – cask – yusum – kesht*,' between breaths, but Mike understood him all the same. Although he didn't answer the question.

'You dumb asshole, I thought Eagle had followed me. You should be asleep.'

This time Casey took a deep breath before trying to talk

between gasps. 'Well. I'm not. Something. Woke me. Saw you. Sneaking out.' He frowned. 'Eagle.'

Mike matched his expression. 'What about him?'

Casey didn't have time to answer before Eagle grabbed Mike from behind and threw him against a tree. Mike landed near his phone – he'd left it on the ground, the screen still glowing – and scrambled to reach it. Before he could, Eagle kicked him hard in the ribs and shouted angrily in a language Casey didn't understand. Mike yelped in pain, and Casey didn't know what the hell was going on, but he didn't like it. He struggled to his feet, clutching his abdomen, and staggered over to put himself between Eagle and Mike.

'Hold on. Eagle. What the fuck. He's just.' Before he could finish Eagle pushed him aside and, to Casey's horror, drew a pistol. The moment's space Casey had bought was enough for Mike to scoop up the phone and begin running deeper into the woods. Casey was so turned around by now he couldn't tell if Mike was running back to the camp or away from it, but Eagle didn't care. He aimed, fired – the pistol crack deafening, echoing off the trees and into the sky – and between those echoes Casey heard Mike cry out.

At least that meant he was alive, right?

Eagle jogged in the direction Mike had run, and Casey followed as fast as he could with fire still burning in his stomach. Where the hell did Mike learn to punch like that?

Mike lay on the ground, clutching his shoulder. The phone had fallen nearby, screen cracked but somehow still glowing. Eagle picked it up, keeping his gun trained on Mike. Casey got there in time to see him hold the phone out to Mike.

'Unlock it.'

'Fuck you…' Mike said through gritted teeth, blood pumping from his shoulder. 'Psycho…asshole.'

'*Unlock it!*' Eagle's voice was almost as loud as the gunshot. He held out the phone, his pistol never wavering. Mike shook his head, his breathing hard and desperate. Casey realised with a start that he'd never seen a person get shot before. This was entirely new to him. Before, he'd have guessed a bullet to the shoulder was something you could shrug off. Painful, but you could keep moving. It seemed not.

'Casey!'

He looked up, startled by Eagle's voice, and saw the big man was holding out his gun, offering it.

'I saw him attack you. You are obviously not a traitor like him. Go ahead.'

Casey couldn't make sense of it. He understood Eagle's words, but their meaning refused to settle in his mind.

Eagle said, 'He is an informant! Probably American government, yes?' Casey looked to Mike for an answer, but none came. 'I should have known.'

Casey shook his head, trying to make the pieces fit. 'No, no, listen, he's a nerd, that's all. You have to understand, he's online twenty-four-seven. He just wanted to check his email, go on Facebook, right, Mike?'

Mike said nothing, his mouth set tight and fixed.

'Facebook? Is that where he learned to disable you with one strike?'

'Hey, he got lucky with a sucker punch, is all.'

'Fucking Americans,' Eagle sneered, and re-sighted his pistol at Mike.

'For Christ's sake, no!' Once again Casey put himself between Eagle and Mike, only this time that meant standing in front of a loaded gun. Another first. His heart pounded as he stared down the barrel. Holy shit, he'd never been so scared in his life. He had absolutely no doubt that Eagle was willing to kill Mike, and would probably kill Casey too if he felt like it. Worse, the veteran was enjoying it. The hint of a smile passed across his face as Casey pleaded with him. 'This man is a goddamn patriot, you hear me? I've known him for three years, and all that time he's proved his dedication to America and the Flag Born. Hell, it was Mike's idea to come over here in the first place!'

This time there was no hint about it as Eagle smiled. 'Of course it was. How else could he infiltrate the Patrios brotherhood?'

'No, no!' Casey shook his head. 'We're here to fight, to help you. Are you blind? He doesn't even look like a Fed!' He said over his shoulder, 'No offence, Mike.'

'I am not the one who is blind,' said Eagle, shoving Casey aside so hard he almost fell to his knees. The veteran stood over Mike, gun trained right at his face. Mike's breathing quickened, and his skin was as pale as the pre-dawn light.

'You're making a big mistake, Eagle,' said Casey. 'You don't know how wrong you are.'

Mike took a deep breath, like he was making a decision. 'No, Casey. It's true.'

Once again, Casey couldn't process the words. He knew them, recognised them, but didn't understand. Maybe he'd misheard. 'What? What's true?'

'I'm FBI... I was embedded...'

'No, no, that's bullshit. Why would you say that?' He turned to Eagle, trying to make him understand. 'He doesn't know what he's saying. He's delirious. We're friends! I know him, he's a patriot!' He turned back to Mike. 'You're a patriot!'

'Yes, I am! For God's sake, don't you get it? I love my country. I serve and protect the United States of America. That's what I've been doing this whole time. All this, the Flag Born, the militias, the riots...it's not right, Casey. You know it's not right.' Casey put his head in his hands, trying to make sense of what Mike was saying, the lies coming out of his mouth, but he wouldn't stop talking. 'Things got twisted, corrupted, poisoned... I *am* a patriot, and I know you are too. So help me stop this. Help your country!'

Casey turned on him, tears burning his eyes. 'Help you? A – a fucking – Jesus Christ, a Fed? This, this is, I don't know, man, I don't know! What the fuck? You betrayed me, you betrayed the Flag Born, you sold us out? Shit!'

'No. I'm trying to *stop* traitors. Traitors to the constitution, the flag, our citizens. Casey, come on. This guy doesn't care about America. He's not your friend.' Mike glared at Eagle, his eyes filled with hatred and tears.

Eagle shrugged. 'I am a soldier doing my duty. Not to a country, but to the superior white race. Surely you understand this, "Sergeant"?' He turned to Casey with a glint in his eye that said everything. The game was up. Eagle knew it was all bullshit. 'Now, Casey Lachlan, you have a choice. To live, and fight for the great cause of Patrios; or to stand beside your traitor friend and die. I would respect that. There is honour in it.'

Casey looked from Eagle to Mike and back again, his vision swimming. Honour in death? More than once he'd told people that was all he wanted from life. But then he'd also told people he was a veteran, and one lie was much like another. In that moment, he finally understood. There was no such thing as a 'good death'. He gritted his teeth, clenched his fists, and stood next to Mike.

Then held out his hand to Eagle.

'Give me the fucking gun.'

All hope fled Mike's eyes in the dim grey light. A second shot echoed through the forest's empty branches to herald a cold new day.

39

From: ChinesePrisoner
   That MIT letter is bullshit. Of course they
say it's fake, they're part of Soros' Zionist
deep state network to cover up the extermination
program. Do your own research and follow the
connections. They don't want you to see what's
happening right in front of your own eyes.

If MIT thought their debunking of the video would make a
difference to people in the right-wing community, they were
sorely mistaken. Bridge hadn't even needed to raise the subject
herself. She was now on almost twenty boards under various
permutations of the 'Prosper' identity, and as soon as MIT's
release hit the press every board started debating it, determined
to debunk the debunkers. Scouring posts made when the first
video of the president had been released, she found a few daring
souls who'd suggested it could be a deepfake. But they were soon
shouted down by the true believers, and the second video only
convinced people further.

Now those same true believers insisted the MIT statement was
itself a hoax, to throw people off. Bridge wasn't entirely clear how
the 'Jewish-funded deep state' would benefit from such a hoax,
but the mere possibility that someone might try to persuade
Americans *not* to fly to Europe and kill immigrants seemed

sufficiently offensive to white supremacists.

Then again, Bridge wasn't here to try and convince them they were wrong. She'd engaged in flame wars and arguments about whether white genocide was real, whether the Great Replacement Theory was supported by secret communications leaked from Shin Bet, whether science had proven Africans had lower IQ than Europeans. It was exhausting, and she hated every minute of it, but it was necessary. Every horrible post she made on those threads added to Prosper's credibility, and allowed her to push conversations in the direction she wanted.

From: Prosper
   Also, who would fake this video? We all know
the message is true, so what is the point? The
leftists couldn't do it, and we don't need it to
know what is the necessary action. Why???

From: OldGlory
   Exactly!!! Total hoax!!! Makes no ducking
sense!!!!
   Hey Prosper, I thought you were in France.
Crazy early for you!!???

Bridge wasn't in France, of course, but that didn't change the fact that it really was early – or late, depending on your point of view. Soon after dinner she'd climbed on top of Karl on the sofa, then led him to the bedroom, where they tore off each other's clothes and spent a blissful hour building up a sweat and forgetting all about work, racists, and Russians. He'd brought it up again briefly as they lay side-by-side afterwards, talking over theories about the Twitter account. But soon he'd succumbed to sleep, leaving Bridge staring at the ceiling with her mind racing. She'd set Radio

Three playing softly, quiet enough not to wake Karl, but it had still taken another hour before she finally dozed off – only to find herself back in Estonia, telling herself not to open the car door, *don't do it Bridge*, but how could she stop herself when it had already happened? And then Maxim shot her again, and she was awake again, and there'd be no more sleeping tonight, despite only managing forty minutes in the first place. Now at three in the morning she was back on the sofa, this time lit by the glow of her laptop, sipping a cup of tea and pretending to be a racist former soldier.

From: Prosper
  It's none of your business, but some nights
I don't sleep very good. The memories I have.
Sometimes they're not easy to ignore, understand?
As a veteran.

She had to tread carefully here. On the one hand she wanted to convince them of her adopted persona. On the other she couldn't risk getting kicked off the board for revealing too much about 'her' life or past. Being overly generous with details would raise suspicions. But Bridge was confident she could draw on her real experience to find that balance. It wasn't even much of a lie.

From: OldGlory
  Jesus duck just asking q question!!! I'm the
godalm king of france, right??? Anyone can say
anything on the internet, doesn't prove its
real!!!!

That was more true than 'OldGlory' knew, and Bridge let the matter drop. If he – she was pretty confident it was a he, and probably American – wanted to keep ranting it would say more about him than 'Prosper'.

She wondered if the rant was rooted in him being a militiaman, envious of veterans – or of those recruited to Patrios. If the CIA's assumption about a mandated comms blackout was accurate, nobody currently undergoing Patrios training would be posting on these boards. He might feel frustrated at being left out.

Karl had shown her an FBI list of known militias, and explained it had grown threefold in the last few years. It read like a random generator programmed to spit out fascist buzzwords: *Lightning Wolf*, *Viking Shield*, *Blue Patriots*, *Blood Scourge*, *Dawn Crusade*, *Loyal Boys*... 'Worst heavy metal festival ever,' she'd joked at the time, and those were only the ones the Bureau knew about and could track. The FBI assumed there were many more groups they weren't aware of; armed and dangerous, but absent from no-fly lists everywhere.

The same was happening in Europe. Access to firearms was more difficult here than in America, but far from impossible, especially in former eastern bloc countries. A combination of hangover from the old USSR and influence of the new Russian Federation ensured a steady supply of black market weapons, from handguns to rifles and everything in between. There would be no shortage of armaments for Patrios soldiers.

```
From: ChinesePrisoner
    Hope you find peace, Prosper. Mindful meditation
could work for you - I know soldiers who find it
useful, it helps clear their minds
```

Bridge saw an opening in the conversation. One way or another she had to try and gain the attention of the Patrios organisers.

From: Prosper

> Thank you, CP. I will try. I think sometimes, maybe the only way I can truly make it stop is by holding a gun once more. Maybe Patrios could give me some target practice, LOL!

A minute later, a direct message from ChinesePrisoner landed in her inbox:

> I hope you get your wish. I'm stuck inside myself, going stir-crazy thanks to lockdown. Posting this from a fucking TV, LOL! But Patrios is a good plan. I should know.

Bridge paused before replying and re-read the message. Had she lucked out and caught the attention of someone organising Patrios? Considering their suggestion of meditation, could this even be a woman? She chided herself for thinking in stereotypes, but it was no more of one than assuming the Patrios organisers were men in the first place. She replied:

> How do you know? Are you involved? I think I would like to be involved, too. But I don't know how.

They responded immediately:

> LOL, I don't know who is behind Patrios. But it's a good plan. I can't say more.

A reply as intriguing as it was disappointing, but Bridge didn't want to risk pushing too far. If this person was connected to the project, however tangentially, they'd be a good contact to cultivate.

She logged out and sat in the gloom, drinking tea and listening to Karl's gentle snoring from the bedroom. It wasn't long since the last full moon, so there was enough light to dimly illuminate the lounge while she waited for sunrise.

Bridge's instincts told her she was getting close, and she realised with an inward curiosity that Karl had been right: she was excited by the prospect of going undercover again. The ghost of the bullet she'd taken in Tallinn – the one in her shoulder, that could so easily have been a few inches lower and ended her – protested, a phantom pain to remind her of danger. But Dr Nayar had said Bridge should find something to do, to stop obsessing over her relationship. She doubted going undercover with a bunch of armed fascists in Europe was what the good doctor had in mind, but it would surely fit the bill.

40

@ToTheFathers
3:00 PM February 21

NÁŠ TATÍČKU MASARYKU
TY JSI NAŠE MOC A SÍLA
69999698453540359
85373606769521268
41976458535343636
53271752689028240
02510331731879544
70213198258924049
42590889628508058
08577050844117179
06561160878688294
83423863997538660

Posted via Tweetdeck for Android

41

Following that close shave when the guard entered suddenly, Sasha had designed a better way. Now when he heard the door unlock he only had to press a keyboard shortcut – a combination of four keys that would never otherwise be pressed simultaneously, not even by accident – to trigger a short script which killed the web browser, launched Netflix, found a random movie within the *Action* category, skipped to forty-five minutes in, and began playing at moderate volume. Loud enough to be heard on the couch, quiet enough not to be heard by anyone standing outside the door.

Sometimes the script selected a movie it had picked before. That happened, with truly random numbers. He could have fixed it, but it would require writing to a database and doing a recursive check of the random selection against the populated list, and... he couldn't be bothered. When he was younger he'd watched *Iron Man* every day for a month. That he might occasionally re-watch the same terrible Steven Seagal movie on Netflix wasn't beyond belief.

This time he was spared Americans with bad wigs, instead being shown Americans in space with bad special effects. When the surly guard opened the door, Sasha was already chilling against the arm of the couch, with the bluetooth keyboard stuffed between two cushions.

The guard wasn't alone. He stood aside to let past one of the staff, a junior diplomat if Sasha recalled correctly.

'You are transported next Wednesday night,' the diplomat said in English. 'By then your vaccine is fully effective. You are allowed one suitcase only. Make sure you are ready, as there is no delay.'

Sasha asked, 'How are we leaving? Remember that I have no passport.' The diplomat looked confused. 'Documents,' Sasha explained, miming opening and stamping a passport. 'I have no documents to travel.'

Finally, the diplomat understood. He smiled and shook his head. 'No documents. We are ready. Make sure you are ready. Next Wednesday.' He turned and left. The guard scowled at Sasha, closed the door, and locked it.

Next Wednesday. A new life awaited him, whether he wanted it or not.

42

@ToTheFathers
3:01 PM February 21

NÁŠ TATÍČKU MASARYKU
TY JSI NAŠE MOC A SÍLA
69999698453540359
85373606769521268
41976458535343636
53271752689028240
02510331731879544
70213198258924049
42590889628508058
08577050844117179
06561160878688294
83423863997538660

Posted via Twitter on the web

'So much for them not repeating the same message twice. Look at this.'

Bridge sat upright on the sofa and showed Karl her screen. He put his own laptop down on the coffee table and leaned over to look.

She'd been looking at a spreadsheet of *@ToTheFathers* tweets.

As Karl had suggested, that morning she'd written a script that would archive all the tweets to date, then continue monitoring the account and automatically add every new post to the spreadsheet. To ensure it was always up-to-date she'd set it running from a web server Karl operated, rather than a laptop. The server didn't host any websites, but Karl used it to host his email account, store files, and run scripts. Within minutes of uploading, the script had filled a spreadsheet with data – a comprehensive archive of the tweets to date, plus their associated metadata dumped into an overflow column. Then it continued watching for further activity, ready to hoover up new posts as soon as they appeared.

'Look at these two entries from earlier today,' she said, pointing. 'They sent a tweet at four pm Central European Time, as expected. But then they sent the same message one minute later. It looks identical.'

'What are the lyrics this time?'

Bridge copied the text into a search engine and scanned the results. 'Czech nationalist song. *The father is our source of strength*, the usual Patrios crap.'

Karl peered at the two messages. 'Are we sure it's not a scripting error? You somehow pulled down the same message twice?' He shrugged off Bridge's indignant, offended look. 'C'mon, we all make mistakes. Gotta check the work.'

She pouted, but he was right. Occam's razor meant human error was always the most likely explanation when something went awry, and that was doubly true in code. She visited the account's Twitter page and was disappointed to find only one tweet, not two of the same.

'See?' said Karl. 'Simple error. Let's look at that script, see what could have—'

'Oh! Shit. Wait.' Bridge had been navigating to the script, but on a hunch she switched back to Twitter. This time she clicked on the tweet itself, opening it to its own page. 'There.' She pointed triumphantly at the timestamp: *3:01 PM*.

Karl shrugged. 'Which is four in Europe, like we said. So?'

Bridge shook her head. 'But it's not, is it? Four-oh-one is not four-oh-oh. And previous tweets, hold on…' She called up the spreadsheet again to double check. 'Yes, look. Every other tweet is right on the dot of eight am, noon, and four pm. To be so consistently precise they're almost certainly scheduled in advance. That's easy to do via the web interface, which is how the tweets are sent. The footer information is always "via Twitter for the web". But now look at these entries in the spreadsheet. The live entry, sent at four-oh-one and matching what's on the site, is via the web as normal. But the *previous* entry – the duplicate that doesn't appear online – has a time stamp of four precisely, and was sent via Tweetdeck from an Android phone.'

Karl stared at the data. 'You're saying they posted at the usual time, but from a phone…then deleted it?'

'Exactly. One minute later they replaced it with the exact same tweet, this time sent from the web as usual.'

He smiled with pride. 'Good thing you set the script to download everything including metadata, or we'd have missed it.'

Bridge felt her cheeks flush, embarrassed at how a few measly words of praise from him made her feel like a gangly teenager all over again. Annoyed with herself, she glared at the screen, willing it to reveal its secrets. 'The question is: why? If they were different it would make sense, but they're not. Why suddenly tweet from a phone, after weeks of sending via the web? And why then delete it, only to replace it with the same tweet anyway?'

'Are we jumping to conclusions? Maybe someone's finger slipped and they accidentally scheduled it twice. Then they saw their mistake when the second tweet showed up, and…' He trailed off, then shook his head. 'No, that doesn't make sense. If that happened you'd delete the second tweet, not the first.'

Bridge pictured the steps in her mind, trying to put herself in the shoes of someone sending coded messages. Why delete a message, only to replace it with the same one? It didn't make sense, unless...

'Unless they're not the same.' She was finishing a sentence she hadn't started out loud, but Karl nodded, understanding. Bridge copied both tweets and pasted them into a plain text editor to compare, wondering if one version might use zero-width characters, invisible accents, or extended text encoding to hide something. But that wasn't it; both tweets really were identical, even when rendered as plain text. 'Dammit. Surely there must be something in that first tweet they didn't want people to see. Why else go to the trouble? It might not even have been a "real" message, it could have been filler.'

'Then why care about a mistake?' said Karl. 'It would be gibberish anyhow. Maybe this is a real message, something important enough to make sure they got it right even though it messed up their schedule.'

'But they're the same.' Bridge clenched her fists in frustration. 'Whatever message they encoded was already broadcast just fine by the first tweet. There was nothing extra in the second tweet.'

They sat in silence, pondering the conundrum. Then Bridge suddenly cried out, startling Karl.

'Jesus, don't do that. What—?'

She silenced him with a raised finger and navigated to the spreadsheet's overflow column, the dump of metadata which the script sucked up along with each tweet's text. She expanded the column to full screen width and peered at its contents. Each cell contained a mass of seemingly-random technical gobbledegook attached to each tweet, much of which even Bridge didn't understand. But she didn't need to understand it to play spot the difference, and grinned when she saw it.

'We had it the wrong way around,' she said. 'They didn't delete the first tweet so they could add something extra to the second. They deleted it to *remove* something that shouldn't have been in the first one. It might be a filler message, after all. But *this* is real.' She pointed at one line of metadata, the line someone had scrambled to expunge the moment they realised it had been transmitted. A string of numbers, by itself innocent and indecipherable. Much of the metadata was beyond Bridge, but she recognised the format of this line well enough. *Co-ordinates.*

'Geolocation. Holy shit.' Karl laughed. 'Holy shit!'

Bridge typed the numbers into a map. 'It will only give us a rough location,' she warned. 'An ISP relay, or maybe a cellular tower at best. But it's better than nothing... There.' The map zoomed over Europe, then focused in close to the regional level. She jabbed her finger at the screen.

'They're in Hungary. Somewhere north of Budapest.'

43

He'd killed Mike. Casey sat at a camp table, alone in the dark, and pulled his jacket close against the cold. Lights in the dorm block and command quarters suggested he wasn't the only person awake, but nobody joined him at the table. He didn't want them to. What could he say to them? He'd killed his friend.

Except: Mike hadn't been his friend, had he? Was Mike even his real name?

Three years, it had been. Almost from the very beginning of the Flag Born, that time Casey and the squad had gone to the range for some Sunday morning shooting, and got talking to the nerdy-looking guy with the AR-16 about Q theories. Turned out he was a computer guy who understood the internet way better than Casey or anyone else in the Flag Born, and he was kind of funny in that sarcastic way nerds often were, and before they knew it he was part of the squad. Part of the team.

Except: he hadn't been part of the team, had he?

He'd been a spy, a traitor, a goddamn straight-up Federal Agent, sent to infiltrate them, to…what? To stop them staging a revolution? The Flag Born couldn't organise a trip to Burger King. None of them had got it together enough to attend the Jan 6 rally, and they'd all had their excuses, including Casey. He'd said he thought it would be all talk, which was something Mike had said first, but Casey couldn't lie to himself any more. He'd been secretly grateful Mike said that, because then he could agree and blow it off without admitting to anyone – least of all himself – that he was scared. With new clarity he saw that had been true of the others, too. It was so obvious now. None of them were veterans. The closest thing any Flag Born had to combat experience was one guy who'd been a cop for three years, but even he'd spent most of his time attending domestic calls and occasionally busting a corner kid for dope, before quitting to work in private security because it paid better.

Well, Casey was pretty sure he had them all beat now. Give someone like Eagle a knife, put him up against the whole Flag Born militia with rifles, and Casey knew who he'd bet on. Even the kids here were more prepared to fight, more eager, than anyone back home.

He'd been filled with fury and sickness at the betrayal. He couldn't say pulling the trigger was easy – no more lies, remember – but the anger sure made it easier than it would have been. Casey didn't even recall walking back to the camp with Eagle. Or had he returned alone? There was a loss there, a gap in his memory to match the hole in his humanity. How did soldiers do it? Was it easier because they hadn't spent three years hanging out with the people they killed? Or did the ghosts cling to them like weights, dragging them down and whispering reminders of what they'd done?

He thought about his father, the man who believed in shooting clean, a crack shot in the hunt. But he'd shot for sport, for game. Never killed a man. What about *his* old man, Casey's grandfather? He'd served in Vietnam. Chances were good he'd done the deed. But he'd never talked about that time, and Casey learned to stop asking.

The European recruits had shunned him all day. Damaged goods, friend of a traitor, call it what you want but they didn't trust him any more. Eagle had told them they should, that Casey had proven himself by taking care of Mike, and they'd nodded and said sure, of course, no problem. But it didn't change anything. They didn't speak to him now, not even to practise their broken English. He'd tripped and fallen during a sweep-and-advance exercise this morning; not unusual in the tightly-packed chaos of the practice houses, it happened to everyone. But when Casey had flipped onto his back and raised his arm for a helping hand to pull him up, all he saw was the backs of his so-called colleagues moving on without him.

Had any of those pricks looked their friend in the eye while they pulled the trigger? He fucking doubted it.

Could he leave? He doubted that too. But he'd lost all taste for Patrios; the reality of what he'd done, what he assumed they wanted him to do all over again, didn't sit easy. He still believed in the cause. The third world was taking the west for a ride, slowly but surely creeping in and taking over. If someone didn't take action, before long the white man would be a minority in his own homelands. That was unacceptable; but now the solution, at least the solution Casey had previously assumed was the only viable option, seemed just as impossible. He couldn't say that out loud around here. Maybe not anywhere. He could try to get out, grab his bag and walk into the forest, but how far would he get? Even assuming a couple of trips hiking in the Rockies had prepared him for what might be days walking through a Hungarian forest in winter, would Eagle and the others simply let him go? No way. They'd hunt him down through the trees, and they knew this terrain better than he ever could. He wouldn't last a day, or even an hour.

No, he had to keep his head down, go along with whatever crazy shit they were planning to pull off, and then on the 'night of Patrios' or whatever the hell they finally called it, maybe he could slip away. Wait until everyone else was distracted. Maybe he'd get lucky and some streetlights would be out. Back away, leave them to it, ditch the gun and the fatigues and catch the next plane home. His phone would still be here, locked in that damn Ferrari bag or whatever it was called, but he could live without that. They hadn't taken his wallet or passport. Those were all he needed to buy a flight back and try to forget any of this had ever happened.

Jesus Christ, what would he say to the guys? Would they even believe that Mike was a Fed? Or should he tell them Eagle killed him, and that was why Casey returned home? Even if Mike's real identity hit the news, that would still fly, wouldn't it?

He wondered if any of the other Americans who'd come over to help lead Patrios were having problems like this. Jesus, there could even be more Feds like Mike. He'd said other groups were sent money too, but was that another lie? He had no way of knowing. Even if he'd been able to get to his phone, it was Mike who knew how to find out things like that.

Casey shivered in the cold, but made no move to go back inside.

* * *

Inside the command quarters, Dmitri turned away from the window. Eagle glanced up from the book he was reading, a history of the Soviet Air Forces. 'Is he still out there?'

Dmitri nodded. 'I think you broke him.'

'Maybe he'll rebuild himself into a stronger man.' Eagle shrugged. 'Our so-called "Sergeant" obviously has a spine in there somewhere. He just needs to find it. What did you do with the body?'

Dmitri sat heavily in the office's only other chair, a plastic and metal contraption that belonged in a school, not a mission-critical training camp. He lit a cigarette and pulled the desk's tin ashtray towards him. 'The ground's frozen solid, but I took care of it. I removed his wallet and phone and burned them along with his possessions.'

Eagle nodded approvingly. 'Good. By the time anyone looks for him we'll have moved on anyway. You sent the message, yes? The, the tweeting thing?'

'Of course.' Dmitri didn't mention his screw-up. The scheduled noon post had originally been filler, and randomised accordingly. But uncovering the FBI agent had necessitated a last-minute change to alert the other camps, so Dmitri had quickly sent it from his phone and, in his haste, forgotten to disable the geolocation setting. Luckily he saw the error immediately, and rectified it a minute later with a post from the laptop. The message was the same, and if anyone noticed the time discrepancy he would blame it on having to rush out a replacement in unusual circumstances.

'That's good,' said Eagle, either oblivious to or unconcerned with Dmitri's mistake. 'It's not a big problem if the other camps have a rat, anyway. Hungary is what matters.'

'Should we replace him? What does the boss say?'

Eagle shrugged. 'The boss tore my fucking ear off for letting the FBI into the camp, so we're definitely not bringing in another Yankee. Someone with more experience to lead the kids probably isn't a bad idea. Who knows, you might even find someone who isn't a government agent this time.' He put his feet up on the desk and returned to his book.

Dmitri pulled hard on his cigarette and frowned.

44

'What do you know about Hungary?'

Edison Hill's face filled the tiny video screen. Broom Nine was all Giles had been able to book at short notice, so Bridge was grateful it was only the two of them on this side of the screen. Anyone else would have had to stand by the door and breathe in.

'Is this a general question,' asked Hill, 'or are you fishing for something in particular?'

Giles sighed. 'For heaven's sake, Eddy, if we don't start talking to one another like adults this will take forever.' He ignored Hill's surprise at the shortening of his name, and Bridge suppressed a smile. It was a regular tactic Giles used to distract people from focusing on his ulterior motives. Talking like an adult, indeed.

She spoke up. 'The Twitter account is based there, but we don't know if it's the command centre, or if they're feeding instructions to a script kiddie in Budapest who posts on their behalf.'

'How sure are you about that location?' asked Hill.

'Pretty sure. Karl and I figured it out together. Didn't he already tell you?' After finding what they now called the *geolocation tweet*, Bridge and Karl had agreed to inform their respective bosses when they arrived at work. Hill should have known by now.

'I'll come to that in a moment. First I want to verify this location. Couldn't they have spoofed it?'

Giles turned to her. 'It's a fair question. You do that sort of thing all the time. The Hungarian security rep claims there's nothing going on within their borders.'

Bridge shrugged. 'It doesn't make sense as a bluff. This information was only live for one minute before they deleted it and sent a replacement without the location metadata. If my scraper hadn't automatically archived every tweet from the account, even I wouldn't have seen it. That's shitty misdirection.' Giles raised an eyebrow at her Americanism, but she ignored it.

'I agree,' said Hill, 'and it jibes with what we've heard from the FBI. They received a message from one of their guys at last, an embedded special agent who previously reported he was flying to Budapest.'

'When exactly were you planning on sharing this information?' Giles threw up his hands and turned to Bridge. 'Did you know this already?'

'No! I would have told you. Agent Hill, was that his final destination?'

'More importantly, how many other bloody agents are out there?' Giles grumbled.

Hill spoke carefully, biting his tongue. 'These are extraordinary circumstances, Agent Finlay, otherwise I doubt we'd have got anything at all from Quantico. The message reached them yesterday, and they passed it to us this morning. It was the first time they'd heard from the agent in question since he flew out, and there's been nothing since. As we suspected, these camps are keeping a lid on comms.'

'What was the message?' asked Bridge.

'*Old paintball can.*'

A moment of silence expanded to fill the small room, until Giles broke it with a loud exhale. 'Safe to assume that wasn't a report he'd stumbled across out-of-date decorating paraphernalia, but rather it should have said *camp*?'

'Agreed. That was the whole message.'

Bridge nodded. 'Perhaps he only had a few seconds to get something out before having to hide the phone. Or he might have been typing blind, so nobody saw. Did the FBI trace the signal?'

'Sorry. Stymied by our own tech security. He was using a Bureau-issue phone; looks identical to a regular iPhone, but can't be tracked.'

While Bridge and Hill talked, Giles had been thinking. Finally he said, 'It makes sense, doesn't it? Paintball camps, I mean.'

Bridge nodded, counting off the advantages on her fingers. 'Isolated location, passing locals are used to the sound of gunfire, and seeing young men run around with guns.'

'So either they're training with paintball guns, or the camp owners are in on it,' said Hill. 'You have to figure they'd notice people using real rifles.'

'That's if the owners are even present,' said Bridge. '*Old* paintball camp, it said. Lots of "experience event" businesses went under during the pandemic, and I doubt many have re-opened yet. A lot of them might have cut their losses and shut down permanently. What if Patrios has walked in and taken over those abandoned camps for a few weeks? Who would even notice?'

Giles drummed his fingers on the table. 'It's better than nothing. I'll work with MI5 to update the local agencies in Europe.'

'Andrea should look for camps here in the UK, too,' said Bridge. 'Remember that Steve Wicker said there are domestic agitators involved in Patrios chatter.' For the first time all week, she felt optimistic. They might get out in front of this one and stop the whole thing before it started.

Giles turned to the screen. 'Does your embedded FBI man have previous experience working abroad?'

Hill shrugged. 'Agent Finlay, I haven't even been told the agent's name. But he's there under the guise of a redneck American. Short of straight-up declaring he works for the Bureau, I doubt there's much he can do to blow his cover.'

Giles turned to Bridge. 'Redouble your efforts to get recruited. At least now you know you'll have a friend out there.'

45

When in doubt, make yourself useful.

Bridge had twenty years of experience in anonymous online communities, from the moment she first got online and pretended to be an adult. Later, learning to navigate the personalities and quirks of the *uk.london.gothic-netizens* newsgroup, in which everyone remained anonymous, had been an invaluable trial by fire. Over the years she'd honed and refined those skills, putting them to use for both social and work purposes. It all helped her build 'Prosper' into someone regarded as a source of wisdom, from time to time even held up as a voice of authority. Her account predated the surge of new posters arriving in the wake of the deepfake videos, so everyone 'knew' Prosper was no fair-weather fascist.

In the days following her discovery of the geolocation tweet, she turned things up even further and made herself very useful indeed – by openly teaching the moderators how to increase security, and hide the boards from snooping authorities. She even used the influx of newbies to justify her concerns. She taught the owners how to regularly purge user details so that if they were hacked, accounts couldn't be matched to real-world identities.

She was taking a unique risk. By giving the board owners ways and means to fly under the radar, Bridge was making it more difficult for people like Steve Wicker, GCHQ, and other agencies monitoring these boards to gather valuable intel. She was even potentially making her own job more difficult.

But that was a problem for Future Bridge. Right now she was focused on Present Bridge's problem of making the Patrios operators recruit her to Hungary, while letting them believe it was their idea. Very publicly aiding the cause was a good way to further build trust and make Prosper indispensable.

Not everyone was convinced.

From: WHITECHAOS
    Arent you a veteran, Prosper? Where did you
learn this technologically shit from?

She was quietly pleased with her comeback, though.

From: Prosper
    A good soldier understands that technology IS
the modern battlefield

That shut him up, and moments later she received a direct message:

SilentType: The cause needs good men who can lead.
What is your location?

'Fuuuuck.' Bridge's hands hovered over the keyboard as she considered how to reply.

Ciaran looked up from his screen. 'Problem?'

She sat back in her chair, twiddled her novelty lightsaber pen between her fingers, and puffed out her cheeks. 'The opposite. I think they want to recruit me.'

She'd half-expected the invitation to come from ChinesePrisoner, the user who claimed to know the Patrios action plan. She'd tried to trace CP following their private message conversation, to see where and who they might be, and found they were disguising their IP in a way that suggested CP was a professional. Their posting frequency and times were also sporadic, though mostly fitted with someone in eastern Europe. Bridge had begun to think that despite their denials ChinesePrisoner really was part of Patrios, maybe even a senior figure. But now here was someone else, a user she'd never seen post on the boards before.

She hesitated, thinking ahead to the problem of expectations. Everyone thought Prosper was a middle-aged Frenchman. When the Patrios organisers met her in person she'd have to persuade them it had been a cover, a way of hiding herself from the authorities. Or perhaps to avoid being hit on by men online. What better disguise than to pretend she was one of them? She hoped they wouldn't assume that if she lied about one persona, she might be lying about another.

Prosper: Travelling. Currently in Hungary. Where
are you?

That was deliberately cheeky. She didn't expect SilentType would tell her, but it suited her persona to ask. It also might distract them from the coincidence of her being in the same country as what she hoped was the primary Patrios camp.

SilentType: You don't need to know that. Are you
ready to fight for the fathers?

Prosper: I was born ready. This is the most
important fight of our lives.

No response. Had she gone overboard? She hadn't thought so. 'Too far' didn't seem to be in their vocabulary.

SilentType: The old bus stop outside Ferences Templom, Erd. Tomorrow, 1900 local.

Prosper: I'll be there.

SilentType: Complete comms blackout starting immediately. Contact will offer you a ride. Your response: "I am waiting for the Admiral." Any other response will be rejected. Acknowledge.

Prosper: Acknowledged. I understand.

SilentType: For the fathers.

* * *

'Have you ever been to Budapest?' asked Giles.

'No, but the contact speaks English. Besides, I won't be hanging around in suburbia ordering cocktails.'

Bridge looked over the Thames from the tall windows of Giles' office. It was a brisk day, cold but bright, and London bustled. All over Europe cities were undergoing the same re-emergence, rebuilding and re-engaging with their social, cultural, and political lives. Operation Patrios threatened to throw a massive wrench into all of that.

'How confident are you they're for real?' Giles asked.

She didn't know. How could she? It was just someone on a message board. But the timing, the detail of the pickup, the insistence on speed… 'Maybe sixty, seventy per cent? I'm willing to gamble on it.'

'I don't doubt it, but it's more than your own neck on the line if you're wrong.'

She turned to see him steepling his fingers in thought. Giles had an excellent poker face, and she worried he might call the whole thing off. A few days ago Bridge might have been relieved at that prospect, but now she found herself leaning in the opposite direction. 'I want to go, Giles. We're running out of time.'

He harrumphed. 'I know. All right, I'll book us an appointment with OpPrep in the morning. It's often said they can work miracles, but even divine power can't turn you into a fifty-year-old man, you know.'

She shrugged. 'I'll tell them I didn't want to get hit on. Lots of women adopt an online persona to stave off internet creeps sliding into their DMs.'

'Careful how you word that. For all you know, those same creeps are the ones who recruited you.'

Bridge smiled. 'I can handle myself. Let's get this show on the road.'

46

Once again the former president sat at his desk, framed by flags, and spoke to the camera.

'My fellow patriots. Make no mistake, this is war. And we didn't start it, no we did not, but when people invade your homeland, and want to destroy your way of life, there's only one appropriate response and we all know what it is. You, all of you, all of us, everyone, we have a duty to protect our lands and our culture, because they are in danger, yes they are. They're threatened every minute of every day so long as these cockroaches, these invaders – and by the way, this has been happening for years. This isn't a new thing. For generations they've been trying to replace us. Look around you, you know who I'm talking about. They're not patriots like you and me, no they're not. They might not even have a gun in their hands, but that doesn't mean they're unarmed. Doesn't mean they're not a soldier. Doesn't mean they won't slaughter you without hesitation if you turn your back, if you let your guard down for even a second. Look at all the good, kind, white people killed in Africa every day when we're just trying to help. We're just trying to make things better. Is that so bad? But they don't care, because they know the truth, the truth the media doesn't want you to hear. This is war. We didn't start it, but we will finish it. You will finish it, yes you will. God bless me, and God bless us all.'

47

Wondering why this sort of thing still had to be done on paper rather than a PDF, Bridge put down the pen, sighed, and texted Izzy.

House forms signed. I'll put them in the post.

Actually she'd asked Karl to post them after she'd left, but Izzy didn't need to know that. Bad operational form to tell her sister she was going abroad, regardless of how much she already knew about Bridge's work.

Good. I'm sending over that box of things from Maman's place for you.

She didn't want it. She'd told Izzy she didn't want it. But, like the mother whose house their relationship now revolved around, her sister either didn't listen or didn't care. Bridge wished she was surprised.

Karl would keep an eye out for the delivery. They had keys to each other's flats, so it shouldn't be a problem. She considered telling him to immediately take it for recycling, but had a strong suspicion he'd side with Izzy on this matter.

She pocketed her phone, took a last look around the flat, then headed out.

* * *

'Élodie Brunier,' Bridge read off the passport. A little younger than Bridge's real age, born in Lyon but educated in Paris according to the supplementary documents. Dropped out when she got involved with neo-Nazi gangs, had a spotted work history ever since. 'What do you want me to tell them about the work gaps if they ask? That I was squatting with fascists in Poland, or something?'

Giles peered at her. 'I can't tell if you're being sarcastic, but yes. We have a cheat sheet of European groups long defunct that you can safely name-drop.'

Debbie, the middle-aged lady from OpPrep tasked with arranging Bridge's cover legend and briefing her on it, passed the relevant sheet of paper across the meeting table. 'Élodie's an ice queen, but she can't hold down a job because when her temper boils over it normally ends in her beating someone up.'

'Definitely a challenging role,' said Giles.

Bridge gave him a withering glance. 'Unlike you, Giles, I have no problem detecting sarcasm. I assume the places that are supposed to have fired me will corroborate?'

Debbie nodded. 'We've given you friendly backups we know are reliable, even if we can't backstop as thoroughly as we'd like considering the unusually short notice under which we've had to work.' Giles shrugged off her accusing expression. 'Now, as to equipment.' She removed a worn-looking black backpack from the cardboard box she'd brought with her, unzipped it, and removed a Samsung phone. 'Given your legend, and how little knowledge we have of what you'll find when you arrive' – another disapproving glance at Giles – 'we daren't give you a standard ziploc kit in case you're searched. So you have this phone, which is prepaid and registered with a French provider. It's a regular model, none of

GCHQ's fancy stuff here, again in case you're searched. What we can give you, though, is a hidden locator beacon.' Debbie passed the pack to Bridge and indicated the interior lining near the flap.

Bridge ran her fingers over the material until she felt a small, hard disc sewn into it. 'If this is GPS, a scanner will pick it up.'

'Not yet it won't,' said Debbie, smiling. 'It's completely inert until activated. To do so, grip through the material and crack that disc in half. Don't worry, it's tough enough not to happen by accident. Breaking the disc triggers a tiny exothermic reaction, like a hand warmer, that powers a miniature GPS inside the disc and a cellular antenna sewn into the seams for twenty-four hours.'

Giles said, 'I suggested this because the chances of you getting to call us from your phone seem to be zero, as we've observed. Activation is your decision. Use best judgement.'

Bridge understood. There might be good reason to activate the beacon as soon as she arrived at the camp, if the threat was significant enough. But there might be an equal argument to wait until she'd gathered more intel. 'In case of emergency, break cotton,' she murmured. The pack contained a few other items: wallet, Swiss army knife, underwear, make-up bag, toiletries, and two well-thumbed books: a French-language *Mein Kampf*, and an English *Das Kapital*. 'Doesn't Élodie read anything for fun?' she asked.

'Depends on your definition of fun, I suppose.' Debbie patted the cardboard box. 'Change of clothes in there for you, too. Good luck.'

After she left, Giles initiated a secure video call while Bridge read over the legend again, committing details to memory. Then the call began and she found herself looking at an older man, grey and glum-looking, in a nondescript office.

'Ian Jameson, senior advisor at the British embassy in Budapest and regional station chief,' said Giles by way of introduction. He indicated Bridge. 'Brigitte Sharp OIT, cover name Élodie Brunier.'

'How do you do,' said Jameson with no enthusiasm whatsoever. 'I hope whatever's going on here can be nipped in the bud with a minimum of fuss.'

'If wishes were horses, beggars would ride. What's the situation out there, Ian? Any racial tension, neo-fascist activity?'

Jameson shrugged. 'It's Hungary, Giles. We barely have any non-whites to begin with, and the place all but runs on authoritarianism. It will take more than whatever these Patrios rumours are to make a dent. I'm keeping an ear out, but there's no indication local security is preparing for any kind of attack. I fear your girl there will come up empty-handed.'

Bridge bristled at his dismissive tone, but tried not to let it show. 'Better safe than sorry, Mr Jameson,' she said. 'Both SIS and the CIA have evidence pointing to an area north of Budapest, while Hungary denies Patrios even exists, let alone that their country might be involved. Which would you trust?'

'Yes, yes, point taken. I'm no green youngster, Ms Sharp, but I can't tell you things I haven't heard.'

Giles intervened to calm the waters. 'We're operating somewhat in the dark on this one, but when isn't that the case? Bridge, if you need to call on the embassy, Jameson is your man. Ian, if you hear anything at all contact me soonest.'

'Understood.'

Giles ended the call and turned to Bridge. 'Don't be fooled, Ian was an action man in his youth. That's why he's waiting out his retirement in a nice quiet posting. The local security he mentioned is *Terrorelhárítási Központ*, or TEK. Skilled counter-terror operators, but corrupt as all get-out, so I'm not taking their word for anything. And there's one more item, courtesy of your friends and mine across the pond.' He removed a photo printout from his operations folder. A group of armed men wearing fatigues and sunglasses, standing in front of a truck from which hung a stars-and-stripes. Two faces were circled by marker pen.

'I can't tell if I'm looking at Helmand or Arizona,' said Bridge.

'No accident, I'm sure. These chancers call themselves the Flag Born, US-based militia outfit. This one here goes by the name Mike Alessi.' Giles pointed to one of the circled men, short and wiry, smiling at the camera with a Glock in his hand. 'Not his real name, because he's the FBI's embedded agent who sent the message from Hungary. His travel companion was one of the militia's founders, name of Casey Lachlan.' He pointed to the other circled man, taller and broad of shoulder with a thick neck.

'Have they heard any more from Alessi since that paintball message?'

'Not a thing. You'd be advised to make contact as early as you can.'

'Assuming he's still there.'

Giles didn't have an answer for that. Instead he said, 'Flight via Zurich is booked from City Airport in four hours' time. Come home in one piece.'

* * *

First she called Henri Mourad and asked him to look in on Fréderic at Marseille's Camp Sud, if he had time. Bridge had apologised a thousand times for endangering Fred back at the farm, and still felt guilty for it. He wouldn't listen to her, but perhaps Henri could persuade him to return home until the potential danger passed.

With that burden lifted she changed into the clothes supplied by OpPrep. Jeans, sturdy boots, some t-shirts of heavy metal bands, a black hoodie, and a choice of accessories; cheap Casio watch, silver bangles, skull rings, friendship bracelets. She said 'fuck it' and wore them all. The black lipstick they'd given her was too much, though. She tossed it, opting for *au naturel*.

After leaving Vauxhall she bought two packs of cigarettes and a disposable lighter, then called at Any Amount of Books on Charing Cross Road, where she bought a second-hand copy of *The Da Vinci Code* to replace *Das Kapital*. Even a young neo-Nazi had to read something for fun, and a poorly written globe-spanning conspiracy theory sounded about right.

Finally, Bridge found a place that could fit her in right away and had her hair cut to a close crop. Like the novel, it felt more in keeping with her cover identity. It also meant she wouldn't look exactly like the picture in her fake passport, which could only help it seem more real.

Karl wouldn't like it, but it wasn't his bloody hair.

48

The second time the old military jeep passed the bus stop at a crawl, then sped up again, Bridge grew suspicious. When it came around a third time she looked directly at the occupants and exaggerated a shrug as they crept by, as if challenging them to say something.

The jeep stopped.

The passenger window rolled down to show two men inside, both in beanies; the passenger kept his eyes fixed ahead while the driver leaned over and called out. 'There is…no bus tonight. Can we offer you a ride?' It was too dark to make out his expression, but even through his accent – vaguely Balkan, she couldn't quite place it – the tone of voice was obviously uncertain.

'I am waiting for the Admiral,' Bridge replied, imitating her mother's heavy French accent to disguise her own.

The driver said something in a language she didn't know. Then he switched back to English and said, 'Tell me your name.'

'Élodie,' she replied. 'Also called *Prosper.*'

The man shook his head, laughed quietly, then opened the door and climbed out of the car. He was the same height as Bridge, wearing the standard army casual of plain fatigues and t-shirt under a zip jacket. The passenger, with a heavier, squatter frame, stayed inside.

'We expected a man,' he said. 'A veteran.'

She shrugged. 'I expected someone with more brains than to

drive past three times. Let's start again. I'm Élodie. Who are you?'

'Captain Popescu, but everyone calls me Eagle,' he said, not offering his hand. The Romanian name confirmed her guess at his origin. 'So you are truly French, at least.'

'And I know how to fight,' said Bridge. 'I learned the hard way, on the streets of Paris and Warsaw.'

'How do you sleep?' said the passenger suddenly. It was the first time he'd spoken, and he didn't bother turning to look at Bridge. But the question was enough. This was *SilentType*, the board user who'd recruited her, and if he knew about Prosper's sleep issues he must have been watching her posts for some time.

'Still poorly,' she replied. 'Like I said, I learned the hard way.'

Eagle unbuttoned a pocket in his fatigues and pulled out a Makarov pistol. He ejected the magazine, handed it to SilentType through the jeep window, then turned back to Bridge and said, 'Take this from me.'

So this was the test. Did they make the male recruits prove themselves like this, too? She doubted it.

Bridge knew several ways to get the gun from Eagle, all tried and tested. She could feint in one direction, then move with his reaction to get inside the shot line and strip it. She could step into him, take him by surprise with a slap to the face, and take advantage of it to prise the gun from his hand. She could kick him in the balls, grab his wrist to make the aim safe, then break his arm as he doubled over.

But these were all standard approaches, and this man looked no stranger to a battlefield. He'd anticipate them.

'Hey, silent type,' Bridge called out to the passenger. Unexpected enough that Eagle glanced to the side, and in that split second she grabbed his wrist with her left hand, stepped inside his range, and slammed her elbow into his solar plexus. Eagle staggered back, gasping for breath, but the stubborn bastard didn't ease his grip on the pistol. She focused her strength on prising it out of his hand, but the effort distracted her. He wrapped his free arm around her in a bear hug, squeezing Bridge's own breath out. She instinctively dropped to a crouch, and as he followed her down she used his momentum against him, throwing Eagle over her shoulder. She had to sacrifice grip on the gun arm, but as he landed she stepped on it. She looked down to see tattooed wings wrapped around his wrist.

'Enough!' came a shout from behind her. It was SilentType, leaning out of the jeep window. He smiled down at Eagle. 'And she knows computers, too. Better than the American, for sure.'

Bridge stepped back and held up her hands in peace. Eagle got to his feet and dusted himself off. 'All right,' he said, replacing the pistol. 'But understand, you are the only woman.'

'Nothing new,' she said, and spat on the ground.

Eagle nodded. 'The bag, Dmitri.' The passenger handed him a silver mesh bag through the window. For a moment Bridge expected they'd make her wear it over her head for the drive to camp, but then she recognised it as a Faraday pouch. 'Your phone,' said Eagle, holding the bag open.

'Why?' she asked, knowing the answer but playing ignorant.

'For security, so we can't be traced,' said Eagle.

'I can turn it off.'

'That is not enough,' said Dmitri through the window. 'Have you heard of Pegasus?'

She had. Pegasus was the invisible spyware favoured by governments and agencies everywhere to track persons of interest. The British, the Israelis, the Russians and more all used it. But again Bridge feigned ignorance.

'It is how they spy on you, all the time. Even switching off the phone is not enough. The bag is non-negotiable.'

The pouch would block all signals, both in and out. As far as cell towers and GPS were concerned anything inside it simply didn't exist. It explained why Mike Alessi couldn't send messages to the FBI, and why they in turn couldn't trace his phone.

Bridge dropped her mission-issue Samsung into the bag. 'When do I get it back?' she asked. Alessi had been able to send at least a short message, days after he'd arrived in Europe, so he must have retrieved his phone at some point.

'When the mission is completed,' said Eagle, stony-faced. 'For the fathers.'

'For the fathers,' Bridge echoed, and picked up her backpack. She let Eagle check inside it, which he quickly did, then he gestured for her to get inside the jeep.

'You have no other luggage?'

'I travel light. Who is "the American"?'

In the mirror she saw Eagle scowl at Dmitri, but the passenger shrugged and said, 'It will come out at the camp.'

'Someone we had to let go,' Eagle explained to Bridge. 'He was supposed to help lead the young recruits, but he was not suitable.'

'You think I am?'

'I suppose we will find out. Welcome to *Patrios*.'

* * *

There was no need for a bag over her head. Without her phone to check GPS, in a foreign country at night, Bridge couldn't possibly follow the jeep's route. When they began driving along an unlit forest road she stopped trying.

They finally turned off the road and pulled into the camp. Even in the dark Bridge could see the FBI agent's message had been correct. She glimpsed a sign with the very English word *paintball* at the entrance, and the buildings fitted the description.

The jeep shuddered to a stop. Dmitri got out and walked to

a small building lit from within. Eagle waited for Bridge to exit the vehicle, then led her to a long, low breeze block structure with only an external light at either end, all dark inside. A young man in fatigues stood smoking by the doors, watching them with unabashed curiosity. She'd already guessed it was the dorm block when Eagle said, 'I will show you your bed.' The smoker discarded his cigarette and hurried inside.

The wolf whistles began the moment she entered. The smoker had rushed to tell his comrades, no doubt. At the end of a short corridor was a doorway, through which a dozen or more young men sat on rows of metal-framed beds, grinning and whistling at her. If she was going to sleep in there, she'd need to find a weapon and stash it under her pillow.

But Eagle pointed instead to an earlier door off the corridor, which opened into a cell-like room with two bunk beds. A bleary-eyed man in the top bunk sat up and murmured, 'The fuck...?' She recognised Casey Lachlan from the Flag Born militia photo. But where was Mike Alessi?

'I thought you said the American left,' she said to Eagle.

He shrugged. 'We started with two. Sergeant Casey, this is Élodie. She will take this bunk.' Bridge expected Casey to object, but he grunted and laid back down, pulling the covers over his head.

The main door opened behind them and Dmitri tossed something to Eagle, who caught it and handed it to Bridge. A canvas jumpsuit. She held it up and was pleased to see it would fit, more or less. Bonus for not being a shortarse.

Eagle said goodbye and left. Casey was either asleep or pretending to be, and while Bridge had a hundred questions to ask, Élodie wouldn't know or care about any of them. So she threw the jumpsuit and her backpack on the bed, hung her hoodie on the room's wardrobe rail, and used the en suite. The term somewhat oversold the chilly, broken-tiled bathroom, but after a couple of hours of sitting in the cold at a bus stop, then in an equally cold rattling jeep, she was bursting.

They were waiting for her when she opened the door.

She'd half-expected it; it wasn't paranoia if they really were out to get you. The question was whether these half-dozen young men from the dorm block, now standing inside the room entrance, just wanted to beat her up or had something else in mind. They looked so young to her she couldn't tell, but that youth also made them cocky and eager to mouth off.

Bridge didn't give them chance. Without breaking stride she slammed her fist into the nearest recruit's nose. He fell back, forcing those behind him to retreat momentarily.

One recruit stood to the side, thus avoiding the fallout, and now took a step towards Bridge. She was rusty from a lack of sparring, but as he drew back his fist to swing it, he might as well have written a letter stating his intentions. She weaved inside the arc of his swing, clamped her hand on the back of his head as he moved past, and smashed his skull into the bunk's metal corner upright. He cried out and collapsed, blood flowing. Casey sat up to watch, but didn't lift a finger to help.

Bridge had seen two cans of deodorant in the bathroom. One of them, plus her lighter, could improvise a flamethrower. But there was no time to get them, or the Swiss army knife from her pack. The recruits she'd knocked back were already reassessing, inching forward. One wide-shouldered thug slowly, deliberately rolled up a thick magazine, while another prepared to come at her with bare hands. She heard shouts from the dorm block. If she didn't end this soon it would become a spectator sport.

Bare-hands feinted at her, out of range but close enough that she couldn't ignore it. Magazine guy used the distraction to come at Bridge from the side, swinging his improvised club. She put out an arm to block, but mistimed it and the magazine hit her in the side of the head. Not solid enough to do real damage, but it hurt and disorientated her all the same. She kept her arm outstretched and grabbed a handful of T-shirt, twisting around to slam an elbow into his head, but he was already pushing her sideways. She stumbled, shin barking on the corner of the desk frame, and before she could regain her footing he was on her, knees on her chest, hand on her throat, bringing the magazine down over and over, and behind him were more of them, cowards bringing up the rear, ready to join in now the hard work was done—

'*That's enough!*' Loud and sudden, the shout cut through the yelled urges, even through the blows to her head. She forced her eyes open, only then realising she'd shut them tight, and saw two onlookers lifted off their feet and out of her vision. Magazine-guy paused and turned, wide-eyed, as Eagle stepped into view and hauled him to his feet. The young man protested to no avail; then his cries changed to a different sort when Eagle slammed his fist into the recruit's face. Even from down on the floor Bridge heard bone snap, and she quickly rolled out of the way as blood poured from magazine guy's nose.

Another man, older like Eagle and with a similar ex-military bearing, shoved his way through the recruits to offer Bridge a hand. She took it, and he pulled her upright. Two more veteran-looking men handled the recruits like sacks of potatoes, pulling them out of the room and tossing them back into the dorm. The men looked like they were itching for someone to argue, but nobody did. Behind them, the main exterior door stood open. Had they been standing there, anticipating this and waiting for the right moment to come in?

She began to wish that someone like Tolbert had come in her place after all. He wouldn't have had to deal with this shit.

'Élodie!' Eagle's voice carried from the dorm, summoning

her. She ran her hands through her hair, rolled her shoulders, and walked through with her head held high. He stood in the middle of the dorm, berating her attackers in front of the other recruits. 'You are weak and undisciplined,' he shouted. 'That girl' – he pointed unnecessarily at Bridge, who bristled at being called *girl*, but let it go – 'put two of you on the ground without a second thought. Are you a moron?'

It took a moment to realise the question was aimed at her. 'Uh...*non*,' she answered.

'Only a moron would come here and think this might not happen. But she came anyway, because she is dedicated to the cause. She has more balls than all of you combined.' A few of the recruits jeered in protest. 'Oh, am I wrong? Then prove it tomorrow, where it matters – in training. Not here.'

He turned to her again. 'Are you ready to fight to honour your fathers?'

Bridge raised a fist in salute. 'Forever!'

'Good soldier,' Eagle nodded. 'Is there anything you want to say to these children?'

All eyes turned to her. 'I require no special treatment,' she said carefully. 'But I will cut the prick off any man who tries that again.' She exchanged glares with magazine guy.

Eagle laughed. 'Excellent. Now behave, or I will break more than noses.' He turned to leave, the other veteran-looking men having already vacated. 'That door locks,' he said quietly to Bridge as he passed. 'Just in case.'

She retreated into the bunk room, locked the door as suggested, then rummaged in her backpack to find the Swiss army knife. She unfolded the primary blade and placed it under her pillow. Better than nothing.

'Thanks for your fucking help,' she said to Casey as she removed her boots. He didn't answer.

49

Fred answered on the second ring. 'It's late, Louis. What's up?'

'Sorry to bother you, boss. There's a guy at the south gate asking for you. Diplomatic ID, British embassy.'

'What the hell does he want?'

'Won't say, but claims it's "a matter of urgency" and he'll only speak to you.'

A knot formed in the pit of Fred's stomach. Had something happened to his family? He could imagine no other reason why a British diplomat would travel all the way from Paris to see him. 'On my way,' he said, shoving his phone into his pocket and his feet into a pair of shoes. He closed his laptop and rushed out of the trailer.

Despite the hour, Camp Sud bustled with activity, thanks to a boat that had capsized two nights earlier. The coastguard had rescued as many as they could, and the refugees were now being processed as quickly as camp staff could manage. As if that wasn't enough, the operation to right the boat and clear it from the bay had caused chaos and delays at the docks, and the mayor had berated the camp administrators as if it was somehow their fault.

All of this fell away from Fred's mind as it ran wild, instead imagining the bad news this diplomat had come to deliver. He'd drop everything and fly home immediately if anything had happened to Isabelle and the children.

He turned the final corner around a low tent and saw the man waiting at the gate. A slim North African, he could have been one of the camp's residents if not for his smart-casual dress. Nice clothes and a good pair of shoes; how little separated the destitute from the government official.

Behind the waiting diplomat stood the protestors and their signs. Their numbers normally diminished at night, to be renewed each morning. But the capsized boat, and the efforts to which Marseille had gone to rescue the survivors, so offended the hardcore contingent that recent nights had remained 'lively', as one camp administrator put it.

Fred didn't wait to be introduced. 'I'm Fréderic Baudin. What's this about? Is my family OK?'

The diplomat seemed confused by the question. 'They're absolutely fine, Mr Baudin. It's you I'm here to talk about.'

Relief washed through Fred's body like a cooling wave, easing the tension that had built inside him. 'We're kind of busy, as I'm sure you can see.'

'I sure can,' said the stranger. He gestured around them. 'Fallout from the capsized boat?'

'Amongst other things. You haven't told me your name.'

The man opened an identity wallet for Fred to read. 'Henri Mourad. Can we step inside for some privacy?'

Fred sighed and ushered him through the gate. They stepped away from the occupants' tents and spoke quietly.

'Before we go any further,' said Mourad, 'I'm obliged to remind you that you signed and continue to be bound by the Official Secrets Act 1989 of the United Kingdom.'

Fred rolled his eyes. 'What now?'

'I work with your sister-in-law. She asked me to come and see you.'

'Brigitte?' said Fred, incredulous. 'What the hell does this have to do with all of…what you people do?' Fred regarded this man

Mourad, this spy from England, with suspicion.

Mourad looked a little sheepish. 'I can't say too much, but we have reason to believe immigrant communities and places like this are under a real threat of attack. Bridge is worried your camp may be a target, and suggested you consider returning to safety in England.'

Fred scoffed. 'Camp Sud has been a target since the first boat came ashore, and we've been dealing with racists ever since. Or did you not see the protestors outside?'

'I'm talking about people with guns, not placards.'

'Listen, the boat that capsized? Thirty dead, forty survived. Everyone has abandoned those people already, and now they must deal with that as well. Every single survivor was related to someone who died. Not one of them escaped without loss. Can you imagine how much they need us? There's more to do here than ever, and if Brigitte thinks—' Mourad was spared the rest of Fred's invective as they became aware of a commotion going on around them. Not in reaction to their argument, but to something the staff were reading on their phones and relaying to each other in appalled tones. Whatever it was, the protestors outside were equally agitated. Fred called out to Louis. 'What's going on?'

'They found another container,' replied Louis, not looking up from his screen. 'At the new port.'

Fred swore and began walking back to his trailer. 'Sorry, Mr Mourad, but your time's up. As I said, we're rather busy.'

'No, no,' said Louis, waving at Fred to stop. 'Not more refugees; a murder scene. My guy at the port says it's like something from a horror movie.'

50

God, the stench.

It hit Henri when he was still twenty metres from the shipping container, a rancid combination of rot, charring, and industrial disinfectant. For the first time in months he was glad someone told him to put on a mask before approaching further. The pathologist said that, ironically, the smell was the result of someone's attempt to reduce the scent of putrefaction by destroying the body. It had not been what anyone could call a success.

Port security initially assumed the container was full of refugees. With Camp Sud a short drive away and several prior incidents of stowaways, it was a logical guess. The head of security had been ready to call both the police and Camp Sud once more. But then they opened the container and realised their mistake.

Henri had left Fréderic Baudin and his staff to their work. Fred was right, they had plenty to do and Henri was only getting in the way. Besides, while the camp lacked security it looked safe enough. The fence was tall, the protestors were outside that fence, and so was the police presence. Surely even a mob of white people wouldn't try to go straight through the armed *nationales*.

Henri could be useful here at the port, though. A body in a container implied it had come ashore, which implied it was from abroad, and that was within his interest. He'd rushed over here, flashed his ID, and had a quiet word with the senior policeman in charge. The policeman warned him the sight wasn't for the faint of heart, and he hadn't lied.

'Some kind of caustic agent, by the look of things,' said the pathologist as Henri peered into the container. The doctor insisted nobody except himself enter, and Henri wasn't about to protest. He saw corroded metal restraints fixed to the roof, melted insulation around the upper parts of the walls, and then the small matter of the lower half of a human body in a rusty, blackened chair, surrounded by what appeared to be vomit.

'Not fire?' Henri asked, sniffing the charred air. The victim's wrists were fixed to the chair, and his hands had the raw, red appearance of burned flesh.

'Fire doesn't do *that*,' said the pathologist, gesturing at the half-corpse. Everything from the sternum upwards was simply missing, and the edges of the wound – a laughably insufficient word, but what else could he call it? – resembled the melted insulation on the walls of the container more than the blackened remains of a fire. Henri suddenly understood that the substance on the floor wasn't vomit, and crossed himself instinctively. The pathologist continued, 'My guess is the gas cloud rose quickly, damaging the flesh in passing, then ate away at the upper body while it remained in the top of the container before venting fully.'

'But that was a mistake, right? The gas was supposed to destroy the whole body.'

The pathologist nodded. 'That's my assumption, but we'll never know for sure.'

Henri had limited experience of pathologists, but he was yet to meet one who would commit to being sure about anything. It was all *perhaps* this, *perhaps* that, and *the evidence suggests*. Impossible to pin down. But Henri was sure enough. According to port records, this container was less than six months into a pre-arranged journey that should have taken it around the world several times over for at least another year. Whoever did this had wanted it to remain hidden for a long time, long enough that when it was found no evidence would remain. But the capsized refugee boat two nights ago, less than two hundred metres from shore, had caused a delay to onward shipping. It also prompted security to increase their patrols, and that's when they'd noticed the smell from this particular container. Being tragically familiar with the scent of decomposition, they'd insisted it be opened.

They'd also discovered that finding someone to take responsibility for the container was impossible. The shipping company that booked its round-trip mystery tour was based in Belize, a typically anonymous company with a name Henri had already forgotten – something like *Global Integrated Solutions Inc.* – and had paid its transshipment fees in advance, from a Swiss bank account that no longer existed. No more information was forthcoming, and if Henri's experience was any guide it never would be.

If by some miracle they could trace the container's origins, though, he was confident it would turn up a connection to Russia because he'd seen something like it before. Not the attempt to dispose of the body by liquefaction – that was a new technique and, judging by the results, one yet to be perfected. But the SVR's ingenious repurposing of shipping containers as mobile prisons and torture chambers was known in the intelligence community. There was little doubt this man had been a prisoner, and while the state of his body made it impossible to definitively say he'd been tortured, the restraints and disposal attempt were enough for Henri to call it a safe bet.

Which left two inevitable questions: who was he, and why had the Russians done this to him?

51

The other recruits had decided the Americans were secretly gay lovers – why else would they have a private room together? – who'd argued, so one of them left, and now the other was walking around like a zombie because he was heartbroken. One claimed to have heard Casey crying not long after Mike disappeared.

When Bridge said she'd been told the Americans had their own room because they were veterans in charge of the other recruits, the responses ranged from shrugs to disbelief to outright laughter. She had her own doubts about whether or not Casey Lachlan really was a former Sergeant, but regardless of the truth he didn't command any respect.

Bridge had quickly realised this, and thrown in her lot – or rather Élodie's – with the local recruits. It was partly a survival tactic; she'd embarrassed and insulted them that first night, and the simplest way to ensure they didn't seek further revenge was to become one of the boys. The first morning at breakfast she'd found magazine guy, nursing a bandage over his broken nose, and challenged him to an arm wrestle. Even if she could have won she would have thrown it, but she didn't need to. He had enough bulk behind him to wear her down, and when her hand touched the table a cheer went up. She laughed, reached across to grab the big guy's can of Coke, drained it, and treated them all to a loud belch. More cheers and laughter reassured her that she'd made the right call. Bridge would have to work twice as hard here to prove herself and be accepted, but she'd been doing that her whole career at SIS.

The food situation was more difficult. Arm wrestling over, the recruits stood in line to fill their plates. Looking down the counter of available food, she had a sickening realisation that she was the only vegetarian. It hadn't been a problem on previous undercover missions, but Hungary was already proving unlike anything she'd done before. She could technically live on bread and cheese for a while, but the others would inevitably mock her for it while tucking in to sausages and bacon. A wave of nausea threatened her stomach, but she forced it down along with two of the greasy tubes and covered the taste with more fizzy drinks, reminding herself this wasn't about her. It was about the mission.

Bridge didn't buy that Casey and Mike had been a couple, but she couldn't tell the recruits why: they didn't know Mike was FBI. She doubted he'd have embarked on a romantic relationship with someone he was supposed to be spying on. That he'd been 'let go' was concerning, but neither Casey nor Eagle would talk about it, and as Élodie had no reason to care Bridge couldn't push too hard for answers.

In fact, Casey would barely talk to anyone about anything. He went through the motions, taking part in group exercises, but something was off. The man wore a thousand-yard-stare everywhere he went, one uncomfortably familiar to Bridge. What could have happened to leave him so traumatised? One time during shooting range practice, she noticed Eagle and Dmitri quietly talking about Casey. Whatever was going on, they knew but weren't sharing.

They weren't sharing what was going on in the woods, either. That first morning, Dmitri led the older camp soldiers – the half-dozen men who'd pulled the recruits off Bridge the night before, all plainly former soldiers – into the forest, armed and loaded up.

When she mentioned it, the recruits said it was normal. But all they knew was that the older men were undergoing specialised training, and aside from Eagle and Dmitri they had almost no contact with the young recruits.

That only made Bridge even more interested, and when the men returned that evening she burned through half a pack of cigarettes trying to eavesdrop without causing suspicion. The first thing she noticed was that they communicated in English, all heavily accented but suggesting they hailed from a variety of countries. Much like in programming, English was the lingua franca of international military operations – particularly among mercenaries.

Some of them called Eagle '*Vultur*'. She didn't speak Romanian, but knew it meant the same thing. She also knew the Romanian Land Forces 1st Spec Ops Battalion were nicknamed *Vulturii*. If that was the source of his nickname, and these men were all veterans on a similar level, things were more serious than she'd realised – but also more confusing. Why did they need the young recruits at all, with experienced mercenaries on hand? Any of these men could beat a dozen recruits to a pulp without breaking sweat. Finding and killing immigrant civilians would be child's play.

Yet here they were, handing out weaponry to fresh-faced race warriors, recruited online through the deepfake videos and message boards. One of the young men had run with Nazi gangs in Szeged. Another spent two months in a Croatian prison for beating up a Syrian immigrant. Yet another was deep into online conspiracies, the sort of person she'd debated on the message boards. They all had their story, their reason for being here, but the common root was frustration at not feeling in control of their lives. Bridge could relate to an extent, but instead of looking to their own governments' failings these young men fell for the oldest trick in the book; blaming foreigners. A political sleight of hand as old and subtle as a Neanderthal tribe.

Speaking of old and tired, the weaponry in question was practically antique. But older equipment was easy and cheap to buy on the black market, and if her fellow recruits cared, they didn't show it. They were giddy to be here, playing at being soldiers and indulging confused fantasies about honouring their white forefathers.

Bridge wasn't normally one for playing at anything, least of all soldiers, and the lack of skills training among her fellow recruits meant she had to tone down her own performance. On the one hand she wanted Eagle to regard her as a good recruit, to get over his obvious initial reticence at her being a woman. She might even be able to draw him into her confidence. On the other hand, if she was too good it would be obvious to someone with training – like Eagle, Dmitri, and the other veterans – that she was a professional. No matter how many times Élodie was supposed to have fought police during neo-fascist protests, it wouldn't explain the kind of training Bridge had undergone. She almost blew it on her first rifle shooting test, throwing out several near-bullseyes without thinking. When she saw none of the locals were even close to that level she quickly adjusted down on further attempts, and let everyone laugh off her first round as beginner's luck. She was relieved to see that Casey was a crack shot with a rifle, which took some attention off her. From then on she aimed to deliver a solid fourth or fifth place in all exercises; good enough, but not so good she'd draw suspicion.

Following sparring, the recruits filed into the dorm block showers. The en suite in her shared room didn't have one, so Bridge stayed outside with a cigarette and waited for them to finish. The bathroom was communal, with a separate row of toilet cubicles across a dividing wall. One in ten tiles was cracked or missing, and the floor looked like it would give anyone who tried to wipe it down tetanus out of spite. Half the cubicles had no locks, but Bridge found a wet room with shower and toilet originally built for disabled patrons. It was no more sanitary than the others, but it had a working lock so she'd adopted it as her own.

Lock notwithstanding, she also adopted a habit of taking her backpack with her and placing her now always-open Swiss army knife within easy reach. 'One of the lads' or not, she couldn't let her guard down.

As she showered, Bridge's thoughts turned again to Eagle, Dmitri, and their band of mercenaries. Why were they here? What were they doing in the woods? And what did it have to do with Operation Patrios?

52

They went in at first light.

Penetration squads led the way, battering open the doors to all three occupied buildings simultaneously, then getting the hell out of the way as the Armed Response units moved inside, guns raised and ready.

Andrea Thomson heard it all unfold from her car, an earpiece hooked up to the first unit commander's radio broadcasting shouts of, '*Armed police! Lie down on the ground!*' loud and clear.

They'd been waiting since midnight, when they rolled through these innocent-seeming Somerset woods with lights off and minimum comms. Thermal imaging confirmed which of the former paintball camp's buildings were occupied. Most of those inside slept in bunks, judging by their positions, while one building housed only three bodies sleeping apart from each other. The camp leaders, no doubt.

Following Andrea's order to look for strange goings-on in remote woodlands, particularly related to former paintball sites, the analyst Paul Granger had found the site. Results were hardly pouring in, but he assessed each that did and passed it to her along with his estimated likelihood that it was what they were looking for. Andrea liaised with local CID to have them checked out, and they'd all drawn blanks. Until this one.

An old facility, put out of business by the pandemic and left abandoned. But a few weeks ago, local dog walkers began hearing gunfire again. They assumed new owners had taken it over and resumed business. *Not entirely incorrect*, thought Andrea.

Her attention was brought back to the present by the sudden, relative silence in her ear. A minute ago it had all been shouts, threats, and stomping about, three things the AR boys did better than anyone. Now that was over, and the commander's voice sounded in her ear.

'All locations secure, I repeat, all locations secure. Beginning to escort suspects from the premises. Ready for you in ten minutes, ma'am.'

Andrea exited the car and made for the primary SOCO van, patiently waiting until they could enter the scene and begin collecting forensic evidence. She used the time to get suited, booted, and gloved up like the other investigators, then followed them in when all suspects had been cleared from the site. By that time an armed response unit had confirmed at least one cache of illegal firearms on the premises, a hodge-podge of live-fire rifles and pistols. Harmless paintball lookalikes, these were not.

The commander directed her to the building where the camp leaders had slept. There'd be time to interrogate them later; right now she wanted to see if anything in that building could help her counterparts in Europe. They still knew woefully little about this operation.

Inside she found a ground floor manager's office, cramped and spartan. Andrea and a forensics investigator both made a beeline for the desk, upon which sat a closed Acer laptop. The SOCO opened it, only to be presented with a password login field.

'Shite,' said Andrea, disappointed.

'Always worth a try,' said the investigator with a shrug. He closed the laptop and placed it inside an evidence bag.

Andrea looked around for anything else that might shed some light, but it didn't look like the camp leader spent a lot of time in here. An address book was probably too much to hope for, but she'd hoped there might at least be a paper record or two, or perhaps a phone they could crack open and get some numbers. She opened a storage cabinet at the back of the room, finding a couple of old walkie-talkie kits and a locked metal box. The box was a decent weight, and its contents rattled and shifted when she lifted it.

'Get this open, would you?' she said to the investigator. He looked the box over, stepped out of the room, and returned a moment later with a crowbar. Andrea laughed. 'No skeleton key?'

He held up the crowbar. 'What do you think we call this? Now, stand back.' He braced it against the box lid and prised it open with a screech of metal.

Andrea peered inside and whistled. She'd hoped for a phone, but hadn't expected this. Twenty phones, everything from iPhones and Samsung Notes to Huaweis and Oppos. The box itself looked reinforced, lined with layers of wire mesh on every side, but lacking padding to protect the phones.

'Huh. Baffle box,' said the forensics investigator. Andrea shrugged, none the wiser, so he explained. 'Prevents wireless signals from escaping or penetrating. Even with the screen off, your phone's always talking to local cell towers. Some still transmit GPS when they're powered down. Put them in a Faraday cage like this, though, and you block the signal.'

'It stops us tracking them.'

'Precisely.'

Andrea cursed. If he was right, the camp had probably insisted everyone put their phone in the box while on-site, which meant they hadn't been using them. Her tech people might crack every phone here but get nothing for it. 'Take them anyway,' she said. 'You never know, we might get lucky.'

She returned to the desk and opened each drawer in turn. They were pretty bare; pens, pencils, a pad of Sudoku puzzles, business cards from local taxi firms, empty hanging files. She peeked in the wastepaper basket; a few crumpled pieces of paper, from the puzzle pad by the looks of things. There really wasn't much evidence of planning or discipline. Was Patrios truly this ramshackle and uncoordinated? Maybe it was her ex-Army bias, but Andrea had expected something more akin to a well organised field operation. From what she'd seen so far they seemed to be making it up as they went along.

Something caught her eye when she turned back to the drawers. The puzzles – that wasn't right, was it? It was a square pad, full of number grids, but the grids were odd. Andrea didn't do Sudoku herself, but she'd seen Joan engrossed in enough puzzle books to know what they looked like, and this wasn't it. These were square blocks of numbers, a hundred or more, one block to a sheet. The numbers looked completely random, there were too many, and no blanks.

She almost gasped as an idea came to her. Hardly daring to believe it, she reached into the wastepaper basket and retrieved a crumpled sheet. Sure enough, it was from the same pad and someone had scribbled on it with a pencil. But they weren't filling in blanks. Instead several numbers were circled or underlined, and in the margins were simple sums:

$$6$$
$$+9$$
$$=15$$
$$1$$
$$+5$$
$$= 6$$

Another sum showed a similar progression:

```
   3
  +8
 =11
   1
  +1
 = 2
```

Andrea took every used sheet from the bin and flattened them on the desk. Each had similar margin sums, successively reducing two-digit numbers to a single digit. Then she found what was presumably the top sheet, with something that wasn't a sum written at the top, and she laughed.

'Ma'am?' The forensic investigator was still in the room, taking photographs. Andrea waved him over, enjoying the chance to return the favour and explain something to him. She placed the pad alongside the used sheets.

'It's called a *one-time pad*,' she said. 'Used for sending and received coded messages. Every message uses a different sheet of the pad, turning a string of numbers back into letters for that message only. After a single use you discard it and move on to the next sheet, so the code never repeats.'

'Hence *one-time*,' said the investigator, nodding. 'That makes sense, but what's so funny?'

'One-time pads have been around for two hundred years. They've lasted that long because they're incredibly simple but impossible to crack, *if* you follow a few simple rules.' She held up the flattened pieces of paper. 'The most important of which is… destroy every sheet after use.'

***

She was still laughing as she called Giles Finlay from inside her car on a secure line. 'They threw the old sheets in the bin,' she told him. 'Didn't burn them, or shred them; nothing. Just scrunched them up.'

Giles sounded equally amused. 'We're not dealing with the cream of the crop, here, are we?'

'Absolutely not,' she agreed. 'But it makes me wonder, what *are* we dealing with? Who sets up something like this, puts in the effort and expense, then leaves an amateur in charge? Is it all a decoy? Did they want us to find this camp, to distract us from looking elsewhere?'

'Perhaps someone else got hold of the FBI agent's phone and sent that message, to throw us off.'

She told him about the baffle box. 'If there's one of those at every camp, it would explain why their agent's been incommunicado. I'd guess you shouldn't bank on hearing from Sharp much, either.'

'It suggests the camp isn't a red herring, though. Why make it impossible to track if you're setting it up as a decoy?'

She shrugged. 'Double bluff, so we wouldn't think it was too easy? Anyway, I think we might be about to get a lot of answers thanks to this pad.'

'What do you mean? It's great that you found the pad, but we don't know what messages they sent with it.'

'Actually, I think we do.' Andrea smiled and looked again at the top used sheet. At the top, in careful handwriting, someone had written: *twitter.com/@ToTheFathers*.

53

The battery, the battery. Of all the stupid things.

Yuri had arrived in Prague more than a week ago, expecting to depart again a day or two later. Everything was pre-arranged on that assumption. But the engineer had shaken his head, apologised, and explained that things moved slowly. Many people were still working at home, and deliveries were slow, and a dozen other excuses that Yuri didn't care about in the slightest because this man had him over a barrel. Strictly speaking he wasn't the only engineer who could perform the task. But he was best-placed, best-connected, and had a previous history of co-operation and collaboration with Moscow. And now there wasn't enough time to go anywhere else.

It would happen soon. It had to. The plan had many other pieces, many other people and schemes. They worked in concert, like the delicate movement of a fine watch. If one part did not move in the right direction at the right time, the whole mechanism would fail. Yuri couldn't allow that – couldn't afford it – and made this very clear to the engineer. But he knew Yuri had no choice. When one was tasked at great expense to secretly build a prototype of a highly-advanced miniaturised weapon from stolen plans, it didn't take a genius to understand the centrality of one's role. The engineer never came out and said, 'Where else are you going to go?' Perhaps even he could tell this would be unwise, with Yuri's fraying temper. But his daily shrug said it for him, loud and clear.

It was so close, so very nearly complete. They just needed the fucking battery. Of course, it wasn't something you could buy at the store or borrow from a spare flashlight. It had to be made by a specialist, a man in another country altogether with access to materials and techniques not found on the high street. To ask the specialist how he came by them would be an insult, the mark of an amateur. Nobody cared where anything came from if it could be turned to one's advantage.

The specialist had assured the engineer it was almost complete two days ago. Since then he had been incommunicado, but the engineer didn't think this unusual.

'How well do you know this man?' Yuri had asked.

'A little,' said the engineer. 'I've worked with him twice...no, three times before. He always delivers.'

'Has he ever dropped off the radar like this?'

'It's not unusual for men like him. They can become obsessed.'

He saw no point in continuing the conversation, so Yuri left the engineer's workshop and returned to his hotel, near-silent thanks to the season and slow recovery from quarantine. There had been days when he was the only person eating at breakfast, and evenings when he'd seen nobody except glum staff in the corridors. Things were better now than they had been before the vaccines, but a world in hiding was a poor fit for men whose success relied on not being seen. Empty streets threw few shadows.

Still, all those layers of watch mechanism protected and insulated him. The longer he stayed here, the more he was exposed, yes. But there was nothing to link Yuri to any trail. He hadn't yet bought his ticket back to the camp, and the engineers and specialists upon whom he now depended were professionals like him. They didn't know his name, and they didn't ask, and even if he'd given one it would be as false as the name on his hotel booking.

Lie upon lie upon lie, because the only thing that mattered in their world was cash in exchange for results. Everything else was of no consequence.

* * *

As if waiting days for the battery wasn't bad enough, the British had to go and ruin his breakfast.

Somehow, the camp in England had been found and shut down. In itself, this wasn't a disaster. A single camp made little difference, although Yuri always enjoyed sowing chaos in that country and watching them flounder. He regretted that he wouldn't get to see that now, but ultimately it didn't matter. More concerning was the information from his English source that the idiot who'd been put in charge of the camp failed to follow encryption protocol.

When this was over, he would make sure the English soldier was eliminated. Not because Yuri was worried he might talk – the man didn't know anything useful – but as a matter of principle.

For now, though, he must give a different order. He prepared the message while watching a new guest, one he hadn't previously seen, enter the restaurant for breakfast.

Yuri had never truly dropped his guard, even in this city of half-filled streets and empty hotels. It would have been easy to feel far from danger, but that wasn't his way and vigilance had saved him many times in the past. What most people called paranoia, experienced operators called common sense.

So he watched this new man, a modern business-type with short dark hair and glasses. Jeans and a polo shirt to breakfast, with faded deck shoes and no socks. A non-smoker, then, because surely nobody would venture outside in this cold with bare ankles. That matched the man's physique, of someone who kept in shape but lacked the bulk of a professional fighter. His watch was an anomaly, gleaming silver steel and almost half an inch thick. Yuri couldn't identify the brand from this distance, but instinctively knew it was one that loudly declared itself as an investment. As if anyone able to spend seventy thousand euros on a watch needed to make ten thousand profit on it when he retired. The watch stood out on this otherwise casual man, suggesting he would change into something more formal after breakfast. Or perhaps not. Perhaps that was the point, like the rock stars who dressed like vagrants because nobody dared tell them not to.

But clothes and accessories could all be bought, borrowed, and adopted. Yuri had done it many times himself, to effect disguise. What ultimately rendered the man safe was his behaviour; sitting with his back to a window, breakfast slowly cooling as he scrolled and tapped his iPhone like a child, more interested in its enticing glow than the world around him. Anyone could stand outside that window and observe the screen over his shoulder. The only time the man looked up from his phone was to switch his attention to the lukewarm food. Even the coffee waitress, an attractive blonde in a short skirt, didn't pull the man's attention away from his screen.

Yuri briefly entertained a fantasy that the man was reading the *@ToTheFathers* feed on Twitter; that he was a supporter, a believer, one of the many who would spin theories and willingly serve a master who didn't even know he existed, all because his hatred ran so deep. The further east you came, the easier it was to find such men. Put a gun in their hand, tell them they'd been right about those brown bastards all along, and let slip the dogs of war.

But if so, the man would soon be disappointed. Yuri returned to his own phone and sent the necessary message.

IMMEDIATE: Shut down Twitter account. Delete all history. Cancel future posts.

He replaced the phone in his pocket and raised his cup at the waitress for a coffee refill. She obliged, and as he watched her walk away he entertained a very different fantasy. But then his phone buzzed with a new message. Annoyed, because his own message hadn't required a reply, he removed it and glanced at the screen.

Package arrived

Ah, well. That was different.

It was tempting to go immediately. To leave his coffee and toast, check out, and make his way to the engineer's workshop. But 'arrived' didn't mean 'fitted'. The plans were technical gobbledygook he barely understood, but even Yuri knew this wasn't a matter of plugging the battery into a socket and declaring the job finished. It would be ready today – he would make sure of that, if he had to stand over the engineer's shoulder the whole time – but there was no reason to rush, and good reason not to in case he was being watched after all.

He returned his phone to his pocket once again, resolving to destroy it after leaving the hotel. He would buy a new one before catching a train to the camp this evening.

54

'*Grenade!*'

The cry came from upstairs, so Bridge ignored it. She completed her three-sixty as someone on the next floor shouted, '*bang!*' followed by several loud thumps as people dropped to the ground. She rolled her eyes, and turned to find herself facing down the barrel of an AK-47. Before she could react, she took a shot straight in the chest.

Eagle called the exercise 'Sweep and Advance', which she guessed was the Romanian Land Forces term for it. It had a hundred different names in armies and units around the world, but was always the same. Enter a house, methodically kill everything inside, then move on to the next building. The camp contained a fake street of empty buildings, on the opposite side from the firing range, built for the exercise. The militia recruits were masked up and given Kalashnikovs with modified paint ammo, marked by orange tape wrapped around the magazines. Eagle's men, the veterans, were also masked but wore additional padding and armour to take multiple shots, as they played the hostiles. After being 'shot', each would leap back to his feet and move on to the next house, ready to play another part.

It was fun, but Bridge couldn't fathom what it had to do with Operation Patrios. This was Hungary, not Helmand or even Homs.

The more she saw of Patrios, the less she understood. Why were the recruits needed, if they had half a dozen veterans like Eagle? Why did Dmitri lead those veterans into the woods for secretive special training, leaving Eagle behind to train the recruits? Why did they take care not to be tracked by mobile phone signals, and send out carefully coded Twitter messages, but blindly recruit strangers off the internet? And why hadn't the recruits been told what their target was, or even when the attack would take place?

She'd begun to wonder if it was an elaborate joke merely designed to sow chaos. Was the aim to confuse Europe's security services and keep them occupied as a distraction for something else? That seemed plausible, but what? And why go to such lengths?

Outside she removed her mask and joined the other recruits eliminated so far, including the group who'd been 'blown up' by the grenade above her. She accepted a cigarette, then noticed Casey sitting against an unused building, also eliminated. She walked over and sat next to him, backs against the wall.

'You know,' she said in her heavy French accent, 'you look like a man who's seen some shit.' He didn't respond, so she continued. 'I know the look. You think nothing will change, that you will always feel like this, and there is no hope. But let me tell you what a friend told me: there is always hope, because people can change. When people change, the world changes. All things pass in time.'

He remained silent but she stayed there with him, smoking and listening to the last of the gunfire from the buildings opposite, watching veterans run from one house to the next and eliminated recruits join the others, shoulders slumped.

Eventually Casey turned to her and said, 'What are you, a philosopher?'

Bridge shrugged. 'I'm French. Same thing.' She smiled, and he smiled back, and then they sniggered like schoolchildren.

A shout from Eagle interrupted further conversation. He didn't take part – instead he watched the exercise from the command quarters, through cameras installed in the fake houses. Evidently he'd seen enough.

Bridge and Casey joined the others as Eagle called out performances worth noting – a good shot here, a bad sweep there – then sent the recruits off to shower. The veterans hung back around the fake houses, laughing and smoking.

As always, while the recruits took their communal showers Bridge waited outside, nursing her own cigarette and thoughts. She continued turning over the mystery of the exercises. Group sparring, sweep and advance...these were military tactics. Sure, they bred comradeship in the recruits. Each exercise built trust, so they would have each others' backs in a real combat situation.

But as far as anyone knew their targets would be immigrants, refugees, foreigners. Surely they weren't planning to go door to door in downtown Budapest, killing everything in their way. Were these exercises all that men like Eagle and his fellow veterans knew? But if so, why put them in charge of the camp? Bridge was missing something, some puzzle piece of understanding that would let her make sense of this strange, contradictory chaos.

Shouts and laughter from the dorm block told her the recruits were finishing their showers. She lit another cigarette for good measure, smoked it in isolated silence, then headed inside and carried her toilet bag into the disabled cubicle. She locked the door, laid out her sparse toiletries on the shelf, and placed her ever-present knife next to them. But as she reached to turn the water lever, voices from outside drifted through the cubicle's half-open window, talking in English.

'Most of them would be dead within five seconds of a real fight. I don't understand why we need them.'

'Because that's the plan. The boss is paying for it, so why do you give a fuck?' She recognised Eagle's voice.

'I don't want them getting in the way. I like a clean job, and I don't like amateurs.'

'He's right. I had contact with Chinese squads on the Indian border. They don't fuck around.'

'Keep your voices down. God, you whine like old women. Relax, OK? These kids have a part to play, and so do we. Take it up with the boss when he gets here.' Eagle again, and Bridge recognised the implicit threat that 'taking it up with the boss' would be unwise. But that was a new development; while Eagle was in charge around here, the former soldier took his own orders from someone else. A metaphorical general, or maybe even a real one.

The mens' voices faded as they moved on, presumably back to the command quarters. Bridge waited another minute before turning on the water and washing herself clean at last.

Army exercises for a bunch of untrained kids who would never carry them out for real. Americans shipped over to be in charge, but then sidelined. A group of real veterans who had their own 'part to play'. And something about the Chinese?

What the hell was going on?

Bridge shoved her head under the hard spray of tepid water and focused on one thing: an impending visit from someone higher up the chain of command. She couldn't wait to see who it was.

55

Good news: the intel from Mike Alessi, the FBI man, was accurate. The UK operation had been at an old paintball facility, and now several other Patrios training camps across the continent had been located in similar places and shut down.

Bad news: the few men willing to talk knew very little, and the ones who undoubtedly knew more – like Sanders, the former Para arrested at the Somerset camp – weren't talking, presumably fearing reprisals from whoever was behind Patrios. More of the one-time pads had been found at European camps, though. Those pads had all been properly maintained, their previous pages destroyed after use, but that didn't matter. Their presence was all the proof Giles needed to know that Bridge's strange theory about the Twitter account had proven correct, and he only required one full pad to decode whatever was being transmitted from the Hungarian base.

Giles closed the report summary file and stood at his office windows, watching the river below. It was another bright and chill morning, the Thames reflecting bursts of sunlight like winking stars in a cheap special effect. Nothing cheap about this corner office, though. It had taken him a good deal of time and work to get here, with the occasional helping hand from a friendly senior officer or valuable operative. Like Brigitte Sharp.

Bridge had been incommunicado since arriving in Hungary. They'd expected that, but Giles remained nervous. Many variables and unknowns were at play. They didn't know for sure if the Hungarian camp was the Patrios nerve centre; they didn't know exactly when the Patrios event was supposed to take place; while they had their suspicions, they didn't know for certain who was behind it; and they didn't even know for sure who or what Bridge might have found at the camp. Was it the same as the others they'd begun to shut down? Or, if Hungary was the epicentre, would it be something quite different?

The one thing Giles was confident of – which, ironically, made him less confident about the mission – was that women would be thin on the ground at these camps. So far they'd mostly been sausage-fests, a combination of young wannabe foot soldiers and a few senior figures to train them, all pumping with excess testosterone. Only a handful of women had been involved. He knew well that Bridge could hold her own; she'd once killed an experienced Russian thug with her more-or-less bare hands. But that was a single opponent. If her cover was blown, and twenty men decided she had to go…well, it wouldn't be pretty.

Deaths in the field never were.

Giles returned to his desk and opened his laptop. Andrea had distributed limited copies of the seized code pad to SIS and GCHQ, opting not to tell the Europeans they had what might be a full pad in their possession until they'd made some headway. There were many more tweets than used pages, which fitted with Bridge's theory that some were filler to obfuscate the real messages, like transmissions from an old numbers station. At present, though, they had no way to tell which were filler and which were real. Had MI5 missed a piece at the site, something that told the recipients when to look for real messages? Or was there something in the messages themselves to differentiate real from fake? Any such identifier would also have to be encoded, to maintain the deception. Finding it could take a while.

Still, no time like the present. He opened the file of photocopies, and typed the Twitter account's address into his web browser.

The account was empty.

Giles refreshed the page, assuming something had gone wrong with Vauxhall's internet connection – even intelligence services sometimes fell foul of the network – but to no avail. He clicked on another random account, and it filled with tweets. Back to *@ToTheFathers*; nothing. The account was still there, and it hadn't gone private. To do so would defeat the point of being able to access it without arousing suspicion; otherwise they might as well have used an encrypted messaging service like Telegram.

He frowned and stroked his beard, twitching his nostrils at the scent of hazelnut. Perhaps whoever ran the account had made that very switch, in response to the raids. But then why not use it from the start? Giles, Bridge, and everyone else assumed that if the tweets really were coded messages, they used this method to avoid incriminating the people reading them. Telegram messages themselves might be secret, but the mere fact of having them on your phone spoke volumes, especially under the murky legal standards of national security interests. So what were they playing at?

One more unknown, one more variable.

He still had the pad, and the used pages. Even if he'd lost the chance to monitor future messages, if he could decode those already sent then surely it must yield something of value. What he needed was a copy of the vanished tweets. He didn't know how to get that, but he employed several people who would.

* * *

The Cyber Threat Analytics office was two floors below his own, and Giles would normally summon them upstairs. But he knew they did their best brainstorming when they worked as a team. They were one down, with Bridge abroad, but hopefully it would suffice. He flung open the door (it crashed into the back of Monica's desk; he sometimes forgot how small the room was) and looked from her to Ciaran as they waited to hear what merited a visit from above.

'How do we get someone's tweets back?' Giles asked.

Monica exchanged a look with Ciaran and said, 'Be more specific.'

'The Twitter account that we think is linked to Patrios, @ToTheFathers. MI5 found a decoder pad at the UK camp they shut down, which we believe is for those tweets.'

'What makes you say that?' asked Ciaran.

'A number of things, not least of which is that the account's entire Twitter feed has since been deleted.'

Monica turned back to her screen and began typing. 'Deleted their feed, or their account…? Ah, here we are. So the account is still there, but no content.'

Ciaran laced his hands behind his head. 'Tricky. Wayback Machine doesn't record Twitter, and the Library of Congress stopped making full copies because the volume grew too much. Now they only preserve "historically significant" tweets.'

Giles took two steps across the small room and pulled Bridge's chair from under her desk. He sat in it, trying not to be distracted by the chaos of pens, paper, coffee mugs, chargers, and books threatening to bury her keyboard. 'Must be nice to know what will or won't be "historically significant" in advance.'

'It mostly means posts by US politicians and a few world leaders,' said Ciaran.

'Why am I not the least bit surprised?'

Monica continued typing. 'There are amateur efforts, too. People who keep copies of the full public feed, mainly in order to troll people by finding embarrassing old posts. The Nazis fucking love it; they dig up vaguely illiberal tweets politicians made ten years ago so they can get faux-outraged and bang on about hypocrisy.' She made a disappointed grunt. 'But Twitter's huge. Like, almost incomprehensibly huge. The sheer amount of storage you need is prohibitive, which is why even GCHQ doesn't keep a copy...' She scrolled a little, then made an even more annoyed noise.

'Problem?' said Giles.

'...And none of the amateur efforts are up to date. Maybe they finally realised they were spending a small fortune on storage for zero benefit.'

'No doubt a relief for politicians everywhere, but bad news for us, given the Patrios account was only created on New Year's Day. Double-edged sword.' Giles picked up Bridge's lightsaber pen from her desk and twirled it between his fingers. He'd often seen her use it in meetings with a note pad, in lieu of her laptop...

He sat upright, pen poised in the air.

Monica raised an eyebrow at him. 'Not a bad impression. Have you been practising, or is it something about that desk?'

'Bridge's laptop,' said Giles, ignoring her mockery. 'She said she'd "scraped" the Twitter account in order to analyse it. That's how she traced the location. I assume that means she has a copy?'

Ciaran nodded carefully. 'So long as she didn't erase it once she'd found what she was looking for. Where's her machine?'

Giles stood up, clapped his hands, and strode out of the office. 'I'll give you one guess.'

56

'The man in the container was *William Gow*,' said Henri Mourad. 'Or rather, Gao Weibo. Born in Harbin, north-east China. Two dozen aliases, but Gow appears to have been the most commonly used. Thirty-five years old.'

'And never to see thirty-six,' said Emily Dunston. 'Presumably he anglicised his name to sound like a second-gen immigrant?'

'Or an international businessman. Which he was, in a way.'

Henri had forwarded the identification file to Dunston as soon as it arrived in his own inbox. But she was old-fashioned enough to want to hear it from her officer, even as he knew she was clicking through the same information on her screen in Vauxhall.

'International fence and fixer,' she read aloud. 'No wonder Interpol has a file. What are your thoughts, Henri? Why would the SVR care enough about an art fence and occasional gun trafficker to torture him to death and then half-liquefy his body in a shipping container?'

'That's still the big unknown, and unfortunately there's nothing in Interpol's file to suggest a reason. Maybe the container isn't one of Moscow's? It wouldn't be the first time others adopted their methods.'

Dunston snorted. 'If you're going to try and convince me, you could at least sound like you believe it yourself.'

She was right. This had the SVR's metaphorical fingerprints all over it. But even if it hadn't and someone else was responsible, it didn't change the central question: *why*?

'You'll see on the index page that Gow was on the Interpol *Personnes Toujours Surveillées* list,' he said. 'I can request that from the local bureau and dig through it for anything likely. Do we have our own dossier on him?'

Henri heard typing as Dunston paused for a moment. 'Yes,' she said at last, 'and listed as a probable Beijing asset. Mind you, anyone with a criminal record and the wrong colour skin gets marked down these days.'

Henri knew that was true. A pitfall of SIS itself being full of spies, not to mention its troubled history of failing to recognise moles and double agents within its own ranks. Overcompensating by assuming *everyone* was a spook did a fine job of covering Vauxhall's collective backside, but was less effective at identifying genuine foreign state actors.

Dunston continued, 'In his case there's supporting intel. Gow seen in locations where we suspect Western secrets were sold to China; popping up in the same cities as known Beijing operatives; happening to be in town when a Chinese trade delegation comes to visit, and so on. It's no smoking gun, but it's not nothing.'

Henri agreed. Like all spies he was suspicious of coincidences, especially centred around a single person. The evidence was compelling, but... 'Even if it's all true, and he had a sideline as a government fixer, it doesn't tell us what Gow could have bought or sold that so offended Moscow they booked him a permanent stay in a specialist torture box.'

'That's for you to figure out, my boy. Grab a copy of our internal file and request his PTS from Interpol, citing me if you need to. Good luck.'

* * *

Henri appreciated the thought, but it wasn't luck that finally answered the question. It was old-fashioned hard work, hours spent digging into those Interpol records, as well as SIS' own archives, to see what connections he could turn up.

Gow's many arrests ranged from theft and fencing to transnational fraud, and while few charges had ever stuck (for a low-rent criminal, he apparently had no difficulty retaining high-rent lawyers) Interpol placed him on the surveillance list all the same, generating a global report of sightings, notable appearances, and contact with known criminals. It was a report as long as Gow's criminal career…until it suddenly stopped a little over six weeks ago. Henri, and the stench that still lingered in his nostrils, could guess the reason.

Most of it was standard criminal stuff. Gow seen meeting a suspected agent; spotted in the same city hosting an international arms fair; observed moving between five European countries in as many days soon after a high-profile art theft. Henri focused on more recent entries. During the pandemic Gow went to ground, like most crooks whose enterprises relied on social contact rather than smash-and-grab. But not entirely. His report contained a few entries from eastern Europe. That in itself wasn't surprising, as many of those countries' lockdowns and quarantine rules had been less stringent than in western Europe. In places such as Poland, Slovakia, and Azerbaijan, a man like Gow could continue to move around unobtrusively. Fortunately, not so much that he wasn't recognised by the occasional detective or national security officer.

Henri scanned the list for connections to Russia, or Gow meeting with people who'd made recent headlines, or even just meeting the same person twice…

It was gone midnight when he found it, but he called Dunston immediately.

57

Yuri finally reached the camp at two in the morning, after waking Eagle with a call from Gyor station. Well, he could hardly catch a cab. Eagle had no doubt silently cursed him a hundred ways, but had the good sense not to do it out loud. Yuri apologised for his late arrival, once only, to settle the matter. Eagle merely grunted in reply, saying nothing more during the drive into the forest.

So the camp was dark, and quiet, which suited Yuri. Eagle opened a small room in the command quarters, one that had remained unused until now, and secured it again behind them. Yuri retrieved a lockbox from behind the room's desk, opened it with a key in his possession, and placed the briefcase he'd been carrying inside it. Only then did he allow himself to relax. He hadn't even been in Paris with Kazhdan, but the events of that day had begun a ticking clock, its tightly-wound mainspring slowly uncoiling inside Yuri. He'd hoped for more days here at the camp, to plan and verify, but the ticking was now too urgent. There were final arrangements to make, and they would have to get it right first time.

As if there had ever been any other option.

'Some of the other camps have been shut down,' he said, sitting behind the desk.

The room contained no other chair, so Eagle leaned against the door. 'How many?'

'Three for sure, including the British camp. There may be others, but communication is obviously restricted.' It was an unfortunate side-effect of operational security; the same protocols which prevented captured Patrios soldiers from identifying men like Yuri and Eagle also meant they couldn't simply call each camp for a progress report.

'Do you want to bring the timeline forward?' asked Eagle.

Yuri shook his head. 'No, we're already short on time. But now we know we can move when ready.'

'What about the computer attack? You know I don't understand that side of things.'

'You make sure everything here is ready, and let me worry about the computers.'

'So you're not joining the strike team?'

'No. But do you really think I'd let any of you loose with this?' Yuri reached down and patted the lockbox. 'How are our would-be Führers?'

Eagle shrugged. 'They know one end of a gun from the other, and I think some of them will actually pull the trigger. It'll be enough.'

'You'd better hope so. We need casualties, here most of all.'

'Then let me put some real men in with them. They'll pop whatever heads you tell them to.'

Yuri shook his head. 'No. Think about it: when the shooting starts, these amateurs will shit themselves, but if they're all in it together they'll have to see it through. Not if they see your men step up and respond, though. Then the children will happily leave it to the professionals while they run away calling for mama.'

'The American might be the first to run anyway. He talks big, and he's good on the range, but ever since that business with the FBI agent he's looked sick. I thought he might fuck the woman and cheer up, but if he has she must be a terrible lay.'

'I don't care if he sits with his cock in his hand so long as he's there,' said Yuri. 'The Yanks are all toy soldiers, but what matters is they're painted red, white, and blue. We make sure word gets out that they're the ringleaders, we leak pictures of them with guns to the right people, and the rest does itself.' He looked out across the compound to the dorm block. 'Is everyone here really that useless?'

'A few can fight, and show potential. You should watch them do simulation tomorrow night; the good ones are easy to spot. A few of the locals, plus a Latvian who can kick the shit out of anyone. The French Nazi woman can handle herself, too.'

* * *

She certainly could, but it took Yuri all of the next evening to understand why.

The recruits performed a 'sweep and advance' exercise through the camp's fake houses under cover of darkness. Eagle had mounted night-vision cameras inside the houses, and monitored the live feeds from a room in the command quarters. Yuri watched over his shoulder.

Eagle's men were instructed to offer only token resistance. The point of these exercises wasn't to make the recruits better soldiers; they merely needed enough confidence to pull the trigger when required. Yuri observed that doing so had required making them *over*-confident, with an inflated sense of their own abilities, but so be it. It didn't matter if they came back. Not that there would be anything to come back to. On the night of the mission this camp would be broken down, cleared out, and burned to the ground – a scene repeated all over Europe while chaos reigned on the streets.

As Eagle had said, not all the recruits were hopeless cases. Some showed signs of training or experience and acquitted themselves well. The 'French Nazi' woman was a good example. Yuri didn't even see her at first; as tall as the men and wearing a mask, he'd never have known if Eagle hadn't pointed her out. She swept well, staying within the safety of her squad, letting the more reckless members go first. This included one man who foolishly kicked open a door in one house, then failed to duck and cover. Token resistance or not, the waiting 'hostile' couldn't pass up a chance to shoot him square in the chest. The woman waited for her squad mate to fall, then leaned out from behind the door and calmly shot the enemy. The eliminated recruit ripped off his mask in fury, and Eagle laughed. It was the American, and if he and the French woman were indeed sleeping together it hadn't stopped her using him as a human shield. Perhaps he wasn't sufficiently Aryan.

The odd thing was that she seemed to be holding back. It was plain to Yuri that she was capable, yet she was inconsistent and often hesitated. Was it a lack of confidence? A woman struggling to assert herself in a world dominated by men? Or something else?

'Tell me about her,' he said.

Eagle cocked his head. 'Élodie? Not much to tell. We found her on the internet pretending to be a middle-aged veteran, ex-*Armée de Terre*. You can understand why. She's a dropout, got involved with gangs, says Hitler's only problem was being ahead of his time. Same story as half the kids here.'

'Which gangs? Where?'

'Paris and Warsaw, I think she said. Does it matter?'

When the exercise was over, Eagle went to give the recruits their assessments and a pep talk. Make them think they were training for something important. Yuri watched from the command quarters doorway, keeping his distance. The recruits who hadn't been eliminated removed their masks and high-fived each other, laughing and swaggering as if they'd survived a day in Afghanistan. The woman joined in, joking around with them and playfully mocking the American whom she'd sacrificed like a pawn. It was then, somehow, that it happened. A flicker of expression, an angle of her face catching the evening light; some small thing that shook loose a memory, and Yuri knew they had a situation to deal with.

She'd changed her hair, and dressed very differently to the last time he'd seen her, but he was certain. 'Élodie the French Nazi', his dimpled Russian arse. That was Brigitte Sharp of SIS.

* * *

He also had a different name, now. When he first encountered Sharp he'd been called *Maxim*. Not long before the pandemic, both recently and a lifetime ago, as so many things now felt. He had chased her through the streets of Paris in a car and killed the journalist under her protection; then in Tallinn he'd shot her when her meddling forced him to eliminate his hacking team; and finally he almost fell into a clever trap she laid. But not quite.

It had been enough to make her a target, and Maxim prepared to task some Moscow grunts in London with finding out more about this Brigitte Sharp. Where she lived, her routine, the identity of her family and lovers. But then came Sasha Petrov's betrayal, which made all other matters irrelevant, and fast on its heels came the pandemic which prevented all but the most rudimentary activity.

Marooned in Belarus with his new name, Yuri had made a half-hearted attempt to research Sharp online, but her digital security was too good. He was more capable with computers than many of his colleagues, but he was no hacker. Without a dedicated group of teenagers ready to do his bidding Yuri had been unable to make progress, and so consigned Sharp to the back of his mind.

Instead he focused on Sasha Petrov. After releasing thousands of secret Kremlin documents into the wild the turncoat hacker had become Moscow's first priority, which made him *everyone's* first priority. Yuri began planning Red Admiral, and finally at new year he'd been able to put it into action. He couldn't wait to see Petrov's face when he realised his own scheme had been used against him.

All of which meant that when Ilya Kazhdan stood on a bridge in Zurich and said the British man had been followed by a woman, Yuri hadn't given it the attention he should have. These days many women worked in security and intelligence. Even the SVR now used them for more than merely honey pots and intel gathering. But that lack of attention was a mistake. Kazhdan wouldn't have known or recognised her, but if Yuri had asked for a description, 'a tall, dark-haired young woman shadowing a British traitor through Paris' would have set alarm bells ringing in his mind. They should have sounded anyway, and he cursed himself for a fool who now had a big mess to clean up.

Had Sharp infiltrated this camp because she knew he would bring the EMP device here? Unlikely. Only five people in the world besides Yuri knew that; two of them were Eagle and Dmitri, and the other three were Kremlin apparatchiks. But he couldn't accept the woman's arrival as a mere coincidence. Perhaps she was looking for the FBI man.

The presence of SIS in the camp wasn't itself a problem. Yuri had always assumed that some Patrios camps would be infiltrated by local intelligence officers, and Eagle wouldn't even have had to kill the FBI agent if he hadn't tried to communicate with his handlers. The shutdown of those other camps didn't bother Yuri much either, besides the encryption cock-up in England. In a way, arrests helped bolster the mythology. Let the governments of Europe waste time and energy chasing armed young fascists, missing the truth under their noses. It only required a few camps to slip through their fingers for the deception to succeed. When the dust settled they would be confused and bewildered, unable to understand what had truly happened and why. Certainly, none of the young recruits would be able to tell them.

Still, Brigitte Sharp concerned him. If it was only about infiltrating Patrios, surely SIS had people in eastern Europe, even native Hungarians, who would have been a better fit? Instead they had sent her all the way from England. She didn't appear to have recognised Yuri – he supposed his new beard was the match to her terrible new haircut – but it was only a matter of time. If her mind was like his, she would not forget the face of a man who had shot her at close range.

She couldn't possibly know where the device was, though. He'd only brought it to the camp the night before. That gave him time to deal with this unexpected problem before Sharp learned enough to pose a threat.

58

'Nice weather if you're an ice cream, I suppose. Or Scottish.'

Andrea laughed. 'And a squaddie, to boot. Anything above minus five is summer holidays for me.'

Giles fell in beside her, walking along the northern embankment past the Tate. Not a route he would have chosen, but being more or less halfway between Vauxhall and Thames House it sufficed in a pinch. His coat, scarf, and gloves were all woefully insufficient protection against the biting cold coming off the river.

'What's on your mind, Andrea?'

She frowned in thought. Giles knew her well enough to see that she was considering how to phrase something, and didn't press. Finally she said, 'Remember I mentioned I was caught in a power blackout recently, up in the Fens?' Giles nodded. 'Not long after, there was another blackout in East Kilbride.'

'Both rural areas. Not unusual, at first blush. But…?'

'Exactly. *But.* Something about it didn't sit right with me. I had our infrastructure analysts and GCHQ look into it. Had to go through a ton of paperwork to get National Grid records, but I did, and sent it to Sunny Patel. He called me back this morning.' Giles waited patiently as she built to the point. 'We're now certain they weren't accidents. They were cyber-attacks, hacking the software that controls substations. Somehow they activated a failsafe mechanism that knocked out power for several hours until it could be reset.'

She paused, and leaned on the wall to look out across the river as a brace of tourists walked by, loudly complaining about the cold. Giles shivered in sympathy. 'I assume you're telling me because you think the attacker was foreign.'

'Almost certainly Russian. They keep cropping up lately, don't they?'

'Indeed. I'll talk to Patel and see if the CTA can render some kind of defence against future attacks.'

'No, no, that's not it. Here, look.'

Andrea took out her phone and opened an email attachment. Giles saw a map of Europe. Black dots began appearing all over the map, expanding into circles of different sizes, many large enough to overlap. When the animation finished fully half the continent had turned black, and the hair on Giles' neck stood on end. He raised an eyebrow at Andrea. 'Explain.'

'The software those attacks targeted isn't some proprietary National Grid thing. It's a standard package, used in substations all over the continent.' She nodded at her screen, still displaying the blackened map. 'This is a simulation run by our infrastructure team to show the area blackout if all of those substations went down at exactly the same time. It's my understanding that a software virus attack could do exactly that.'

Giles nodded, already making connections in his mind. 'You think the two blackouts here were a dry run for a wider attack. But why?' No sooner had the question passed his lips than he knew the answer. 'Patrios. Steve Wicker's "simultaneous event", working in tandem with this.'

Andrea shrugged. 'I'll grant you there's no guarantee we're right, but it makes sense. On the one hand we have a group of fascist agitators recruiting and training young men to go forth and attack immigrants. On the other hand we have what appears to be hackers ready to plunge half the continent into a blackout.'

'Which, assuming they conduct the attacks at night, would make the Patrios soldiers' job both easier to carry out, and harder for security to monitor. No CCTV cameras, no streetlights, no public transport.'

Andrea snorted. 'I'll thank you not to call those wankers *soldiers*. Amateur white supremacists, more like.'

Giles grunted in assent and shivered again. 'Let's say they are indeed connected. We'll need to warn European security and formulate a cyber-response to harden the targets. That could take weeks, maybe months, to get through the red tape and install it everywhere.'

'Can't your pet geeks write their own virus to attack the first one? Fight fire with fire? Sharp's done that before.'

Giles exhaled, considering it. 'It's not something to be done lightly. Besides, Bridge isn't here.' He quickly explained the mission to Hungary to infiltrate Patrios.

Andrea swore and sucked her teeth. 'Pity you can't clone her. Did you see that the Twitter account's vanished, by the way? Now we can't even decode what they're planning.'

'I might have a solution to that. I'm due to make a call about it today...and you've given me an idea.' Giles smiled at Andrea's quizzical expression. 'We can't clone Bridge, but we may have the next best thing.'

* * *

'I can't authorise a joint operation like this without going up the chain,' said Edison Hill.

Giles could never get a handle on the Americans. One day they were happily trampling over rules and regulations, revelling in their elephantine power and daring anyone to stop them. The next they were walking on eggshells because the observance of some obscure procedural rule was apparently more important than getting the job done. 'I don't recall needing to wait for authorisation when Agent Dominic and Bridge worked together to kill that virus at the G8.'

'That was an emergency, with extenuating circumstances I could use to justify it to Langley.'

'I assure you this is no less an emergency. One in which, I'm sure I don't need to remind you, American citizens may be involved.'

Giles was glad this was an old-fashioned phone call rather than video. It meant Hill couldn't see his rolling eyes, and he in turn couldn't see the CIA officer's contempt. Paradoxically, it was somehow more honest than if they were maintaining poker faces on camera.

'That's low, Agent Finlay.'

'Put it down to extenuating circumstances.' Giles took a breath and relaxed his tone. 'You and I both know Bridge and Dominic are the best either of us have at this stuff, and if she were here I'd have set her to work already. But she's in theatre – a ball that your agency began rolling, remember – and if our theory about these blackouts is correct we are *all* in deep shit.'

Hill didn't respond, which Giles took as a good sign. Anything other than immediate outright refusal meant the American was thinking about it, and that meant he could be persuaded.

Finally Hill said, 'You really think this is connected to Patrios? They're going to cut the power all over Europe, then go on a killing spree?'

'I do, and so does MI5. We've already begun warning our European counterparts.' That was a lie; Hill was the first call Giles had made upon returning to his office. But letting the CIA believe it was the only agency not already in the loop was a gamble to get their buy-in. Nobody liked being last to the table, least of all America.

'How long will you need him for?'

'I honestly don't know. But that Patrios deadline we discussed previously is the end of this week.'

Hill thought for a while. 'All right. But I expect regular updates from both of you. Don't keep me in the dark.'

Giles grimaced. 'That's precisely what we're hoping to prevent.'

59

'Bridge told me the place was small, but...wow.'

'We can't all have the CIA's resources,' said Giles, closing the CTA office door behind them. He indicated Bridge's desk. 'I would say make yourself at home, but I assume she keeps her flat in a better state than her workspace.'

Karl smiled as he sat in her chair. 'Barely. So first of all, here's the laptop.' He pulled Bridge's HP out of his backpack, which had already passed through a security scan when he entered the SIS building, and handed it to Giles. 'I should warn you, I don't know what her password is.'

Ciaran looked up from his monitor. 'I thought you were practically married.'

'Gotta keep some secrets,' said Karl with a smile. 'Besides, this is work.'

'Our tech team have access anyway,' said Giles. 'Now, I want the three of you working on a response to this power station attack. Agent Dominic—'

'Oh, come on. Karl, please.'

'—Karl, I've briefed Ciaran and Monica. They'll bring you up to speed.'

Monica began typing, not looking up. 'We're building a worm to infect sub-stations and defend against attacks by another worm.'

'Oh, so like installing black ice.'

'Black what?' Giles asked.

'It's an acronym,' Karl explained, ticking off the letters on his fingers. '*Intrusion Countermeasures Electronics*. ICE. Comes from old cyberpunk sci-fi. It's the stuff that fries people's brains through the head jack when they hack into corporations.'

Giles stared at him for a moment, then shook his head. 'I can see why you and Bridge get along,' he said, turning to leave. 'I want updates twice daily, and at any significant milestones. In the meantime, I have tweets to decode.'

'Isn't that a job for GCHQ?' Monica suggested.

'Did they make an archive, too?' asked Karl. 'I saw the Twitter account's been emptied, but if you've figured out the cipher I guess you can at least decode past tweets.'

'Indeed,' said Giles, holding up Bridge's laptop. 'That's why we need this, it may be the only copy we have.'

Karl realised what Giles meant and shook his head. 'Oh, no. They're not on there.'

'Bloody hell,' said Giles in frustration. 'After all that, she deleted them?'

'No, you don't understand. They were never on her laptop. The script runs on a server, for twenty-four-seven uptime. You just need to log in.'

Ciaran looked at Karl in disbelief. 'You're running it on a public server.'

'OK, first of all, that server is absolutely secure and definitely not public,' said Karl, offended. 'But even if it was, so what? All the script does is archive publicly accessible tweets and metadata into a spreadsheet. It's not classified or sensitive.'

Giles all but threw Bridge's laptop down on her desk. 'This is my fault for not telling you why I wanted it in the first place,' he grumbled. 'Now come and log me in, or whatever you need to do so I can make a copy of that spreadsheet and begin decoding.'

'I still think you should hand it off to GHCQ,' said Monica.

'And I think you should focus on doing what I told you to, which is designing that anti-worm. Hop to it.'

Giles beckoned Karl to follow him upstairs. He told his assistant to allow only the highest priority interruptions, then sat at his desk, opened his own laptop, and moved aside. Karl didn't need telling twice; he launched a web browser, logged in to a server, and clicked through a couple of directories.

'You want a local copy to work from, right?'

'Correct. Best log me out from your server when you've done so.'

'Already done.' Karl pointed to a file on the desktop called *TTF_archive.xls*. 'There you go. Should be all good.'

Giles opened the file, mentally crossing his fingers. To his relief he was greeted by an Excel spreadsheet filled with the *@ToTheFathers* tweets, in chronological order, from the first to the last before the account was deleted. A 'notes' column contained extra data from each tweet, and near the bottom one entry also had a third column with the single word *HUNGARY!!!*

Giles became aware that Karl was not only still in the room, but watching over his shoulder. 'Don't you have a computer worm to be writing downstairs?'

'Oh. Sorry. But, uh, I don't know where...'

'My assistant will escort you.' He waved the American out of his office and returned to the spreadsheet.

It had been some time since Giles had decoded anything, let alone a one-time pad cipher, and it was true that he probably should have handed it to GCHQ. But he had a fondness for codes, and given its potential importance he didn't want to wait any longer than necessary.

Once again he took the photocopies of the one-time pad sheets, filled with number grids, from their folder. But this time he had something to compare them with. The difficult part would be working out which tweets were real messages, and which were nonsense 'filler'. He had no indication of what order the pad sheets had been in; one-time pads were simply used in sequence, from the first sheet to the last, so contained no page numbers or markings. He would have to 'brute-force it,' as Bridge might have said, by trying each sheet against each message until he came up with something that made sense. He shuffled through the photocopies, seeking inspiration—

Oh, of course.

The reason they believed this pad decoded the tweets was because the camp leader had written the account name at the top of one page. Surely therefore that was the pad's first sheet, which by definition must apply to the first genuine message.

Giles located the sheet in question, then scrolled to the very first tweet posted to the account. January 1st, 0800 hours CET:

```
LAND OF HOPE AND GLORY
NEVER TO BE SLAVES
66408726102204878
16611636666158410
81760216047699996
98452426655275963
31678602813496935
24266552759633167
86028134969356107
29596332133951796
56964998345629311
30163096284016047
```

Every post started with some form of reference to a national anthem or populist song. Those probably weren't part of the code; nothing on the pad sheets related to them, and using them in a form of encoding seemed impossible. If they were lines of gibberish he might have assumed they were *modulo-26*, a plain letter-exchange cipher. But no such method he was aware of could produce intelligible words, let alone pre-existing lyrics.

The numbers, then. Each sheet worked as a key to encode letters to numbers, and back again, in the same format as the grid in each tweet. Seventeen characters per each of ten lines: one hundred and seventy characters, which was plenty for coded instructions. That would be the maximum length it was possible to send using this method, but not the minimum. Shorter messages would fill any remaining space with zeroes, thereby ensuring the final encoded output was always the same length. This made it impossible to simply guess at the content of a message, or tell whether it was real or filler; as did the lack of spaces and punctuation in the numeric code, leaving no way to gain a head start by identifying single-character words like *I* or *a*.

As the coded output was numbers the cipher must be *modulo-10*, but that was only part of the solution. There were many different ways to turn twenty-six letters into the numbers 0-9. All Giles could do was pick a value system, try it out on several random tweets, and see if any of them made sense.

He started with the most basic key, where *A=01* and *Z=26*, and set to work.

* * *

When he looked up from his desk the light was fading outside, and his room was dark. He'd been working by the glow of the laptop screen, not realising his overhead lights were off. Giles removed his glasses, rubbed his eyes, stood up and stretched out his back, switched on the lights, then returned to his desk.

After the first simple value key found nothing he'd moved on to common 'checkerboard' keys, where the most common letters were encoded with a single number, leaving the remaining letters with two-number combinations. One of those, called the *AT-ONE-SIR* key, had proven out – using it in combination with the top sheet he was able to decode the fortieth tweet, sent two weeks after the account began.

```
WENN ES STETS ZU SCHUTZ UND TRUTZE
BRÜDERLICH ZUSAMMENHÄLT
PATER BE READY LOCAL RECRUITING BEGINS SOON
ALSO WELCOME AND FLATTER INCOMING US PATRIOTS
```

'Pater' was strange; an unusual anachronism that bore no relation to the rest of the phrase. But this was Operation *Patrios*, so perhaps odd synonyms for 'father' were the order of the day.

Giles was bothered by the implication that all of the tweets from the first two weeks were filler, but if you wanted to fool people you had to put in the effort. Or perhaps, he thought grimly, they were real but decoded with a completely different pad.

He didn't know the correct order for the remaining sheets of the pad he had, but now he'd identified the correct checkerboard key, things moved faster. He chose another used numbers sheet at random and worked through the later tweets, now able to tell within the first few characters if it was producing something readable. Soon enough he found a match, decoding a tweet from the week before last:

```
GLORIA A LA PATRIA
ALZAD LOS BRAZOS HIJOS
PATER ENGAGE ONLINE AND ENCOURAGE CIVILIAN
ATTACKS AS PROTOCOL MEANWHILE PREPARATIONS AND
```

This plain text was from the Franco-era lyrics to *La Marcha Real*, the Spanish national anthem. None of the song lyrics seemed significant beyond their obvious symbolism and nationalist appeal – in this case, extolling the glories of the fatherland during an era of brutal dictatorship. Whoever composed these tweets wasn't subtle.

The decoded message, though, suggested 'Pater' was a signal that a real message would follow. A clever modification. With a traditional numbers station, agents knew which messages were real because they listened to the radios on a pre-arranged schedule. The station transmitted regardless, but the agent only listened when they knew they'd receive a genuine message. With this Twitter account, that was unnecessary. The agents at each camp could look at it whenever they liked, and simply use the next sheet on the pad to decode the first letter of each new tweet. If that first letter was anything other than *P* they could stop immediately, knowing it was filler. But if it was a *P*, followed by an *A*, and so on they could decode and read the whole message, then destroy the cipher sheet. Once again he thanked his lucky stars that Sanders, the British camp leader, had skipped that final step.

Giles raced through the remaining code sheets. The account averaged one real message every two or three days and they confirmed what he, Andrea, and others had suspected. The deepfakes of the former president were designed to sow discord and rile up European racists. The American militia members who'd been paid to fly over were to be handed weapons and lead the local recruits in a wave of violence throughout the continent. Power would indeed be cut across Europe that night, allowing attackers to fight under cover of darkness. Finally, the 'T-minus' references confirmed a date: this coming Friday evening, as they'd suspected. It wasn't much time to prepare a response, but at least now they knew the deadline. Ciaran, Monica, and Karl would have several days to build their 'anti-worm'.

One thing the tweets lacked, though, was any clue to motivation. Part of it was surely to embarrass America and increase tension with the EU by involving US citizens in deadly attacks. But was that all? The encoded tweets, the one-time pads, the camps, the deepfakes, the funded flights... Could the people behind Patrios really be such faithful white supremacists that they would go to these lengths?

It was the kind of intel he'd ordinarily hope the Americans could supply via someone like Mike Alessi, as with the message about the paintball camps – which had in turn given them the one-time pad and allowed Giles to decode these messages.

How ironic, then, that the post with co-ordinates in the notes column – the one which had prompted Bridge to gamble on the Patrios HQ location, and took her to Hungary – was a real encoded message that explained why they'd heard nothing more from the embedded FBI agent...and why Bridge was in grave danger.

```
NÁŠ TATÍČKU MASARYKU
TY JSI NAŠE MOC A SÍLA
PATER FBI INFILTRATOR FOUND AT HQ BE ALERT FOR
OTHERS AND MAINTAIN SILENT PROTOCOL REMEMBER THEY
CANNOT SPEAK WHAT THEY DO NOT KNOW T-12
```

Giles picked up the phone and hoped Edison Hill was still in his office.

60

Until now, Eagle had been in charge. He'd led the exercises and ordered his own squad of veterans around. To what end, Bridge still wasn't sure; like those she'd overheard arguing with Eagle, she didn't understand why they needed the young recruits if they had the veteran squad. Eagle said the recruits 'had their part to play', but they were keen-eyed and fresh-faced young men, some little more than children. Bridge didn't know much about military operations, but she knew about manpower; the notorious Brook's Law, coined in the '70s, said adding more people to a project to speed up development actually slowed it down and caused delays. Surely the same applied here. Adding untrained amateurs to an attack squad was worse than just using a small but highly-trained unit.

Then Yuri arrived, and things began falling into place.

He was obviously the 'boss' Eagle had mentioned. Not a high-ranking soldier who barked orders, necessarily. Eagle hadn't even introduced him to the recruits. But as they'd set off for an evening sweep and advance exercise she saw them both talking at the command quarters, and Yuri carried himself like a man whose word was never to be questioned.

Casey was slowly coming out of his shell following their chat against the wall, and seeing Bridge's look he said, 'New guy looks like a professor. That beard sure ain't regulation.' He forced a laugh, and Bridge did likewise.

'Perhaps he is the one in charge, *oui? Le cerveau de l'opération.*' At Casey's blank look she translated, 'In English you say: *the man with the plan.*' His presence here, now, suggested they'd been right about the deadline for Operation Patrios; this coming Friday, which was the end of the period the Americans had been told to book as vacation.

But Casey was right. Despite his stocky build, Yuri looked less like a soldier and more like an academic...or a spy. The kind of man who pulled strings and issued orders, not the kind who strode onto the battlefield himself.

All of which preoccupied Bridge's mind during training. Luckily, by now the sweep-and-advance exercises were second nature, which itself bothered her. She had trained at the Loch under a military instructor, but her training hadn't involved anything like this. That she'd picked it up so easily, and could now almost sleepwalk through the houses, suggested things were intentionally dumbed down for the recruits. Again, the question: what was the point, besides inflating the young mens' egos?

The theory came to her while she kicked down a door, Casey covering from behind. The idea struck with such force that it made her hesitate, and the veteran waiting inside the room 'shot' her like a sitting duck. Casey took him down in retaliation, but Bridge was eliminated. She seized the opportunity to have a quiet cigarette outside and assemble her thoughts. Eagle had said the young recruits had their part to play; but he'd also said, '*and so do we,*' meaning his squad of veterans.

What if they were two different parts?

She replayed the overheard conversation in her mind, noting Eagle's insistence that the 'amateurs' wouldn't get in the way, that they had an important role to play despite their lack of experience and training – not to mention a lack of modern equipment. Was that because they were setting the recruits up for deliberate failure?

Perhaps their oh-so-important role was to be patsies, hung out to dry while Eagle, Dmitri, and the other veterans carried out the real mission on Yuri's orders. Wind up the recruits, point them at an immigrant community, let them attract the attention of the police and other authorities...while the real Operation Patrios happened elsewhere, unnoticed.

Bridge needed to know more, and Yuri's arrival presented her with an opportunity. After showering she threw on a coat and went outside, passing a few recruits smoking outside the dorm block. She ignored their whispers and walked around the command quarters to lean against its back wall, facing the trees, where she took out her own cigarettes and lighter. She'd made this a semi-regular smoking spot since arriving. Going it alone rather than smoking with the other recruits was in keeping with the chilly persona she'd adopted, and it gave her time to think.

The moment she lit up they'd smell it inside the building; a nearby window stood half-open. Instead she held a cigarette loose in her hand and listened to the voices inside, catching snatches of conversation. She recognised Eagle when he spoke.

'Going to be a blast...like the Mossad job...the hotel.'

The reply came from a voice she hadn't heard before in the camp: Russian, with a St Petersburg accent. Presumably the mysterious Yuri.

'Easier...won't...deal with CCTV.'

Bridge knew which 'job' they meant; the killing of Mahmoud Al-Mabhouh, a Hamas officer, in a Dubai hotel. Mossad hadn't been officially tied to the mission, least of all by Israel, but nobody seriously doubted they were behind it. The job was so successful nobody even knew it had happened until Al-Mabhouh was found dead the following morning.

It gave further weight to her suspicion that the recruits were being sent to shoot up immigrant communities and make a lot of attention-grabbing noise while Eagle and his men undertook a separate mission the recruits knew nothing about. An assassination, precise and clandestine.

'But you're…are you?' asked another voice she didn't recognise, fading in and out from a distance.

'No,' replied Yuri, 'I've got…delivery to make…out of there before…stop you.'

Were there *three* missions taking place, here? The recruits as distraction, Eagle leading a kill squad, and Yuri making some kind of delivery?

She heard approaching footsteps and quickly lit her cigarette, making plenty of noise with her lighter. She took her first drag and blew out a cloud of smoke as Casey turned the corner.

'There you are.'

She nodded in reply and continued smoking.

'What you doing?'

Bridge shrugged. 'Having a quiet smoke.' She turned to him and said, 'Not so quiet, any more. And you?'

It took him a moment to understand what she was asking. Then he said, 'I was wondering where you were. Curfew's in five minutes.'

Bridge checked her watch casually, but inside she admonished herself for losing track of time. Although breaking curfew felt in keeping with the Élodie persona.

A noise from the window made them both turn to look. She glimpsed disappearing white hair as Yuri pulled his head back inside, then heard quiet voices saying things she couldn't make out before someone closed the window. She shrugged and resumed smoking as if it was the most natural thing in the world, while Casey watched her expectantly. 'Are you my policeman, now?' she said. 'I'll be only one minute.'

Before Casey could answer, Eagle rounded the corner and

regarded them both.

'It is almost curfew,' he said. Bridge held up her cigarette in response, as if no civilised person would force her to abandon an unfinished smoke.

Casey took the opposite approach. 'I already told her,' he said to Eagle. 'That's why I'm here, I was trying to get her inside.'

'Do the wolves set alarms to come out of the forest and kill us all at one minute past?' she said to nobody in particular. 'Why do we need a fucking curfew anyway?'

Eagle put a hand on Casey's shoulder and said, 'Go on. I'll deal with her.' Casey gratefully scurried away. The veteran watched him go, then turned back to Bridge. 'You froze up during exercise this evening, Élodie. That's not like you.'

She responded by dropping her cigarette and grinding it under her heel. Then she lit another, to make a point.

'You're normally one of the best,' he continued. 'Something on your mind?'

Now or never, Bridge. She took the plunge. 'I just wonder why we bother? In the real world, these boys will run away from a baby with a water pistol. But you have five, six soldiers like you who can handle anything.' She shrugged. 'You don't need us.'

Eagle lowered his voice. 'They have their part to play. We all do. But...' He paused, considering something. Bridge tried not to let her anticipation show, despite noting that he referred to the recruits as *they*, not *you*. Finally he said, 'Maybe you deserve something more. Something special.'

For the first time she allowed real intrigue to show in her expression, as if excited by his proposal. 'Do I get to shoot a rifle that isn't forty years old?'

'Perhaps,' Eagle laughed. 'But not now, not here. Be ready tomorrow morning. Dmitri will explain.' He reached over and plucked the cigarette from her mouth. After taking a drag he extinguished it on the ground. 'Now, though: lights out.'

She returned to the dorm block, grabbed her backpack, and took it with her into the room's en suite. She brushed her teeth and changed into nightclothes, giving Casey time to lose interest, then ran her fingers over the backpack's lining to find the small, hard disc sewn inside. With the tap running to cover the sound she broke the seal, beginning the micro-exothermic reaction to power the GPS beacon's tiny battery. She hoped there was enough local cellular reception for it to broadcast. Whatever was happening here at the Hungarian camp seemed an order of magnitude more serious than they'd originally thought. Giles had said to use her best judgement, and to her mind the safest course of action was a security services raid to put Eagle, Yuri, and everyone else out of commission before the operation even began.

Bridge finished changing and returned to her bed. She missed being able to fall asleep to the quiet sounds of Radio 3, but the knife under her pillow was comfort enough.

61

Giles squinted at the glowing phone screen. Next to him, his wife Sam groaned and rolled away, disturbed by the buzzing but still asleep. He threw back the covers, stood, and left the room as quietly as he could before answering the secure call.

'Giles. Go ahead.'

'Sir, this is Ops.'

'I'm aware. Do you think I'd have answered at this time of night otherwise?'

'Sharp has activated her beacon.'

Giles swore quietly. 'Call me back in two minutes.' He ended the call and tiptoed back into the bedroom, where first he retrieved his glasses, then threw on a gown and slippers. He backed out again and headed downstairs to his study, closing the door to minimise noise. He waited for the call, considering what might have happened.

SIS had received no contact from Bridge since she landed in Hungary, which they'd expected. Andrea's discovery of a 'baffle box' at the UK camp had confirmed they were keeping a tight lid on comms signals. But Bridge hadn't set off the emergency GPS tracker as soon as she arrived. She'd waited several days, before now sending up a flare late at night. He thought back to the coded messages, and the deadline. It was now Tuesday evening, and the countdown confirmed whatever Patrios was planning would take place on Friday. Had the deadline changed, and the camp now posed an imminent danger? Or had Bridge activated the beacon because *she* was in imminent danger?

He answered his phone on the first ring. 'Where is it?'

'Heavily forested area north of Budapest, sir. I've already requested the most recent satellite observation of the position.'

'What was local time of activation?'

A pause while the Ops officer checked. 'Signal received at twenty-three-fifteen local. But it might have been activated earlier, if cellular reception in the area is sporadic. The device is low-powered by design.'

'Let's call it our assumed time, then. When do you expect the sat obs?'

'Arriving now, sir. Stand by.' He heard the officer muffle his headset microphone and have a brief conversation with a colleague. Giles caught snatches of words; they were discussing what the satellite photos looked like. A moment later the photos appeared on his own screen, and he studied them. One at day, one at night, taken three and four weeks prior according to their timestamps.

The night photo was useless. A couple of lights suggesting activity, but no detail. The day photo was clear, though. A cluster of buildings nestled deep in the forest, at the end of a single road that was barely visible even through bare winter branches. Two vehicles stood by the buildings.

'Another paintball camp?' Giles asked.

More muffled voices, then the officer returned loud and clear. 'That's correct, sir. Apparently closed down two years ago, and we can find no record of it re-opening. Photos do imply someone's there, though.'

'Which Bridge has now confirmed, and I'll wager those vehicles don't belong to their estate agent. Forward me the co-ordinates and whatever else we have on the location immediately. I'll put in a call to Budapest.'

He wasn't looking forward to this. László Kovács from TEK had been nothing but obstinate regarding Patrios, but Giles had to try. He found the number while waiting for Bridge's co-ordinates to arrive, then made the call. As Giles had expected, Kovács didn't share his sense of urgency.

'What crime has been committed here?' said the Hungarian. 'Occupying an abandoned camp in the middle of the forest? Hardly a threat to national security.'

Giles worked to keep the frustration out of his voice. 'The threat, as I've explained before, is Operation Patrios itself. There have been several raids on such camps throughout Europe already, and we believe danger is imminent.' He almost mentioned their belief it was Russian-backed, but Giles had met too many old warhorses from eastern Europe with an unhealthy nostalgia for the USSR. If they suspected Moscow was running things, they might turn a blind eye entirely.

'You believe, but you have no proof. This so-called operation is a fantasy. I know you think it's still bread lines and *babushkas* here, but no. Anyone driving around Hungary shooting people will find our police are better shots, not to mention better equipped. Besides, we expect many centimetres of snow this week.'

'That won't stop them if the targets are in urban areas, where snow ploughs have cleared the roads. I assure you, my officer wouldn't send up a flare like this without good reason.'

'Your officer should not even be here,' said Kovács angrily. 'You send one of your people to operate in sovereign Hungarian territory without informing us, then when he pisses his pants you want us to run and help? We are not your servants, Mr Finlay.'

'Of course not, but we are supposed to be colleagues and partners. Personally I care more about catching terrorists than protocol.'

'Then you should be grateful I do not care enough about this to call your ambassador. Collect your "officer" and return him to England immediately. Leave Hungary's security to Hungarians.'

'For God's sake, man, at least promise me you'll keep an eye on things. I can send you the exact co-ordinates.'

'We keep an eye on everything, Mr Finlay. And we are quite capable of doing it ourselves.' Kovács ended the call, leaving Giles seething helplessly at his phone.

When he returned to bed Sam murmured and rolled towards him in her sleep. He took her hand in his and stared at the ceiling.

62

The next morning came too soon. Bridge had barely slept, alternating between anticipating a security raid on the camp at any moment and wondering what Eagle had in store for her. If she could get an idea of what he and his fellow veterans were planning before the raid took place, it might be useful.

There had been no raid during the night, so she trudged bleary-eyed to breakfast with the other recruits, waiting for Eagle to say something. But she saw no sign of him until they'd finished and began filing back toward the dorm block. Then he and Dmitri walked out of the command quarters together, and Eagle beckoned Bridge to one side.

'Good morning,' he said. 'Today is the day, I think.'

He handed her a loaded Makarov, which she tucked into her waistband like an amateur. She glanced over at the recruits and saw Dmitri had pulled Casey aside for a similar one-on-one.

'Is Casey joining us?' she asked with genuine surprise.

'Dmitri will explain everything. Follow him, and do exactly as he says.'

The 'silent type' soldier finished talking to Casey and approached Bridge. With a nod, he walked into the forest and she followed, leaving everyone else at the camp.

'Where are we going?' she asked casually. Dmitri kept a good pace, staying ahead of her. This was the same direction in which she'd seen him take the other veterans when they entered the forest for their specialist training. She hadn't seen them leave that morning, though. Were they waiting for her? Or would they follow on later?

'Be patient, and you will see,' Dmitri replied. 'I was excited when Eagle asked me to bring you here.'

Something moved in Bridge's peripheral vision, but when she turned to look it was gone. Aside from the occasional cluster of evergreens most of the trees were bare, so she assumed the forest's hibernating wildlife would still be asleep. But any wildcats in the area would be active. The Makarov pressed into the small of her back was a cold, hard comfort.

They walked in silence for another five minutes, until Dmitri stopped at the edge of a clearing. 'You see?' he said, spreading his arms to present their destination. 'Special training area.'

Not special in terms of its facilities, that was for sure. A large natural clearing, with cheap folding tables propped against trees at its perimeter. Cut logs and fallen branches had been piled together to form a combined firing mark and low cover, while further downrange wooden posts stood ready to hold paper targets, as evidenced by splintered holes near their tops. A blue tarpaulin lay against a wide tree on the clearing's downrange side, covering something low. Surely vets like Dmitri and his men wouldn't risk leaving an ammo stash out here, would they?

Or perhaps they would, because the two most unusual and impressive features of the clearing suggested they were confident nobody else would visit.

First, they'd used cut logs to lay out a maze on the ground. No, not a maze – it was more like a building plan, with narrow corridors running between wide rooms. Dmitri and his veteran squad might come here for some light target practice, but surely this was its primary use; to practise a co-ordinated assault on a building. Which building? Impossible to say.

Besides, even the ad hoc layout was overshadowed by the single most unexpected thing in the clearing, something far more high-tech than any of the improvised equipment: an unmarked helicopter, standing alone to one side.

She remembered tattooed wings, visible under a jacket sleeve. Was this the real root of Eagle's nickname? Could he fly this thing? What the hell had she got herself into?

Another movement in the trees caught her peripheral attention. Again, the Makarov reassured her. But there was something about Dmitri's manner, and the timing of this invitation so soon after Yuri had arrived, and the way he now invited her to get comfortable at the firing mark before he'd even set up a target...

Eagle wouldn't have armed her if this wasn't on the level, would he? If they suspected something, they could have killed her at the camp. Nobody would run to the police; more likely the recruits would join in. She remembered Eagle and Yuri talking the night before. *Like the Mossad job...at the hotel. Nobody will even...until it's too late. Out of there before...stop you.* Then Eagle offering her a place on a special mission. She'd thought she had persuaded him to take her into his confidence. But had he already intended to? What was it about Yuri's arrival that—

Memory flooded Bridge's mind. Paris. Tallinn. He had been clean-shaven then, with shorter hair, but his eyes were haunted by that same perpetually sad look, above a wide Russian nose. *Maxim.*

At that moment Bridge became certain of several things. The Makarov she'd been given was a useless decoy loaded with blanks; Yuri/Maxim had recognised her at the camp; the movements she'd seen in the forest were not wildlife, but one of Dmitri's fellow veterans acting as backup; and he was 'excited' to bring her here so he could put a bullet through Bridge's skull. The only uncertainty was whether her death would come before or after rape and mutilation.

The decision was made, her body moving, almost before she'd consciously completed the thought. She turned, pulling out the Makarov, and covered the ground between herself and Dmitri in three long strides. He was turning too, his own instincts telling him something was wrong, reaching for his own firearm. But Bridge was a fraction ahead of him, perhaps because he'd expected her to hesitate. Hesitation and fractions were the difference between life and death.

She fired three shots into his face.

Even blanks could injure, sometimes kill, when fired up close. The shockwave from their explosive powder was powerful enough to crack bone at point-blank range. Bridge wasn't that close; waiting to make contact would have given Dmitri time to raise his own weapon. But she was only a metre away, and the rapid, loud reports startled and disorientated the veteran. Give him credit, thought Bridge – even when recoiling from the light and thunder blinding him, he didn't drop his own gun. But she'd expected that and kept moving, taking her Makarov by its barrel and pistol-whipping him in the side of the head. He fell to one knee, firing two blind shots at where his instincts told him she was standing.

Her ears rang as the shots whistled by her, already swinging a boot at Dmitri's face. She wasn't sure if it was teeth or nose, but something broke under the blow and he collapsed onto his back.

A third shot, and this time Dmitri fired so fast she didn't even see it. No, wait – it wasn't him. She'd forgotten about the backup soldier. Bridge threw herself to the ground, unable to tell the direction of the shot's origin. It was barely audible above her ringing ears anyway. Meanwhile Dmitri was recovering and still had his Beretta. One good shot from that would end it all, making her a forest feast for those wildcats. The absurd question of whether or not that was a fitting end for a vegetarian flashed through her mind as she scrabbled over cold dirt and leaves to reach Dmitri and climb on top of him, slamming the butt of the Makarov into his already-smashed face as she grabbed for his gun arm with the other.

He howled in pain, but Bridge barely heard it. She was on top of him partly because she assumed his backup in the trees wouldn't fire and risk hitting Dmitri if they were entangled. But mainly she had to get that damn gun away from him. She took his wrist in her hand and slammed it into the hard, frozen ground. The Beretta didn't budge, and while she had leverage in this position, she wouldn't stand a chance against him in a straight contest of strength. He was beating on her with his other fist, blow after blow against her kidneys, putting all his energy into both of his hands rather than waste any trying to move or throw Bridge off. She could have made things easier on herself by sitting up, though that would present whoever was hiding in the trees with a clear target. But Dmitri's backup man could be making an approach right now while Bridge was distracted. At any moment she might feel a bullet in her back, or even a knife if they wanted to keep it quiet.

Dmitri sensed her distraction and took advantage, changing aim and delivering a solid fist to the side of Bridge's head. She recoiled, sliding off him, and figured she had about five seconds before he shot her like a dog.

Or even a knife...

Even as the thought surfaced she dropped the useless Makarov, brought up her leg, and reached for it with her now-empty hand. Her fingertips closed around reassuring secret metal.

Bridge had kept her Swiss army knife within reach since that first night at the camp. It was just an eight-centimetre blade but she'd ground and honed it whenever the chance arose, taking it with her everywhere, slipping it inside her boot every morning in case one of the recruits tried something again.

Not, she thought with sudden clarity, that she could return to the camp after this. If she survived, only one course of action remained, and that was to get the hell away from here. One step at a time, though.

The first step was pulling the knife from her boot. The next was to once again do the unexpected. As soon as she had rolled off Dmitri he struggled upright, getting his feet under him to hold a steady aim and execute her. It was only natural that he'd expect her to retreat, to try and escape. Instead Bridge rose herself, uncoiling like a spring, ignoring the burning pain in her kidneys as she drove the knife into his abdomen.

Like the blank shots, it wouldn't kill him. But once again it was enough to shock and disorientate him. This time, instead of following through, she pulled back the blade to plunge it in twice, three times, four times. By then it was slick with blood and she lost her grip, but the damage was done. Dmitri fell to one knee, gasping with pain, and the Beretta finally slipped from his hand. Bridge pounced on it and shot him in the chest. When he collapsed to the ground she shot him again, in the face.

Staying low, she raised the pistol and scanned the trees for Dmitri's backup. Whoever it was had fired only one shot, but she daren't hope they'd retreated to the camp afterwards. If the execution order had come from Yuri, they would be under orders to finish the job.

As if to confirm her thoughts, another shot rang out. Dmitri's body jerked as the bullet hit his leg, inches from Bridge. She leapt for cover behind the nearest tree and scanned the forest, catching a glimpse of the backup, and nearly froze in surprise when she recognised Casey Lachlan. Of all the people to send, why him?

A backup was sensible – close quarters combat was a messy

business, as Dmitri's battered body showed, and things rarely went to plan. Here, the plan had been to shoot Bridge in the back of the head while she took position at the firing mark. She'd never even have known it, much less been able to somehow dodge or fight back. But she did, and now it was Casey's job to do what Dmitri had not. Did they think she wouldn't fight him?

She shivered, her body suddenly cold, and not only from fear. She looked up to see snow falling from the slate-grey sky. The cold, hard ground of the Hungarian forest was in no mood to melt it away.

On the bright side, now Bridge not only knew the truth but was armed with Dmitri's own gun. Casey must have seen that, so it would be a shootout. Staying low, ignoring the pain in her side, she ducked behind the nearest tree.

A movement further around the clearing. She raised the Beretta, but stopped herself before firing. The M9 had a capacity of fifteen rounds, but Dmitri might have practised on the range before coming out for a little morning execution. The only way to check was to eject the mag and count, and Bridge wasn't inclined to disarm her only weapon while someone was trying to kill her. The pain in her kidneys burned slow, flaring up when she moved too fast, and her ears still rang from the close shots. She'd have to rely on seeing Casey approach rather than hearing him, and falling snow would make that twice as difficult.

She chided herself for not recognising Yuri/Maxim earlier, despite the beard and longer hair. If he was behind Patrios, it all but confirmed her suspicion that the Hungarian camp recruits were a smokescreen, their planned attack a diversion from the *real* mission carried out by Eagle and his squad of veterans on Yuri's orders. What was that mission? Now wasn't the time to try and figure it out.

Bridge moved through the trees as stealthily as she could, trying not to follow Casey's route directly but keeping him in front of her. This was now a game of cat and mouse, except each of them simultaneously played both roles, neither knew the terrain, the snow blinded everything, and one of them was temporarily deaf.

She moved around the edge of the clearing, from trunk to bush to trunk, trying to watch both the trees across the open space and the woods behind her. Snow was now coming down thick and fast. The ground crunched underfoot, potentially giving away her position.

She drew level with the target posts. Still no sign of Casey or any shots fired. She moved behind a wide tree, looking around for better cover, but the area held nothing except the wooden stakes.

One of which exploded in splinters as a shot whistled past her, somehow passing between Bridge and the tree but hitting a target pole square in the high centre. Seeing the impact point so clearly meant the shot had originated behind her—

She pirouetted around the tree, putting its thick trunk between her and Casey as he ran at her. She stumbled over a tree root and lost her balance, falling heavily to the ground. The Beretta slipped from her hands, but as she scrabbled to retrieve it Bridge saw it wasn't a tree root she'd tripped on. It was the blue tarpaulin she'd seen earlier, and her fall had pulled the canvas aside to reveal what it covered.

The wide, dead eyes of FBI Special Agent Mike Alessi stared up at her.

She recognised him from the Flag Born photo, and now they knew why Alessi hadn't sent any further messages.

'Don't m—what the fuck? I said *don't move*! Drop the gun!' Casey stood over her, his pistol aimed directly at her but his attention distracted by Alessi's corpse.

'Did you know?' asked Bridge. 'Did you know he was here?' She didn't bother with the fake accent any more. They were well beyond that.

'They didn't even fucking bury him…' Casey whispered, staring at the body. Bridge couldn't get a handle on his reaction; surprised, horrified even, but not shocked. Then she understood.

'This is what's keeping you up at nights, isn't it? Did they make you watch? I know he was your friend.'

'Watch?' Casey echoed, his voice bitter. 'They didn't make me do anything, you idiot. I did it because – because…' His voice cracked, leaving him unable to finish.

I did it. The pieces fell into place and Bridge almost felt sorry for him, this wannabe soldier so far out of his depth. But regrets couldn't absolve him. 'It's not easy to take a life, Casey. Believe me, I know. Come with me, and I'll help you get through it. We can go together, right now.' She spoke softly, trying to reassure him. 'Neither of us belong here, you know that. This isn't our war.'

'You don't know shit!' he shouted, returning all his attention to Bridge. The gun wavered in his trembling hand. Even if he didn't plan to shoot her, he was boiling over with so much rage it might go off accidentally. 'You don't know me – you didn't know him – you don't – *fuuuuuck*!'

Casey screamed, and fired.

63

'You're asking the impossible,' said Maria Schmidt from the BfV. 'We can't cover every location. Our grid operators say there are hundreds of power substations running this software in northern Germany alone.'

Andrea sighed. 'Believe me, we're all in the same situation.' Once again she sat beside Giles on a joint call with the European security agencies to update them on her blackout theory, this time without their bosses watching over their shoulders. She continued, 'We're focusing on areas with significant communities of immigrants and refugees, which generally means cities and larger towns. I don't think any of us expect neo-fascist gangs to start roaming the streets of small villages.'

'Why not?' asked Tolbert irritably. 'There are many such places with foreigners.'

'Because this is about spectacle,' said Giles. 'Everything connected to Patrios so far has been an attention grab, to make headlines and get people talking. We see no reason this should be any different. In a blackout, maximum exposure requires eyewitnesses. If you want some of those witnesses to be journalists and reporters, that means the cities where they live and work.'

'We have already shut down two camps,' said García. 'We don't think there are any more.'

Andrea frowned. 'I wish I shared your confidence. But even without the camps, neo-fascists everywhere are emboldened.

Incidents here in the UK are up. They're not co-ordinated, but we know at least some have been fuelled and inspired by the Patrios movement. So let's not get complacent and call it job done because we rounded up a few young lads who don't know any better.'

'Any Americans among the arrested?' Giles asked García.

'Arrested? They did nothing illegal. We shut down the camps and sent them home. All Spanish and French.'

Giles pinched the bridge of his nose. So it wasn't just the Hungarians who saw things that way. 'I'm sure that will be a great comfort to the people they turn on back home.'

'We found three Americans at a camp outside Gdansk,' said Dabrowski from Poland. 'We worked with the US embassy to hasten their return flights. The ambassador was very co-operative.'

'I bet he was,' said Andrea. 'Even with the current climate in the US, they won't be keen on headlines of Americans being detained alongside European fascist groups.'

Rossi from Italy shrugged. 'But my Spanish friend is right. At this moment, these people have committed no crime. We cannot detain people for target practice.'

'Don't any of you people have anti-hate laws?' said Giles. 'The rhetoric alone should be enough to get them twenty-four hours in a cell, which might make them think twice.'

'Or it might, as you say, embolden them,' said Kovács from Hungary. Giles had the distinct impression he, and some of their other counterparts, wilfully refused to acknowledge the danger. Or perhaps they simply didn't care if the only people in danger were immigrants.

'We're getting rather off track,' he said. 'All of you, please, ask your infrastructure people to watch for unusual activity on the grid and be ready to implement emergency measures. At this time, with such limited short notice, there's nothing more we can do.'

Andrea glanced at him and raised an eyebrow. Giles responded with a tiny cautionary shake of the head, small enough for her alone to see and understand.

'The good news,' she said, turning back to the video screen, 'is that the attacks seem to be a relatively simple fix. The tripped relay is easy to replace, so if your utility staff are standing by, these blackouts could potentially be short-lived and Patrios-related activity could be minimised.'

The meeting went on for another twenty minutes, but Giles' mind was already on other matters. When it was over, after the agency representatives all signed off, Andrea turned to him.

'You don't think we should have told them your people are working on a cyber solution?'

'Absolutely not. What the CTA's proposing is effectively another worm to eat the attacking worm. Pragmatic as they may be, I doubt any of our friends will be thrilled to learn that our solution to Russia infecting their system is for us to do it instead.'

Andrea smiled. 'Some of them might even think that's worse.' She checked her watch. 'SCAR next, right?'

Before he could answer, a knock at the door preceded Devon Chisholme's appearance. Giles frowned. 'Devon, the *In Use* light is on.'

'Oh, I thought you'd started without me.'

'Perish the thought.' While Chisholme found a seat, Giles pulled the room keyboard towards him and set up a new secure call with Edison Hill and Steve Wicker. This was going to be a very long day.

* * *

Giles Finlay had been at SIS for many years before he recruited Brigitte Sharp. He'd run countless missions during that time, and continued to oversee many in which she wasn't involved at all. He'd attended hundreds of meetings at which she wasn't present, including CTA meetings, and even SCAR committees back when he'd been working overtime to get the unit set up. He didn't normally think twice about her absence. Today, he did.

Today he reflected on how this meeting was perhaps the first true demonstration of why they'd argued for the committee's formation. Some years back, Bridge and the CTA had foiled a terrorist attack in central London that could have killed hundreds, including members of Parliament, senior civil servants, and high-ranking military officers. The attack had its roots in cyber-espionage – which, even now, Giles still struggled to convince C and the upper floors merited better funding – and his team had prevented the attack only by the skin of their teeth. During the inevitable debriefs and post-mortem analyses, it became abundantly clear they would have had skin to spare if many branches of government and security had been more open with one another. A 'joined-up task force' had been an idea on Giles' mind for some time, so he seized the chance to make it real. He knew his reputation in these corridors, what they said about him in not-so-subtle whispers. *Overly ambitious, control freak, power hungry.* He made no apologies. Intelligence work was no place for the lackadaisical, which was why he put Bridge through the wringer every now and then; he had to know he could rely on her, so gave her the occasional jab to make her prove herself and bolster her self-confidence.

Today, he wondered if he'd gone too far.

'Bridge not here?' asked Steve Wicker from the split video screen.

'All in good time,' Giles said. 'Thank you all for attending at short notice. First, an update on Operation Patrios. Two weeks ago parties unknown created so-called deepfake videos of the former president, encouraging Americans to travel to Europe to participate in a coming race war. Simultaneously, someone using the Patrios name financed right-wing militia groups in the US to do precisely that.'

'Langley is still trying to trace those payments,' said Hill, 'but the holding company belongs to a holding company, belongs to a holding company, and they're all registered in tax havens.'

Giles nodded. 'I think we can lay that one to rest in a different way, and that brings me to my absent officer. I disapproved of the CIA persuading Bridge to infiltrate the online fascist communities in the first place—'

'Now hold on,' Hill interrupted. 'She wasn't doing anything classified, and besides, the results were worth it.'

Giles nodded. 'Which brings me to my point. Much as I disapproved, it may turn out to be what saves us. At this very moment Brigitte Sharp is inside a Patrios camp somewhere in Hungary. She identified that camp as the source of the *@ToTheFathers* Twitter account, which, as you know, we suspected of sending coded instructions to Patrios leaders. That has since been confirmed, thanks to an encryption pad found at the camp in Somerset. I've decoded the messages and they point to an attack occurring this Friday, facilitated by cyber-attacks on power stations that will black out large areas of Europe.' He looked to Steve Wicker. 'There's your *simultaneous event*, Steve. We've informed our counterpart European agencies, and while a frustrating number refuse to take the threat seriously, we're working on our own solution to counter the cyber-attacks. Karl Dominic of the CIA is collaborating with my CTA team to put that into action. Meanwhile, last night, Bridge activated an emergency tracking beacon, giving us the co-ordinates of a former paintball camp north of Budapest which appears to have been commandeered by Patrios.'

'When's the raid scheduled?' asked Hill.

'Unfortunately, the Hungarians are one of the agencies not taking this seriously. They say the camp isn't illegal, and refuse to move in. Does the CIA have any officers on the ground in Hungary?'

'Don't you have your own?'

Giles shrugged. 'One man counting the days till retirement, I'm afraid.'

'One man more than us,' said Hill. 'Our closest Delta squad is embedded in Kyiv. I could redirect them, but it would take twenty-four hours minimum to reach Budapest, and then what? We have no jurisdiction.'

'Since when has that bothered the CIA?' said Andrea, only a smidgen too harshly in Giles' opinion.

'I'll pretend I didn't hear that. I won't authorise an armed assault on a camp of people who technically haven't committed any crimes.'

'And who themselves are armed and indoctrinated, remember,' said Steve. 'It'd be another Waco.'

Hill nodded. 'Exactly. If shit like that's going down, it has to be led by domestic authorities.'

Giles pinched the bridge of his nose. 'Could you at least point an NSA satellite at the area for real-time observation? Bridge wouldn't have sounded the alarm without good reason.'

'I'll make a request, but otherwise it's down to Sharp. That's the job.'

A silence fell across the room. Callous as it was, they knew Hill was right. Bridge would, too.

Giles cleared his throat. 'Moving on: the main reason I called this meeting. As you'll recall, it was also two weeks ago that Simon Kennedy attempted to sell the plans for our new EMP device to Boštjan Majer.' He nodded at Chisholme. 'Instead, the meeting was intercepted and both men were killed, we believe by known SVR operator Ilya Kazhdan. He was seen in Zurich soon after, where we further believe he passed the plans to a contact before dropping off radar.'

Chisholme leaned back in his chair. 'As you say, this is old news. Presumably you have an update?'

Giles tapped the room's computer keyboard, and a slideshow of images appeared on the screen. The first was an open shipping container surrounded by port security, *gendarmes*, and forensic examiners.

'Marseille port, last week. Be warned, the next few are pretty grisly.' He tapped to advance and heard several groans at the images of a half-corroded corpse inside the container, still strapped to a blackened, twisted chair. 'As you may be aware, shipping containers are the *en vogue* location for mobile torture rooms, and particularly favoured by Russia. Our man was present when the locals found this one, and thanks to Interpol we now know who the unfortunate victim was. Not that he was an innocent soul – far from it – but I think we can all agree very few people deserve such a fate.' A murmur of assent rippled around the room.

'So who was he?' asked Andrea.

Giles tapped the keyboard in response, and the gory photos were mercifully replaced by an Interpol file. 'William Gow, real name Gao Weibo. Ring any bells?' Everyone shook their heads. 'No reason he should; he mostly operated on the continent. Fixer and fence, long suspected of being a Beijing plant. Disappeared seven weeks ago.'

Andrea squinted at the screen. 'Says there he's on Interpol's PTS list. So if nobody sighted him for seven weeks...'

'We assume that's how long he was in the container,' Giles nodded. 'It was apparently pre-booked on a two-year world tour, going from port to port.' He glanced up at Edison Hill. 'And paid for by another untraceable shell within a shell within a shell.'

'That's not a connection,' said Hill. 'Pretty much standard MO.'

'Indeed, but now look at this.' Giles tapped again, to show records from Gow's Interpol file. 'Several sightings were made during the pandemic in eastern countries. They include two in Slovakia, and one each in Poland and Hungary, where he made contact with the same individual. An individual with his own surveillance record, as it happens.' Never afraid of a little dramatic flair, Giles paused for a moment, enjoying their collective anticipation. 'Boštjan Majer.'

Everyone exhaled. 'Our EMP-buying fence,' said Chisholme, leaning forward. 'Surely that's no coincidence.'

'Gow met with Majer four times in two months, not long after lockdown conditions spread across the world,' said Giles. 'Gow later vanished into thin air, presumably for ten rounds of torture Moscow style, while six weeks later Majer was killed by a known Russian officer as he attempted to buy our stolen EMP plans. Plans which appear to have subsequently been handed off in Zurich.'

Steve Wicker whistled. 'What the fuck is going on?'

'We still don't know,' Giles admitted. 'I can't help feeling that we're missing a piece of the puzzle. But if this isn't all connected somehow I'll eat my desk.'

64

As the snow eased off, Bridge located the low sun behind clouds and picked a direction. The Twitter co-ordinates located the camp north of Budapest, and Dmitri had led her even further north from the camp. That placed it directly between her and safety, and she couldn't risk skirting too close. Instead she chose east and set off at a steady pace.

Casey had missed. At first she could hardly believe it; they were less than two metres apart. But then she'd seen the frustration, anguish, and relived trauma on his face, and realised he'd missed on purpose because he couldn't face killing again. He was the one who'd shot Mike Alessi, after the FBI infiltrator's cover was blown. It explained so much about Casey's behaviour, and his reaction on seeing the body. The brief message Alessi had sent must have been all he could manage before being caught. It could well have been *why* he was caught.

'Go!' Casey had screamed at her. 'Just go.'

Bridge considered fighting him for the Beretta, even turning it on him. He was in such a state her chances were fifty-fifty. But why look a gift horse in the mouth? So instead she became a ghost in the snow, running into the forest without looking back.

According to her watch, that had been an hour ago. She wondered if Casey had returned to the camp by now, and what he'd tell Yuri and Eagle. Would they have time to do anything before local security raided the place in response to the GPS beacon?

She couldn't think about that at the moment. She had to focus on moving, staying warm, staying alive, and somehow reaching the British embassy. She needed to find a town or village, hope to hell someone there spoke either English or French, and persuade them to take her to Budapest without attracting the attention of the police or Yuri.

Oh, is that all? Sure, Bridge, no problem. Christ.

Trudging through virgin snow and surrounded by silence, she imagined wandering out here for days, unable to find a road, dying of hypothermia long before starvation got her. She'd studied this region a little after cracking the geolocation tweet, but hadn't been able to bring any kind of map with her to Hungary. What she remembered suggested it might be possible to walk for days in these hills without encountering civilisation. Would her body be found? Would they even look for her?

Stop it, Bridge. Absolutely zero help thinking like that. But what was she to think of instead? Fluffy bunnies and prancing ponies? That had never been her, not even when she was a child. And who was she now, this woman who turned to violence not as a last resort but as a first option? She remembered her fantasy in the Metro, wanting to hurt those racist idiots.

No. She shook her head. She wasn't like Dmitri, or even Yuri. Oh, she could take care of herself. It was why she'd taken up karate all those years ago, to defend against the bullies at her new English school. That was an indelible part of her that couldn't be erased even if she wanted to. But every instructor she'd had, from her first *sensei* to her last, from Sgt Major Hard Man to the kickboxing instructor at her gym, preached the same mantra: *the best way to win a fight is not to have one.* Violence as a last resort, when all other avenues – including walking away – had failed. Some practitioners, mostly young men, interpreted the mantra to mean they were living weapons, whose awesome power was a danger to everyone should it be unleashed. But that was a childish delusion. The instructors' point was that fights were unpredictable. When a confrontation turned to violence – real violence, unconcerned by rules, regulations, and referees – nobody could truly know the outcome. All the black belts in Japan wouldn't heal a broken bottle to the neck, or dry a slippery floor, or defend against an unseen second attacker in the forest—

She retched, doubling over. Her grasping hand found a tree and held her upright as her body acted reflexively, dry heaving spittle on the snow-covered ground. It was like the adrenaline leaving her body was taking the shortest route out, while the comedown insistently replayed events in her mind. A yawning, endless falling sensation, fully understanding her actions without the shield of a survival instinct to hide behind.

Bridge had pulled the trigger first.

Yes, they were blanks. Yes, the ensuing fight with Dmitri had proven her instincts correct, and if she hadn't pulled that trigger she'd be lying dead instead of him. But what did it say about her that she hadn't hesitated or waited for confirmation? To escape the predictability of execution she'd risked the unpredictability of violence, and it was like crossing a Rubicon.

She stopped, listening. Was that the sound of a helicopter? No, it was a trick of her still-damaged hearing. But the sun rode high in the sky now, and anyone flying overhead would see her easily.

She pressed on through the snow.

65

'She got away,' said the American. 'She killed Dmitri, took his gun, shot at me, and ran into the forest.'

Yuri leaned back in his chair and regarded Casey. Eagle stood in the doorway behind him, red-faced with anger.

'You were Dmitri's backup,' said Eagle. 'She was unarmed, for fuck's sake.'

Casey stared at the ground, obviously embarrassed. Yuri was tempted to shoot him there and then – as he should have done with Brigitte Sharp the moment he recognised her – but the American was still useful, and would play his part.

Eagle turned to Yuri. 'You said she was a computer geek, not a fucking soldier.'

'I also said she was British intelligence. But blame is pointless now.' He fixed Casey with a serious look. 'Tell nobody of this. If anyone asks, Dmitri and Élodie are conducting a secret operation, and that is all you know. Understand?' The American nodded. 'Good. Leave us.' Eagle looked ready to protest, but Yuri silenced him with a glance and the Romanian stood aside to let Casey stumble back to the dorm block. 'So much for your killer American.'

Eagle shook his head in disbelief. 'He shot his countryman right in front of me. He's been moody ever since, so I thought this would get his confidence back.'

'Maybe in future leave the armchair psychology to me. I don't believe he even tried to stop her escaping.' Yuri checked his watch. 'She will have immediately begun walking to find a town or road. We must assume she's already sounded an alarm.'

'Impossible,' said Eagle. 'Her phone and belongings are still here. I'll take the chopper up, locate her, and the team can move in to eliminate her before she gets any further.'

'No!' Yuri slapped his open hand on the desk, making Eagle flinch. He knew these men wouldn't be physically intimidated by him, but they were still soldiers at heart. Take control, show authority, give orders. Some things never changed. 'We still have the advantage. Sharp thinks the recruits are the main attraction, and that's what she'll tell London.'

Eagle seethed in silence.

Yuri considered their options, then opened his laptop. 'We go tonight. Prepare to burn down the camp. I will send the message.'

'Tonight? Impossible. Everything is arranged for Friday. My police contact has already paid bribes.'

Yuri unlocked a drawer in his desk and removed two bricks of plastic-wrapped banknotes. 'Then it is Christmas again for them,' he said, tossing the cash to Eagle. 'All government officials claim you ask the impossible until you pay them. Use however much it takes.'

Eagle surreptitiously peered at the drawer. Yuri caught the look and pulled it open to show more bricks of cash, identically stacked and wrapped, along with a pistol and ammunition cartridges. He gestured at the contents, as if presenting them on a game show, and locked eyes with the Romanian. 'Yes, Eagle. I have no doubt you could overpower me, take the key, and steal all this cash. There's maybe enough here to buy, what, half a Ferrari? Or you could do what you were hired to do, and wake up next week with enough in your Swiss account to buy ten Ferraris and a whore who'll pretend she's impressed by them.' He slammed the drawer shut and locked it. 'Do you want to avenge your fallen comrade? Then do the job, get paid, and raise a drink to him from a beach in Venezuela.'

Eagle turned to go, then turned back again. 'You recognised the woman. Did she recognise you?'

'No. I looked very different then. Now get out and make the necessary arrangements.' Eagle nodded and left. Yuri leaned back in the chair and exhaled heavily. He'd told the veteran what he wanted and needed to hear, but he had lied twice.

First, Sharp's escape troubled him. Of all the Patrios camps across Europe, this was the one that truly mattered. Red Admiral, and the manufactured confusion around it to distract the authorities and misdirect their attention away from the truth, relied on everything here running smoothly. Now, because of her, he must speed up the clock. Was it possible she knew the truth after all? He couldn't imagine how, but he wouldn't underestimate her again. The next chance he got, he would kill her without warning.

Second, despite what he told Eagle, Yuri assumed Sharp had indeed recognised him. How else could she have escaped execution? She was tougher than she looked, but dodging bullets and overpowering Dmitri was beyond any woman. If she'd anticipated it and surprised him, though... Yuri should have blown her brains out as soon as he recognised her. It would have required some explanation to the other recruits, but now so did Dmitri's sudden disappearance. At least a public execution would have kept the morons in line. He could have told them she was an undercover policewoman.

Not that they had anything to fear from the local police, thanks to the large bribes Eagle was paying out. But the recruits didn't know that, and Yuri had no intention of telling them. Better they maintain an air of rebellion against the state, of insurrection and patriotism in the face of jackboots. Never mind that given the chance every recruit would pull on those same boots, pin a badge to their chest, and use them as licence to grind an immigrant's face into the dirt – all while whining that they were being oppressed.

Tonight, though, they would be rebels. With the camp all-male again it would be easy to transform them into a mob. Take control, show authority, give orders. Some things never changed.

Yuri unlocked his computer and prepared to send a message.

66

'There's been another tweet.'

Giles looked up from his desk as Ciaran burst in, breathless. Then he returned to his laptop and quickly navigated to Twitter. He didn't need to ask what Ciaran was talking about.

@ToTheFathers
11:00 AM March 2

CROWN THY GOOD WITH BROTHERHOOD
FROM SEA TO SHINING SEA
17414724592531064
00186396188176711
99949732800188581
74761042216202672
96986227841639899
73099416775521177
18167037738353538
89551780977573822
38507683565067960
07105627848183688

Posted via Twitter on the web

'Close the door and sit,' he said, taking a screen grab of the tweet in case this one suddenly vanished like its predecessors. He switched on the wall-mounted flatscreen and shared his desktop to it so they could easily read the encoded message.

'That's *America the Beautiful*,' said Ciaran, the sofa creaking as he sat down. 'Unofficial national anthem of the US. Weren't the others all European songs?'

Giles nodded, pulling the one-time pad photocopies from their folder on his desk. 'They were, but we now believe all this business with the presidential deepfakes and flying Americans over is to scapegoat them and turn the EU against the USA.'

'Don't think they need much prompting,' Ciaran snorted.

'This is the first tweet since they deleted them all, yes? So let's try the first unused sheet of the pad and assume they're using the same value key. First digit, *one...*' Giles roughed out the key and decoded the first digit. It was a *P*. 'Encouraging,' he said. 'Read the next four digits for me.'

Ciaran did, and Giles noted each down, converting and calculating them into letters. 'Is it real?' asked Ciaran.

'I should bloody well coco,' said Giles, holding up his jotter pad to reveal the word *PATER*. 'Continue.'

Ciaran did, reading the digits from the large screen while Giles decoded them using the number grid. Eventually he said, 'Stop. The last half-dozen digits have all been zeroes, which means end of message. It's a short one.'

'What does it say?'

Giles frowned. 'That we have less time than we thought.'

PATER COMMENCE OPERATION TONIGHT
FOR THE FATHERS

***

'We've hardly begun basic bug tests,' Karl protested. 'You said we had until Friday.' Monica nodded in agreement.

Giles held up the decoded message so they could both read it. '*Shit happens*, isn't that what your lot always say? Well, this is the shit, and here it is, happening.'

'Fuck.' Monica turned back to her computer and began typing fast. 'Fuck fuck fuck. How long do you think we've got?'

'That rather depends on how quickly their attack inflicts damage.'

Karl shrugged. 'We think it's pretty instant. It doesn't appear to be all that sophisticated. The worm hits the system, it sends a false signal out across the wires, and boom. From someone hitting *go* to a relay tripping takes ten seconds, tops.'

'So we might still have time,' said Ciaran. 'Didn't the prior tweets indicate the attacks would begin late in the evening? Prime nightlife time, like?'

'They did,' Giles agreed, 'but they were also, as has been said, planned for Friday. All they really need to begin is the cover of night.' He checked his watch. 'Central Europe will go dark in a little over two hours. Next question: how long will *our* worm take to deploy?'

'A couple of minutes,' said Karl. 'We're using a stack buffer overflow to trigger a shellcode injection and target the resource files.'

'Fascinating. Do whatever you need to make it ready and send it at least thirty minutes before sunset in Paris. I'll inform everyone it's happening.' He made for the door, but stopped when Monica spoke up.

'Giles…' She took a deep breath. 'If they deleted the old tweets because they know we've got a decoder pad, maybe they sent this one expecting us to decode it, too. What if it's disinformation?'

Giles nodded. 'I had the same thought, but we have little choice. If we assume this is a bluff and get it wrong, the cost could be disastrous.'

'It could be disastrous anyway,' said Monica. 'You do understand that if this goes arse-up we might take down Europe's power grid even before the attacking worm is released? God, I wish Bridge was here to do this. No offence,' she added to Karl.

'Oh, I'm right there with you.' The American turned to Giles. 'Monica's right. The cure could be worse than the disease.'

Giles had been aware of that since he asked Karl to help them. But it was important to show confidence. There'd be time enough later for regrets and buck-passing.

'If that happens, we can always fall back on blaming Moscow,' he said with a half-smile. 'But try to make sure it doesn't.'

67

It was a half-surfaced track of cracked tarmac, weather damage, and deep ruts. To Bridge it was the yellow brick road. She'd been walking for hours, picking her way through undergrowth and fallen branches, staying alert for pursuers, her body temperature stubbornly dropping, wondering if she might have to spend the night among the trees and whether she'd survive if she did. She hadn't travelled much in this part of the world, but she'd spent enough of her youth obsessed with gothic tales to know the legends of endless Transylvanian forests had plenty of truth behind them.

But here was a road, and no matter how poorly made, that it was made at all was enough. Roads came from places, places with people, and anywhere with normal people was the safest place she could be right now. She followed it down into a valley.

Relieved as she was, Bridge only relaxed a little. Yuri and his men might still be searching for her, and this road might wind through the forest for miles before reaching civilisation. The sun was low in the sky, and night would soon fall. But a part of her mind could now consider the wider implications of what she'd seen and heard at the camp, and the secret training area in the forest.

Bridge was sure now that the recruits were a distraction, a decoy to draw attention away from the real mission carried out by Eagle and his veteran squad. A kill squad, judging by the reference to the Dubai hotel hit. An assassination inside a building, the one mapped out with logs in the clearing. If it also involved the helicopter, surely they weren't going for subtlety. Perhaps they wouldn't need to; if she'd heard right, Yuri had implied it would be easier because they wouldn't have to deal with CCTV. So it was somewhere that normally *would* have security cameras, but they'd be deactivated.

Was that Yuri's job? He was a technical specialist, a man who set up hacking workshops on Moscow's behalf. The deepfakes and coded Twitter messages felt like him, as did disabling CCTV. But not storming a building to kill a target. Then again, hadn't he also said he'd be making a 'delivery'?

Her thoughts were interrupted by a winking light in the trees. The sun was low enough that anyone walking through the forest would use a flashlight. Had Eagle found her?

No. It was stationary, the strobing effect made by tree branches between Bridge and the light as she walked. She saw another, then another, and finally understood she was looking at a village below her in the valley. Lights. Houses. Civilisation. Maybe a phone.

She suddenly remembered Andrea Thomson asking about a blackout at a SCAR meeting, and now pieces began slotting into place. Disabling CCTV; distracting security with racist attacks; executing a kill mission while everyone looks the other way; forty-year-old AK-47s; making a delivery.

She hurried towards the village with renewed urgency. If she was right, only one question remained: who was the target?

68

Sasha Petrov was going to China.

Some might say he was swapping one prison for another. When they arrived in Beijing it would be no safer for him to walk the streets than it was here in Budapest. He wondered if the party would assign him a place with guards, maybe a villa with personal security to escort him when he wanted to go out.

If they let him go out.

They would, wouldn't they? He assumed they'd paid a lot for him. Boštjan Majer wasn't the type of man to give anything away for free. Sasha had sought him out because of this reputation, believing Majer's network of contacts could help him escape his former SVR employers and find a new home. Plus, he figured an old troublemaker like Majer would enjoy giving Moscow a poke in the eye.

North Korea, Venezuela, and Colombia had all made encouraging noises, and Britain said they would consider it. But North Korea sounded like a death sentence; the South American countries could not protect Sasha from Moscow's wrath; and Britain was mired in endless bureaucracy. It became moot anyway when the pandemic made long-distance travel all but impossible. Majer had to quickly find somewhere for Sasha to stay, to keep him below the radar until the world re-opened. The Chinese were the only people willing to take him at such short notice.

Majer had contacted a man called...Bow? Lao? Dow?

Whatever, he'd arranged to keep Sasha here, effectively making the decision. Beijing it would be, once they could safely transport him there. Like everyone else in the world, Sasha had expected to wait a couple of months at most while governments and scientists eradicated the virus. Instead, all this time later, he remained a prisoner; locked in his suite and unable to leave for fear of being seen.

At first he'd wondered if it was a trick, the sort of mind game the Chinese liked to play, to keep him in the dark while outside the world returned to normal. The state TV news he'd been permitted to watch insisted that wasn't the case, that the virus had continued to spread. But they had the wherewithal, and the inclination, to run a fake news channel if it suited them. After hacking the TV and editing the fake security video, Sasha's first move had been to check the real news. Turned out it wasn't a lie. The world had well and truly fucked up dealing with the virus. That was bad, but it helped him trust his captors a little more.

They were captors, weren't they? He understood that now. Maybe they wouldn't let him leave his house in Beijing after all. He'd entertained fantasies of being lauded, interviewed on state TV, asked to sit in on high-level government discussions about the Great Firewall and the state of China's cyber-security.

He supposed that was still possible, but now it seemed a child's dream. Was his purpose to be merely a trophy for them to wheel out every so often and thumb their noses at Moscow? He'd told them a lot about Russian cyber intelligence ops, information not found in the huge file of documents he'd released.

Operation Patrios wasn't in those documents, either. Because the Kremlin rejected his plan, it never made it into the official records he'd leaked to the world. Sasha never expected anyone would revive Patrios and go through with it. But he also never expected to be trapped in Budapest, waiting to be smuggled into

China under forged documents.

Out of idle curiosity, he searched for Majer online. It wouldn't be easy – the Slovenian would hardly be on LinkedIn, or posting selfies to Instagram. But with no access to a phone, Sasha couldn't just call him on a whim.

Four pages of search results and several news reports later Sasha knew he wouldn't be calling Majer at all. He and two Englishmen had been found dead in a Paris apartment. Details were scarce, but speculation was rife, and while nobody outright called Majer a criminal it was heavily implied with monikers like 'international businessman' and 'political broker'. Meanwhile the Englishmen were 'government functionaries' and 'civil servants'. In Paris? Lying dead next to an *international businessman*? Pull the other one.

Sasha hit his custom keyboard shortcut to switch to Netflix. While actors played at war, his mind raced. What had Majer got himself into? Did it have anything to do with Sasha's situation now?

The door unlocked. He had a moment of panic, then remembered he'd already switched to a movie. The diplomat entered again behind a guard, wearing an almost apologetic expression.

'Transport could be delayed,' the man said with the tiniest shrug of his shoulders. 'The weather is bad. It is snowing.'

The secure suite had no windows, so Sasha was perpetually unaware of the weather. It didn't normally matter.

'So when are we going?' he asked.

The diplomat smiled. 'Soon. We don't know. Soon. Make sure your bag is packed. One suitcase only.'

He left, and the guard locked the door behind him. Sasha immediately switched back to his makeshift TV computer and checked the weather forecast. It was true. Here in Hungary snow could come down heavily at a moment's notice, and while the country was well practised at coping with it, clearing roads of even a few inches took time. If the fall continued then inches could soon become feet, and it might be days before he was able to leave.

He shut off the TV and crawled fully clothed under the bed covers. Nothing was going to happen tonight.

69

Thirty minutes before sunset in Paris, Monica deployed the anti-worm.

Giles shrugged. 'Always something of an anticlimax, wouldn't you say?' Monica and the others muttered in agreement. 'So now we wait. I've booked out Broom Two for us to keep an eye on things.'

'Wait, am I allowed in there?' asked Karl.

'It's a briefing room, not our secret archive of classified black files. Come along.'

The American delivered his thousand-watt smile. 'So what you're saying is, there *is* an archive of classified black files.'

'Or maybe that's what we want you to think.'

Ciaran and Monica brought their laptops, Karl followed empty-handed. Giles caught Monica directing a subtle head shake at the CIA officer, but couldn't tell if it was a warning not to take the joke too far, or simply in despair at his humour. Either way suited Giles. He wasn't feeling especially jovial.

On the way there his mobile rang with a call from Edison Hill. Giles answered as he walked. 'Make it quick. I'm outside the situation room.'

'Appropriate, because we've got a situation. Sat obs says the paintball camp is on fire.'

Giles stopped. The others stopped with him, but he waved them on. Ciaran and Monica knew the way perfectly well, they could escort Karl.

'Define *on fire*.'

'What I said. The Hungarian camp is ablaze.'

'Any signs of life? My officer's in there.'

'Can't tell, thermal is useless until it burns out. But on a hunch I asked them to do a wide view of the whole continent.'

'Don't tell me,' Giles groaned. 'Multiple fires, scattered across Europe, all started this evening.'

'Bingo.'

Giles took a deep breath. 'Very well. That suggests it's part of the plan, which in turn suggests we're not looking at a bizarre suicide pact in Budapest.'

'You were right, though. This is happening now.'

'Indeed.' He ended the call and entered Vauxhall's second-largest briefing room, with an enormous central table and standing room to spare. When empty the place felt cavernous, outdone only by the lecture hall that was Broom One. But tonight a crowd of analysts, assistants, and liaisons to desks and departments all over Europe filled the room with a hum of activity and conversation. Brooms One and Two, often re-tasked as situation rooms, were uniquely equipped with online connections to the outside world. Giles recognised most of the analysts. More importantly they all recognised him, so he didn't have to waste time on introductory pleasantries. He took the head of the table, made a few assistants shuffle around so Ciaran, Monica, and Karl could take positions beside him, and wished everyone good luck.

Now the waiting game began.

On the far wall, a grid of large connected screens displayed a patchwork of security officers on webcam from European countries, and status lists of cities across the continent that could potentially be affected by the blackouts. Andrea Thomson, representing London, occupied one slot. Giles knew her own monitoring team was watching the UK, and London in particular, for tripped relays. The other agency heads on-screen would be doing the same with their teams – at least, Giles hoped so. He was still concerned that not enough of them were taking this seriously.

The next few minutes were a repetitive march of status updates, all saying everything was fine and there was no sign of anything untoward. Then reports began trickling in of suspicious activity: here a convoy of young white men in SUVs, there a matching convoy in anonymous trucks. All were checked, and facial recognition attempted where feasible. Some would inevitably be nothing more than joyriders out for a spin, but in Giles' opinion caution was underrated. Better to check them all out and be disappointed than skip one and miss potential danger.

They didn't know for sure if things would kick off at the top of the hour. It was an educated guess, nothing more. But the anticipation in the room continued to build, with everyone focused on that time marker.

With fifteen minutes to go, Giles' assistant entered the room wearing an urgent expression. 'Sir...'

'What is it?'

'I think Brigitte Sharp is trying to reach you from Budapest.'

70

'Return home by safest route,' said Giles over the phone. 'I'll instruct the suits to work up papers for you.'

The suits in question were the staff of the British embassy in Budapest, one of whom currently stood guard in the doorway of the tiny back room into which Bridge had been directed to take a secure call. He wasn't a normal diplomat, though. This was Jameson, the veteran SIS officer Bridge had spoken to before she came to Hungary. Being the country's sole officer made him Budapest station chief, despite having no juniors. Grey and wiry, he looked every bit like a man counting the days until his retirement – which explained his unhappy expression, having taken an earful from Giles moments before. Bridge had asked for Jameson upon arriving at the embassy, but they'd made her wait while staff called multiple London departments to confirm her identity and story. Eventually word reached Giles, who called Jameson and roared down the line at him to stop fucking about and put Bridge on the phone.

Getting to the embassy in the first place had been nerve-wracking. Nobody in the village Bridge found spoke a word of English or French, but luckily they did have phones, and one young man downloaded a translation app. Through it she was able to make him understand she needed to call the embassy, and after a game of pass-the-phone in two languages between the man, herself, and embassy staff, he finally offered her a lift. Snow was falling again and she remained on edge throughout the drive, wondering if she'd be in time. But after just half an hour they reached the outskirts of Budapest, and fifteen minutes later she almost cried with relief at the sight of a union jack flying from the British embassy. She had nothing to pay the man with, not even her Swiss army knife, which she'd left stuck in Dmitri's body. She patted herself down apologetically to show she was penniless. He smiled and waved her out of the car. The kindness of strangers.

'Have you shut the camp down?' asked Bridge. The first few minutes of their conversation had been a simple intel dump, with Bridge summarising what she'd seen and learned at the camp, and her speculation that Eagle's men were carrying out the real mission. 'I activated the beacon, but I was long gone before anyone arrived.'

'I'm afraid it's toast anyway,' Giles said. 'According to satellite all the Patrios camps are on fire this evening. We're now certain the attacks will take place tonight rather than Friday.' He explained the deleted tweets, the one-time pad, and the single tweet sent earlier that day.

Bridge groaned. 'Shit, it's my fault, isn't it? Yuri – Maxim – he moved up the schedule because I escaped.'

'Possibly, but without you we wouldn't have had eyes on him or his base camp, and might never have found that poor FBI fellow.'

'Some consolation. Listen, I've got a theory. Remember Andrea asking if a power cut could have been an attack? Well, Russia's no stranger to hacking power stations to cause blackouts. They did it before, in Ukraine.'

'Let me stop you there,' Giles interrupted. 'While you were away, we were able to decode those tweets. We now know the blackouts weren't accidents.'

'They were dry runs for a Europe-wide attack, right? Black out the cities, let the Patrios recruits loose under literal cover of darkness, chaos reigns. Which brings me to part two—'

Giles interrupted again. 'Monica and your pet American already created an "anti-worm" countermeasure to protect against the attack. They released it a short while ago.'

Bridge took a moment to be confused by this, then digested it and moved on. 'I think the blackouts are a cover. Or at least the one here in Budapest. Their kit is all ancient – antique AK-47s, Makarovs, old jeeps. If Patrios is so well-funded, and with Yuri being there too, it didn't make sense. But then I remembered what he said about making a delivery, and Eagle's men not worrying about CCTV.'

'Go on.'

'Think about it. Whoever they're targeting has enough security to require a kill squad, and operates their own CCTV. But wouldn't any place fitting that bill also have a backup generator?'

'Almost certainly,' said Jameson from the doorway, listening in. 'We have several ourselves, capable of maintaining power for up to twenty-four hours.'

'Meaning they wouldn't be affected by a power blackout,' Giles agreed.

'Exactly. But do you know what would affect them?' Bridge took a deep breath. 'An EMP burst.'

Giles said nothing.

'I know it's a little out there, but it makes sense and explains the old-fashioned weapons,' Bridge continue. 'No fancy night scopes or targeting circuitry that would be destroyed by a burst.'

Now Giles spoke up. 'There may be a connection here; William Gow and Boštjan Majer.' He related the story of Gow's corpse found in the Marseille shipping container, and the Chinese fixer's contact with Majer in Budapest. Bridge became all the more concerned for Frédéric, and hoped Henri had been able to persuade him to go home. Giles continued, 'If killing Gow and

Majer cleaned up Yuri's loose ends from stealing the EMP plans, who's left? Who's the target?'

Bridge turned everything over in her mind, trying to shake loose an answer. 'It doesn't make sense,' she said. 'If your timeline is right, Gow was dead in a container before Kennedy even took the plans. One of Eagle's men implied they're going up against the Chinese, but they can't have meant him.'

'Then who? Hungary has a large Asian immigrant population, but no Chinese dissidents that we're aware of.' They sat in silence for a moment, then Giles gave up and said, 'Look, you've done all you can. Let's get you out of there and home.'

'Sometimes I wish you were a little more like Dunston.' She ignored Giles' responding *harrumph*. 'I'm the officer in theatre, and the only person able to positively identify Yuri. If we can figure out the target, I can stop this and maybe even get the EMP device from him.'

'From the man who shot you. Nothing to do with wanting revenge, of course.'

'That's just a nice bonus.' She wouldn't insult Giles' intelligence by pretending it wasn't true, but it also wasn't the point.

'You really think he's built the device?' asked Giles. 'Devon said it wasn't easy.'

'Difficult isn't impossible, and what better proof of it working than to use it in a live op?'

'Surely it would be rather conspicuous.'

'That's my point. Set off a burst in the middle of the city and yes, Patrios distraction or not, armed police would be on the scene in minutes. But if you did it somewhere that's already blacked out, who would know? People might not even realise what had happened until hours later.'

'So the blackouts act as cover for the EMP.'

'Exactly. The question is, who does Moscow want badly enough to expend resources like this? Look at the lengths they've gone to. They sent an assassin to kill three men, steal the EMP plans, and escape halfway across Europe. They organised deepfakes to recruit young fascists, and even financed Americans to fly over and take part. They set up camps with supplies of food, weapons, and equipment. They tasked hackers to carry out attacks on power stations. And all of that is a distraction from the real op, for which they've had to build a bloody EMP and train for weeks. This has to be a major, high-value target.'

'A single target, you mean? Do you really think Russia would do all this just to cover up one assassination?'

'I think people like us doubting they'd go this far is precisely what Yuri is banking on. But who's offended them so badly?' Bridge glanced at Jameson, whose eyes were practically on stalks hearing everything involved. She tried to connect the puzzle pieces in her mind. Was there a link to Majer meeting with a fixer for the Chinese government? The veterans had talked about attacking the Chinese, but for what? And why would Yuri of all people care? He ran cyber operations, part of Moscow's hybrid war footing. It made sense that he'd be behind stoking online activism like the far-right message boards Bridge had infiltrated, or even the deepfake videos. But Giles was right – all of this to distract from an assassination? She laughed inwardly at the thought of the board denizens trying to untangle *this* conspiracy, all bad punctuation and broken English, searching for connections in classified data dumps…

She sat bolt upright and shouted, 'Sasha Petrov!'

'I beg your pardon?'

'The whistleblower who dumped the classified Kremlin documents. You said before that Majer wasn't just an arms trader, right? He was also a fixer, and he handled Petrov.'

She heard rustling as Giles stroked his beard. 'Petrov certainly embarrassed Moscow. They burned a good number of agents in response, to plug further leaks. No doubt he's on their list.'

'At the time there were hacker theories that Petrov had been "disappeared", or gone to ground. Cozy Bear conducted a big disinformation campaign to discredit him and the data; propaganda all over the place. But it was forgotten when everyone went into lockdown.'

'You think he's the reason Majer met with Gow.'

'Why not? Beijing and Moscow's rivalry keeps growing, and if there's two things China loves to hoard it's intel and leverage. Imagine how much Petrov could give them. Here's a man who knows Russia's systems, has seen the operational procedures... For all we know he might have been part of Cozy Bear before he went rogue.'

'There's been no word recently. If Petrov is in China, surely it would have come to our attention by now.'

'But what if he's *not* in China yet? What if they had to hide somewhere quickly because of the pandemic, no questions asked? As a Beijing fixer, Gow would have access to diplomats and Chinese nationals abroad. People who could hide Petrov at a secret location until he could be moved again.'

Giles sighed, understanding. 'A location Gow might well have given up under torture in a shipping container. But where?'

Bridge remembered the logs in the forest clearing. Like the plan of a large building, corridors and rooms... she turned to Jameson. 'Do all embassies have backup generators like yours?'

The old SIS officer shrugged. 'It's a pretty safe bet.'

'Ah,' said Giles, following Bridge's train of thought. 'The Chinese embassy, hiding out like Assange.'

'Hardly. Assange sent out a press release every time he sneezed. If the Chinese have Petrov tucked away inside their embassy, they won't breathe a word until he's safely in China. With travel opening back up, that could be any day now.'

'But not before the Russians get to him.' Giles fell silent for a moment. 'You really think they plan to storm a foreign embassy and kill a target? Think of the diplomatic fallout.'

Bridge shook her head. 'Who can prove it's them? The kill squad is all Balkan special forces, not Russian. First they black out cities and launch the Patrios attacks to distract everyone, including here in Hungary. While everyone's busy dealing with that, the squad sets off the EMP to fry the embassy's backup power and cameras, kicks the door in, takes out Petrov, and scarpers. The only witnesses will be Chinese diplomats, and the last thing they want is local cops investigating their embassy. They might not even admit they had Petrov in the first place.'

Giles swore under his breath. 'There's no time to prepare for this. I'll have to make an emergency call to London's Chinese embassy so they can relay warning to Budapest. Maybe they can get Petrov out before the Patrios squad arrives.'

'Doubtful. We're already several inches deep in snow.'

'Then they'll have to harden defences as best they can. All assuming your theory is correct, of course.'

'Oh, suddenly it's all on me when international relations are at stake?'

Giles grunted. 'Rest assured that every neck from yours through mine and up to the Foreign Secretary's is on the block for this one. In the meantime, proceed as ordered. Return home by safest route.'

'I told you, I'm already here and I can recognise several of the players.'

'I rather think the AK-47s and antique jeeps will make them stand out, Bridge. If they've built the EMP device then we're already screwed on keeping those plans under wraps, and Petrov is not our priority or problem. There's nothing more you can do.'

'Not our problem?' she protested. 'If we'd pulled our bloody fingers out and given him asylum he wouldn't be facing a Romanian death squad—'

The light disappeared. Bridge instinctively looked up to see if the room bulb had blown, but through the doorway into the corridor she saw the whole building was dark. A glance out of the window confirmed it wasn't just them.

As Jameson had predicted, the backup generators kicked in to restore power and dim emergency lighting. He exhaled with relief and leaned out into the corridor, hearing shouts from elsewhere in the building.

'Giles, it's happening. Budapest is blacked out.' She turned to Jameson. 'How far is the Chinese embassy from here?'

The officer pointed out of the window. 'South-east, no more than a ten-minute walk.'

Bridge ended the call before Giles could protest. 'Or a three-minute jog,' she said. 'Let's stop by your armoury on the way.'

71

The tip-off came from a jogger. Someone pounding the road on the south-west edge of Paris who claimed to have seen a bizarre caravan of three urban SUVs speeding along a back road, crammed full of young men wearing balaclavas and apparently holding rifles. The jogger used a smart watch to call the police, who called DGSI, who mobilised a greeting party. Henri's contact at *l'intérieure* asked if he'd accompany them, particularly in case they encountered Americans.

Henri raced to meet them, anticipating a power blackout at any moment. Every SIS officer in Europe had been briefed by Giles Finlay and their head of station on Operation Patrios, though many were skeptical as to whether it was real. Henri had been even more skeptical when Emily Dunston called him a couple of hours previously to warn that it could happen that night, rather than at the end of the week. This tip-off and the DGSI's response quelled some of his doubts, but the city's power remained on.

The DGSI ordered the *gendarmerie* to organise a roadblock – under the guise of a regular traffic check for undisclosed security reasons – at a bottleneck heading into the city from the region where the vehicles were spotted. Their car headlights blared into the night, obscuring Henri and the other security officers waiting behind them. Suddenly he wondered if this was a decoy; a hoax called in by the attackers themselves to concentrate DGSI's response on this area, while the real culprits entered the city from the north.

Then three pairs of headlights approached at once, and Henri braced for attack. If these men really were armed, they might simply open fire on the roadblock and smash through, taking their chances. He heard at least one vehicle speed up, and instinctively reached for his pistol. But the *gendarmes* were more forthright with their weaponry, and the sight of several large guns trained on the approaching vehicles had the desired effect. The SUVs stopped short of the roadblock, leaving enough distance between them that Henri feared an all-out firefight. For a tense moment the situation remained at a stand-off, each side waiting for the other to make its move.

The lead SUV moved first, reversing in an arc. The others followed suit, preparing to turn around and head back the way they came. This might have been a good decision, if not for two things. First, the lead SUV misjudged the road width and overshot the tarmac, dropping backwards into a drainage ditch and grounding its rear axle. Second, the officers waiting behind the roadblock with Henri were only half of the DGSI presence. The other half now sped out of a side road two hundred metres behind the SUVs and formed a matching roadblock to foil retreat. For good measure several officers stepped out, drew weapons, and took cover behind their cars. *If there are any Americans in the SUVs at least they'll feel at home*, thought Henri.

The SUVs stopped. Two men leapt out and opened fire on the new roadblock. Henri and the DGSI officers all dropped into cover behind the *gendarmerie* cars to return fire. He couldn't tell from his position whether they or the officers at the other roadblock were the ones to take down the shooters, but down they went all the same, collapsing like puppets whose strings had been cut.

A stark silence followed the blast of gunfire but was soon

broken by jumbled shouts of surrender and compliance, the air filled with cries of '*Ne tirez pas*', '*Je me rends*', and an American asking if anyone spoke English. The so-called Patrios soldiers tumbled out of the cars, empty hands raised as they fell to their knees and begged for mercy.

Henri watched the arrests, taking satisfaction from their expressions when they saw him and assumed this dark-skinned man was DGSI. He'd spoken to the lone American, who all the others insisted was in charge, while the man protested innocence and claimed he'd been forced into taking part against his will. Henri didn't believe that for a second, though it made about as much sense as anything else in this bizarre episode. For one thing, it was now confirmed: no blackout in Paris. If these men hadn't been so obvious, or if the jogger simply hadn't seen them, what then? Would they really have driven onto the Champs Élysées and opened fire on foreign tourists, while knowing they risked being caught on camera? Had they really thought they could do so without drawing the DGSI's attention? They didn't look like trained soldiers. They were barely more than children, given guns and vehicles and orders to be good little murderers – an operation so half-baked it had been scuppered by a roadblock.

Henri really hoped he could get copies of their interrogations.

Glad as he was that things had turned out well here in Paris, he was all too aware that this confirmed Patrios was real, and operational. What, he wondered, was happening elsewhere across Europe? Was every group involved this amateurish? He'd been led to understand Patrios was a well-funded, probably Russian-backed operation. Surely some of the branches knew what they were doing.

He thought of Fred Baudin in Marseille's Camp Sud, and wished he could have done more to help.

72

In Munich, the lights were out in half the city and all the surrounding areas. At an out-of-town refugee-processing centre, a sympathetic guard who had previously told his colleagues to take a smoke break watched the rapidly approaching headlights of several large cars and took cover. They'd told him they wanted to make it look as if they'd broken through the gates, even though that would be impossible if he hadn't unlocked them. He braced himself as the cars slammed into the heavy steel barriers, flinging them open and smashing the lead car's headlights. By the time his colleagues reached the guard post, having abandoned their cigarettes, the shooting had already begun.

In Belgrade, the lights stayed on. That didn't stop a group of armed young men driving to Luke Ćelovića, locally called *Afghani Park* after its population of rough-sleeping refugees and asylum seekers; the city couldn't or wouldn't accommodate them, and the park was within easy walking distance of the central bus and train stations. It was an obvious target for the young men – so obvious that as soon as their cars came under suspicion, the local police called the Security Intelligence Agency for advice and informed volunteer groups working in the park. The would-be attackers were arrested without a shot being fired.

In Stockholm, and across the archipelago, the lights were out.

Outside the city, near Gustavsberg, three SUVs took the island-hopping roads to a secluded modern shanty town of prefabricated housing for north African refugees. The 'Värmdö solution' was supposed to be temporary, though the houses always seemed to be full, and their thin corrugated metal walls stood no chance against bullets. But the young men driving the SUVs lost their nerve as they drew near. A week later, police would find a curious submerged cache of discarded rifles and ammunition near the shore.

In Naples, the night was lit like any other. North of the city, though, Castel Volturno wasn't so lucky. Much of the run-down town, home to thousands of 'invisible' undocumented refugees, did without electricity and running water as a matter of course; when the lights went out in even the better parts of town, the controlling mafia assumed the incoming Nigerian gangs were to blame, while the Nigerians believed the mafia was preparing for another massacre. The lightly-armed young men driving into the resulting crossfire never knew what hit them.

* * *

'I'd call it a half-win,' said Karl Dominic as Giles rushed back into Broom Two. 'A lot of big hitters like Paris, Rome, Vienna, Zurich, and Barcelona are all good. Of course, we can't know for sure if that's because the anti-worm worked, or if they weren't vulnerable.'

'Just tell me who's gone dark. I already know about Budapest.' Seeing the immediate concern on Karl's face, he quickly added, 'Bridge is fine. Holed up at the British embassy.' While Karl processed this news, Giles turned to Ciaran instead. 'Report.'

'Berlin, Munich, Gdansk, Minsk, Belgrade, Marseille, Zagreb, and yes, Budapest, all went dark in the last two minutes. There may be other, smaller locations still to report. London is fine, as we can see.' Ciaran gestured to the room screen, where some of the European agency heads were now only black tiles on a grid. Giles saw Andrea Thomson on mute, talking rapidly into her phone from her office across the river.

'Shit,' said Karl, 'Did you say Marseille is dark? Bridge's brother-in-law works with refugees there.'

Giles grimaced, remembering his conversation with Tolbert. 'Let's hope their police are clued in.' He raised his voice to be heard by everyone at the table. 'How are those facial ID scans and arrests going?' Several analysts and assistants tried to answer at once, so Giles held up a hand for silence. 'Let's keep it simple. Hands up if your region desk reports attacks by Patrios hostiles.' Eight people raised their hand. 'Keep them up if any of those hostiles have been identified.' Three people. 'About what I expected, thank you. Let's not forget to update the board, shall we?' They responded with a flurry of typing, changing and shifting the on-screen status lists.

Giles doubted the night would pass without fatalities, but with luck any deaths would be on the other side – not innocent people like Fréderic Baudin. He hoped Bridge had the sense to stay safe inside the Budapest embassy.

73

'Hurry up, will you? Grab a couple of guns and let's get a bloody move on,' said Bridge as Jameson hesitated. The embassy's emergency power generators dimly illuminated the building interior with reduced lighting to conserve energy, and after jogging through darkened corridors they stood in a small secure room before the armoury wall safe.

'If you're right about this, you can't seriously expect to stop an assassination team by yourself.'

'I won't be by myself, because you're coming with me. And we don't need to stop the kill squad. We just have to prevent Yuri setting off the EMP. When they see the embassy still has emergency power, the squad will abort.' It meant she'd only be able to arrest Yuri, but like Jameson, she didn't fancy their chances against Eagle's squad anyway. If she could just prevent carnage at the Chinese embassy and an actual, for-real EMP blast inside a modern city, she'd consider that a job well done.

'What makes you think this Yuri fellow will be there to set it off? Surely he'll give it to the squad to operate.'

Bridge shook her head. 'I've run into this man before.' The phantom wound in her shoulder twinged in sympathy. 'I don't see him trusting anyone else to carry it out.'

Jameson locked eyes with her, as if trying to judge her soundness of mind. Then he sighed and unlocked the safe. 'This is a quiet posting, you know. The country may be going down the drain, but my job these days is nothing but paperwork.'

'It wasn't always, though?' Bridge asked hopefully. 'Where were you before?'

He ignored the question and opened the safe to reveal a small rack of identical Glock 17 pistols. He handed one to Bridge and took another for himself, followed by two ammunition magazines each. 'I'll need to sign these out.' Bridge rolled her eyes, but before she could complain he added with a wink, 'Emergency measures, though. It can wait until we get back.'

74

In Marseille, the lights went out.

Fréderic Baudin was finishing up the day's paperwork, two hours late as usual. Louis had poked his head around the door and asked him to join a game of pétanque with the residents. As usual, Fred said he'd come along later if he had time, with no real intention of doing so. Knowing this, Louis said he'd see him in the morning and Fred returned to his paperwork.

Five minutes later, he swore at the tell-tale click of the power going out in his trailer. At least his laptop still had some battery, so even if this lasted for a while he could continue working.

Shouts from outside drew his attention, and now he saw power was down throughout the camp. He opened his door and heard people calling out that it was even more widespread; the whole city was dark, now lit only by the thin moon. Fred pulled out his phone to call someone at the mayor's office. Like his laptop, it had enough juice to run for a few hours before needing a charge. But as he was about to dial, he saw there was no signal. Not merely a bad signal, but nothing at all. No reception, no wifi.

An eerie, unsettled silence filled the air. Fred stepped into the cool evening and marvelled at the quiet as he walked the 'streets' of Camp Sud with his phone in flashlight mode. Normally the camp had a persistent low murmur, even in the dead of night, but now everyone looked around in silent confusion. He wondered if the refugees found the idea of losing power in France absurd. The home of nuclear energy, supposedly a plentiful haven far from the famine and rubble they'd left behind.

Then laughter came from one tent, joined by another, and shouts in a language he didn't know. Others responded in kind, and with more giggles. Fred was glad they could see the funny side. Laughter was a blessing that visited only the relaxed mind.

But then among the laughs he heard angry cries in French, and as he drew close to the north perimeter they were joined by chants beyond the fence. The damn protestors. Fred caught snatches in the tumult: 'leeches', 'freeloaders', 'it's their fault', and more, as if the penniless refugees of Camp Sud were to blame for a power cut in France's second-largest city. Did they even really believe it? Or was it a convenient scapegoat, one more thing they could blame on immigrants, knowing nobody would demand evidence for their accusations?

Lights approached from behind. Fred turned to see, but was blinded by them. Then Louis identified himself and said, 'Phone network is down, boss. We should ask the police guard how long this will last.'

'If the towers are down, I doubt they'll be able to get through to anyone either,' Fred replied. 'Their radios will be out of range of headquarters. What we need is a landline.'

The unmistakeable triple-bark of automatic gunfire rang out.

Fred wished he didn't recognise it so easily, but after years of working for MSF he and his staff knew that sound too well. Without words, Louis and Fred's wary expressions said all that needed to pass between them. Gunfire was invariably followed by shouts and screams, and tonight was no exception. It became a tumult as they ran to the south entrance, the camp's refugees rushing back inside their tents and away from the gates, toward the seaward side of the camp.

Every muscle in Fred's body wanted to join them. Some nights his gut still ached from being shot while protecting his son Hugo from a crazed Russian agent Isabelle's sister had led to their farmhouse. Doctors insisted his recovery was full and complete and what he experienced was merely a sense memory, but it didn't feel any less real. Now, as he rushed to the camp perimeter in the dark, he felt it again and stumbled. Louis caught him, told him to stay back, but Fred insisted he was fine. Up ahead, flashlights illuminated the scene, and he despaired to see they were all held by protestors. The police who normally guarded the camp were nowhere to be seen – were they dealing with other emergencies in the city, or had they simply stood aside? He'd long suspected that if push came to shove, the police wouldn't stop the placards. *The enemy of my enemy.*

These protestors no longer held placards, though. Instead they shepherded a group of young men, bizarrely wearing green-and-brown camouflage fatigues, carrying machine guns. At any other time Fred would have assumed the rifles were fake, replicas designed merely to intimidate. But there was no faking the sound they made. Had they shot someone outside the camp? Or simply fired into the air to announce their arrival?

With a sinking feeling, he recognised two of the young punks who'd tried to muscle their way inside the camp the previous week. This time they'd brought backup.

'Halt,' he called out, shining his phone flashlight directly in their faces. 'This is criminal trespass. You have no right to enter.' Appealing to their compassionate nature would be a hiding to nothing, but perhaps they still feared the law.

'Fuck off, old man,' said the nearest one, shouldering his rifle. 'We've had enough of filthy towelheads sucking France dry, and pricks like you helping them. We are the true patriots!' The others took up his cry.

'No! You're babies who don't know any better.' Fred was only in his late thirties, but if they wanted to call him old he was only too happy to return the compliment. 'You are lied to, every day, by the people you call heroes. But where are they? Why aren't they here, beside you, holding a gun? I'll tell you. They don't care about you. You're nothing to them. You could die like a dog where you stand and they wouldn't shed a tear. They don't even know your name.' Louis stood beside him and linked arms. A UN medic did the same on his other side. Fred saw more colleagues, and other camp staff, step up to form a human wall. It was a performative shield, to be sure. A few well-placed bullets would destroy them in an instant. But it spoke loudly.

The placard-wavers were loud too, shouting insults and obscenities, more raucous by the moment. Fred feared they might rush the gate and break into the camp, but they held their own line behind the young men. No matter whose side you were on, you didn't willingly step in front of a gun barrel.

But Fred also refused to move aside, even when the young 'patriot' at the front pointed his rifle directly at his face. 'This is a war, old man, and you're siding with the enemy.'

Every cell in Fred's body trembled, his temperature so low he could have imagined he was in the Arctic, not the easy cool of a Mediterranean evening. But in a way, this wasn't as bad as the farm. Knowing Isabelle and the children were safe gave him the confidence to say, simply: 'No. *You* are the enemy.'

The two men glared at each other, framed by chiaroscuro phone light. Over the young man's shoulder Fred glimpsed protestors moving forward, breaking away from the mass of the crowd.

A single shot rang out.

Instantly the tension broke, becoming shouts, cries, and panic. Fred fell inexorably to the ground, unable to stay upright, as if the earth itself pulled him down. Then he realised he *had* been pulled, though not by the earth. The human wall on either side of him had dropped instinctively in reaction to the gunshot, but he was unharmed.

Which was more than he could say for the young man who, until a second ago, had been pointing a gun at him.

Fred shifted his position and looked around, trying to understand what was happening. The protestors who'd emerged from the crowd were armed, and...arresting the young men? He saw punches thrown, tasers fired, guns raised. Zip ties pulled hard around camouflaged wrists, now helpless on the ground.

One of them – a big, bearded man, the one he now understood had emerged from the crowd to shoot the punk threatening him – called out, 'Where's Fréderic Baudin?'

He sat up and raised his hand. The bearded man took it and pulled Fred to his feet. 'Your British friend had a hunch,' said the man, and winked. 'Luckily they're all amateurs, as we suspected. When you thank Brigitte, tell her Serge says hi.'

All Fred could do was nod in response and watch dumbfounded as Serge, undercover policeman or whatever he was, returned to his colleagues.

75

'Vienna,' said Jameson as he led them around a corner. 'Berlin, before that. Prague, before that.'

Bridge realised he was answering her earlier question of where he'd been posted. 'Hell of a list. No wonder you wanted a quiet life to end on.'

'Yes, well, let's hope this isn't the end. I'd rather see that out back in England, if it's all the same to you.'

Already three inches deep, the snow continued falling as they ran through the dark streets. The unlit city at night was unnerving and eerie, especially as the moon was little more than a waning sliver. At least it gave them some light in addition to the glaring headlights of cars struggling through the snow and dark. It occurred to Bridge that the lunar cycle had been part of the plan. By Friday, when the Patrios attacks were originally scheduled to take place, it would be a new moon. No moonlight, and no respite from the blackouts for anyone.

Traffic was less snarled up than she'd expected, but there were plenty of confused shouts and horn blasts. Casey and the recruits might be shooting up a neighbourhood somewhere across town right now, and Bridge would never hear it. The fate of those people was in the hands of the local police. Jameson assured her they'd been briefed after MI5 and SIS alerted the local agencies to the danger, but he didn't sound confident that they were taking it seriously. Bridge remembered his own earlier skepticism and wondered how hard he'd really tried to convince them. Perhaps the blackout would do the job. It had certainly convinced Jameson; before they set off he'd called his contact at TEK and told them to get to the Chinese embassy as soon as possible. They'd argued about jurisdiction and authority – apparently the *Terrorelhárítási Központ* normally only intervened when formally requested by the national police – and, not speaking Hungarian, Bridge could only go by what Jameson told her. He said they'd promised to discuss it with the police, but she didn't need local knowledge to guess that meant even a good decision would come too late.

They rounded a corner onto a wide road, and Jameson stopped. 'There,' he said, pointing. In the dim light Bridge made out high railings in front of several wide, low buildings in tree-lined grounds. 'Embassy row, as it were. China is the large central one, with guards.'

Two torch beams swept across the path in front of the embassy gates at waist height, moving like searchlights. Bridge and Jameson were in no danger of being spotted this far away, on the other side of the road; the beams were focused on the guards' immediate vicinity. As predicted, the embassies along the road had dim lighting still in effect, running from emergency generator power. She wondered if they would all last as long as the British generators.

'Now what?' asked Jameson.

It was a good question. Was Yuri already here? What about Eagle and his veterans? Even if Bridge was right about this being their target, she wasn't privy to the plan. She assumed Yuri would set off the EMP to disable the embassy's security, and the veterans would go in to kill Petrov. Now she was here, it seemed crazy. Storm a foreign embassy? How could they possibly hope to get away with it?

She knew the answer. The EMP would disable immediate

communications, fry recording equipment, take out the emergency lights, and prevent anyone in the embassy from escaping quickly. The staff inside would be caught off guard and unprepared for attack. The pulse would disable any nearby car with a controlling microprocessor, which, in practical terms, meant all of them and surely included the embassy's vehicles. Someone in Eagle's squad would be waiting beyond its range, ready to move in after breach and serve as a getaway driver.

All while the police and security services were distracted by a group of young fascists causing havoc among the local Asian community.

Before she could answer Jameson, a car turned into the street behind them. It passed them, then pulled up at the curb and killed its lights. That was unusual. The snow was easing off, but everyone continued to abandon the city centre in a bid for home. Not this driver, who parked far enough from the embassy not to be seen by the searching flashlight beams, but by Bridge's estimation within range of the EMP. She checked her watch; three minutes to nine. Was that the mark?

Fuck it.

'Walk normally,' she said to Jameson and set off. He followed, approaching the car from the rear. 'Take this side,' she said, meaning the pavement, while she stepped out into the road and drew the Glock he'd given her at the embassy. The old spy saw the movement and mirrored it.

Bridge knew little about cars and cared less, but even she could tell this one was decades old. All mechanical, like the old-fashioned jeeps. Seeing it was dark inside, Bridge hesitated. If this was Yuri, wouldn't he switch on the reading light to see what he was doing? Maybe he didn't need to. She hadn't actually seen the EMP plans, and was no electrical engineer anyway. Code was one thing, but schematics and circuit diagrams were beyond her.

Perhaps the device had a glowing red button labelled *Press Me.*

She drew level with the driver window and leaned in, gun out of view, to get a look at the person inside. The car door slammed open and flung Bridge sideways. She staggered and lost her balance, landing on her back in the wet, slushy snow. She brought her gun up in time to stare down the barrel of another as the driver stepped out, his aim never wavering. Behind the gun she recognised a sad-eyed face with a wide nose. Yuri.

Suddenly she was back in Tallinn again, watching helplessly as she wrenched open the door of Maxim's car and the bullet burned into her shoulder, pain and shock spreading across her chest—

A car door slammed, startling them both. Bridge saw a blur of movement behind the car and smiled, watching Jameson run away down the street with a newly-acquired backpack slung over his shoulder. Yuri turned, realising what had happened; the station chief had reached in and taken the EMP device. Bridge took advantage of the distraction and kicked the driver's door hard into Yuri. As he winced in pain she scrambled to her feet and relieved him of his gun. Another Beretta, like the veterans carried. She stuffed it into her waistband.

'Better make up your mind, Miss Sharp,' he said through gritted teeth. 'I think the Chinese are taking an interest.'

His eyes looked past her, but Bridge made no move to turn around. That would give him an opening. He was probably telling the truth anyway, and she'd already rejected the idea of simply shooting him. This man had twice tried to kill her, had undoubtedly killed others, and was about to do it again. But if they hadn't caught the Chinese guards' attention yet, shooting him definitely would. With a grunt of frustration Bridge pulled Yuri away from the car, kicked the door closed, and marched him at gunpoint after Jameson. The SIS officer waited at the corner, and as they approached he pulled a plastic cable tie from his pocket to tie Yuri's wrists behind his back.

Yes, Bridge thought, this would be fine. Return to the British embassy with the EMP device, place Yuri under arrest, and wait out the power cut. When the veterans arrived at the Chinese embassy and saw the lights were still on they'd abort and retreat to base, or simply disperse. She could give local police rough directions to the training camp, and hope the recruits hadn't caused too much trouble elsewhere in the city. All in all, it wasn't a bad result. She exhaled with relief.

Just as she heard the distinctive sound of an AK-47 being fired.

76

Casey had been first to the jeeps that evening. Several recruits expressed surprise he was even coming along, let alone at the vehicle and checking the loadout before anyone else. He shrugged it off and said nothing. His reputation was still tainted by Mike's disappearance, even though nobody else knew the truth. His failure to stop Élodie, or Brenda, or whatever her real name was ate away at him too, but for different reasons. Even Dmitri hadn't stopped her.

Besides, he now understood a little better why Élodie had seen through him, but backed off when he'd made it clear he didn't want to talk about it. Who would understand better than someone who'd seen the same shit? *I know it's not easy to take a life,* she'd said, and obviously hadn't been talking about killing Dmitri two minutes earlier. She'd done it before, but had somehow got over it. Maybe she saw herself reflected in him.

Maybe that's why he couldn't bring himself to kill her.

It didn't matter now. Water under the bridge, and there was new shit to do. Élodie's betrayal had made Yuri furious, and brought the whole operation forward. Hence the jeep loadout, hence Casey being there first, because he knew he was the only one who'd do what needed to be done. *Shoot clean.*

Now here they were, rolling through dark streets on the edge of Budapest. Once or twice they passed police cars, patrolling in the blackout, but nobody stopped them. Why should they? Just some young men taking a ride. Nothing to see here, officer.

They headed for what the locals called Chinatown. Eagle had explained that Asians made up most of the country's non-white immigrants because of something called 'golden visas'. Casey hadn't really paid attention. Maybe he should have, because when one of the recruits suddenly announced they'd arrived he figured there'd been a mistake. He'd been waiting to roll through a golden arch, drive along a red-lanterned street with gift stores, restaurants, and street hawkers. Sure, the power blackout would have rendered lanterns and neon useless, but even in the dark he could see this wasn't what he'd imagined at all. This was... suburbia. A street of regular small houses with lawns, driveways, and yards.

'The hell kind of Chinatown is this?' he said out loud.

He hadn't expected an answer, but one of the recruits who spoke English said, 'They buy their way into our country; visas for big money. They turn this into a ghetto. Then they fill places in our schools that should be for white children, because our schools are better than theirs. They will not replace us! Drive! Them! Out!'

Shouts of 'Drive them out', 'For the fathers', and other chants in Hungarian filled the air as the recruits armed themselves, pulling AK-47s and ammo from under tarpaulins, slotting magazines into place with practised ease following their weeks of training under Eagle and Dmitri. They grinned, cocky and confident. And why not? Wasn't this what all the preparation was for? Weren't they doing exactly what Eagle, the American president, and Operation Patrios asked of them? Weren't they discharging their duty to the forefathers of the white European race?

Casey didn't take a rifle; instead he had a pistol, a Makarov, tucked in his jacket. He removed it, thumbed the safety off, and climbed out of the jeep like the others. The street didn't look like any ghetto he'd ever seen, but it didn't matter. He watched the recruits fan out from the jeep, spreading in a wide arc with rifles raised as they closed in on the houses. Some looked like they wanted to do a sweep and advance, even though it would be slower.

One of them counted down: '*Három... kettő... egy... tűz!*'

As one, they opened fire. The sound was violent and deafening, like standing in the middle of Fourth of July fireworks. The damage inflicted was a different story.

The recruits' first reaction was confusion. Several fired again, while others tried removing and re-seating the ammo magazines before unleashing another burst. Casey leaned against the jeep and quietly laughed. When bursts of gunfire were replaced by arguments and shouting, he wasn't so quiet any more. One recruit shot directly down at the ground, then crouched to examine the result. When he stood up again he turned to Casey, who didn't need streetlights to guess at his expression.

It had been so easy. They'd already stopped paying attention to him after Mike, and Élodie's disappearance made Casey even more invisible. Nobody wondered where he was for the fifteen minutes it took to remove orange tape from the paint-filled practice magazines. Nobody noticed him swap them for the live round mags. Nobody cared that he'd been first at the jeeps to make sure they hadn't been swapped back.

Doors opened as the street's occupants came to see what the noise was. People shouted from their houses in Hungarian and Chinese, neither of which Casey knew, but he understood the universal tone of '*What the fuck is going on*?' Suddenly uncertain, the recruits hesitated, giving Casey enough time to draw Élodie's Swiss army knife – *why let a good knife go to waste*, he'd thought before returning to camp from the forest – and slash a tyre on each jeep. As the recruits ran back he held the Makarov above his head and pulled the trigger.

'These ain't paint,' he said, sweeping the pistol across them, their advance halted. All except one, whom he saw coming from the corner of his eye, a movement in the dark. He turned and fired without hesitation, aiming low. His would-be attacker screamed and dropped to the ground, clutching his leg.

Casey laughed again. By now more doors were opening, more people were shouting. Most of the recruits stood dumbfounded. Some turned and ran, escaping into the night. He saw one tackled to the ground by a furious resident before they could get that far. Casey turned, hearing movement behind him, in time to see someone climb over the jeep and smash the butt of their rifle across his head. He dropped hard, firing blind, heard the pistol shot ricochet off the side of the jeep. Someone wrestled it from his grip, shouting in Hungarian, and then the beating really began.

He was still laughing through broken teeth and bloody lips when the police arrived to arrest everyone.

77

The rattle of AK-47 shots echoed through the dark streets, barely covering the simultaneous sound of roaring engines and grinding metal. After a few seconds, it was over.

Bridge turned on Yuri. 'Is that Eagle and the others? Weren't they supposed to wait till you set that off?' She pointed at the backpack with the EMP device slung over Jameson's shoulder.

Yuri broke into a wolfish grin. 'Perhaps they have not realised. They are soldiers, not scientists.'

Bridge found it hard to believe he wouldn't have briefed them on the EMP's effects. But whatever the reason, they hadn't aborted or dispersed as she'd expected.

'Who cares why?' said Jameson, pulling at Yuri's arm. 'We've got what we need. Let the Chinese worry about their own embassy. I already called Hungarian security. The locals can deal with it when they get here.'

Yuri laughed; a barbed, involuntary outburst. Bridge looked from him to Jameson, to the street corner leading back to the Chinese embassy, and groaned. Giles' description of the *Terrorelhárítási Központ* rang in her ears: *skilled operators, but corrupt as all get-out.*

When planning an audacious attack in enemy territory, what simpler way to keep the security services away than good old-fashioned bribery? Yuri had already backed up the Patrios money truck to bring over American patsies. Here, in a country where graft was woven into the fabric of government, why not empty a second load and buy yourself a non-response?

Jameson was right. It wasn't their problem. They now had, Bridge presumed, the only working EMP device based on the stolen plans. They might even have got lucky and reached Yuri before he uploaded the plans anywhere else. They'd warned local security about Patrios, and Bridge had disrupted the camp enough to hope its recruits wouldn't cause much trouble. On top of all that, she'd barely slept and was running on fumes. There was nothing more she could do, was there?

But she remembered her words to Izzy. *I make the world a better place, too.*

If Yuri's squad got to Petrov, it was all over for the whistleblower. He might not be entirely innocent – nobody working in Russian cyber-ops could claim to be – but his death would send a message to the world that Moscow could do what it liked, where it liked, and nobody would stand up in defiance. The British government had already left Petrov out in the cold, dithering over whether to upset the oligarchs who held half of Parliament in their pockets. He'd paid the price by living underground, and for what? So Russia could kill him anyway and ensure no one would ever blow the whistle again?

Bridge had hesitated in Paris, giving Ilya Kazhdan enough time to murder three men and create this whole mess. She knew it wasn't her fault, but that didn't change the simple fact that if she'd entered that apartment right away this wouldn't be happening.

Fuck it.

She turned to Jameson and said, 'I'm going in after them. Take this one back to the British embassy and hole up until the power comes back on. Do not take your eyes off him.'

The SIS man looked at Bridge like she'd lost her mind. Perhaps she had. Yuri's expression was unreadable; incredulous, impressed, or maybe both.

The Russian leered at her. 'I am sorry I will not be there to see you die. But I am glad I will, perhaps indirectly, be the reason for it.'

'Oh, put a sock in it, you old villain,' she said, already running back to Embassy Row. She rounded the corner and crossed the road, dodging cars churning through snow, looking for the twin-torch searchlight beams outside the embassy. But all was dark on the pavement, and if not for passing headlights she would have stumbled blindly across the first dead body. Behind it a bulky shape pressed up against the security railings, which, upon drawing closer, she saw was a humvee, reinforced with front impact bars. This was the pedestrian entrance to the building. Vehicles entered around the back, where presumably security barriers were in place to carry out traffic stops. On this side there were no such barriers, only the guards, because there was no room for vehicles to enter. Eagle's squad had made room – by ramming the humvee into the railings hard enough to bring down the gate and surrounding metal, then shooting any guard they hadn't run down.

The railings had put up a good fight, though. The vehicle was a write-off. The shattered windscreen had exploded over its crumpled bonnet and both front tyres were blown, making it impossible for the veterans to leave the same way they came. But doubling back was a risky tactic anyway; better to move forward and through. In the meantime a getaway driver who'd waited beyond EMP range was probably now en route to collect the squad and exfiltrate them out of the country, or perhaps to a local private airfield where a plane stood ready.

Gunfire barked from inside, prompting Bridge to get a move on. She stepped carefully over the downed railings, relying on good balance as much as her sight in the darkness. The backup generator didn't run to external security lights, which allowed her to move unseen, but she'd be no use to anyone with a twisted ankle.

Inside the grounds, low auxiliary lighting emanated from the embassy windows. The main door remained shut but the dim glow revealed two bodies lying in front, fallen where they'd stood. Moving around the building she found three consecutive windows with the tell-tale white impact points and spider-web cracks of bulletproof glass, signalling failed breach attempts. Further along a fire exit door swung wide on its hinges, illuminated by the interior emergency lights.

Bridge entered, following in the squad's footsteps. She heard gunfire, amid screams and shouts. Four dead guards before she'd even stepped inside, and now more shots. What kind of body count would these maniacs rack up to eliminate a single target? She slowly pushed open a door at the far end of the corridor, wary of anyone standing watch. Nobody was, but the scene that greeted her – two dead Chinese people, one man, one woman – answered her question. They didn't look like embassy security. The low amber lighting gave it a surreal air, like moving through a living *giallo* film, following a trail of violence. Eagle and his veterans weren't the kind to employ fancy methods or waste time tying up prisoners. Especially foreigners.

She picked up her pace to follow the cries, gunfire, and sounds of movement. Where would Petrov be? She dismissed the ground floor as too exposed, too difficult to hide someone, and climbed a narrow flight of enclosed stairs. It struck her that Petrov would be somewhere like this; kept away from the outside world, with no windows through which he could be seen or targeted. Giles had made a comparison to Assange, but that wasn't the same; his self-imposed exile at the Ecuadorian embassy had been public, staged in protest. Petrov was being held here to keep him out of the public eye, cut off from the world so Moscow couldn't find him. It was ironic that the pandemic had simultaneously made it necessary, but also easier to pull off. No tours of the embassy during quarantine.

If Bridge was right, she could narrow her search to rooms in the core of the building. But surely Eagle was following the same logic – and his squad had spent weeks learning the layout of this building with their logs in the forest. By contrast, Bridge was fumbling in the literal dark. How could she hope to reach Petrov before the veterans?

She swept the corridor at the top of the stairs and turned another corner, heading away from the building exterior. A dead staffer lay on the floor, bleeding into the carpet. Shouts of alarm and panic came from all around, disorientating her as she tried to mentally map what she'd seen of the building so far. Behind the screams was another sound, a kind of throbbing she couldn't make out.

Whatever it was, the cacophony covered the sounds of Bridge's own movement. Nobody would hear her coming if she kept her cool and worked methodically. Around the next corner she'd find the rooms she was looking for, fully internal with no windows.

She turned, gun raised, and found herself face to face with a scared young man.

78

Sasha didn't know anything was wrong until the lights went out.

He'd been on the message boards, using the hacked television to browse around with the ChinesePrisoner account for any news about Operation Patrios. There was plenty. The boards were buzzing with conversation about the new Twitter post from @ToTheFathers, speculating what the quote from an American song meant and trying to decode the numbers. Nobody knew for certain, least of all the gematria idiots. Any fool could see it was an encoded message, and without the means to decode it they were merely guessing.

Sasha had tried to decode some tweets himself, before they were deleted, but it was impossible. They didn't share a consistent encoding method. It probably changed for every message, which made it very secure, but laborious to decode and read without a computer. Not that anyone going to such lengths would keep the encryption method in a computer, where it could easily be hacked or leaked.

Instead he amused himself joining in the conversation and screwing with everyone, posting random made-up shit he'd 'decoded' from the messages, refusing to divulge his methods. He was surprised how many fell for it and started quoting Sasha's 'revelations' to shore up their own arguments in other conversations.

Then the TV had blinked off, along with all the lights, before low-wattage emergency bulbs kicked in to paint the room a dim red. The emergency power didn't extend to the TV, though. That could be a problem – if Sasha couldn't restart it before a guard entered the room, it might reboot in front of them and display the message boards rather than its default of shitty Chinese state news. Then he'd be in real trouble.

But that paled into insignificance against the prospect of being shot, which the gunfire and screams told him was a possibility. Unless the Chinese had a second fugitive tucked away here, in Hungary of all places, what else could it be? Why would anyone cut the power to an international embassy and stage an armed assault, with all the risk and political damage it entailed, if not for someone like him? It didn't take a genius.

Nevertheless Sasha was a genius, if he did say so himself, and had spent the past week learning the embassy's security systems. Including the electronic lock on his door, which had been added when the suite became his prison, and required power to its electromagnet to operate. Power that, like the TV, came from a secondary feed.

He walked to the door, took a deep breath, and pulled it open.

The corridor was empty. He heard shouts, cries, and more gunfire. Where was his guard? Wasn't protecting him their fucking job?

On the other hand, with the guard gone Sasha was free to grab his go-bag from under the bed, be thankful he'd kept it, and leave the room.

He wished he'd thought of rooting the TV earlier; given more than a week to monitor the internal CCTV he could have learned the building's layout properly. Instead he was running blind, just trying to get away from the gunfire and screams. It didn't matter if they were SVR, or someone working on their behalf. He knew they were here to kill him.

In the corridor he passed several staff, but they paid him no attention, focused on their own escape. How many of the people working here knew who he was, or even that he'd been here all this time? It was probably classified information.

Elevators were death traps, he knew that. Instead he headed for the other side of the building. He came across a dead guard with a gaping, bloody wound in the back of his head. But the dead man still held a pistol, and Sasha overcame his disgust to prise it out of his lifeless hand. He'd never held anything more than a BB gun before, and the weapon's weight surprised him. But even without training, wasn't a gun better than no gun?

Wiping blood from the pistol grip on his T-shirt, he heard movement from around a corner up ahead. He held the weapon with both hands and raised it in front of him, approaching the corner as quietly as he could. His heart hammered in his chest, the blood and adrenaline rushing through his body seeming so loud it might give him away. He struggled to keep the pistol steady in his trembling hands, but at point-blank range that shouldn't matter. Should it?

A dark figure appeared around the corner, catching him off guard. He recoiled in surprise, yelping involuntarily, only remembering he had a gun in time for the man to strip it from his hands, wrap an arm around Petrov's neck, and clamp a gloved hand over his mouth.

Suddenly he was on his knees, his go-bag dropped beside him, with his head pushed forward and hands pulled behind while a second man – where the hell did he come from? – pulled zip ties hard around Sasha's wrists. They hauled him upright and pushed him along the corridor.

They were here; they'd found him; but they hadn't killed him. That could only mean one thing, and as realisation bloomed through the fog in his mind, Sasha finally tried to resist. 'Wait, my clothes…!' He twisted around, looking for his bag.

The one who'd taken his gun, a big man with a permanent scowl, shoved Sasha back around. 'You won't need them,' said the soldier in perfect Russian.

79

'Ne lőjön! Kérem, ne lőjön!'

The young Chinese man looked scared out of his mind, and Bridge was impressed he'd had the presence of mind to say what she assumed was 'don't shoot' in Hungarian rather than his native language. Then she reminded herself he was young enough that he might have been born here. He froze to the spot with his hands raised high in surrender, lifting his cheap suit jacket enough for her to see he wasn't armed. Just a junior functionary, presumably wondering why foreigners were rampaging through his embassy.

'Petrov?' she said, gesturing around them and miming in what she hoped were universal signs of 'looking for someone'. He returned a blank look, not understanding. 'The Russian?' she tried, but he shook his head. 'Prisoner!' she shouted in exasperation, and finally he understood. He said something in Chinese she didn't understand, and pointed back the way he'd come, then raised his pointed finger. *Along here, then upstairs.* Thank goodness some languages were universal.

She gave him a thumbs-up, then jerked it back over her shoulder to indicate he should leave the way she'd entered. He didn't need telling twice, and hurried past her. Bridge moved along the corridor, came to a junction, and saw stairs to the left. There had been no gunfire for the past thirty seconds. Good for embassy staff, potentially very bad for Petrov. She took the stairs two at a time, passing a window halfway up that looked out over the embassy grounds. The throbbing sound was louder here, and she finally understood that it was a helicopter overhead. Had the police realised something was wrong? Had the TEK finally decided to send in a squad? It was a nice thought, but she was out of time.

Reaching the top of the stairs, she moved room by room. The unbidden memory of sweep-and-advance exercises at the Patrios camp came to mind, and she wondered what had happened to Casey Lachlan. Her sympathy for the American was distinctly limited, but in letting her escape he'd shown he wasn't a natural killer. How was he coping? Mike Alessi may have been an FBI agent, but he and Casey must have grown close while he was embedded.

Empty room, empty room, empty room. Not truly empty, of course, but offices, meeting rooms, and libraries devoid of people. Some had a *Marie Celeste* air, still-steaming cups of tea hastily abandoned at the first sound of gunfire. Did the embassy have a panic room? Almost certainly. Perhaps more than one.

The thought stayed with her as she stumbled over a duffel bag on the floor in the corridor. She crouched and unzipped it; nothing but men's clothes and toiletries. Did it belong to the dead staffer, lying face down further ahead? She stepped over him, and not long after turned a corner to find a door different to others she'd seen – reinforced steel, with a grip handle instead of a door knob, and a CCTV camera pointed directly at it from high across the corridor. It was open.

Bridge edged to the doorway, recognising a magnetic lock mechanism that must have automatically disengaged when the power failed. She cautiously peered in, but there was nobody inside. Moving through it she knew instinctively it was Petrov's room. It resembled a hotel suite with couch, TV, small table, sleeping area, bathroom, and absolutely no sign of a phone or computer. That made sense; giving a hacker any means of communication with the outside world would be like leaving the door unlocked. The closest thing to a computer was a bluetooth keyboard on the couch, presumably to control the TV.

She paused, looked at it again, and groaned as memories slotted into place. *Posting this from a fucking TV, LOL.* That's what the forum poster ChinesePrisoner had said in a private message. She hadn't given it much thought at the time, but now she understood. Bridge had rooted TVs herself in the past, and Petrov could probably do it with his eyes closed. All he'd need was a keyboard.

But the Russian whistleblower wasn't here. Had he escaped before the kill squad found him? In the quiet of the room, the circling helicopter sounded closer…and Bridge mentally kicked herself again.

'Bollocks,' she hissed in frustration. She'd assumed Eagle and his fellow veterans were here to execute Petrov, but what if they weren't? What if the objective was to return him to Moscow? A fate far worse than death for a traitor to the motherland. So that wasn't a police helicopter circling overhead. It was Eagle, the former soldier with a winged tattoo, flying the chopper hidden in the forest. *He* was the getaway driver, waiting outside the EMP's burst range – except he wasn't driving, he was flying. Where the hell did he plan to land? The street outside was lined with trees. Bare or not, those branches would rip a rotor to pieces.

It didn't matter. This had all been a big mistake, and the best thing Bridge could do now was get the hell out. She should have stayed outside, returned to the British embassy with Jameson and their own prisoner. Losing Petrov was unfortunate, but gaining Yuri more than made up for it. She wondered if she'd be allowed to watch the tapes of his interrogation, deep in the bowels of Vauxhall. Prime-time Saturday night viewing.

She retraced her steps, coming upon the fallen duffel bag again. This time she emptied it out on the floor, hoping to find a phone. No such luck. But from her crouched position she could see inside the nearest room, a library, where the main reading desk held piles of papers and reference books... and an old-fashioned wired telephone. Bridge ran inside, picked up the handset, and almost laughed when she heard a dial tone. It wouldn't have survived an EMP, but a normal blackout didn't stop good old copper phone lines from working.

She placed her gun on the desk and dialled a number from memory, waiting for the international connection to take hold. It was answered on the second ring.

'*Giles. Line?*'

'More insecure than you can possibly imagine, but it's too late to worry about that and there's too much to explain. We're going to need diplomatic transport back to England, with a prisoner in tow. We prevented them setting off the EMP, and Jameson has Yuri in custody, but—'

A stumbling noise from the corridor outside, the sound of a man cursing quietly in Russian, and Bridge instinctively threw herself behind the desk. The phone clattered to the floor as two shots buried themselves in the wood. A book on the shelf behind her exploded, tossing scraps of pages into the air.

The solid desk blocked her view, but she didn't need to see to know it was Yuri. Somehow he'd escaped Jameson's plastic restraints and followed her inside. Christ, was Jameson dead now too? If not for the Russian stumbling over the duffel bag's contents she'd have taken a bullet herself.

She was trapped behind the desk, forced to quickly guess which side he'd favour. A younger man might have climbed over the top, but that wasn't Yuri's style. Bridge tried to remember the moment he'd shot her in Tallinn, and in which hand he held the gun. *Fuck!*

That image had woken her in the dead of night more times than she could count, but now she actually wanted to picture it she saw only a blur of pain and shock.

Her Glock lay on the desk, out of reach.

But she had another.

Bridge drew the Beretta from her waistband, the pistol she'd confiscated from Yuri himself outside. She flicked off the safety and took her own third option, standing up directly behind the desk and firing at movement to her right. He'd tried to bluff her, coming around on his off side. Had she subconsciously guessed that? No way to know. But he'd been expecting her to come out low from the side of the desk, not stand up straight.

Her first shot was wide. So was his. Her second hit square in his chest, and he fell.

Keeping the gun trained on him, Bridge approached Yuri. His own gun – or rather, Jameson's – lay on the floor beyond his grasping reach. Blood spread across his shirt in waves. Drawing closer she saw welts from the cable ties circled his wrists. He wore a backpack, the one Jameson had taken from his car. The EMP device.

She crouched beside the dying Russian, watching his chest hitch and eyes widen. Blood gargled in his mouth with each strained, gasping breath.

'Don't think you'll be taking that to Moscow,' she said, nodding at the backpack. 'No medal for you.'

Yuri laughed, coughing blood as he whispered something. Bridge had to lean in close to hear him over the noise of the circling chopper, now louder than ever.

'Fucking… kill you…' he hissed.

Bridge pulled the backpack off him and threw it over her shoulder. 'Funny,' she said, levelling the Beretta at Yuri's face. 'I was thinking the same thing.'

*** * ***

She stood at the staircase window overlooking the embassy grounds and watched the helicopter descend. Downdraught from its rotor blades made a blizzard of the surrounding air, rushing pulses of displaced snow in all directions. Bridge glimpsed white lines on the ground, picked out by the chopper's own lights, and realised where it was setting down. A tennis court. Eagle slowed the rotors as it landed but kept them moving, ready to spin up again in a hurry.

Below her the squad of mercenaries was already moving across the grounds, to the tennis court and their escape. They operated like a well-oiled machine; five men in combat blacks, some walking backwards to cover all angles of attack. They stood out against the snow like a stark shadow, obscuring detail. But from up here Bridge could see the small, helpless figure of Sasha Petrov at their centre. In less than a minute he'd be on that chopper and in the air.

She shouldn't care. Petrov wasn't part of her mission. Taking him in would poke Russia in the eye, which was always fun, but if the government cared enough about that they would have granted him asylum when he asked. Then she remembered something else 'ChinesePrisoner' had said to her on the message board:

Patrios is a good plan. I should know.

At the time she'd thought he might be one of its organisers, a camp co-ordinator like Eagle or Dmitri, proud that he knew what was going on. Now she wondered: what if he wasn't proud, but boasting? What if Patrios had been his plan? It wasn't in the records Petrov leaked to the world. She'd only skimmed the papers, but analysts at SIS, MI5, and GCHQ – not to mention their sister agencies around the world – had scoured every word. If anything in them resembled Patrios, SIS would have been alerted by now.

So Petrov knew at least one major plan not contained in the leak – and if he knew one, he might know more. That made him valuable.

Bridge's options, though, were depressingly few. She could run downstairs and rush the soldiers, but they'd be at the chopper before she reached ground level. She'd be lucky to get off a single shot before they returned fire and cut her down.

She could break this staircase window and fire down, with a chance to hit two or three before they determined the direction of fire. But at this range, in these conditions, and with only a handgun, the sheer wind force from the chopper blades could easily make her miss. She might even hit Petrov by accident.

She could aim for Eagle himself, try to take him out in the cockpit. But that was twice the range, through armoured glass, and even if she made a miraculous shot, who was to say the squad didn't contain a second pilot?

Only one option remained. Giles wouldn't like it – hell, she wasn't keen on it herself – but there was no other way.

80

Sasha continued struggling for about ten seconds. That was how long it took before the big man with the scowl punched him in the face, and he didn't struggle again after that. The other man, the one who'd zip-tied Sasha's hands and now pulled him through the building, had a grip like iron anyway.

The men led him downstairs to the embassy's rear grounds. Sasha had seen this area once before when he first arrived, though not since. That had also been at night, but it looked very different now. The trees were bare, snow covered the ground, no guards or diplomats walked the gardens (though backup security lamps illuminated bodies lying face down) and no city lights shone beyond the grounds.

The enormous black helicopter idling on the tennis court was also new, but in a way that was the least surprising thing.

Sasha had concluded his captors weren't entirely Russian. When the rest of the squad arrived, orders were quickly issued in a bewildering mixture of English, Russian, and what sounded like Romanian. He didn't need to understand it all to recognise words like 'Moscow', 'rendezvous', and 'deliver'. They were taking him back to face the music.

The men formed up close around Sasha, backs to him, with their guns ready, protecting him while simultaneously moving across the grounds and compelling him towards the chopper. Even in the cold, bitter night their sweat and body odour assaulted his senses, cloying and rank. He thought he might faint. It wouldn't save him – they pressed against him so tightly he would surely be dragged the rest of the way before they noticed he was unconscious – but it might afford a blissful ignorance.

The protective shell broke apart when they reached the chopper. Two of the men stood either side of Sasha, holding his arms and pushing his head down as another pulled open the vehicle's door. He'd once watched a documentary on Russian maximum-security prisons, holding prisoners so dangerous they were made to walk with their backs bent and heads bowed, arms shackled behind them. But he was no deadly prisoner, no risk to any guard or mercenary like these men. He contemplated making a run for it, a final attempt to flee for the gate. Undoubtedly it would be final; they would shoot him in the back without a second thought.

Would he rather die than be taken back to Moscow? It was a romantic notion, but the truth was he wanted to live. There was always a chance he could somehow make it out to fight another day. Maybe even take revenge.

They bundled him inside the cabin. Two secured his harness while another closed the door, and yet another shouted to the pilot. The rotors gathered speed, and Sasha's stomach lurched as the helicopter rose into the air.

Nothing could save him now.

81

Bridge placed the backpack against the wall underneath the window as the squad reached the chopper. Two of them took hold of Petrov and forced his head down as another opened the door. They threw him inside the cabin while the others covered, guns raised and ready to lay suppressive fire. Then they followed inside, one by one. The last man heaved the door closed and immediately the rotor cycle increased, its rising whine signalling imminent take-off.

She watched as the chopper rose into the air, carefully avoiding the trees. Slowly it gained height, five metres, ten metres—

When it reached fifteen metres Bridge set off the EMP.

At the time she would have sworn she felt the pulse pass through her. Later she'd acknowledge the sensation was merely psychosomatic, but in the moment it seemed real. As real as the chopper's lights winking out in the dark, and its lowering rotor pitch as the aircraft's engine shut down.

It dropped like a stone. There was no graceful decline, no gliding moment before the dive. One minute the helicopter was rising through the air; the next it was a crumpled wreck on the blackened ground.

Crouched in the sudden dark, with even emergency lighting now disabled, Bridge was dimly aware of an acrid scent; the smell of a thousand microchips and circuits inside the building quietly frying. But nothing could tear her gaze from the silent behemoth of twisted metal lying on the tennis court.

82

'Sometimes, Giles, trying to get a straight answer out of you is like knotting one's tie in a crooked mirror.'

This time they were in Leicester Square, where lunchtime crowds watched acrobats and buskers earn their crust. A much more comfortable place to have such a conversation, from Giles' perspective, even if Devon Chisholme stood out like a crooked reflection himself.

'I don't see what's hard to understand,' said Giles. 'The thumb drive was in the same backpack as the device. When the device was used, the drive was wiped.'

'Don't you know if copies were made beforehand?'

'There's no way to tell. But while we don't have the Kremlin sources we used to, we're not entirely out of that game and so far we've heard nothing. So either it's at a level of classification to which even our agents are unsighted...'

'Or we got away with it,' said Devon, completing the thought. 'Bloody hell.' A busker's hawker approached him carrying an empty Starbucks cup, but the civil servant's expression made him reconsider and retreat. Devon continued, 'I wonder if we can slip this in a footnote somewhere. My minister seldom reads past the headlines.'

Giles smiled. 'That might be rather difficult, considering what role the device ultimately played. But don't worry. Always remember that history is written by the victors.'

'Ah, your *retrospective corrections*. Better for both our sakes, I'm sure.'

'Rather more for yours than mine, Devon. The Service saved the day, saved your face, and obtained a valuable asset into the bargain. I'll expect you to remember that in times of trouble. Corrections can always be further amended.'

Giles left Chisholme watching a street dancer gyrate to a boom box. As he hailed a cab back to Vauxhall, he checked his phone and regretted it immediately. There was another video.

83

Once again, the former president faced the camera from his darkened room. The flag hung behind him as always. The presidential seal could be seen at the bottom of the screen. His face was grave and serious.

'My fellow patriots, I've got great news, the best and most amazing news. You succeeded beyond our wildest dreams. All over Europe, people are seeing the light. You might see a lot of fake news about what happened, but you know you can't believe it, don't believe what the media tells you. Believe me, I've had calls – so many calls – from presidents and leaders thanking me, which of course I accepted, but I also want to thank you, because your support means a lot, of course it does. Now I need you all to stand down, go home, and stop fighting. You've done enough, the world owes you its thanks, and now you can rest. I won't rest, of course. I'll be working very hard, taking many phone calls and having many meetings, every day. Last night I talked to my good friend President Putin, of Russia, and by the way, he told me he's going to pardon that great patriot, Sasha Petrov, who's been so unfairly treated by the mainstream media. So unfair. But now I have to return to my great work. You won't see it because it's secret work, hidden work. Sit back, trust me, and leave it all to me. I know how to fix this. Your job is done.

Mission accomplished. I salute you. God bless me, and God bless us all.'

Giles pressed a key on the remote to shut off the screen in his office, then peered at Bridge.

'I mean, really. Even if people think the others were real, the Petrov line rather gives this one away.'

Bridge relaxed back into the leather couch, triggering a series of creaks. 'I know. Imagine if Putin is compelled to denounce all of these videos as fake, so people don't think he's pardoned a traitor. How embarrassing for everyone concerned.'

Despite her sarcastic front, watching it back now Bridge would admit she'd laid it on a bit thick. Too late to change, though; the video was already spreading in the usual places. Besides, she was a coder, not a speech writer. Trying to replicate the staging from the previous videos had been difficult enough, and it still wasn't quite right. The flag hung differently, the seal was cut off at the bottom of the frame, and the synthetic voice made it sound like he had a head cold. The same people who spun mythologies out of everything from coded Twitter posts to classified data dumps would pick up on those differences and scrutinise the video frame-by-frame.

But as Bridge had said before, you couldn't disprove a conspiracy theory. The Patrios faithful would willingly incorporate it as a new facet of the grand plan. Bigger, deeper, and wider. She'd already seen them try to make sense of how the recruits across Europe were mostly ineffective; abandoned by the operation's leaders once they'd served their purpose as a distraction and political football. Some local communities had even fought back, standing alongside their immigrant and refugee neighbours against the young Patrios men.

That wasn't how the message board denizens saw it, of course.

In their minds the recruits were heroes of the white race, fighting to stop the Great Replacement and refusing to bow down to the liberal European elite. Some of the men arrested had spoken to the press to declare their pride in having taken part, insisting they wouldn't hesitate to do it again. Online rumours circulated that this was the plan all along, to gain press coverage for the cause and recruit new members.

Against all that, a low-quality deepfake video trying to persuade them to lay down their arms didn't stand much chance. But if it kept them busy fighting each other so they had less time to, say, foment race war in Europe? Bridge would call that mission accomplished.

Giles leaned forward. 'Hungarian media is telling everyone the attack was part of Patrios. That a pack of amateurs stormed a foreign embassy, killed several guards, then escaped. The helicopter was an unrelated private craft that ran into trouble due to the snow and crashed in the embassy grounds. It's a miracle those on board escaped with only broken bones.'

Bridge snorted. It wasn't a miracle, it was her own good judgement estimating from what height a drop would disable the chopper and its occupants without crushing them to death. But nobody would ever know that.

'Where's Casey Lachlan in this cock-and-bull story? Leading the amateurs to storm the embassy, or still with the other group who were arrested before they began?'

'Casey who?' said Giles with a shrug. 'No news reports have mentioned any Americans being involved. My understanding is that the State Department is working very hard to ensure that remains the case, and those involved have been given ample incentive not to run counter to their wishes. On the bright side, our own silence on the matter has afforded us a reciprocal understanding concerning the EMP device.'

Bridge took a moment to untangle his word salad, then understood he was describing a tit-for-tat. 'So nobody knows a device was used, or that our plans were even stolen.'

Giles nodded. 'Apparently, computers are at risk of short-circuit from power surges if left plugged in during blackouts. Who knew?'

'Nobody, because it's not true.'

'It is now.'

She sighed. 'And Mike Alessi's body in the forest?'

'Hiking accident while on holiday. Private funeral, closed coffin. Bear attacks make a terrible mess.'

Bridge almost laughed at the absurdity. But that was the nature of cover-ups; with enough political grease, any wheel could be turned whichever way those in power saw fit. The public would never be told that members of Hungary's own security service were bribed to look the other way. They would never learn a federal agent died while serving vital information, or that another American had tried to kill a British officer. Ignorance was bliss.

'How's Jameson?' she asked.

'Recovering, thanks to you. He'll remain on station for the time being. Considering his role in this, he may even secure a late-career promotion.'

Bridge had found Jameson lying in the street, losing blood and in shock, after she made it out of the embassy herself. Yuri had overpowered and shot him, but Jameson was sensible enough to play dead, correctly guessing the Russian was more concerned with escaping than verifying a kill. It had saved the older officer's life, buying enough time for Bridge to reach him and flag down one of the many emergency vehicles arriving on the scene after the chopper crash.

'I'm glad, but he shouldn't be on station if he can't handle himself,' she said.

'When you're pushing sixty and looking for a quiet posting you might feel differently,' Giles mused. 'If we had call for a safe harbour in Budapest I'd set one up and make him caretaker. Mind you, that's not the promise of boredom it used to be.'

Bridge ignored the bait and changed the subject. 'Where's Petrov?'

'Touched down on British soil even before you did. A few broken bones, but nothing time won't heal. Rest assured he's being thoroughly debriefed.'

Bridge's own debriefing had been rather less courteous than when she'd returned from Paris, considering the carnage in Budapest. In the plus column, Yuri was gone for good and Petrov was safe. Bridge had been surprised to find the mission records now included speculation about the young hacker being held in Budapest, and confirmation of her being tasked to retrieve him for SIS if possible. It wasn't the first time Giles had retroactively amended OpPrep files to suit an unexpected outcome, but this took the biscuit, considering it wasn't long ago that the same government had consigned Petrov to limbo.

She hadn't mentioned the altered records in her post-mission session with Dr Nayar. The therapist had wanted to focus on her reaction to the assault in the camp, the fight in the forest, killing Yuri. Bridge had wanted to focus on anything but.

There was some good news, though. Henri Mourad confirmed he'd alerted the DGSI about Camp Sud in Marseille being a potential target, and they'd taken action. A group of Patrios recruits were arrested at the refugee camp, achieved with 'minimal violence and casualties'. That could describe anything from a fist-fight to a shoot-out, but the important thing was that the camp staff had all been OK.

'Take some time off,' Giles was saying. 'Ask Agent Dominic to give you a foot rub or something.'

'Classy. Does this mean my weekend is now a right?'

Giles regarded her over his glasses. 'Maybe for the next couple of weeks. Don't push it.'

84

Bridge's finger hovered over the Enter key.

Silence filled her apartment. She'd gone straight from Giles' office to Karl's bed, shutting out the world and her own thoughts for a night. He was relieved to see her safe and unharmed, and didn't even mention her haircut as he held her so tightly she could hardly breathe. But it hadn't helped her sleep. She dozed for an hour here, thirty minutes there, always waking with a gasp from nightmares of blood and violence.

Yuri's dead face, grinning like a wolf. Artjom Kallas' panicked expression in the back seat of her Paris car as it crashed and crashed again. Unable to tear her eyes from Marko Novak while crows tore flesh and vein from his body on the ground outside Izzy's farm. Dmitri's surprised face as Bridge fired blanks into his face, trying to empty the gun but it was endless, ten shots, twenty shots, fifty, a hundred.

At dawn she left Karl snoring in bed, dressed in the spare workout clothes she kept at his flat, shoved her day clothes into a backpack, and ran to Hampstead Heath. Her Aftershokz vibrated to the pounding melancholy of Covenant's *Europa* while the air clawed at her throat and emptiness filled her mind. Nothing but movement and music, weaving between dog walkers and other runners. She could run all day, here, among these ordinary people.

Eventually she turned for East Finchley and ran home.

The box of junk from Maman's house awaited her, filled with

forgotten souvenirs of her childhood and adolescence. Old read-along CDs of fairy tales, a toy kaleidoscope, a stuffed tiger with one eye missing, exercise books from school in Lyon... She'd had no idea her mother kept this stuff, and if asked at the time whether to bother, Bridge would have answered no. But now she was grateful. She didn't know where in her tiny flat she could keep it all, but she'd figure something out.

One item gave her pause. Not a toy, or book, or anything that stood by itself. She wasn't even sure why Maman had kept it, let alone taken it back with her to Lyon. It was Bridge's yellow karate belt. The first qualification she'd earned as a teenager. She wrapped the thick woven fabric around her hand and remembered her early sparring tournaments, where Maman had watched from the stands; dressed for the opera but shouting full-throated Gallic encouragement like she was at a prize fight.

Giles' words rang in her ears. *When you're pushing sixty and looking for a quiet posting...* Bridge hadn't expected to make it past thirty in the first place. Was she really going to spend another thirty working for SIS at Vauxhall? Or posted to a distant country like Jameson, praying every day that nothing would happen until she shuffled into retirement?

For too long she'd felt trapped – not only by the pandemic and lockdown, but by her position. Why had she fallen out with Izzy? Because of her work. Why had she not been there when her mother was dying? Because of her work. What kept her awake at night, re-living trauma in a state of constant stress? Work that she couldn't avoid, couldn't refuse. She'd spent years begging for her OIT status, and now it stood revealed as a poisoned chalice. Oh, there was no question she'd done good with it. Without Bridge in the field, who could say what horrors SIS might have failed to prevent? Even if she'd been given a choice whether to accept missions, she would have said yes. Half the time she took action in spite of Giles' orders, not because of them. And through it she'd found Karl, of course.

But now she understood that it would destroy her. Even if she asked to be chained to a desk, Giles wouldn't do it. Bridge had proven herself too valuable, too capable of taking action. Of taking lives.

Ordinary people didn't do that, because nobody asked them to. Nobody expected them to. Nobody ordered them to.

Giles E Finlay
Director, CTA, SIS

Dear Giles,
    I write to formally offer my resignation from the Service. While this may seem sudden, I've given it lengthy consideration...

Last night was better; she slept for two or three hours at a time, and each time she woke it was more of a flinch than a howl. This morning she'd taped up the junk box and placed it under the spare bed, next to a crate of PC parts and hard drives left over from old computers. She'd always sworn that one day she'd go through that box to salvage anything she could re-use. Now she knew better. She put the kettle on, set Karna's *The Raven* playing on low, and watched the world go by out of her lounge window, tea in hand.

Maman had by all accounts enjoyed a swinging youth; had even been a muse to the occasional photographer. But then she'd met Arthur, and party girl Sophie Trichet became dedicated mother Sophie Sharp. From that point, besides occasional vacations in Spain or Italy, the dutiful wife and mother had barely left Lyon or London. Izzy was damned to the same fate – formerly a fun-loving girl, brought down to earth and domesticity by the death of their father when she and Bridge were still teenagers, now spending all her time in London or Côte-d'Or, raising children and playing housewife.

Bridge had always refused that path. She didn't want children, didn't want to marry, didn't want to see nothing but the streets of her own home town. She'd succeeded, too; no kids, no husband, a job that flung her to the corners of Europe. But in other ways she was more hemmed in than any of her family. She didn't even have much of a wild youth to look back on with nostalgia. She'd always nurtured a vague notion, more of an expectation than a conscious plan, that once she'd achieved some kind of settled status or senior post at SIS she could relax and take time to see the world. There was always tomorrow, wasn't there?

The last few years had put the lie to that.

Her phone buzzed as she hit Enter. She picked it up to answer, expecting Karl. Bridge hadn't spoken to him about this, and didn't feel ready to. Would she ever?

But to her surprise, it wasn't him.

'Izzy?' she answered.

Her sister took a moment to speak, then said, 'Fréderic told me what you did. The undercover policeman, Serge, that you sent to Marseille.'

Bridge imagined Tolbert and Fred trying to out-gruff each other, and smiled. 'He wasn't just there for Fréderic. The whole camp was in danger.'

'I know, but still. Thank you.' Another pause. 'How are you doing, sis?'

Her printer whispered from across the room. She stared at the single sheet of printed paper and said, 'I think I'm OK.'

They talked until Bridge's phone battery ran out. That night, she slept like a free woman.

Author's note

Like other Brigitte Sharp books, *The Patrios Network* features many things that either exist or are only a short hop away.

EMP weapons exist, though not yet on the scale of miniaturisation I've imagined. Likewise, while everything Bridge says about the stunning/alarming (delete as appropriate) progress of deepfake technology is accurate, it's not quite as convincing as seen here...yet. The vulnerability of power stations to cyber-attack, however, is worryingly real – as was the assault on Ukraine's grid in 2015. The 'missing 9s' Cuban numbers station is a true story, and so is the use of shipping containers as impromptu torture chambers. Finally, if you know what you're doing you can indeed root your television and turn it into a mini-computer.

More importantly, the book also features social and political phenomena which are all too present in our world. Refugees from war-torn and impoverished countries continue to seek a better life, but are demonised by those to whom they turn. Did you find the opinions of my fictional online denizens reprehensible? Not only do such message boards exist, but the opinions found therein – and sometimes even on public platforms like Twitter and Facebook – sadly outstrip anything I've written here.

At time of writing we're emerging from the global Covid pandemic at last. Planning and writing a Brigitte book, with its reliance on foreign travel and geopolitics, while unable to predict the state of the world even six months hence, was challenging to say the least. It required assuming that things will eventually return to normal. If I'm wrong, I can only hope you enjoyed this wild fantasy of people taking trains and flying abroad.

Antony Johnston
October 2021

Acknowledgements

The generosity of others never ceases to amaze me. I couldn't have written this book without the time, advice, and expertise many people gave to make it better. As always, though, I took their knowledge and corrupted it for the sake of drama; any errors or distortions are mine alone.

James Thomson and Fiona Pollard gave invaluable technical advice and inspiration. James also, along with fellow tech-head Kelly Guimont, helped rescue my working computer from a catastrophic mid-manuscript meltdown.

Andy Diggle helped untangle several plot threads in which I'd wrapped myself. When writing action scenes I tend to ask, 'What Would Diggle Do?' and it's surprising how often the answer involves a helicopter.

Thanks to Mihir Joshi for his inside knowledge of shipping, ports, and containers; to Éva Cserháti, Zita Sőregi, and Ziad Wakim for translations; and to Shane Waley, Jeff Quest, and the 'Spybrary' community for their support and commitment.

My agent Sarah Such combines shrewd judgement with patience and understanding, and I can't thank her enough for all three. Scott Pack (who commissioned the book), Simon Edge (who edited it), and all at Lightning Books believed in Bridge and once again helped sand down my rougher edges.

Finally, I couldn't do any of this without Marcia, who somehow continues to put up with me and my music collection.

The Exphoria Code

Brigitte Sharp, a cyber-espionage specialist with MI6, has been deskbound and in therapy for three years, after her first field mission in Syria went disastrously wrong. But now one of her best friends has been murdered, and Bridge believes his death is connected to strange posts appearing on the internet, carrying encrypted hidden messages.

When Bridge decodes the messages, she discovers evidence of a mole inside a top-secret Anglo-French military drone project. Her MI6 bosses force her back into the field, sending her undercover in France to find and expose the mole...who may also be her friend's killer. But the truth behind the Exphoria code is worse than she could have imagined.

Soon she's on the run, desperate and alone – as a nuclear terrorist plot unfolds and threatens everything Bridge has left to live for.

Very possibly the definitive espionage thriller of the early 21st century
– **Alan Moore**

Antony Johnston is a talent to look out for and this, his latest entry into the world of espionage, is a treat
– **Anthony Horowitz**

Johnston's first novel immediately establishes him as a fresh voice in spy thriller writing... An engaging character, top flight technological expertise made easy for the reader, fast action and a web of intrigue make this a propulsive read
– **Maxim Jakubowski**, *Crime Time*

The Tempus Project

MI6 officer and elite hacker Brigitte Sharp is back, battling a series of hacks and ransom-ware attacks, masterminded by a hacker known only as 'Tempus', who is targeting politicians and government officials with impunity.

Discovering that this campaign is linked to a cyber-attack on the London G20 summit, she is drawn into the dark-web world of crypto-currencies, Russian hackers and an African rebel militia. In another compelling cyber-thriller from the creator of *Atomic Blonde*, Bridge races against time to prevent a disaster that could alter the balance of global power forever.

Absolutely awesome – one of the best techno-thrillers I've read for a very long time
– M.W. Craven

Johnston manages to make the world of "runtime executables" and "rootkits" thrilling – no mean feat – while also featuring car chases and old-fashioned mole-hunts on the streets of Tallinn
– The Times

Forget about Lisbeth Salander. Here comes Brigitte Sharp
– Johana Gustawsson

Atomic Antony Johnston amazes as always
– Barry Forshaw

If you have enjoyed *The Patrios Network*, do please help us spread the word – by putting a review online; by posting something on social media; or in the old-fashioned way by simply telling your friends or family about it.

Book publishing is a very competitive business these days, in a saturated market, and small independent presses such as ourselves are often crowded out by the big houses. Support from readers like you can make all the difference to a book's success.

Many thanks.
Dan Hiscocks
Publisher
Lightning Books